Secret Life

Violet Grant

G. P. PUTNAM'S SONS
NEW YORK

The

Secret Life

of

Violet Grant

B E A T R I Z   W I L L I A M S

G. P. PUTNAM'S SONS
Publishers Since 1838
Published by the Penguin Group
Penguin Group (USA) LLC
375 Hudson Street
New York, New York 10014

USA · Canada · UK · Ireland · Australia
New Zealand · India · South Africa · China

penguin.com
A Penguin Random House Company

Library of Congress Cataloging-in-Publication Data

Williams, Beatriz.
The secret life of Violet Grant / Beatriz Williams.
p.   cm.
ISBN 978-0-399-16217-6
1. Nieces—Fiction.   2. Aunts—Fiction.   3. Family secrets—Fiction.
4. World War, 1914–1918—Fiction.   I. Title.
PS3623.I55643S48   2014   2013043630
813'.6—dc23

Printed in the United States of America
1   3   5   7   9   10   8   6   4   2

BOOK DESIGN BY AMANDA DEWEY

To my beautiful grandmother,
Sarena Merle Baker

1924–2013

Secret Life

Violet Grant

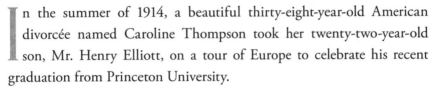

In the summer of 1914, a beautiful thirty-eight-year-old American divorcée named Caroline Thompson took her twenty-two-year-old son, Mr. Henry Elliott, on a tour of Europe to celebrate his recent graduation from Princeton University.

The outbreak of the First World War turned the family into refugees, and according to legend, Mrs. Thompson ingeniously negotiated her own fair person in exchange for safe passage across the final border from Germany.

A suitcase, however, was inadvertently left behind.

In 1950, the German government tracked down a surprised Mr. Elliott and issued him a check in the amount of one hundred deutsche marks as compensation for "lost luggage."

This is not their story.

PART ONE

"Gravitation is not responsible for people
falling in love."

—Albert Einstein

Vivian, 1964

NEW YORK CITY

I nearly missed that card from the post office, stuck up as it was against the side of the mail slot. Just imagine. Of such little accidents is history made.

I'd moved into the apartment only a week ago, and I didn't know all the little tricks yet: the way the water collects in a slight depression below the bottom step on rainy days, causing you to slip on the chipped marble tiles if you aren't careful; the way the butcher's boy steps inside the superintendent's apartment at five-fifteen on Wednesday afternoons, when the super's shift runs late at the cigar factory, and spends twenty minutes jiggling his sausage with the super's wife while the chops sit unguarded in the vestibule.

And—this is important, now—the way postcards have a habit of sticking to the side of the mail slot, just out of view if you're bending to retrieve your mail instead of crouching all the way down, as I did that Friday evening after work, not wanting to soil my new coat on the perpetually filthy floor.

But luck or fate or God intervened. My fingers found the postcard, even if my eyes didn't. And though I tossed the mail on the table when I burst into the apartment and didn't sort through it all until late Saturday morning, wrapped in my dressing gown, drinking a filthy concoction of tomato juice and the-devil-knew-what to counteract the several martinis and one neat Scotch I'd drunk the night before, not even I, Vivian Schuyler, could elude the wicked ways of the higher powers forever.

Mind you, I'm not here to complain.

"What's that?" asked my roommate, Sally, from the sofa, such as it was. The dear little tart appeared even more horizontally inclined than I did. My face was merely sallow; hers was chartreuse.

"Card from the post office." I turned it over in my hand. "There's a parcel waiting."

"For you or for me?"

"For me."

"Well, thank God for that, anyway."

I looked at the card. I looked at the clock. I had twenty-three minutes until the post office on West Tenth Street closed for the weekend. My hair was unbrushed, my face bare, my mouth still coated in a sticky film of hangover and tomato juice.

On the other hand: a parcel. Who could resist a parcel? A mysterious one, yet. All sorts of brown-paper possibilities danced in my head. Too early for Christmas, too late for my twenty-first birthday (too late for my twenty-second, if you're going to split hairs), too uncharacteristic to come from my parents. But there it was, misspelled in cheap purple ink: *Miss Vivien Schuyler, 52 Christopher Street, apt. 5C, New York City*. I'd been here only a week. Who would have mailed me a parcel already? Perhaps my great-aunt Julie, submitting a housewarming gift? In which case I'd have to skedaddle on down to the P.O. hasty-posty before somebody there drank my parcel.

The clock again. Twenty-two minutes.

"If you're going," said Sally, hand draped over her eyes, "you'd better go now."

Of such little choices is history made.

. . .

I DARTED into the post office building at eight minutes to twelve—yes, my dears, I have good reason to remember the exact time of arrival—shook off the rain from my umbrella, and caught my sinking heart at the last instant. The place was crammed. Not only crammed, but wet. Not only wet, but stinking wet: sour wool overlaid by piss overlaid by cigarettes. I folded my umbrella and joined the line behind a blond-haired man in blue surgical scrubs. This was New York, after all: you took the smell and the humanity—oh, the humanity!—as part of the whole sublime package.

Well, all right.

Amendment: You didn't *have* to take the smell and the humanity and the ratty Greenwich Village apartment with the horny butcher's boy on Wednesday afternoons and the beautifully alcoholic roommate who might just pick up the occasional weekend client to keep body and Givenchy together. Not if you were Miss Vivian Schuyler, late of Park Avenue and East Hampton, even later of Bryn Mawr College of Bryn Mawr, Pennsylvania. In fact, you courted astonishment and not a little scorn by so choosing. Picture us all, the affectionate Schuylers, lounging about the breakfast table with our eggs and Bloody Marys at eleven o'clock in the morning, as the summer sun melts like honey through the windows and the uniformed maid delivers a fresh batch of toast to absorb the arsenic.

Mums (lovingly): You aren't really going to take that filthy job at the magazine, are you?

Me: Why, yes. I really am.

Dadums (tenderly): Only bitches work, Vivian.

So it was my own fault that I found myself standing there in the piss-scented post office on West Tenth Street, with my elegant Schuyler nose pressed up between the shoulder blades of the blue scrubs in front of me. I just couldn't leave well enough alone. Could not accept my gilded lot.

Could not turn this unearned Schuyler privilege into the least necessary degree of satisfaction.

And less satisfied by the moment, really, as the clock counted down to quitting time and the clerks showed no signs of hurry and the line showed no sign of advancing. The foot-shifting began. The man behind me swore and lit a cigarette. Someone let loose a theatrical sigh. I inched my nose a little deeper toward the olfactory oasis of the blue scrubs, because this man at least smelled of disinfectant instead of piss, and blond was my favorite color.

A customer left the counter. The first man in line launched himself toward the clerk. The rest of us took a united step forward.

Except the man in blue scrubs. His brown leather feet remained planted, but I realized this only after I'd thrust myself into the center of his back and knocked him right smack down to the stained linoleum.

"I'm so sorry," I said, holding out my hand. He looked up at me and blinked, like my childhood dog Quincy used to do when roused unexpectedly from his after-breakfast beauty snooze. "My word. Were you *asleep*?"

He ignored my hand and rose to his feet. "Looks that way."

"I'm very sorry. Are you all right?"

"Yes, thanks." That was all. He turned and faced front.

Well, I would have dropped it right there, but the man was eye-wateringly handsome, stop-in-your-tracks handsome, Paul Newman handsome, sunny blue eyes and sunny blond hair, and this was New York, where you took your opportunities wherever you found them. "Ah. You must be an intern or a resident, or whatever they are. Saint Vincent's, is it? I've heard they keep you poor boys up three days at a stretch. Are you sure you're all right?"

"Yes." Taciturn. But he was blushing, right the way up his sweet sunny neck.

"Unless you're narcoleptic," I went on. "It's fine, really. You can admit it. My second cousin Richard was like that. He fell asleep at his own wedding, right there at the altar. The organist was so rattled she switched from the Wedding March to the Death March."

The old pregnant pause. Someone stifled a laugh behind me. I thought I'd overplayed my hand, and then:

"He did not."

Nice voice. Sort of Bing Crosby with a bass chord.

"Did too. We had to sprinkle him with holy water to wake him up, and by sprinkle I mean tip-turn the whole basin over his head. He's the only one in the family to have been baptized twice."

The counter shed two more people. We were cooking now. I glanced at the lopsided black-and-white clock on the wall: two minutes to twelve. Blue Scrubs still wasn't looking at me, but I could see from his sturdy jaw—lanterns, *psht*—he was trying very hard not to smile.

"Hence his nickname, Holy Dick," I said.

"Give it up, lady," muttered the man behind me.

"And then there's my aunt Mildred. You can't wake her up at all. She settled in for an afternoon nap once and didn't come downstairs again until bridge the next day."

No answer.

"So, during the night, we switched the furniture in her room with the red bordello set in the attic," I said, undaunted. "She was so shaken, she led an unsupported ace against a suit contract."

The neck above the blue scrubs was now as red as tomato bisque, minus the oyster crackers. He lifted one hand to his mouth and coughed delicately.

"We called her Aunt van Winkle."

The shoulder blades shivered.

"I'm just trying to tell you, you have no cause for embarrassment for your little disorder," I said. "These things can happen to anyone."

"Next," said a counter clerk, eminently bored.

Blue Scrubs leapt forward. My time was up.

I looked regretfully down the row of counter stations and saw, to my dismay, that all except one were now fronted by malicious little engraved signs reading COUNTER CLOSED.

The one man remaining—other than Blue Scrubs, who was having a pair of letters weighed for air mail, not that I was taking note of any details whatsoever—stood fatly at the last open counter, locked in a spirited discussion with the clerk regarding his proficiency with brown paper and Scotch tape.

Man (affectionately): YOU WANT I SHOULD JUMP THE COUNTER AND BREAK YOUR KNEECAPS, GOOBER?

Clerk (amused): YOU WANT I SHOULD CALL THE COPS, MORON?

I checked my watch. One minute to go. Behind me, I heard people sighing and breaking away, the weighty doors opening and closing, the snatches of merciless October rain on the sidewalk.

Ahead, the man threw up his hands, grabbed back his ramshackle package, and stormed off.

I took a step. The clerk stared at me, looked at the clock, and took out a silver sign engraved COUNTER CLOSED.

"You've got to be kidding me," I said.

The clerk smiled, tapped his watch, and walked away.

"Excuse me," I called out, "I'd like to see the manager. I've been waiting here for ages, I have a very urgent parcel—"

The clerk turned his head. "It's noon, lady. The post office is closed. See you Monday."

"I will not see you Monday. I demand my parcel."

"Do you want me to call the manager, lady?"

"Yes. Yes, I should very much like you to call the manager. I should very much—"

Blue Scrubs looked up from his air-mail envelopes. "Excuse me."

I planted my hands on my hips. "I'm terribly sorry to disturb the serenity of your transaction, sir, but some of us aren't lucky enough to catch the very last post-office clerk before the gong sounds at noon. Some of us are going to have to wait until Monday morning to receive our rightful parcels—"

"Give it a rest, lady," said the clerk.

"I'm not going to give it a rest. I pay my taxes. I buy my stamps and lick them myself, God help me. I'm not going to stand for this kind of lousy service, not for a single—"

"That's *it*," said the clerk.

"No, that's *not* it. I haven't even started—"

"Look here," said Blue Scrubs.

I turned my head. "You stay out of this, Blue Scrubs. I'm trying to conduct a perfectly civilized argument with a perfectly uncivil post-office employee—"

He cleared his Bing Crosby throat. His eyes matched his scrubs, too blue to be real. "I was only going to say, it seems there's been a mistake made here. This young lady was ahead of me in line. I apologize, Miss . . ."

"Schuyler," I whispered.

". . . Miss Schuyler, for being so very rude as to jump in front of you." He stepped back from the counter and waved me in.

And then he smiled, all crinkly and Paul Newman, and I could have sworn a little sparkle flashed out from his white teeth.

"Since you put it that way," I said.

"I do."

I drifted past him to the counter and held out my card. "I think I have a parcel."

"You *think* you have a parcel?" The clerk smirked.

Yes. Smirked. At me.

Well! I shook the card at his post-office smirk, nice and sassy. "That's Miss Vivian Schuyler on Christopher Street. Make it snappy."

"Make it snappy, *please*," said Blue Scrubs.

"*Please*. With whipped cream and a cherry," I said.

The clerk snatched the card and stalked to the back.

My hero cleared his throat.

"My name isn't Blue Scrubs, by the way," he said. "It's Paul."

"Paul?" I tested the word on my tongue to make sure I'd really heard it. "You don't say."

"Is that a problem?

I liked the way his eyebrows lifted. I liked his eyebrows, a few shades darker than his hair, slashing sturdily above his eyes, ever so blue. "No, no. Actually, it suits you." *Smile, Vivian.* I held out my hand. "Vivian Schuyler."

"Of Christopher Street." He took my hand and sort of held it there, no shaking allowed.

"Oh, you heard that?"

"Lady, the whole building heard that," said the clerk, returning to the counter. Well. He might have been the clerk. From my vantage, it seemed as if an enormous brown box had sprouted legs and arms and learned to walk, a square-bellied Mr. Potato Head.

"Great guns," I said. "Is that for me?"

"No, it's for the Queen of Sheba." The parcel landed before me with enough heft to rattle all the little silver COUNTER CLOSED signs for miles around. "Sign here."

"Just how am I supposed to get this box back to my apartment?"

"Your problem, lady. Sign."

I maneuvered my hand around Big Bertha and signed the slip of paper. "Do you have one of those little hand trucks for me?"

"Oh, yeah, lady. And a basket of fruit to welcome home the new arrival. Now get this thing off my counter, will you?"

I looped my pocketbook over my elbow and wrapped my arms around the parcel. "Some people."

"Look, can I help you with that?" asked Paul.

"No, no. I can manage." I slid the parcel off the counter and staggered backward. "On the other hand, if you're not busy saving any lives at the moment . . ."

Paul plucked the parcel from my arms, not without brushing my fingers first, almost as if by accident. "After all, I already know where you live. If I'm a homicidal psychopath, it's too late for regrets."

"Excellent diagnosis, Dr. Paul. You'll find the knives in the kitchen drawer next to the icebox, by the way."

He hoisted the massive box to his shoulder. "Thanks for the tip. Lead on."

"Just don't fall asleep on the way."

GIDDY might have been too strong a word for my state of mind as I led my spanking new friend home with my spanking new parcel, but not by much. New York complied agreeably with my mood. The crumbling stoops gleamed with rain; the air had taken on that lightening quality of a storm on the point of lifting.

Mind you. I still took care to stand close, so I could hold my umbrella over the good doctor's glowing blond head.

"Why didn't you wear a coat, at least?" I tried to sound scolding, but my heart wasn't in it.

"I just meant to dash out. I didn't realize it was raining; I hadn't been outside for a day and a half."

I whistled. "Nice life you've made for yourself."

"Isn't it, though."

We turned the corner of Christopher Street. The door stood open at my favorite delicatessen, sending a friendly matzo-ball welcome into the air. Next door, the Apple Tree stood quiet and shuttered, waiting for Manhattan's classiest queens to liven it up by night. My neighborhood. I loved it already; I loved it even more at this moment. I loved the whole damned city. Where else but New York would a Doctor Paul pop up in your post office, packaged in blue scrubs, fully assembled and with high-voltage batteries included free of charge?

By the time we reached my building, the rain had stopped entirely, and the droplets glittered with sunshine on the turning leaves. I whisked my umbrella aside and winked an affectionate hello to the grime in the creases of the front door. The lock gave way with only a rusty minimum of rattling. Doctor Paul ducked below the lintel and paused in the vestibule. A patch of new sunlight shone through the transom onto his hair. I nearly wept.

"This is you?" he said.

"Only good girls live at the Barbizon. Did I mention I'm on the fifth floor?"

"Of course you are." He turned his doughty shoulders to the stairwell and began to climb. I followed his blue-scrubbed derriere upward, marveling anew as we achieved each landing, wondering when my alarm clock would clamor through the rainbows and unicorns and I would open my eyes to the tea-stained ceiling above my bed.

"May I ask what unconscionably heavy apparatus I'm carrying up to your attic? Cast-iron stove? Cadaver?"

Oh! The parcel.

"My money's on the cadaver."

"You don't know?"

"I have no idea. I don't even know who it's from."

He rested his foot on the next step and cocked his head toward the box. "No ticking, anyway. That's a good sign."

"No funny smell, either."

He resumed the climb with a precious little flex of his shoulder. The landscape grew more dismal as we went, until the luxurious rips in the chintz wallpaper and the incandescent nakedness of the lightbulbs announced that we had reached the unsavory entrance to my unsuitable abode. I made a swift calculation of dishes left unwashed and roommates left unclothed.

"You know, you could just leave it right here on the landing," I said. "I can manage from here."

"Just open the door, will you?"

"So commanding." I shoved the key in the lock and opened the door.

Well, it could have been worse. The dishes had disappeared—sink, perhaps?—and so had the roommate. Only the bottle of vodka remained, sitting proudly on the radiator shelf next to the tomato juice and an elegant black lace slip. Sally's, by my sacred honor. I hurried over and draped my scarf over the shameful tableau.

A thump ensued as Doctor Paul laid the parcel to rest on the table. "Whew. I thought I wasn't going to make it up that last flight."

"Don't worry. I would have caught you."

He was looking at the parcel: one hand on his hip, the other raking through his hair in that way we girls adore. "Well?"

"Well, what?"

"Aren't you going to open it?"

"It's my parcel. Can't a girl have a little privacy?"

"Now, see here. I carried that . . . that *object* up five flights of Manhattan stairs. Can't a man have a little curiosity?"

Again with the glittery smile. I pushed myself off the radiator. "Since you put it that way. Make yourself comfortable. Can I take your coat and hat?"

"That hurt."

I slipped off my wet raincoat and slung it on Sally's hat tree, a hundred years old at least and undoubtedly purloined. I placed my hat on the hook above my coat, taking care to give my curls an artful little shake. Well, you can't blame me for that, at least. My hair was my best feature: brown and glossy, a hint of red, falling just so around my ears, a saucy flip. It distracted from my multitude of flaws, Monday to Sunday. Why not shake for all I was worth?

I turned around and sashayed the two steps to the table. Also purloined. Sally had told me the story yesterday, over our second round of martinis: the restaurant owner, the jealous wife, the police raid. I'll spare you the ugly details. In any case, our table was far more important than either of us had a right to own—solid, square, genuine imitation wood—which now proved positively providential, because my mysterious gift from the post office (the parcel, not the blonde) would have overwhelmed a lesser piece of furniture. As it was, the beast sat brown and hulking in the center, battered in one corner, stained in another, patched with an assortment of foreign stamps.

"Well, well." I peered over the top. "What have we here?"

Miss Vivian Schuyler, read the label. Of *52 Christopher Street,* et cetera, et cetera, except that my first name appeared over a scribbled-out original, and my building address likewise.

"It looks as if it's been forwarded," I said.

"The plot thickens."

"My mother's handwriting." I ran my finger over the jagged remains of *Fifth Avenue.* "My parents' address, too."

"That sounds reasonable." He remained a few respectful feet away, arms crossed against his blue chest. "Someone must have sent it to your parents' house."

"Apparently. Someone from Zurich, Switzerland."

"Switzerland?" He uncrossed his arms and stepped forward at last. "Really? You have friends in Switzerland?"

"Not that I can remember." I was trying to read the original name, beneath my mother's black scribble. *V* something something. "What do you think that is?"

"It's not Vivian?"

"No, it ends with a *t.*"

An instant's reflection. "Violet? Someone had your name wrong, I guess."

For a man who'd just walked coatless through the dregs of an October rain, Doctor Paul was awfully warm. I wore a cashmere turtleneck sweater over my torso, ever so snug, and still I could feel the rampant excess wafting from his skin, an unconscionable waste of thermal energy. Up close, he smelled like a hospital, which bothered me not at all.

I sashayed to the kitchen drawer and withdrew a knife.

"Ah, now the truth comes out. Make it quick."

"Silly." I waved the knife in a friendly manner. "It's just that I don't have any scissors."

"Scissors! You really are a professional."

"Stand aside, if you will." I examined the parcel before me. Every seam was sealed by multiple layers of Scotch tape, as if the contents were either alive or radioactive, or both. "I don't know where to start."

"You know, I *am* a trained surgeon."

"So you say." I sliced along one seam, and another. Rather expertly, if you must know; but then I had done the honors of the table at college since my sophomore year. Nobody at Bryn Mawr carved up a noble loin like Vivian Schuyler.

The paper shell gave way, and then the box itself. I stood on a chair and dug through the packing paper.

"Steady, there." Doctor Paul's helpful hands closed on the back of the chair, and it ceased its rickety-rocking obediently.

"It's leather," I said, from inside the box. "Leather and quite heavy."

"Do you need any help? A flashlight? Map?"

"No, I've got it. Here we are. Head, shoulders, placenta."

"Boy or girl?"

"Neither." I grasped with both hands and yanked, propelling myself conveniently backward into Doctor Paul's alert arms. We tumbled pleasantly, if rather ungracefully, to the disreputable rug. "It's a suitcase."

I CALLED my mother first. "What is this suitcase you sent me?"

"This is not how ladies greet one another on the telephone, darling."

"*Each* other, not *one* another. *One another* means three or more people. *Chicago Manual of Style*, chapter eight, verse eleven."

A merry clink of ice cubes against glass. "You're so droll, darling. Is that what you do at your magazine every day?"

"Tell me about the suitcase."

"I don't know about any suitcase."

"You sent me a package."

"Did I?" Another clink, prolonged, as of swirling. "Oh, that's right. It arrived last week."

"And you had no idea what was inside?"

"Not the faintest curiosity."

"Who's it from?"

"*From whom*, darling." Oh, the ring of triumph.

"From *whom* is the package, Mums?"

"I haven't the faintest idea."

"Do you know anybody in Zurich, Switzerland?"

"Nobody to you. Vivian, I'm dreadfully bored by this conversation. Can't you simply open the damned thing and find out yourself?"

"I already told you. It's a suitcase. It was sent to Miss Violet Schuyler on Fifth Avenue from somebody in Zurich, Switzerland. If it's not mine—"

"It *is* yours. I don't know any Violet Schuyler."

"*Violet* is not nearly the same as *Vivian*. Doctor Paul agrees with me. There's been a mistake."

A gratifying pause, as Mums was set back on her vodka-drenched heels. "Who is Doctor Paul?"

I swiveled and fastened my eyes on the good doctor. He was leaning against the wall next to the window, smiling at the corner of his mouth, blue scrubs revealed as charmingly rumpled now that the full force of sunlight was upon them. "Oh, just the doctor I met in the post office. The one who carried the parcel back for me."

"You met a doctor at the *post office*, Vivian?" As she might say, *the gay bathhouse on Bleecker Street*.

I leaned my hip against the table, right next to the battered brown valise, trusting the whole works wouldn't give way beneath me. I was wearing slacks, unbelted, as befitted a dull Saturday morning, but Doctor Paul deserved to know that my waist-to-hip ratio wasn't all that bad, really. I couldn't have said that his expression changed, except that I imagined his eyes took on a deeper shade of blue. I treated him to a slow wink and wound the telephone cord around my fingers. "Oh, you'd adore Doctor Paul, Mums. He's a surgeon, *very* handsome, taller than me, seems to have all his teeth. Perfectly eligible, really, unless he's married." I put the phone to my shoulder. "Doctor Paul, are you married?"

"Not yet."

Phone back to ear. "Nope, not married, or so he claims. He's your dream come true, Mums."

"He's not standing right there, is he?"

"Oh, but he is. Would you like to speak to Mums, Doctor Paul?"

He grinned, straightened from the wall, and held out his hand.

"Oh, Vivian, no . . ." But her last words escaped me as I placed the receiver in Doctor Paul's palm. His palm: wide, firm, lightly lined. I liked it already.

"Good afternoon, Mrs. Schuyler. . . . Yes, she's behaving herself. . . . Yes, I carried the parcel all the way up those wretched stairs. That's the sort of gentleman I am, Mrs. Schuyler." He returned my wink. "As a matter of fact, I do think there's been some mistake. Are you certain there's no one named Violet in your family? . . . Quite certain? . . . Well, I *am* a doctor, Mrs. Schuyler. I'm accustomed to making a diagnosis based on the symptoms presented by the subject." A hint of a blush began to climb up his neck. "Hard to say, Mrs. Schuyler, but—"

I snatched the receiver back. "That will be enough of that, Mums. I won't have you embarrassing my Doctor Paul with your remarks. He isn't used to them."

"He *is* a dream, Vivian. My hat's off to you." Clink, clink, rattle. The glass must be almost empty. "Try not to sleep with him right away, will you? It scares them off."

"You would know, Mums."

A deep sigh. Swallowed by the familiar crash of empty vodka glass on bedside table. "You're coming for lunch tomorrow, aren't you?"

"Not if I can help it."

"Good. We'll see you at twelve sharp." *Click.*

I set the receiver in the cradle. "Well, that's Mums. I thought I should warn you from the get-go."

"Duly warned."

"But not scared?"

"Not a lick."

I tapped my fingernails against the telephone. "You're certain there's a Violet Schuyler somewhere in this mess?"

"Well, no. Not absolutely certain. But the fact is, it's not *your* suitcase, is it?"

I cast the old gaze suitcase-ward and shuddered. "Heavens, no."

"A cousin, maybe? On your father's side? Lost her suitcase in Switzerland?"

"You mean a century or so ago?"

"Stranger things have happened."

I set the telephone down on the table and fingered the tarnished brass clasp of my acquisition. As ancient as my mother's virtue, that valise, and just as lost to history: cracked and dusty, bent in all the wrong places. A faint scent of musty leather crept up from its creases. There was no label of any kind.

I don't mean to shock you, but I've never considered myself an especially shy person, now or then. And yet I couldn't quite bring myself to undo that clasp and open the suitcase in the middle of my ramshackle Greenwich Village fifth-floor apartment. There was something odd and sacred about it, something inviolable in all that mustiness. (Quite unlike my mother's virtue, in that respect.)

My hand fell away. I looked back at the telephone. "I think it's time to call Great-aunt Julie."

"VIOLET *SCHUYLER*, DID YOU SAY?"

"Yes, Aunt Julie. Violet Schuyler. Does she exist? Do you know her?"

"Well, well." The line went quiet. I imagined her pacing to the limit of the telephone cord, like a horse on a gilded Park Avenue picket line. I imagined her pristine sixty-two-year-old face, her well-preserved brow making the ultimate sacrifice to this unexpected Saturday-morning conundrum.

"Aunt Julie? Are you there?"

"You're certain the name was Violet? Foreign handwriting can be so atrocious."

"It's definitely Violet. Doctor Paul concurs."

"Who's Doctor Paul?"

"We'll get to him later. Let's talk about Violet. Obviously you know the name."

She exhaled with drama, as if collapsing on the sofa. I heard the scratching of her cigarette lighter. Must be serious, then.

"Yes, I know the name."

"And?"

A long breath against the mouth of the receiver. "Darling, she was my sister. My older sister, Violet. A scientist. She murdered her husband in Berlin in 1914 and ran off with her lover, and nobody's heard from her since."

Violet, 1914

BERLIN

The Englishman walks through the door of Violet's life in the middle of an ordinary May afternoon, smelling of leather and outdoors.

She's not expecting him. In that hour, Berlin is crowded with light, incandescent with sunshine and possibility, but Violet has banished brightness within the thick redbrick walls of her basement laboratory. She closes the door and lowers herself into a wooden chair in the center of the room, where she stares without moving at the heavy blackness surrounding her.

In her blindness, Violet's other senses rise up with primeval sharpness. She counts the careful beats of her heart, sixty-two to the minute; she hears the click of footsteps down the linoleum hallway outside her room. The sterile scents of the laboratory fill her nostrils: cleaning solutions and chemicals, paper and pencil lead. Deeper still, she feels the weight of the furniture around her, interrupting the empty space. The chairs, the table, the radioactive apparatus she is about to employ. The door in the corner, from which she can just begin to detect a few thin lines of light stealing past the cracks.

As she sits and waits, as her pupils dilate by tiny fractions of degrees, the stolen light from the doorway finds the walls and the furniture, and the intricate charcoal shadow of the apparatus atop the table. Violet removes a watch from her pocket and consults the luminous dial. She has been sitting in her shapeless void for ten minutes.

Ten more minutes left.

Violet replaces her watch and resists the urge to rise and check the apparatus. She set it up with her own hands; she has already inspected each detail; she has already performed this experiment countless times. What possible surprise could it hold?

But a trace of unease seems to have stolen into the room with the light from outside the door. It pierces Violet's calm preparation and winds around her chest like the thread behind a needle. She counts her pulse again: sixty-nine beats to the minute.

What an extraordinary anomaly.

She has never experienced this sensation before an experiment. Her nerves are cool and precise; her nerves are the very reason she was first delegated to perform this particular duty. She might go further and say that her nerves had brought her to this point in her life: her work, her unconventional marriage, her existence here in Berlin in this incandescent May of 1914, in a basement laboratory at the Kaiser Wilhelm Institut, waiting for her pupils to dilate to the necessary degree before she can begin an experiment at the frontier of atomic physics.

But she can't deny the existence of this sensation that tightens about her heart. It is real, and it is quantifiable: seven additional beats of her heart in every minute.

A double knock strikes the door.

"Come in," Violet says.

She closes her eyes as the door opens, because she doesn't want the additional light to interrupt the adjustment of her pupils. Footsteps beat against the linoleum; the door clicks shut. Her husband, probably, come to check on her progress. To stand over her and ensure that she gets nothing wrong. That she misses nothing.

But in the split second before he speaks, Violet knows this intruder isn't her husband. These footsteps are too heavy, the leathery air that whirls through the door with him too brash. Her senses recognize his strangeness just before his voice confirms it.

"I hope I'm not disturbing you, Mrs. Grant."

Violet opens her eyes.

"My name is Richardson, Lionel Richardson. Your husband told me you wouldn't mind my observing the experiment."

Your husband told me. Walter sent this stranger to her?

Again, that unsettling sensation in her chest. If only she could see him. His black shape outlines the blacker void around him, obstructing the light from the door without a trace. His voice rumbles from the center of a capacious chest, low and respectful, the syllables clipped by precise British scissors.

I hope I'm not disturbing you.

"Not at all," Violet says crisply. "Are you a colleague of his?"

"No, no. A former student." He makes some movement in the darkness, indicating the apparatus. "Used to do these sorts of things myself."

"Then I need not apologize for the darkness. Would you like to sit?" Her heart is beating even faster now, perhaps seventy-five hard strikes a minute. It must be surprise, that's all. She's rarely interrupted in those experiments, which are long and repetitious and generally unworthy of spectators. Her animal brain is simply reacting to the sudden presence of an unknown organism, a possible threat. An unexpected foreign invader who might be anyone or anything, but whose vital and leathery bulk doesn't belong in the quiet darkness of her laboratory.

"Thank you." A chair scrapes against the linoleum, as if Lionel Richardson can see in the dark. Or perhaps he simply memorized the location of the furniture in the brief flash of light at his entrance. "Are you nearly ready to begin, Mrs. Grant?"

"Almost." Violet consults her watch again. "Another three minutes."

Richardson laughs softly. "I remember it well. No twenty minutes ever passed so strangely. Time seems to stretch out, doesn't it? A sort of black infinity, disconnected from everything else. All sorts of profound thoughts would pass through one's brain. Not that I could ever recall them afterward."

Yes, Violet thinks. *That's it exactly.* "You're here for old times' sake, then?"

Another laugh. "Something like that. Dr. Grant told me someone else was performing my old duties this very minute, and I couldn't resist a peek. Do you mind?"

"Not at all."

Of course she minds. Lionel Richardson seems to take up half the room, as if he's swallowed up the blackness to leave only his own solid limbs, his broad and rumbling chest. Violet is seized with a burst of annoyance at her husband, who surely should have known better than to send this stranger to swallow up her laboratory while she sits waiting in the darkness, alone and unsuspecting.

Richardson says, "I'd be happy to help you with the counting. I know it's something of an eyestrain."

"That's not necessary. It takes some practice, as you know."

"Oh, I remember how. I was the first one, you know, back in ought-nine, when your husband began his experiments. I still see those bloody little exploding lights, sometimes, when I close my eyes."

Violet laughs. "I know what you mean."

"Maddening, isn't it? But I see the crafty doctor has found a permanent replacement for me. A far more agreeable one, at any rate."

This time Violet feels the actual course of acceleration in her chest, the physical sense of quickening. How did one bring one's heart back under proper regulation after a shock? You couldn't simply order it to slow down. You couldn't simply say, in a firm voice, as one spoke to a misbehaving child: *Sixty-two beats is more than sufficient, thank you.* The heart, an organ of instinct rather than reason, had to perceive that there was nothing to fear. The chemical signals of danger, of distress, had to disperse from the blood.

Violet flicks open her watch. "It's time. Are you able to see?"

"Just barely."

"We can wait a few more minutes, if you like."

"No, no. I'm not here to interrupt your progress. Carry on."

Violet rises from her chair and moves to the table in the center of the room, guided more by feel than by sight. She flicks the switch on the lamp, though she doesn't look directly at the feeble low-wattage bulb. It illuminates her notepad and pencil just enough that she can write down her notes.

She casts her eyes over the apparatus: the small box at one end, containing a minute speck of radium; the aperture on the box's side, through which the particles of radiation shoot unseen toward the sheet of gold foil; the glass screen, coated with zinc sulfide; and the eyepiece with its magnifying lenses.

She takes out her watch, settles her right eye on the eyepiece, and squints her left lid shut.

A tiny green-white flash explodes in her vision, a delicate firework of breath-stopping beauty. But Violet's breath is already stopped, already shocked by the unexpected invasion of Lionel Richardson into her laboratory, and the tiny flashes make no impression, other than the scratches of her pencil as she counts them.

Why this oversized reaction? Why this perception of imminent danger?

Has Walter perhaps mentioned Lionel Richardson's name before? Is there some association buried in her subconscious that causes the synapses of her brain to crackle with electricity, to issue these messages of alarm down her neural pathways to the muscles of her heart and lungs? Or maybe it's just that she can't see him, can't inspect his face and clothes and person and confirm that he's speaking the truth, that he's only a man, a visiting former student of her husband's, benignly curious.

Violet takes her eyes from the screen for an instant to check her watch. Nearly five minutes have passed. At five minutes she will draw a line under her counting marks and start again.

"Can I help you? Keep time for you?" asks the invader.

"It's not necessary." She looks at her watch. Five minutes. She draws a line.

"Aren't you missing your count, looking back and forth like that?"

"A few, of course."

"Dr. Grant always had me take a partner to keep time. We switched off to rest our eyes." He offers this information respectfully, without a trace of the usual scientific arrogance.

"We don't have the staff for that here in Berlin."

"You have it now."

Without taking her eye from the eyepiece, Violet grasps the watch in her left hand and holds it out. "Very well. If you insist."

He gathers the watch in a light brush of his fingers against her palm. "Five-minute intervals?"

"Yes." Violet shuts her eyes.

"All right. Ready . . ."

A tranquil leather-scented silence warms the air. Violet breathes it deeply inside her, once, twice.

"Go."

Violet opens her eyes to the glorious flashing blackness, the stars exploding in her own minute universe. Her pencil moves on the paper, counting, counting. Lionel Richardson sits just behind her, unmoving, close enough that she can feel the heat radiating from his body. He holds her watch in his steady palm. Her gold pocket watch, unadorned, almost masculine; the watch her sister Christina gave her four years ago on a smoke-drenched pier on the Hudson River, as the massive transatlantic liner *Olympic* strained against her moorings a few feet away. Her watch: Violet's only parting gift from the disapproving Schuylers.

"Time," says Lionel Richardson.

Violet draws a line to begin a new count.

"And . . . go."

He issues the direction with low-pitched assurance, from his invisible post at her left shoulder. He hasn't simply swallowed the blackness, he's become the dark space itself. Even his scent has absorbed into the air. Violet makes her tireless marks on the notepad. She sinks into the world of electric green-white scintillations, the regular strikes of radioactive particles against atomic nuclei, and somewhere in the rhythmic beauty, her heart returns at last to its usual serene pace, her nerves smooth down their ragged edges. Only the pencil, hard and sharp between her thumb and forefinger, links her to the ordinary world.

"Time," says Richardson, and then: "Would you like me to count this round? Your eyes must be aching."

Her eyes are aching. Her shoulders ache, too, and the small of her back. She straightens herself. "Yes, thank you."

Lionel's chair scrapes lightly. His body slides upward in the darkness behind her. A pressure cups her right elbow: his hand, guiding her around her own chair and into his. He places the watch in her palm and settles into the seat before the eyepiece, hunching himself around the apparatus without complaint, for he's much larger than she is.

She lifts the watch and stares at the face. "Ready?"

"A moment." He adjusts himself, settles his eye back against the lint lining. His profile, lit by the dim bulb next to the notepad, reveals itself at last: firm and regular, the nose a trifle large, the hair short and dark as ink above his white collar. His forehead is high, overhanging the eyepiece, and in the soft yellow light Violet cannot detect a single line. "Ready."

She drops her gaze back to Christina's watch.

"And . . . go."

Vivian

A unt Violet. I had a great-aunt named Violet, an adulteress and murderess, about whom I'd never heard. A scientist. What sort of scientist?

I regarded the valise on my table, and then turned to tell Doctor Paul the extraordinary news.

Alas. Too late.

Inexplicably, unfathomably, he lay upon my sofa, in the hollow left by Sally's debauched corpse an hour or two earlier, so profoundly asleep I was tempted to hold my compact mirror to his mouth and check for signs of life.

Hands to hips. "Well. There's courtship for you."

But then a tiny steel ball bearing of sentiment rolled downward through the chambers of my heart. Poor dear Doctor Paul. One arm crossed atop his chest; the other dangled to the floor. His legs, far too long for the sweeping red Victorian curves of the sofa, propped themselves over the edge of the opposite armrest.

I knelt next to him and touched the lock of hair that drooped in exhaustion to his forehead. Up close, I could see the tiny lines that fanned from the outer corners of his eyes. I bent my nose to his neck. Here, he smelled of salt instead of antiseptic, and perhaps a little long-forgotten soap, too, sweet and damp. I rubbed the tiny golden bristles of his nascent beard with my pinkie. He didn't even flinch.

"Aren't you just too much," I whispered.

AUNT JULIE blew into the apartment half an hour later, smelling of cigarettes and Max Factor pancake foundation. She flung her hat on the stand but kept her coat in place. When you maintained a figure like hers so far past its biblically ordained two score and ten, you lived in a perpetual state of Pleistocene chill.

"Where is this suitcase of yours?" she demanded, lighting a cigarette.

"It's not mine. That's the point. Drink?" I didn't wait for an answer. The liquor filled a cabinet of honor in the kitchen—such as it was—and while Aunt Julie might not admire the quality of the refreshment provided, she had to approve of its quantity.

She whipped off her gloves just in time to accept her Bloody Mary, no celery. "Haven't you opened it yet?"

"Of course not. It's not mine."

"For God's sake, my dear. Did your mother raise you with no standards at all?" She drained down half a glass, set the tumbler on the table, and put her hand on the valise's tarnished brass clasp. "Well, well."

"Now, wait just a minute." I darted over and snatched her hand away.

"What are you doing?"

"I don't think we have any right to look inside."

"Darling, she'll never know."

"How do we know that?"

"Nobody's heard from her for fifty years. I'd say that was a pretty decent indication, wouldn't you?"

"We should make some sort of effort to track her down first."

Aunt Julie rolled her eyes and picked up her pick-me-up. "Ah, that's good. You're the only one of my nieces and nephews to mix a decent drink."

"I had the finest instruction available."

She wagged a finger. "Teach a girl to fish—"

"Look, Aunt Julie, about this Violet of yours . . ."

But Aunt Julie had already turned, aiming for the kitchen and a refill, and stopped with a rattle of dying ice. "Vivian, my dear," she said slowly, "there's a man on your sofa."

"You don't approve?"

"Oh, I approve wholeheartedly. But I do feel compelled to ask, for form's sake, where the hell you picked him up on such short notice, and why he isn't dressed more suitably."

I came up behind her and slipped my arm about her waist. "Isn't he a dream? I found him at the post office."

"Delivered and signed for?"

"*Mmm.* Poor thing, he works such long shifts at the hospital. He carried up the package for me with his last dying surge of energy, and then he just"—I waved my hand helplessly—"collapsed."

"Imagine that. What do you plan to do with him?"

"What do you suggest?"

She resumed her journey to the liquor cabinet. "Just don't sleep with him right away. It scares them off."

"Funny, Mums already warned me. Tell me about Violet."

"There isn't much to tell. Not much that I know, anyway. I was the baby of the family. I was only nine years old when she left for England. That was 1911, I believe." Aunt Julie wandered back from the kitchen and leaned against the table, drink in hand, staring lovingly at Doctor Paul.

"Why did she leave for England? Was she sent away?"

"No, the opposite. She wanted to be a scientist, and naturally that didn't go down well in Schuylerville. I remember the most awful rows. They let her go eventually, I suppose—there's not much you can do with a girl if she's got her heart set on something—and washed their hands of it." Aunt Julie cocked her head. "What color are his eyes?"

"Blue. Exactly the same shade as his scrubs. And stop trying to distract me."

"I've changed my mind. Get him in bed pronto."

"You know, I'll bet he can hear you in his subconscious."

"I hope he does. You could use a good love affair, Vivian. It's the one thing you're missing."

I wagged my finger. "You're the most miserable excuse for a chaperone in the history of maiden aunts."

"I am not a maiden aunt. I've been married *several* times."

"Regardless, I'm not going to sleep with him. Look at the poor darling. He's exhausted."

"I find," said Aunt Julie, swishing her gin, "they can generally summon the energy."

I crossed the floor to my bedroom—it didn't take long—and took the extra blanket from the shelf. I called back: "Now talk. What did Violet do in England?"

"Got married to her professor, like the sane girl she was. She was very pretty, Violet, I'll say that, though she didn't care about anything except her damned atoms and molecules."

I returned and spread the blanket over Doctor Paul, taking extra care with his doughty shoulders. "But then she murdered him."

"Well, I don't know the details of all that. The family hasn't spoken of it since, never even uttered her name. I don't think there was a trial or anything like that. But yes, the fellow was murdered, and Violet ran off with her lover. From a suite at the Adlon, of course. She did have taste." She snapped her fingers. "And poof! That was that."

"There must be more to it."

"Of course there's more."

"And you were never curious?"

"I was young, Vivian. I hardly knew her, really. She was at school, and then she was in England." Aunt Julie set her glass on the table and crossed her arms. "I wondered, of course. Once or twice, when I was in Europe, I asked a few questions. But nothing ever turned up."

She was staring at the valise now, her lips turned down in a crimson crescent moon. She stretched out one claw and touched the lonely leather.

"I don't believe you," I said.

"Of course you don't. You're young and suspicious."

"And I know you, Aunt Julie." I pointed at her duplicitous chest. "Out with it."

She spread her hands. "I've told you all I know."

She played her part well. Round eyes, innocent eyebrows. Mouth set irrevocably shut. I crossed my arms and tapped an arpeggio into my left elbow. "I can't believe I had another great-aunt, all these years, and nobody ever mentioned it."

Aunt offered me with a pitiful smile. "We're the Schuylers, darling. Nobody ever would."

From the window over the back courtyard came the sound of crockery smashing. A baby wailed. My first night in the apartment, with the roommate I'd met only that morning, I hadn't slept a wink: the cramped squalor was so foreign to Fifth Avenue, to Bryn Mawr, to the rarefied quiet of a Long Island summer. I adored every piece of makeshift purloined furniture, every broken cabinet door held together with twine, every sound that shrieked through the window glass and told me I was alive, alive.

"Let's open the valise," said Aunt Julie. "I want to see what's inside."

"God, no. What if it's a skeleton? Her dead husband?"

"All the better."

I shook my head. "I can't open it. Not until I know if she's still alive."

"You sound like a melodrama. If you really want the truth, it's inside that bag." She stabbed it with her finger. "*That's* where you'll find Violet."

"Well, it's locked," I said. "And there's no key."

Doctor Paul stirred on the sofa. "Clamp, not screw," he muttered, and turned his face into the cushion.

I dropped my voice to a whisper. "See what you've done! Now, be quiet. He needs his sleep."

Nobody could invest a standard-issue eye roll with as much withering contempt as Aunt Julie. She did it now, right before she marched to the hat stand and lifted her hat—a droll little orange felt number, perfectly matching her orange wool coat—from its hook. Crimson lips, orange hat: only Aunt Julie could pull that one off.

I followed her and placed a kiss on her cheek. "Stay dry."

She shook her head. "You won't break open the mysterious suitcase sitting on your own kitchen table. You won't go to bed with that adorable doctor sleeping on your sofa."

I opened the door for her and stood back.

Aunt Julie thrust her hat pin just so and swept into the vomit-stained hallway. She called, over her shoulder: "Youth is wasted on the young."

EONS PASSED before the scent of Aunt Julie's Max Factor faded from the air. I spent them tidying up the apartment—as far as feeble human ability could achieve, at any rate—and generally hiding all evidence of sin.

I did this not to favorably impress Doctor Paul when he woke (at least, not exclusively) nor out of a general desire for cleanliness (of which I had little) but because I liked to keep my hands busy while my brain wrestled with a problem.

And my new aunt Violet was a doozy of a problem.

A woman scientist: now, that was interesting, something I could understand. Not that I liked the sciences particularly, but I could see her struggle as vividly as I saw mine, for all the half century of so-called progress between us. Not only was this Violet a female scientist, poor dear. She was also a scientific female. She would have sat at the lonely table, wherever she made her home. I couldn't blame her for marrying her professor.

The question was why she killed him afterward.

My housemaidenly urgings flickered and died. I sank into the chair at the table, feather duster in hand, and touched my finger, as Aunt Julie had, to the sturdy leather. *That's where you'll find Violet,* Aunt Julie had said, but it seemed to me that she existed elsewhere. That the marks and stains of her life's work lay scattered out there, in the wide world, and that the contents of this particular valise were instead private, the detritus of her soul. I had no right to them. What if someone opened up *my* suitcase?

In the wake of the earlier fracas, the courtyard had gone unnaturally still. The clock ticked mechanically in my ear, and for some reason the sound reminded me that I hadn't had lunch, that I had packed an entire week's worth of excitement into a single Saturday afternoon, and for all I knew it might be dinnertime already.

I glanced at the face. Two-thirty-one.

I rose from the table and went to the kitchen, where I measured water and coffee grounds into the percolator. Doctor Paul would need coffee when he woke up, and lots of it.

Two-thirty-one. I'd known the good doctor for two hours and thirty-nine minutes, and he'd been asleep for most of it. I plugged the percolator into the wall socket and opened the refrigerator. Butter, cheese. There must be some bread in the breadbox.

Doctor Paul would be hungry, too.

AH, the scent of brewing coffee. It bolts a man from peaceful slumber faster than the words *Darling, I'm pregnant.*

I watched his big blue eyes blink awake. I savored the astonished little jerk of his big blue body. "Hello, Doctor," I said. "Welcome to heaven."

He looked at me, and his head relaxed against the pillow. "You again."

"I made you grilled cheese and tomato soup. And coffee."

"You didn't."

"You carried my parcel. It was the least I could do."

He smiled and sat up, all blinky and tousley and shaky-heady. "I don't know how I fell asleep."

"It seems pretty straightforward to me. You were exhausted. You made the mistake of lowering your poor overworked backside onto my unconscionably comfortable sofa. Voilà. Have some coffee."

He accepted the cup and took a sip. Eyelids down. "I think I'm in love with you."

"Aw, you big lug. Wait until you taste my grilled cheese."

Another sip. "I'd love to taste your grilled cheese."

Well, well.

I rose to my feet and went to the kitchen, where Doctor Paul's sandwich sat in the oven, keeping warm. When I returned, his eyes lifted hopefully.

I handed him the plate. "So tell me about yourself, Doctor Paul."

"I do have a last name, if you'd care to hear it."

"But, Doctor, we hardly know each other. I'm not sure I'm ready to be on a last-name basis with you."

"It's Salisbury. Paul Salisbury."

"You'll always be Doctor Paul to me. Now eat your sandwich like a good boy."

He smiled and tore away a bite. I perched myself at the edge of the armchair, such as it was, and watched him eat. I was still wearing my frilly white apron, and I smoothed it down my front like any old housewife. "Well?"

"I do believe this is the best grilled cheese I've ever had."

"It's my specialty."

He nodded at the suitcase. "Haven't you opened it yet?"

"Oh, that. You'll never guess. It belonged to my secret great-aunt

Violet, who murdered her husband and ran off with her lover, and the damned thing is, of course, locked tight as an oyster with a lovely fat pearl inside."

Doctor Paul's sandwich paused at his mouth. "You're serious?"

"In this case, I am."

He enclosed a ruminative mouthful of grilled cheese. "I hope you don't mind my asking whether this sort of behavior runs in the family?"

"My behavior, or hers?"

"Both."

I settled back in my armchair and twiddled my thoughtful thumbs. "Well. I can't say the Schuylers are the most virtuous of human beings, though we do put on a good show for outsiders. Still and all, outright psychopathy is generally frowned upon."

"I can't tell you how relieved I am to hear it."

"That being said, and as a general note of caution, psychopaths do make the best liars." I clapped my hands. "But enough about little old me! Let's turn our attention to the alluring Dr. Paul Salisbury, his life and career, and, most important, when he's due back at his hospital."

Doctor Paul set his empty plate on the sofa cushion next to him, rested his elbows on his knees, and leaned forward. His eyes took on that darker shade again, or maybe it was the sudden rush of blood to my head, distorting my vision. "Midnight."

I lost my breath.

"I'm supposed to be sleeping right now. I was supposed to return to the hospital from the post office, change clothes, and go back to my apartment to sleep."

"Where's your apartment?"

"Upper East Side."

"My condolences."

"Thanks. I should have found a place closer to the hospital."

I looked at the clock. "You've lost hours already."

"I wouldn't say that."

I untangled my legs and rose to fetch the tomato soup. "I hope you don't mind the mug. We don't seem to have any bowls yet."

"Whatever you have is fine." He took the mug with a smile of thanks. Oh, the smile of him, as wide and trusting as if the world were empty of sin. "Wonderful, in fact. Sit here." He whisked away the plate and patted the sofa cushion next to him.

I settled deep. I was a tall girl—an unlucky soul or two might have said *coltish* in my impulsive adolescence—and I liked the unfamiliar way his thigh dwarfed mine. The size of his knee. I studied those knees, caught the movement of his elbow as he spooned tomato soup into his mouth. The patient clinks of metal against ceramic said it all: anticipation, discovery, certainty. *The real deal*, something whispered in my head.

When he had put himself on the outside of his tomato soup, Doctor Paul cupped the empty mug in his palms. "What would you like to do now, Vivian?"

"I was hoping you'd say that. Did you have anything particular in mind, Doctor, dear?"

"I was asking *you*."

"Well, Mother said I shouldn't go to bed with you right away. It would scare you off."

I couldn't see for certain, but I'll bet my best lipstick he blushed. If I closed my eyes, I could feel the warmth on my nearby cheek.

"Aunt Julie concurred," I added. "At first, anyway. Until she got a good look at you."

"I'm not saying they're right," he said carefully, "but there's no rush, is there?"

"You tell me."

"No. There's no rush."

We sat there, side by side, legs not quite touching. Doctor Paul rotated the mug in his hands, his competent surgeon's hands. They looked older and wiser than the rest of him. He kept his nails trimmed short, his cuticles tidy. The tiny crescents at the base were extraordinarily white.

He cleared his throat. "Of course, I didn't mean to imply that I'm not tempted. Just to be clear. Extremely tempted."

"Mind over matter?"

"Exactly."

"I'd hate to lead you astray from the well-worn path of virtue."

He cleared his throat again. Blushed again, too, the love. If he kept giving off that kind of thermodynamic spondulics, I was going to have to change into something less comfortable. "Yes, of course," he mumbled.

I lifted my eyes, and the table appeared before me, and my great-aunt Violet's suitcase atop it. Aunt Violet, who ran away with her lover into the Berlin summer. Had they made it to Switzerland together? She would be in her seventies now, if she were still alive. If she had succeeded.

Doctor Paul rose from the sofa in a sudden heave of dilapidated upholstery. His hand stretched toward me, palm upward, open and strong. "Let's go somewhere, Vivian."

"What about your sleep?"

"I'll catch up eventually. This is more important."

I took his hand and let him pull me upward. "If you must. Where do we go?"

He stood close as a whisker, solid as a deep-blue tree. "How about the library?"

"The library."

"Yes, the library." Doctor Paul reached around my back, untied my frilly apron, and lifted it over my head. "We're going to find out all about this aunt of yours."

Violet

Your husband told me you wouldn't mind, Lionel Richardson said. For the life of her, Violet can't imagine why. In the course of their two and a half years together, Walter has only allowed one other man inside the darkened laboratory with her: namely, himself.

But then, like most illicit affairs, theirs was unequal from the beginning. Violet's youth, her loneliness, her awe-swollen gratitude were no match for Dr. Grant's experience. At nineteen—at any age—innocence doesn't know its own power. To know that power, after all, is to lose it.

In Violet's downcast moments—now, for example, as she locks the laboratory door and trudges in the direction of Lionel Richardson's laughter down the hall—she forces herself to recall the instant of their meeting, the instant in which everything changed. When the chains of her attachment were first forged.

She climbs the stairs to her husband's office, from which Richardson's laughter originates, but she sees instead the familiar Oxford room of 1911, richly appointed, and the angular man standing in the doorway before it: the legendary Dr. Walter Grant made manifestly physical. She remembers how every aspect exuded masculine eminence, from his thin-lipped mouth surrounded by its salty trim beard to his graying hair gleaming with pomade under the masterful glow of a multitude of electric lamps.

He wasn't a large man, but neither was he small. He was built like a whip, slender and hard, and the expert tailoring of his clothes to his body gave him an additional substance that, in Violet's eyes, he didn't require.

At the moment of that first meeting, Violet was somewhat out of breath. She had grown agitated, speaking to his private secretary, whose job it was to protect the great man from unforeseen attacks like hers; she was also hot beneath her drab brown clothes, because it was the end of August and the heat lounged about the yellowed university stones, an old beast exhausted by the long summer and refusing to be moved. Damp with perspiration, her chest moving rapidly, Violet pushed back her loosened hair with firm fingers and announced herself.

Clearly, Dr. Grant was annoyed at the disturbance. He turned his grimace to the secretary.

"I'm dreadfully sorry, sir. The young lady will simply not be moved. Shall I call someone?" The secretary's clipped gray voice betrayed not the slightest sense of Violet as a fellow female, as a fellow human being, as anything other than an obstacle to be removed from Dr. Grant's eminent path.

Violet was used to this. She was used to the look of aggravation on Dr. Grant's face. She was used to rooms like this, the smell of wooden furniture and ancient air, the acrid hint of chemicals in some distant laboratory, the *clickety-click* of someone's typewriter interrupting the scholarly quiet. She tilted up her chin and held out her leather portfolio of papers. "With all respect, Dr. Grant, I will not leave until I learn why my application to your institute has once more been sent back, without any sign of its having been read and considered."

"Application to this institute," said the secretary scathingly. "The cheek of these American girls. I shall ring for help at once, Dr. Grant." She lifted the receiver of a dusty black telephone box.

But Dr. Grant held up his hand. He looked at Violet, really *looked*, and his eyes were so genuinely and intensely blue that Violet felt a leap of childlike hope inside her ribs.

"What is your name, madame?" he asked.

"Violet Schuyler, sir. I have recently graduated with highest honors from Radcliffe College in Massachusetts, with bachelor of science degrees conferred in both mathematics and chemistry. My marks are impeccable, I have letters of recommendation from—"

"When did you first make your application to the institute?"

"In March, sir. It was returned in April. I presumed there had been some misdirection, so I sent it again, and—"

He turned to the secretary. "Why have I not seen Miss Schuyler's application?"

The secretary knit her fingers together on the desk and creased her narrow eyes at Violet. "I assumed, sir, that—"

"That I would not consider an application from a female student?"

"Dr. Grant, the institute . . . that is, there is not a single scientist who . . . It's impossible, sir. Of course it is. Your laboratory is no place . . ."

Dr. Grant turned back to Violet with eyes now livid. "I apologize, Miss Schuyler. Your application should have been received with exactly the same attention as any other. If you will please do me the honor of attending me in my office, I shall read it now, with the utmost regard for your tenacity in delivering it against all obstacles." He stood back and motioned with his arm.

And so it began, the awakening of Violet's gratitude, in that instant of triumph over the pinched and gray-suited secretary. She swept into Dr. Grant's office and heard the firm *click* of the door as he closed it behind them, the decisive shutting-out of disapproving secretaries and rigid parents from the territory around them.

"Sit, I beg you," he said, proffering a venerable old leather chair, and Violet sat. He pulled out his pair of rectangular reading glasses and settled into his own chair, behind the desk, while the clock drummed away in the corner and a robin sang from the tree outside the open window. As he read, he remained absolutely still, as if absorbed whole into the papers before him. Violet clenched her fingers around her knee and observed his purposeful energy, the fighting trim of his whip-thin body. Dr. Grant was three years older than her own father, and yet every detail of him belonged so clearly to a newer age, the modern age. Even his graying hair, the color of burnished steel.

How on earth did she get here, in this English building, filled with a race of people to whom she did not belong? Why had she fled her family, her life, her country, her comfortable future? What was she doing?

You're greedy, her mother had said to her quietly, that last night in New York, as she had packed her things. Greedy and selfish. It's not the knowledge you want, you can have that from your journals. You want to be in the newspapers, you want to be Marie Curie, you want to think you're different from all of us. That all other women are silly and complacent and conventional, except you, brilliant you.

Isn't that right, Violet?

"I beg your pardon," Dr. Grant said, raising his head a quarter hour later to part the curtain of silence between them. "I believe a mistake has been made. You are quite the most qualified applicant to this institute in four years."

Despite his heroic vanquishing of the secretary, Violet had somehow been expecting resistance. Resistance was all she knew: from her parents, filling the musty Fifth Avenue air with argument and expostulation; from her brothers, jeering over the silver and crystal. The opposition of the entire world against one embattled island of Violet.

She opened her mouth to return this volley that did not arrive. Instead, on the end of a wary breath, she offered: "I was informed at the outset that it's too late to enter the university for the current term."

He waved that aside in a flash of starched white cuff. "I shall see to it personally. You will have to join one of the women's colleges, of course. Somerville, I think, will be best. I know the principal well; there should be no trouble at all. Have you lodgings?"

"I am at the Crown," she said numbly.

He made a small black note on the paper before him. "I will see to it at once. A quiet, discreet pair of rooms. You have no companion, I take it?"

"No. I am independent."

"Very good."

Very good. Violet absorbed the note of rich satisfaction in his voice, above the glacial white of his collar, the symmetrical dark knot of his necktie. He was wearing a tweed jacket and matching waistcoat, and when he rose to bid her a tidy good afternoon, he unfastened the top button in an absent gesture to let the sides fall apart across his flat stomach.

Violet looked directly into his eyes, at that unsettlingly clear blue in his polished face, but her attention remained at his periphery, at that unfastened horn button, from which the tiny end of a thread dangled perhaps a quarter inch.

Now, as she pauses once more outside her husband's office door, she remembers longing, quite irrationally and against her finest principles, to mend it for him.

Vivian

By the time we reached Twenty-first Street, we were holding hands. I know, I know. I don't consider myself the hand-holding kind of girl, either, but Doctor Paul reached for me when a checker cab screamed illegally around the corner of Fifth Avenue and Twentieth, against the light, and what would you have me do? Shrug the sweet man off?

So I let it stay.

Doctor Paul had suggested walking instead of the subway, once he emerged from the hospital locker room, shiny and soapy and shaven, hair damp, body encased in a light suit of sober gray wool with a dark blue sweater-vest underneath. I would have said yes to anything at that particular instant, so here we were, trudging up Fifth Avenue, linked hands swinging between us, sun fighting to emerge above our heads.

"You're unexpectedly quiet," he said.

"Just taking it all in. I suppose you're used to bringing home blondes from the post office, but I'm all thumbs."

He laughed. "I've never brought home a blonde from the post office, and I never will."

"Promises, promises."

"I happen to prefer brunettes."

"Since when?"

"Since noon today."

"And what did you prefer before that?"

"*Hmm.* The details are strangely hazy now."

I gave his hand a thankful squeeze. "Stunned you with my cosmic ray gun, did I?"

He peered up at the sun. "I said to myself, Paul Salisbury, any girl who can say *Holy Dick* in the middle of a crowded post office in Greenwich Village, that girl is for keeps."

"Nothing to do with my irresistible face, then? My tempting figure?"

"The thought never crossed my mind."

I couldn't see for the galloping unicorns. The Empire State Building lay somewhere ahead, over the rainbow. "The blue scrubs did it for me. I've had a doctor complex since I was thirteen. Just ask my shrink."

"And to think my pops didn't want me to go to medical school."

I stopped in the middle of the sidewalk and turned to him. "You're having me on, aren't you?"

He shook his head.

"But everyone wants his son to be a doctor. No one brags about his son the banker, his son the lawyer."

"Not mine."

I squinted suspiciously. "Are you from earth?"

"I'm from California."

I nodded with understanding and turned us back up the sidewalk. "Aha. That explains everything."

"Everything?"

"Everything. The golden glow, the naive willingness to follow a strange girl upstairs to her squalid Village apartment. I knew you couldn't be a native New Yorker."

"As you are."

"As I eminently am. Tell me about California. I've never been there."

He told me about cliffs and beaches and the cold Pacific current, about his family's house in the East Bay, about the fog that rolled in during the summer afternoons, you could almost set your watch by it, and the bright red-orange of the Golden Gate Bridge against the scrubbed blue sky. Did I know that they never stopped painting that bridge? By the time they had finished the last stroke, they had to start all over again from the beginning. We were just escaping from Alcatraz when the stone lions of the New York Public Library clawed up before us.

"After you," said Doctor Paul.

"SO. I suppose we should start with Violet Schuyler," said Doctor Paul, in his best hushed library whisper.

"How you joke."

"No?"

"My dear boy, don't you know? It's much easier to find out about men. Even if my aunt Violet were the most talented scientist in the Western world, she would probably only rate a small paragraph in the *E.B.* Either no one would have paid her any attention, or some man would have jumped in to take credit for her work."

"Really?" The old lifting eyebrow.

"Really."

"What about Marie Curie?'

"The exception that proves the rule. And she worked with her husband."

"All right, then. So what was Violet's husband's name?"

"That I don't know."

"Shh," said the librarian.

The *New York Times* came to our rescue. "She's a Schuyler," I told Doctor Paul. "Even if the family disowned her, they'd still have put a wedding announcement in the paper."

He shook his head. "And they say Californians are the loonies."

"Oh, you'll learn to love us. And our Labrador retrievers, too."

"I didn't say I didn't love you. I don't suppose you know the wedding date?"

"I do not. But it would have taken at least a few months from meeting to marriage, don't you think?"

He winked. "Would it?"

"You're a shameless flirt, Doctor Paul."

"*Shh,*" said the librarian.

We started with January of 1912, and in half an hour had found our mark. I whistled low, earning myself a sharp look of hatred from the librarian, or perhaps it was jealousy. "April. What, eight months? For a confirmed old bachelor? That was quick work."

"Even for a daughter of the Schuylers. She must have been irresistible. A shame there's no photograph."

"I suppose it's a good thing they didn't have the bright idea to sail home to New York and meet her parents afterward," I said.

He looked at me quizzically.

"The *Titanic.*"

"Oh, right." He turned back to the frail yellow page before us and frowned. "It's awfully concise, isn't it?"

I followed him. The statement was a short one, a compact jewel box of status markers, conveying only and precisely what readers of the *Times* needed to know about the happy bride and groom to place them in the only world that counted.

Miss Violet Schuyler weds Dr. Walter Grant. Miss Violet Schuyler, daughter of Mr. and Mrs. Charles Schuyler of Fifth Avenue, New York City, and Oyster Bay, Long Island, was married last Monday to Dr. Walter Grant of Oxford, England, at the Oxford town hall. A short reception followed the ceremony. The couple will reside in Oxford, where Dr. Grant is chairman of the Devonshire Institute for Physical Chemistry.

"You're right. There should be a photo," I said. "My aunt Julie said she was very pretty. A genuine redhead."

"Funny, the announcement says nothing about Violet's being a scientist, too."

"Well, it wouldn't, would it? The horror."

Doctor Paul straightened from the table. "We have a name now, anyway. Violet Grant, Dr. Walter Grant. The encyclopedia should have a listing, shouldn't it?"

We tackled the *E.B.* shoulder-to-shoulder, oxen in yoke. Did I mention I was enjoying myself immensely? Working with Doctor Paul gave me the most exhilarating sense of equality, the thrill of collaborative discovery. Exactly the way I had pictured my job at the magazine, before I actually entered the office two weeks ago and knocked on my editor's door for that first journalistic assignment. Just imagine me, fresh of face, shiny of pelt, poised of pencil, doing my best Rosalind Russell before the legendary desk of my legendary editor.

Me (humbly): What'll it be, Mr. Tibbs? Murder trial? Corruption investigation? Fashion shoot?

Tibby (cheerfully): No cream, extra sugar, and make it hot.

But this. Doctor Paul's older and wiser fingers flipping through the wispy new pages of the latest *Encyclopaedia Britannica*, his voice muttering *Gramophone, Graves, too far, here it is, Grant*. All on my behalf. All as if I belonged by his side, reading the one-column entry for Dr. Walter Grant in tandem with his own adept brain.

Then, the coup de be-still-my-beating-heart. Doctor Paul turned, knit his devastating brows to an inquisitive point, and said the magic words: "What do you think, Vivian?"

I think we should marry and breed.

"I think it was a shame she killed him."

GRANT, Walter, Ph.D. (1862–1914) Physical chemist, an earlier colleague of Ernest Rutherford before a professional dispute caused a rift between the two, chair of the Devonshire Institute for Physical Chemistry (Oxford), and finally a fellow at the Kaiser Wilhelm Institut für Physikalische Chemie und Elektrochemie in Berlin, Germany, in the years before his death. His early experimentation in the discovery of the atomic nucleus paved the way for numerous advances, though by the time of his death in July 1914, his theories had reached a dead end and he had failed to produce any major original research in several years.

Born on August 7, 1862, the only surviving child of a Manchester solicitor and the daughter of a music teacher, Grant attended first Uppingham School in Rutland, where he excelled in mathematics and Greek and won a scholarship to King's College, Cambridge.

The circumstances of his death have never been established conclusively, due in part to the state of civic confusion as Germany hovered on the brink of the First World War. According to press reports, his body was found in his flat in Kronenstrasse with a single gunshot wound to the chest in the early morning hours of July 26, 1914. Police attempted to apprehend his wife, Violet Grant, but she escaped Berlin with a man widely rumored to have been her lover, and was not seen again. No other suspect was subsequently apprehended, and the case remained open.

"Look how handsome he is." I tapped the tiny gray photograph of a bearded Dr. Walter Grant, right between his smug scientific eyeballs. "A crying shame."

"If she killed him," said Doctor Paul. "The case remains open, it says."

"Who else would have done it?"

"The lover, for one."

A shadow fell over the life, work, and beard of **GRANT, Walter,**

Ph.D. An exasperated shadow, judging by the acute angle of the elbows as hands met hips.

"That was your last warning," the shadow whispered bitterly. "I must ask you to leave."

"I WONDER who he was, this lover of Violet's," I said. "The encyclopedia didn't even give his name."

Doctor Paul stretched out his long legs and fingered the rim of his cup. We were sitting in a booth at an overheated coffee shop on Forty-second Street, a hat toss from Grand Central Terminal, and I, watching the good doctor's lugubrious hand circle its way into infinity, found myself in the absurd position of envying a hunk of white ceramic. "Some good-looking young fellow, I guess. Closer to her own age. She'd probably examined her future, decades of marriage to a man old enough to be her father, and realized it wasn't worth it."

"What wasn't worth it?"

"Whatever she got from it. Money or security." He shrugged and pulled a packet of cigarettes from his jacket pocket. "Do you mind?"

"Oh, thank God." I snatched a cigarette from the pack. "I was hoping you'd ask."

He laughed and lit me up like a gentleman. I might have lingered overmuch near his outstretched fist, though he didn't seem to mind. "I've told myself I'll quit when this damned residency is over with," he said, pulling out one for himself.

"I've told myself I'll quit when I'm good and ready." I took a sweet long drag, just to drive home my point, and drank my coffee in a reckless gulp. And why not? I couldn't fault the coffee, hot hot hot; the same went for Doctor Paul's cigarettes, Winstons, luxurious and masculine. Coffee and tobacco, that fusion of divine creation. I'd ordered a raisin bun some time ago and presumed the kitchen was now sending out to Madagascar for more cinnamon. I didn't care. "I don't think she wanted money from him. She wasn't the type. If she wanted to marry for money, she'd have stayed in New York and done a much better day's work of it."

"Fair enough. Security? She was alone in England. She'd left her family behind."

"Possibly. Or maybe she was in love with him."

"Really?" His voice was so saturated with doubt, I could have stretched out my two hands, wrung it from the air, and mopped it back up with a napkin.

"Really. It's a known phenomenon, after all. A rite of passage. Falling in love with your professor."

"Are you serious? An old man like that?"

"You're sure you want to hear this, golden boy?"

Just before he answered, he checked himself. His blue eyes did that thing again, that darkening, as if the weight of realization brought about some chemical change in him. He picked through his words more carefully and said: "Is this about Violet, or about you?"

Well, now.

I am not a girl who evades a man's gaze without good reason, but I dropped mine then, right through the gentle haze of smoke drifting from my fingers and into the hot black pool of coffee, *kerplop*.

Here we were already, the moment of truth. It usually took a lot longer to arrive, didn't it? Several dates at a minimum. Sometimes never, if the chemistry wasn't bubbling enough to make the effort worthwhile. You circled around it as long as you could, until there was no putting it off, until the suitcases had to be dragged out from under the bed and opened, the contents examined. Had you slept with anyone? When? Why? How many? The answers could be elliptical or coded—*we were engaged*, that was a favorite—and the details left to the imagination, but you had to have your answer ready. Some boys wanted to know you were lily-white; some just wanted to know you weren't a livid scarlet. You needed to know whether he cared about your particular shade of pink, and what that meant, and whether you cared if he cared. You might even be curious about him—Yes? How many? What kind of girls?—and then it was time for the fork in the road, and whether the two of you would take it. It was a funny time, 1964. An in-betweener, a swirling slack tide.

I had no answer ready for Doctor Paul. I had the truth, but what sane person ever wants the truth?

"Never mind," he said. "I didn't mean to pry."

I lifted my head. "Didn't you?"

"Not to make any judgments, Vivian. Just to know about you. What makes you—"

"Tick?"

"What makes you *Vivian*."

I liked the way he said my name, all throaty on the *V*'s, all stretched to its rightful three syllables. The diner was quiet, at least for the middle of Manhattan, only half full, giving me the illusion of privacy, the demi-sanctity of confessional. Something clattered onto the Formica before me. The raisin bun. "Thank you," I said, without looking up.

"Did he hurt you?" asked Doctor Paul, compassionate.

"Did he hurt me." I snatched the raisin bun. "Do I look like the kind of girl who lets herself get hurt?"

"You tell me."

I went on with my mouth full, in a way that would have caused my mother to reach for her third vodka gimlet, no ice. "Look, a girl goes away to college, any girl, every girl, and she's alone. No mother and father, especially no father. She meets a lot of boys, if she's lucky, and they're either painfully awkward or awkwardly pushy, and she wonders where all the men have gone, the ones who know how to speak and act and treat a lady. Oh, wait. Look. There's one! Right at the front of the room, an expert in his field, eminent and confident as all get-out, holding the classroom in his chalk-dusted palm, maybe flashing you a smile, maybe holding your gaze a second or two. You find yourself going to his office to ask a question, to talk about your exam, and lo and behold, he can actually hold a conversation. He pulls out your chair for you and hangs your coat on a hook. He's civilized. He's a grown-up, and he acts as though you're the only woman in the universe." I reached for my pocketbook and shook out another smoke. Doctor Paul went for his lighter, but I waved him away and used my own. "So that's how it happens. Daddy complex, whatever the shrinks want to call it. You think you're safe with him, until you're not. Until you're losing your virginity on his office sofa, oopsy-daisy."

"The difference, of course," said Doctor Paul, in a voice from another century, "is that this Dr. Grant married her afterward."

"Stand down, Lancelot. God forbid I should have married *him*. Anyway, I could have said no, and I didn't. I was curious. I had my own urges. Don't let any girl tell you she doesn't." I let the waitress refill my coffee before I exploded my next little bombshell. "And my mother made it look so easy, having affairs. I thought, well, tiddledywinks. I'm her daughter. It's the family business, isn't it, sleeping with married men."

"He was married?"

"He's not anymore. It turned out he had a thicket of notches on the arm of his office sofa, and eventually the poor wife discovered them while she was plumping the pillows one day. As I said, a rite of passage, and he was more than happy to perform the sacraments."

Doctor Paul sat back and stubbed out his cigarette. His cheeks were faintly pink; so was the tip of his nose. "I don't know what to say."

"Look, I don't regret it. I don't think I do, anyway, except that he was married. That was wrong, that was stupid, and I'd never do that again. It seems I don't have the stomach for adultery, genes or no genes."

"What a relief."

"But I can see the same thing happening to her, to Violet. Seduction, that is. She would have been much more alone than I was, wouldn't she, with her family across the ocean, and no other women to share her midnight cocoa and a good laugh? She'd burned every bridge, God help her. So either Dr. Grant seduced her, because she was innocent and vulnerable, and then he married her out of guilt. Or else she seduced him and made him cough up the ring, ex post coitus."

"Which one do you think it was?"

I licked the sticky from my fingers and finished off the coffee. Half a cigarette remained in the ashtray, burning quietly, but I'd had my fill.

"Maybe a little of both." I ground out the cigarette with a little more force than strictly necessary.

Doctor Paul studied my fingers at their work. "What are you thinking?"

Perceptive, I thought. Maybe he couldn't read my mind yet, but at least he knew when it was chewing on a bone. I folded my arms and leaned forward. "Oh, about what you said. If I'd married my professor, instead of scattering two hundred pages or so of his latest research notes over the new-fallen snow one fine February morning . . ."

Doctor Paul grinned. He picked up my hand and kissed my palm. "And?"

"I think I'd probably have ended up murdering him, too."

Violet

Violet never could pinpoint the moment in which her immense regard, her gratitude, and even awe for Dr. Grant transformed into romantic desire. For some reason, this disturbs her. Shouldn't erotic love make its nature obvious from the beginning? Wasn't sexual attraction the first basis for attachment between men and women?

Possibly the idea of Dr. Grant as a sexual partner simply didn't occur to her. She had been exceptionally innocent when she first came to the institute, for all her air of independence. She'd never been kissed, never even held hands with a man. She'd been too busy, too eager to prove herself, and all the boys she knew in college and in New York were just that: boys, callow and conventional, shallow and unimaginative. She imagined herself proudly as a kind of sexless being, her mind too occupied with complex and abstract thoughts to lower itself to base human instincts. To mere physical titillation. So perhaps all that initial awe and gratitude really was a form of sexual desire, sublimated into something the virginal Violet of September 1911 could recognize and accept.

She has an answer ready, though, in case Walter or anyone else should ask.

This is another of the scenes that remains vivid in her brain, mined frequently for details: Dr. Grant standing in his office, two weeks into the start of the term, and offering her a chair. He had already called for tea, and it was arriving right now in all its lavish plenty, borne on a large tray by the gray-suited secretary. Violet heard his words in her ears: *I have just finished marking your first paper, and I am stunned by the quality of your thought.*

Yes: *stunned,* he said. His exact word. He sat in the chair next to her—not behind his desk but directly next to her, his woolen knee nearly brushing hers—and fixed her with his blue eyes and repeated the word: *stunned.*

When Violet rehearses this story for her imaginary audience, she usually tells them that her heart gave a skip when he said this, and it did. Her memory is exact, and she feels the emotion again, simply remembering it. Her blood tingles in her fingertips, and her breath becomes thready in her chest. She recovers that exact sense of her younger self: as if she's an explorer, catching a glimpse of some new and undiscovered territory, just out of reach.

The scene resumed.

"Thank you," she said.

The secretary left, and the door clicked shut.

Dr. Grant turned to the tea and poured her a cup, asked her if she took cream and sugar. Violet answered him politely, though her nerves were singing.

She had *stunned* Dr. Walter Grant by the quality of her thought.

She watched his elegant hands perform before her. She glanced briefly at his lips, full and rather endearingly pink, framed by his short tabby beard. When he gave her the cup and saucer, the tips of his fingers touched the tips of hers.

"I hope I have not seemed cold, this past fortnight." He took up his own tea. "I was conscious of your peculiar status among the other fellows, and I had no wish to incur their resentment by any particular notice."

"Yes, of course. I didn't expect any favorable treatment, not at all. I'm just another fellow here, after all."

"Not just another fellow, Miss Schuyler. You are by far my most promising student. With your diligence and your elegant mind, you make the others seem like factory drudges."

Violet looked into her muddy tea. "Thank you."

"My dear"—his tone shifted, taking on a sympathetic weight—"believe me, I do know how difficult it is for you, surrounded by these men of narrow and conservative attitudes, who don't understand you. Isn't it?"

"I have no cause to complain." Her eyes stung. She kept them trained on her cup.

He shook his head and leaned in a little. "My dear, dear child. I've seen how they avoid you, how they refuse to include you in any of the usual social activities, lunch and tea and that sort of thing. Did you think I hadn't?"

"I hope you haven't wasted your time with such trivial concerns, Dr. Grant. I'm getting along just fine."

"Tell me, my dear, has any one of them approached you outside of the institute? Has any one of them perhaps offered you any sort of outstretched hand at all?"

"Nothing of any significance."

"Something, then?"

"I've received a note or two at my room. Invitations to tea."

"Have you answered them?"

"No. I thought it improper. I didn't even recognize the names."

"Ah, Violet." He placed his tea on the edge of the desk and took her hand. "You must understand, you're an exceptionally attractive woman, young and quite obviously inexperienced. I'm afraid this university has no shortage of cads wishing to take advantage of that inexperience."

His hand was warm around hers. "I am perfectly capable of understanding the difference, Dr. Grant. As I said, I haven't answered the notes. I don't have the slightest interest that way in any of my colleagues."

"Good." He patted their enclosed hands. "Very good. I'm relieved to hear it. I take a particular interest in you, Violet. I see you as a kind of protégé. I intend to look after your interests with all the zeal in my power."

His kind voice made her eyes prickle with tears. She wouldn't tell him, she couldn't tell him how lonely she'd been, nobody saying a word to her, cold glances and cold lunches, her cramped and empty rooms at the end of the day. Studying, studying. Her coffee delivered hot in the morning by her landlady, accompanied by the only smile she would receive until her return that evening. The alien voices and vehicles and architecture, the September drizzle parted at intervals by a fickle sun. At least at Radcliffe she knew a few other girls like her, ambitious and clever girls, who were always happy to commiserate over hot cocoa at midnight. Here she had nobody, she had less than nobody: a negative space of openly hostile company.

"You are so kind," she said.

"There, now. If you have any trouble, Violet, you're to come to my office immediately. You may ring me at any time, day or night. You're to think of me as an uncle, Violet, a very dear uncle who admires you greatly."

If his words were a little more fulsome than avuncular, Violet was too grateful to notice. She blinked back her tears and returned the squeeze of his warm hands. She looked up into his face—the face of Dr. Grant, brilliant and renowned *Dr. Walter Grant*, gazing at her with such tenderness! She was overcome with gratitude; she was melting with it. "Thank you, sir."

He shook his head, smiling. "You must call me Walter, in these rooms. I'm your uncle, remember? Your nearest relation here."

"Yes, of course." But she couldn't quite bring herself to say *Walter*, not yet.

He gave her hand a last pat and picked up his cup. "You'll come to me every week like this, Violet. You're looking rather thin, rather pale; you must eat better. I shall stuff you with cake and sandwiches and send you on your way. Does that sound agreeable?"

She smiled. "Yes, very much."

And so she and Dr. Grant came to take tea in his sumptuous offices every week, served without comment by his own personal secretary, talking and laughing and calling each other *Dr. Grant* and *Violet*, while the leaves changed color and fell from the trees, and the afternoon sky grew darker and darker, until it began to turn quite black by four o'clock, when she knocked punctually on his door. It was then a week before Christmas, and the air smelled of snow. Dr. Grant stood in his office with a pair of workmen, his white shirtsleeves glowing in the lamplight, wires and plaster everywhere; he was having a new telephone installed, he told her, shaking his head, and the case was hopeless.

Perhaps they should take tea at his house in Norham Gardens instead?

Vivian

Doctor Paul's living room had potential, and I told him so.

"Your living room has potential, if you'd consider unpacking the moving boxes." I waved my chopsticks at said boxes, which were clustered in haphazard stacks about the room, like some sort of ironic modernist furniture set. "Maybe a lick of paint, too. White is so sterile."

"Agreed. It's like being in a hospital."

"How can you stand it?"

"I'm not here often. I usually sleep in an empty examining room."

I *tsk*ed. "And you've lived here four weeks. If I were a shrink, I'd suggest you were having second thoughts."

"About the apartment?"

"About the apartment. About New York."

"Maybe I was."

In the absence of furniture, we were lying on the floor in an exact perpendicular relationship: fully clothed, I hasten to add. Our heads were propped up by a single upholstered cushion, provenance unknown, and the little white boxes of Chinese takeout sat agape between us, like a row of teeth awaiting root canals. I picked up one of them now and dug my chopsticks deep into a shiny tangle of chow mein. "What, the charms of our humble town have worn thin already?"

"I don't mean to offend—"

"Which means you're about to do just that."

"—but I haven't seen much charm to begin with. I work in a hospital, Vivian. All I see is New York's greasy gray underbelly. Do you know what my first patient said to me? My first patient, a little kid of eight years old, in for an appendix—"

I put down my chopsticks. "You're a *kid* surgeon?"

"Yes. He said to me—"

"This is just too much. Perfect Doctor Paul is so perfectly perfect, he saves the lives of nature's little angels."

"I am not perfect."

I rolled my head against the cushion and looked at him, inches away. He was staring at the ceiling, chopsticks idling in one hand, chicken chop suey balanced on his ribs. His adorable hair flopped toward the cushion, a little disordered, close enough to taste. The expression on his face wrecked my chest. I said softly: "From where I'm sitting, you're close enough to divine."

"Don't say that." He sat up, catching the chicken just in time. "My dad. Pops. He's a gambler."

"That's a shame, but it's not your fault."

"No, I mean he really gambles. Deep. Drinks, too. I was lucky, I got out when I could, went to Princeton on scholarship. I have to send him money sometimes."

"What about your mother?"

"Died when I was ten. Cancer. But I just want you to know, my family's not like yours. We're nobody special."

"For God's sake, why would I care about that? My special family's a mess." I removed the white box from his hand and replaced it with my fingers. "Lie down again, will you? You're making me anxious."

He laughed at that and settled back against the cushion, a tiny fraction closer to me. I felt his hair against mine, his mouth disturbing the air as he spoke. "You've never been anxious in your life, Vivian."

"Oh, haven't I? I'm anxious now."

"You shouldn't be."

I let that sit for a moment in perfect tranquility, because I liked the way it sounded. *You shouldn't be.* Shouldn't be anxious, Vivian, because I am the real deal, I am your Doctor Paul, and we two have an understanding, now, don't we.

"Yes," I whispered.

"Yes?"

"Yes, we have an understanding, don't we?"

He squeezed my hand against the bare parquet floor of his sterile white apartment. "We do."

Doctor Paul evidently had a clock somewhere, buried in his boxes or else on an unseen shelf, because I could hear it ticking methodically as we lay there in perpendicular quietude, absorbing the force of our understanding. If I could see that clock, I guessed it would read somewhere between seven and eight o'clock in the evening, which meant that I had now known him for just over seven hours.

I traveled through them all again: the post office, my apartment, the walk to the library, the library itself, the coffee shop. Wandering up the dull weekend stretch of Madison Avenue, bending our way to the park, not caring where we went as long as we remained linked by this pulsing thread, this shimmering ribbon of you-and-me. How we talked. Not of ourselves, of course. We stuck to the things that mattered: books read, places traveled, friends met, ideas discarded. An hour had passed in a minute, and another hour in a few electric seconds, until we'd looked up to a lowering sky in blind amazement. "Where are we?" Doctor Paul asked.

"I think that's the Guggenheim, through the trees over there. The museum."

"I know the Guggenheim. My apartment's only a few blocks away."

"Imagine that," I said.

"Imagine that. Are you hungry?"

"Enough to eat you alive."

"Will Chinese do?"

We ordered takeout from a tiny storefront on Eighty-ninth Street—
THE PEKING DELIGHT, promised the sign above the window, in bright gold
letters on a lucky red background—and Doctor Paul led me to his apartment on Lexington Avenue, on the third floor of an anodyne white-brick
apartment block, the primary virtue of which was its close proximity to
the express subway stop on Eighty-sixth Street. "It's only fair," he told me,
"since I handed you such a gilded opportunity to have your psychopathic
way with me this morning."

He had opened a bottle of cheap red wine, not a good match for the
Chinese, but we drank it anyway in paper Dixie cups, ounce by tannic
ounce.

I listened to the clock, the irreplaceable tick of seconds and minutes.

"I should head home," I said. "You need a few hours of sleep before
you go back to the hospital."

"I suppose I do."

Neither of us moved.

"I don't like it," he said. "It's dark out, and that neighborhood of
yours—"

I laughed. "Oh, nuts. It's the city that never sleeps, remember? I'll be
just fine. Anyway, my parents live around here. I could always sleep
there."

"You could sleep here."

Our hands were still entangled, his right and my left, clinging on for
dear life. Not a muscle twitched in either.

Doctor Paul cleared his throat. "For the record, I meant *sleep* sleep.
Real sleep. I'll take the sofa."

"You have a sofa?"

"Somewhere underneath all these boxes."

"These boxes you won't unpack."

"I will now." Again, he gave his words time to settle in and sink to the bone. I listened to the cadence of his breath and stared at the nubby white ceiling. *I will now.* I will unpack for you, Vivian, because if New York is your home, it must be mine, too.

He spoke softly. "I don't want you to go, Vivian."

"Why not?"

"You know why."

"But I'd love to hear you say it."

He turned on his side to face me. "I'm afraid that if you go, we'll lose it. This." He held up our combined hands. "What happened today."

"No, we won't. We couldn't if we tried." I detached his hand and rose to my feet. "Go to bed. I'll clean up."

He rose, too. "Vivian."

"Go to bed."

"Like hell I will."

We cleaned up together, because he wouldn't hear of anything else, finishing off the wine as we went along. I made him unpack the box marked KITCHEN so we could drink from genuine glassware next time. His kitchen was even smaller than mine, an L cut short by an old wooden table wedged against the wall, and a stack of plates had to be stored atop the asthmatic Frigidaire.

"I have an idea." Doctor Paul folded his dish towel and placed both hands on my shoulders. "I'll nap on the sofa while you take the bed, and when it's time for me to go to work, I can drop you off at your own apartment. For one thing, your roommate will be wondering where you are."

"Sally will be wondering no such thing. Sally will be out earning herself a new pair of shoes, maybe a nice new bracelet if she puts in a little elbow grease. She wouldn't notice if I didn't come home until Monday morning."

Doctor Paul looked stricken. I patted his cheek. "But it's a lovely plan. Where do I sign?"

A look came into his eyes, perilously close to mine: a look that said he knew exactly where I should sign on to his plan. His hands sank into my shoulders. He blinked his blue eyes slowly, like a cat readying for naptime, and I knew by the prickling of my skin that he was about to kiss me.

I've already explained that I'm not a shy girl, but some impulse overcame me as Doctor Paul's warm breath bathed my face in chop suey promise. I wanted to kiss him, I wanted to make a meal of him; I most thoroughly wanted him to make a meal of *me*, and yet, at the last perilous instant, I dodged him.

Yes, you heard that right.

I dodged him.

Instead of tilting my face conveniently upward, parted of lips, closed of eyes, trip-hammer of pulse, I stepped into his chest and crushed my nose into his windpipe. His startled arms wrapped around me. A hearty consolation prize of an embrace.

We stood there in awkward disappointment. I felt the need to explain myself. "If we start now, we'll never stop," I said, next to his ear.

"And we can't have that."

He owned a terribly comfortable chest, my Doctor Paul. Solid and clean-smelling, his breath flavored with wine and dinner. He stroked my hair until I wanted to stretch like a cat.

He whispered to me, "What are you thinking?"

"I was thinking about Violet again."

"She's on your mind, isn't she?"

"I can't stop wondering. What she was like, what happened to her. How she lost that suitcase." I pulled a little more Doctor Paul into my lungs. "I was thinking that maybe she was miserable with her professor. Maybe she had finally found someone to love. Someone to trust."

"Do you think that excuses what she did?"

"I don't know. We don't know what he was like, do we? What he did to *her*. This Dr. Grant of hers."

Doctor Paul kissed my hair. "Time to sleep, Vivian."

"Please take the bed. You won't be able to excavate the sofa in time."

"Where will you sleep?"

"*If* I sleep—which I doubt—I'll just curl up on the cushion."

He pulled back. "It's not very gentlemanly of me."

"Nuts to that. Go put on your pajamas."

We looked at each other for a moment longer, goofy with infatuation, and then he leaned forward to kiss me on the forehead like a good brother.

I AWOKE on the cushion an hour later, one arm stiff beneath my face, one head exploding with bizarre disconnected dreams in which I was my great-aunt Violet, and my chemistry lab was full of jars of old curiosities like two-headed snakes and rabbit fetuses in formaldehyde, and a naked professor chased me around the counter of a post office in Istanbul. And those were just the scenes I remembered.

In case you were wondering, I knew it was an hour later because I had located the source of all that thunderous ticking and discovered a battery alarm clock in a box marked BEDROOM, still set to California time. I had wound the hands ahead three hours and set it next to me so neither I nor Doctor Paul would oversleep. Eight-twenty-two, it said, and in my Violet-tinged confusion I thought perhaps this was morning, and we were doomed.

But the cracks between the metal blinds were still black, and my brain, returning bit by broken bit to the sanity of consciousness, knew an immense and bone-rattling craving to see how my good doctor was faring alone in his bedroom.

I didn't even remember him going to bed. I remembered watching him drink down a few glasses of water to flush the wine out; I remembered taking in an eyeful of Doctor Paul as he opened the bathroom door, half dressed, and slipped away from me. Then the screen turned black and Violet stepped out with her embryonic tortoises and her naked professor.

I rose to my feet, also numb, and padded to the bedroom.

It was a tiny space, just large enough for the metal mattress frame he called a bed, blanketed in an uninspiring white, and a bent metal chair stacked with books. In the glow from the sleepless city outside, I saw Doctor Paul sprawled on his back in the center. He had flung one arm up on the pillow beside him, and his head was turned toward it, as if he were whispering secrets to his elbow. I watched the rise and fall of his white-blanket chest. Even in sleep, his hair achieved a perfect flop that ached to be set right by a loving hand.

I had to turn away.

I had drunk a couple of glasses of water, too. I stopped in the bathroom for relief, and as I stood at Doctor Paul's sink and washed my hands with Doctor Paul's soap and stared into Doctor Paul's mirror, I caught a glimpse not of myself but of Violet: her beauty, her ravenous ambition, her newborn self standing, as I did, on the brink of a jaw-dropping precipice.

I shed my shoes and dress and stockings and folded them neatly. I was surprised to see that my hands were a little shaky. I looked at myself in my shining silk slip, my cat on a hot tin roof. I kissed my finger and touched it to the mirror.

He came awake the instant I slid under the warm white blanket, or maybe he'd never fallen asleep. At any rate, he seemed remarkably lucid. "You again."

"Like a bad penny."

He found the edge of my shining silk slip. He lifted it up and over my head.

I whispered: "I'm not scaring you off, am I?"

"Not even close," he said, that was all, and his skilled surgeon's hands wrapped around me and took me apart, piece by piece, from my face to my throat, to my breasts and hungry young thighs. I took his face and kissed his sweet mouth, his salty skin, the lovely burnished belly of my dear new Doctor Paul, and there was no stopping us now. It was like painting the Golden Gate Bridge: no sooner had we finished, salt-licked and panting, than we had to start all over again from the beginning.

Violet

V iolet knows she had only herself to blame for what happened that day. Walter might have made the invitation, but while the Violet Schuyler of 1911 was still sexually innocent, she was nobody's fool.

As she walked down the darkened paving stones of Magdalen Street, with Dr. Grant at her side keeping up a reassuring stream of chatter, she knew his suggestion of a private meeting had not been made thoughtlessly. They might have gone to a tea shop on the high street, or even a respectable hotel lobby, some public place, well lit and filled with people. There was no need to rendezvous at his house.

He was speaking of telephones. "I've never quite liked the things, to be perfectly honest. As a means of communication, they're wholly unsatisfying. One can't hear the other party properly, one hasn't the assistance of gesture and tone. It has all the disadvantages of communicating by letter, without the advantage of being able to express oneself with any sort of detail or subtlety."

Violet, who hated telephones, found herself saying, "But at least they're immediate. If you want a doctor, or the police—"

"Yes, for emergencies, of course. But it's a disaster for human communication."

"And you pride yourself on being so very modern."

Dr. Grant laughed. "Yes. I suppose one's got to be old-fashioned about *something*."

They crossed Broad Street, under the dull orange glow of an arc lamp, and for an instant, as a motor-omnibus rattled near in a jangling chaos of headlamps and petrol fumes, Dr. Grant laid a protective hand at her elbow.

Violet knew the way; her own rooms were not far from Dr. Grant's imposing house. The buildings slid past the sides of her vision, gray Oxford stone blurred by the settling darkness, illuminated in lurid patches by the arc lamps. People hurried past, buried deep in their overcoats, never looking up, never noticing the pair of them, Violet and Dr. Grant, his hand now permanently affixed to her elbow. The heavy damp chill in the air froze her lungs.

She could have said *no*. She could still stop and say she had changed her mind, she'd rather go to the tea shop, she'd rather go home and study. Dr. Grant's limbs struck out confidently next to her, his voice cheered the frosted air. Dr. Walter Grant, taking her to tea in his private residence.

Red-brown and Gothic outside, Dr. Grant's house surprised Violet on the inside. Its high-ceilinged grace reminded her of home, of the elegantly proportioned rooms over which her mother competently presided, except that these light-colored walls and clean furnishings disdained the cluttered excess of the past. A silent housekeeper took her coat, and Dr. Grant ushered her into a small sitting room at the back, where not a single silver-framed photograph decorated the side table, and a coal fire fizzed comfortably under a mantel nearly bare of objects, except for a pair of small Delftware vases standing at either end. A phonograph horn bellowed upward from a square end table near the wall.

Dr. Grant walked to the fire and spread out his hands. "Ah, that's better. What a devil of a chill out there today. I shouldn't be surprised if it snows."

"It certainly feels like snow."

He turned to her. He was smiling, quite at ease. He spread out his hands behind him, catching the warmth from the fire. "You, of course, have the advantage of youth. A man of my advanced years feels the cold more acutely every year."

"You're hardly that," Violet said, taking her cue. But she meant it, too. Though Dr. Grant was older than her own father, he existed in a separate category altogether from parents and uncles and middle-aged men, whose waistcoats strained over their comfortable bellies. Dr. Grant's stance was elastic, his eyes bright and blue, the mind behind those eyes quick and supple. His brilliant mind: it excited her; it had excited her for years, long before she arrived in England. She couldn't quite believe that she was standing in Dr. Walter Grant's own private sitting room, waiting for his housekeeper to bring tea. That he had chosen to bring *her* to his home.

"The tea should be ready directly," he said, as if he'd read her own mind, "by virtue of that very telephone I've just been reviling. Though perhaps a drink of brandy might not come amiss, in this chill?" He raised his eyebrows hopefully.

"Yes, brandy. Of course."

He poured and offered; Violet sipped hers watchfully. She was not a drinker of brandy. It burned down her throat to her empty stomach. She disguised the shock with a bright smile.

"Drink it down, child," Dr. Grant said. "All of it. Brandy warms the soul."

Violet drank obediently. She was surprised to find that the glass trembled slightly in her hand.

Dr. Grant walked to the phonograph and settled a disc on the turntable. "Do you like Stravinsky?" he asked. Before she could think of a reply, a violin zigzagged tinnily from the scalloped edges of the bell.

A knock, and the door opened. The housekeeper arranged the tea things on the side table. Dr. Grant offered Violet a chair and poured her a cup. She sat and drank her tea, trying to think of something clever to say, while Dr. Grant carried another chair from near the sofa and placed it beside hers. He settled himself into it, tea in hand.

"Here we are, quite comfortable," he said.

Looking back, Violet is never able to pinpoint the moment in which the tenor of the conversation began to change. Perhaps the note had always been there, from the beginning, from the morning she first walked into his office. Perhaps it had only amplified slowly, decibel by decibel, week by week, tea by intimate tea, so that Violet was not quite alarmed when Dr. Grant's hand found its way to her knee, half an hour after she had entered his house, and he asked her whether she had left any admirers languishing behind her in New York.

"No, none at all. I was far too busy for that."

"Surely some young man awakened your interest?"

"No. Not one." She met his gaze honestly. She could feel the pressure of his hand in every nerve of her body, heavy with significance. The music behind her built into an arrhythmic climax, and then fell away again.

His fingers stroked the inside of her knee in languid movements. His other hand reached for his cup, applied it to his lips, and set it back carefully in the saucer. "You were wise, child, not to succumb to your natural physical urges with such unworthy objects. Young men who don't understand you, as I do."

"I don't remember feeling any such urges."

The stroking continued, an inch farther up her leg. "Nonsense, dear child. It's perfectly natural, the sexual instinct. You should never feel ashamed of your desires; you should never feel as if you must deny the existence of these inclinations. Of what you want with me."

Another inch.

Violet was dizzy with disbelief. She had half expected this moment, had at some level determined to accept it, and now that it had arrived, now that the impossible invitation had quite clearly been made, she found that her heart, her presumably logical and scientific heart, was beating too frantically to allow words.

Dr. Grant picked up her hand and kissed it. His beard scratched her fingers. "Have I frightened you, child?"

Violet wanted to sound worldly. "No."

"You are very beautiful. It's natural that men should desire you."

"I . . . I suppose so."

He kissed her hand again, and then leaned his face to hers and kissed her very gently on the lips. His beard tickled her chin; his mouth was soft and tasted like tea. His other hand still lay on her thigh, palpating, gathering the fine wool of her skirt between his fingers. His thumb crawled upward, an astonishingly long thumb. "Let me show you, child. Let me give you what you're longing for. Don't be afraid."

"I'm not afraid."

Dr. Grant took her right hand and guided it to the apex of his trousers.

Violet's memory, usually so clear and precise, turns blurry at this point. She remembers her surprise at the bony hardness of Dr. Grant's flesh beneath her fingers; she knew the theoretical concept of the male erection, of course, but it was another thing to experience it by touch. But she can never afterward remember the true sequence of events after that: whether he kissed her again or led her to the sofa; whether he removed his own clothes first or hers. Hers, probably. He was so eager to uncover her, so explicit in his approval of her sleek newborn skin, her firm breasts, her bottom, the pretty triangle between her legs, which she attempted at first to keep closed in a vestigial show of virgin modesty.

But Dr. Grant ridiculed her clenched muscles. He drew away the fig leaf of her right hand with a murmured, *Come, now, child. Don't be silly. Let me see you.* He climbed on top of her and gripped her round young bottom, and for all Violet's fearful anticipation, the act itself was over quickly: a shove, a stab of pain, the intimate shock of penetration. He heaved once, twice, and went rigid, stretched upward in an arc of ecstasy while the violins shrieked across the room. A groan emerged from between his clenched teeth, and then Dr. Grant collapsed like a dead man atop her chest, vanquished, his tabby beard stabbing her cheek.

She lay beneath him, equally motionless, a little stunned, and observed the pattern of the ceiling plaster above her, the curtains still drawn wide against the darkness of the back garden. The music finished, and the phonograph bell released a steady cyclical scratch into the still air.

She wondered how the two of them might look to any intruder peeping through the glass: Dr. Grant's white back covering her chest, his buttocks fixed in the cradle of her hips; her left knee raised against the cushions and her right leg slipping inexorably down the sofa's narrow edge. The deed done, her shining virginity consigned to the past, like an unneeded relic, like the bric-a-brac on her parents' mantel. A quarter hour ago she had been sipping tea.

Her parents. How horrified they would be, how prostrate with musty horror at her actions, her willing participation in her own seduction. Or perhaps they wouldn't. Perhaps they would simply shake their heads and say, *You see? We knew she would come to a bad end, we knew nothing good would come of all this scientific nonsense.*

Dr. Grant lifted his head and looked at her with affection. His face was flushed, the tip of his nose the color of candied cherries. "Good girl." He kissed her breast. "Brave girl. You did well. At last. God, that was splendid."

What should she say to that? *Thank you?* She smiled instead and touched his damp temple.

Dr. Grant rose and drew on his trousers. He poured her another glass of brandy and returned, balancing himself on the strip of damask next to her naked hip. "Drink."

She sat up and drank the brandy. It burned less this time, spreading instead a comfortable warmth through her middle.

"How do you feel, child?"

"Quite well."

"Good girl." He put his fingertip to the bottom of the brandy glass and nudged it to her lips. When she was finished, he rearranged the sofa cushions at her back, he added coals to the fire and brought her cake and sandwiches from the table, which he shared with her, sitting close, his body actually touching hers, and told her how well she had pleased him, how long he had been imagining this, how he had felt when he was inside her. He spoke with total candor, a complete freedom of vocabulary.

Violet tried to keep her gaze on his face, but she couldn't help stealing glimpses of the delicate graying curls on his chest, the plaited tendons of his forearms as he ate his cake, which was frosted with buttercream and studded with tiny black poppy seeds. She saw the indent of his navel, just above the waist of his checked wool trousers, and his braces dangling down past his hips. An odd thrill ran through her limbs: excitement and a sort of bemused nausea. No turning back now.

After a while, he asked her again how she felt, and she had said again that she was quite well, and she realized that she meant it. The room was warm, and the brandy simmered happily in her veins. The shock had faded, leaving relief in its place. (Relief for what, she wasn't quite sure.) Dr. Grant moved closer. He lifted her hair and kissed it. "This lovely hair. I've pictured it like this, spread out on my sofa cushion, from the first moment you walked into my office, months ago. You must grow it longer for me, child."

"If you like."

Dr. Grant put on his shirt, secured his braces, and left the room. He returned with a black rubber bulb syringe and a jar of vinegar, and told her she should use the lavatory to clean herself, and to do it thoroughly and at once to avoid any consequences of the afternoon's work. Violet, knowing almost nothing about the prevention of pregnancy, presuming Dr. Grant was an expert, obeyed him to the letter, though the vinegar stung horribly on her raw flesh.

By now it was past seven o'clock. Dr. Grant helped her dress and walked her to her lodging house, where they stood close in the chill gloom of the hallway, at the bottom of the stairs. There was no sign of the land-lady. Violet's head was buzzing. She asked him if he wanted to come up-stairs, and he smiled and said no, not this time. He recommended she soak in a warm salt bath for at least half an hour before bed.

Then he ran his hand over her hair and kissed her good night, and told her he was looking very much forward to seeing her again.

Vivian

Doctor Paul was moving invisibly around the edge of the bed, like a certain six-foot rabbit you might or might not have encountered. After all that vigorous exercise I shouldn't have woken up, but I did. We New Yorkers are an alert and suspicious breed.

"Go back to sleep, Vivian," he said.

"What time is it?"

He sank into the mattress next to me. It was too dark to see his face properly, but the Manhattan glow cast rings of white light around his pupils and made him less invisible. "Eleven-thirty. I have to leave for the hospital." He brushed the hair away from my face and tucked it behind my ear, as if I were a child with a trick appendix and not a woman lying naked in his bed, flushed of skin and dreamy of eye.

"That was reckless of us," I said.

"Fraught with danger," he agreed. Now the thumb on my cheekbone. Was there no end to him?

I said: "You aren't new at it, however."

"No." He hesitated. "But never like this."

"No. Not even close."

He might have sighed a little. Probably he did. "Vivian . . ."

"Already with the *Vivian*."

"Stop it, will you? I was just going to say you're dazzling. I'm dazzled, I'm upside down and inside out and . . . God, Vivian. I don't know *what* to say. There aren't words. I just want to crawl back under the blanket and spend my life doing that with you. And everything else we did today."

"Except that you're married? On the lam? You have a dozen ankle-biters back home in San Francisco?"

"None of those things. I just . . . just a loose end or two to tie up, that's all. Nothing for you to worry about."

I nodded. "Everyone has a loose end or two."

"Do you?"

"I might." I looked straight into those light-circled pupils. "But not at the moment."

This time he sighed in earnest. "Well, then. When can I see you again?"

"When does your shift end?"

He laughed. "Twelve long hours. But I need to sleep, actually sleep this time, and clean up. And—"

"Loose ends."

"Just one, really. So . . . Monday evening? Six o'clock? Dinner?"

"You don't have my telephone number."

"I have your address."

I opened my arms. "Kiss me good-bye, Doctor."

THE THIRD TIME I woke up, it was full morning, and my love-struck body was twisted into a cocoon made of Doctor Paul's sheets. I had to untangle myself before I could reach down for the alarm clock, and then I nearly went into cardiac arrest. It was ten a.m. I'd never slept that late in my life. I'd certainly never known the luxury of waking up in a man's bed before.

Oh, ho? You don't believe me, Vivian Schuyler, not for a second?

Very well, then. Picture me, a wise fool of a college sophomore, caressing the dampened nape of my professor's neck, staring up at his office ceiling, moon-eyed as all get-out. I watch him heave himself up, shuck off the Trojan, straighten his trousers, and light the obligatory cigarette.

Me (dreamily): Let's make love at your house next time. I'll bring champagne and make you pancakes in the morning.

Professor (lovingly): Let's just meet at the library and screw in the stacks, shall we?

But that was all in the past, wasn't it? I rose from Doctor Paul's bed, wrapped myself in a sheet, and found my pocketbook in the living room. I lit a cigarette and leaned against a stack of moving boxes. A piece of paper caught my eye, taped to the icebox.

> Vivian
>   Milk in the fridge. Coffee in the pot. Toast in the
> cabinet. Heart in your hands. For unknown reasons,
> the hot water knob in the shower opens to the right.
>   Still dazzled.
>   Paul

Now, this was what I called a love note. I kissed that sweet little scrap of nonsense and slipped it into my pocketbook.

When I'd finished my cigarette, I showered, brief and scalding hot, and dressed again in my shameful clothes. I plugged in the percolator. I found fresh sheets in the box marked BEDROOM and made up Doctor Paul's bed with precision hospital corners and lovingly fluffed-up pillows.

The clock now read eighteen minutes past eleven. I poured myself a hot one, picked up the telephone, and dialed up Margaux Lightfoot.

"Why, hello, Vivs. How was your Saturday night?"

"I met a boy, honey," I said.

Thrilled gasp. "You didn't!"

"I did. I'm over at his place right now, drinking coffee."

Shocked gasp. "You *didn't*!"

"I did, indeed. Twice." I lit another cigarette and leaned back against the cushion on the living room floor, like the tart I was. The telephone cord spiraled around my right foot.

"You'll scare him off," said Gogo.

"Never mind that. I'm off to Sunday lunch right now, and I need your help."

"But what's he like, Vivs? Is he a dreamboat?"

"The absolute boatiest. But listen. I've just discovered I have a long-lost aunt who murdered her husband fifty years ago. Do you think you could get your father to let me look in the archives a bit tomorrow morning?"

"Oh, Vivs, I don't know. It's his holiest of holies. He doesn't even let me go in there unless it's magazine business."

"I could make it magazine business. I could find out what really happened and write up the story, a big investigative piece." I unwound my foot and wound it back again the other way. "The whole thing is just so juicy, Gogo, just too succulent. Her husband was a physicist, a hotshot, entry in the *E.B.* and everything, and she just . . . disappeared. With her lover. Right before the war. Don't you think that's scandalous? And I never even knew!"

A current of hesitation came down the line. Gogo was the dearest of the dear, but some might say she lacked a certain *je ne sais* sense of adventure.

"Well, Gogo? Don't you think it would make a perfect story?"

"Of course I do, Vivs," she said loyally. "But you know . . . you aren't really . . . you're not one of the writers yet. Not officially."

"Oh, I know I'm just fetching old Tibby's coffee for now, but this is large change. Really large change. And you know I can tell a story. Your father knows it. I can do this, Gogo."

"I'll talk to him about it."

"Mix him a martini first. You know he loves your martinis."

"I'll do my best, I promise. But never mind all that! I want more about this boy of yours. What's his name? What does he do?" She lowered her voice to a whisper of guilty curiosity. "What did he do last *night*?"

"Oh, my twinkling stars, what *didn't* he do." I straightened from the cushion. "But I don't have time now, Gogo. Sunday lunch starts at twelve sharp, or I'll be heave-hoed out of the family. Which is a tempting thought, but I'll need my inheritance one day, when my luck runs out."

"I want *details* tomorrow morning, then. Especially the ones I shouldn't hear."

"You'll have your details, if I have my afternoon in the archives."

Despairing sigh. "You're a hard woman, Vivian Schuyler."

"One of us has to be, Gogo, dear. Go give that boy of yours a kiss from me." I *mwa-mwa*'d the receiver, tossed it back in the cradle, and stared at the ceiling while I finished my coffee and cigarette.

Was I speculating about Violet, or recalling my mad honey-stained hour of excess with Doctor Paul?

I'll let you decide that one for yourself.

NOW, you might have assumed that my mother named me Vivian after herself, and technically you'd be right. After all, we're both Vivians, aren't we? And we're mother and daughter, beyond a doubt?

It's a funny story, really. How you'll laugh. I know I did, when my mother explained it to me over vodka gimlets one night, when I was thirteen. You see, she went into labor with me ten whole days before the due date, which was terribly inconvenient because she had this party to go to. Well, it was an important party! The van der Wahls were throwing it, you see, and everybody would be there, and Mums even had the perfect dress to minimize the disgusting bump of me, not that she ever had much bump to speak of, being five-foot-eleven in her stocking feet and always careful not to gain more than fifteen pounds during pregnancy.

Well. Anyway. There I inconveniently arrived, five days before the van der Wahls' party, six pounds, ten ounces, and twenty-two gazelle inches long, and poor Mums had no more girl names because of my two older sisters, so she left unchanged the little card on my bassinet reading Baby Girl Schuyler, put on her party dress and her party shoes, and checked herself out of the hospital. Voilà! Disaster averted.

Except that when the nanny arrived the next day to check me out of the hospital, they needed a name in order to report the birth. I don't know why, they just did. So the nanny said, *hmm*, Vivian seems like a safe choice. And the nurses said, Alrighty, Vivian it is.

Oh, but you'd never guess all this to see us now. Just look at the ardent way I swept into the Schuyler aerie on Fifth Avenue and Sixty-ninth Street, tossed an affectionate kiss on Mums's powdered cheek, and snatched the outstretched glass from her hand.

"You slept with him, didn't you?" she said.

"Of course I did." I sipped delicately. "But don't worry. He practically asked me to marry him on the spot."

"Practically is not actually, Vivian."

I popped the olive down the hatch. "Trust me, Mums. Is Aunt Julie here today?"

"No, she's having lunch with the Greenwalds." Out came the moue, just like that.

"Ooh, and how are our darling Jewish cousins doing these days? Has Kiki had her baby yet?" I watched her consternation with delight. Poor old Mums never could quite accustom herself to what she was pleased to call the Hebrew stain in the Schuyler blood. Of which, more later.

Mums made a triumphant little cluck of her tongue. "Not yet. I hear she's as big as a house."

"Oh, maybe it's twins! Wouldn't that be lovely!" I pitched that one over my shoulder on the way to the living room, where my father wallowed on a sofa with my sister to his left and a fresh pair of trickling gimlets lined up to his right. (The vodka gimlet was one of the few points of agreement between my parents.) He staggered to his feet at the sight of me.

"Dadums! Handsome as ever, I see." I kissed his cheek, right between two converging red capillaries.

"You look like a tramp in that dress." He returned the kiss and crashed back down.

"That's the point, Dad. Two guesses whether it did the trick."

"Don't listen to him, Vivs. You look gorgeous." Pepper pulled me down next to her for a cuddle. "A little creased, though," she added in a whisper.

"Imagine that," I whispered back. We linked arms. Pepper was my favorite sister by a ladies' mile. Neither of us could politely stand Tiny, who had by the grace of God married her Harvard mark last June and now lived in a respectably shabby house in the Back Bay with a little Boston bean in her righteous oven. God only knew how it got there.

"I want details," said Pepper.

"Take a number, sister."

Mums appeared in the doorway with her cigarette poised in its holder. She marched straight to the drinks tray. "Charles, tell your daughter what a man thinks of a girl who jumps into bed with him right away."

He watched her clink away with ice and glass. "Obviously, I have no idea," he drawled.

Pepper jumped to her feet and slapped her hands over her ears. "Not another word. Really. Stop."

Mums turned. The stopper dangled from one hand, the cigarette holder from the other. So very Mumsy. "What are you suggesting, Charles?"

"Dad was only celebrating your renowned virtue, Mums. As do we all."

She turned back to her mixology. "Fine. Do as you like. I'd just like to point out that among the three of you, only Tiny's found a husband."

"Mums, I'd rather die a virgin than marry Franklin Hardcastle," said I.

"No chance of that," muttered Pepper.

"Pot, meet kettle," I muttered back.

Mums was crying. "I miss her."

"Now, now," I said. "No use weeping over spilled milk. Especially when the milk took so excruciatingly long to get spilled."

"At least one of my daughters has a sense of female decorum." Sniff, sip, cigarette.

"I can't imagine where she got it from," said Pepper. God, I loved Pepper. We were simpatico, Pepper and me, perhaps because we'd arrived an unseemly twelve months apart. As a teenager, I'd once spent an entire morning smuggling through Mums's old letters to discover whether we were half sisters or full. I'd have to concede full, given the genetic evidence. Tiny, I'm not so sure.

"Apparently not from our great-aunt Violet." I piped the words cheerfully.

Next to me, Dad exploded into a fit of coughing.

Mums's red eyes peeped over her poisons. "Are you all right, Charles?"

"Who's Aunt Violet?" asked Pepper.

"Oh, this isn't about that package, is it?" said Mums.

I pounded Dad's broad back. The hacking was beginning to break up, thank goodness, just as his face shifted from red to purple. "Deep breaths," I said.

"What package?" asked Pepper.

"Yesterday I picked up a package from the post office. Mums had forwarded it to me." I kept up the pounding as I spoke. "It was a suitcase belonging to a Violet Schuyler. Aunt Julie said she was our aunt, and— this is the best part, Pepper, so listen up—she murdered her husband in 1914 and ran off with her lover. Isn't it delicious?"

Dad renewed his spasm of choking. I turned back to him. "Glass of water, Daddy, dear?"

He shook his head.

"As you see," I told Pepper, "Dad's heard of her. But the point is, we have a precedent in this family for independent women. It's in our blood."

"But Mums isn't an independent woman," said Pepper. "She just has a weakness for parties and married men."

"I'm standing right here, you ungrateful child."

"True, but she's not a real Schuyler, is she?" I turned to Mums. "Not by blood."

"Thank God," said Mums. She found her favorite armchair and angled herself into it like a movie star, drink and smoke balanced exquisitely in each hand. "I have my faults, but I haven't murdered your father. Yet."

"Small mercies." Dad had finally recovered. He reached into his jacket pocket and pulled out his battered gold cigarette case, which had been to Eagle's Nest and back, comforting him in every trial.

"That bad, is it?" I said.

"I don't know what you mean." He lit his cigarette with a shaky hand.

"Now, Dad. It's been fifty years since the alleged crimes. Do spill."

"There's nothing to spill."

"Are you saying she didn't exist?"

"She existed, of course." He exhaled a good-sized therapeutic cloud and inhaled his drink. "But you've just about summed up all I know. Your grandparents never talked about it."

"But you must have heard something else. Names, rumors, something."

A rare sharp look from old Dadums. "Why do you want to know?"

"Curiosity."

My father heaved himself up from the sofa and walked to one of the stately sash windows perched above the park. A magnificent thirty-foot living room, the old Schuyler apartment had, thrown open to guests in 1925 by my grandfather and not much redecorated since. We took our drinks from the same crystal decanters, we wobbled across the same Oriental rugs, we sank our backsides into the same mahogany-framed furniture under the gazes of the same disapproving portraits. Possibly Mums had reupholstered at one point, but the sagging cushions were all Schuyler. Dad jiggled his empty ice. "Well, she was a scientist. Left for Cambridge or Oxford, I forget which, a few years before the war."

"Oxford," I said.

"She married a professor, and then they moved to Berlin at some point. He was at some sort of institute there."

"The Kaiser Wilhelm."

Mums did the daggering thing with her eyebrows. "How do you know all this?"

"It's called a *li-brar-y*, Mums." I dragged out the word. "You go there to read about things. They have encyclopedias, periodicals, *Peyton Place*. You'd be amazed. Proceed, Dad."

"No, you go ahead. Obviously, you know more than I do."

"Just a few facts. Nothing about *her*. What she was like."

"I didn't know her. I was born during the war."

"But Grandfather must have said something about her. You can't have just pretended she never existed."

"Oh, yes, they could," said Pepper.

"She didn't get along with my father," said Dad slowly. He was still looking down at the park, as if it contained the secret to his lost youth: the handsome face that had drawn in my mother's adoration, the mobile spirit that had seen him off to war. I caught glimpses of it sometimes, when we were alone together, just him and me, walking along some quiet path in that self-same Central Park or taking in a rare Yankees game. I could almost see his jowls disappear, his eyelids tighten, his irises regain their storied Schuyler blue. His voice lose its endearing tone of sour-flavored aggression. "Anything I heard about her, I heard from Aunt Christina."

"Well, that's not much use, is it? She died eons ago."

"Vivian, really," said Mums.

But Dad turned to me with a touch of smile. "Twenty-five years may seem like eons to you, my dear, but I can remember that hurricane like it was yesterday."

"And she was close to Aunt Christina?"

"I don't know if they were close." He found the ashtray on the drinks table. "But they wrote to each other. Kept in touch. I remember she said that Violet was an odd bird, a lonely girl. I don't think she was happy."

"Did Aunt Christina know what happened? The murder? The lover? Did she know his name?"

"Oh, for God's sake." Mums rolled her head back to face the ceiling.

"Hardly the kind of thing she would tell *me*," said my father.

"Anything, Dad."

He didn't look surprised at my curiosity. The sacks beneath his eyes hoisted thoughtfully upward, and he folded his arms and leaned against the window frame. "I don't know. There might have been a baby."

"Charles, must you be vulgar?"

"Or not." He shook his head. The fumes wafted. "You'd have to ask Aunt Christina."

"Many thanks."

"I have a Ouija board somewhere," said Pepper helpfully.

At which point the housekeeper saved us, announcing lunch, and we shifted ground to the dining room and a tasteful selection of sliced meats and cooked eggs and salads with mayonnaise. It was not until the end of the meal that the shadow of Aunt Violet cast itself once more upon our protruding eggy bellies. Naturally, Pepper was to blame. She stirred cauldrons like a witch in a Scottish play.

"Here's what I think." She helped herself to Mums's cigarette case. "Vivian should do a story on Aunt Violet for the *Metropolitan*."

"Don't be sarcastic, Pepper," said the pot to the kettle.

"I'm not being sarcastic. The whole thing screams *Metropolitan* feature. Compromising photographs, the works. Don't you think, Vivian?"

I tossed back a final trickle of straw-colored Burgundy. "Already thunk."

"Thought," said Dad.

"Vivian!" said Mums.

"Why not? It could be my breakthrough."

"Because it's vulgar. Because it's . . . it's . . . it's *family*."

Mums, caught in a stammer! Now I knew I was onto something big.

"Why not? The Schuylers haven't given a damn about Violet in half a century. There's no need to start now."

Pepper spoke up. "That's where you're wrong, Vivs. We've obviously done our Schuyler best to ignore Violet out of existence for half a century. It's a completely opposite thing, ignoring versus indifference. Justice for Violet, that's what I say! Down with Schuyler oppression!" She shook her fist.

"You will not write this story, Vivian," said Mums. "I forbid it."

"You can't forbid me; I'm twenty-two years old. Besides, it's freedom of speech. Journalistic integrity. All those darling little Constitutional rights that separate us from the communists." I put my fist down on the mayonnaise-stained tablecloth, right next to Pepper's wineglass. "Violet must have a voice."

"Oh, not your damned women's lib again," said Dad. "I fought the Nazis for this?"

"It's not my damned women's lib, Dadums. It's all-American freedom of the press."

Mums threw up her hands. "You see, Charles? This is what comes of letting your daughter become a career girl." As she might say *call girl*.

"*I* didn't let her become a career girl."

"*I* certainly didn't."

Agreement at last! I gazed lovingly back and forth between the pair of them.

"I hate to interrupt another petty squabble, dear ones, but I'm afraid you can't have the satisfaction of laying blame at each other's doorsteps this time. It just so happens I gave myself permission to start a career. The two of you had nothing to do with it, except to prod me on with all your lovely objections." I dabbed the corners of my mouth with an ancient linen napkin and rose to my feet, orator-style, John Paul Jones in a sleek little red wool number that would have sizzled off the powder from the Founding Fathers' wigs. "And I am damned well going to use said hard-won career to find out what happened to Violet Schuyler."

"Bravo." Pepper clapped her hands. "Count me in."

Dad pulled out his cigarette case. "Here's what I'd like to know, Vivian, my sweet. Whose damned idiot idea was it to send girls off to college?"

Violet

Violet has always supposed that her liaison with Dr. Grant, and the eventual announcement of their marriage, came as a shock to their colleagues at the Devonshire Institute.

And yet how could they not have known what was taking place throughout that long winter of the affair? She was so naive and unguarded, so fearfully young and trustful. She shivers to think of it now, and yet how can she blame herself? If she were that Violet now, and Walter were that Dr. Grant, she would do it again.

The day after Dr. Grant took her virginity with tea and cake in his sitting room, Violet sat alone in the institute's cramped dining hall, eating a typically overboiled and lukewarm lunch, when a young laboratory assistant approached her with a folded note. *Miss Violet Schuyler*, it was labeled, in the brusque black slashes she had come to associate with a concurrent jolt of energy inside her belly. She opened the paper to read that her presence was required in Dr. Grant's office on a matter of immediate urgency. Five minutes later, she lay on the edge of a broad desk with her skirts raised obediently about her hips, while the head of the Devonshire Institute for Physical Chemistry conducted a rigorously invasive experiment between her legs.

That night, he walked her back to her rooms and went upstairs with her, though he was not particularly pleased by the extreme narrowness of her bed and the spartan illumination of the single lamp. He remained only half an hour, including drink and cigarette. That was a Thursday. The next evening, they met at his house and shared an intimate dinner of pheasant and a pair of 1894 Margaux in the sitting room, and afterward Violet followed Dr. Grant upstairs to his wide and well-dressed bed. "Remember, child," he said, as he unbuttoned her shirtwaist, "nothing is unnatural that gives man and woman pleasure together. The sexual instinct is Nature itself."

In the morning, she found three new dresses hanging in the wardrobe, next to Dr. Grant's suits. They were for her, he said, so she would have something to wear when she stopped the night; there were also underthings in the drawer, each of them a perfect fit, and a new toothbrush in the bathroom. The housekeeper brought a tray loaded with breakfast, and Violet found she was terribly hungry.

On New Year's Eve, Dr. Grant surprised her by driving her up to London in his motor, where they rang in the year of grace 1912 at an enormous party at the Ritz hotel and stayed all weekend in a grand suite. He took her to the theater and out to dinner, and on the final evening he presented her with a pair of thick gold bracelets, studded with tiny diamonds on the outside and engraved with his initials—*WG*—in a bold modern typeface on the inside. "One for each wrist," he said, smiling, as he slid them over her amazed hands.

It still felt like a dream in those early weeks; it *was* a dream. Violet had never imagined herself with a lover. She knew she would never marry; she despised the thought of marriage and supposed she would eventually take a partner or two when she had the time, but she hadn't conceived of having a whirlwind love affair like this, complete with weekends in London and extravagant gold bracelets and satiny hotel sheets. These ideas had never occurred to her.

She found, rather shamefully, that she liked it.

She liked the attention and the excitement, the sense of belonging and purpose. The shared secret, as they moved about the institute each day, each knowing what extravagant acts had occurred in Dr. Grant's bedroom the previous night. She liked the way he looked at her when he undressed her, the fervid enjoyment he took in her young body; she liked the way he would call her into his office or wake her up in the night, as if his need for her could not be contained within respectable hours. She liked feeding his appetites. She liked the heavy drunken look of his face after he had taken her, the knowledge that she, Violet Schuyler, and she alone, had given him this intensity of pleasure he could not do without. *Splendid, child, well done, that was a damned splendid fuck,* he would groan, and she thought she might boil over from the joy of having satisfied the worldly and experienced Dr. Grant, of having soldered herself so thoroughly to another human being.

January fled. The afternoons began slowly to lighten as Violet danced along the Oxford streets each day, illuminating the frozen pavement, the occasional blankets of snow, the piles of exhausted slush. She could hardly now remember her despair at the beginning of September. The introductory lectures had ended, and she now worked directly in the laboratory with her eminent lover, unlocking the mysteries of the atom, every day burgeoning with the hope of some electrifying discovery. She gazed in rapture at the exquisite green-white explosions on the scintillating screen, the smacking of individual alpha particles into individual gold atoms, proving beyond doubt the existence of the atomic nucleus and the vast empty space between each one; she counted each spark as if she were counting diamonds in a crown. What did they mean? They were trying to tell her something, these flashes. They were trying to lead her to some unspeakable treasure: What was it? What was it made of, the nucleus of an atom of gold? What did it look like? And how could she find out, short of the impossible act of breaking it apart? She took her measurements, she made and remade her calculations, she ran the experiments over and over again with different isotopes. The immersion thrilled her, the sense of sinking into a three-dimensional puzzle, a new and fabulously minute universe that only a handful of men had ever seen.

And her, Violet Schuyler.

By February, her colleagues at the institute, perhaps encouraged by Dr. Grant's example, began to soften toward her, even to speak with her. One evening, she fell to talking with one of the second-year fellows, a shy and handsome young man with friendly brown eyes, as they happened to leave the institute together. Before she realized it they had walked all the way to her own lodging house.

She had stopped, embarrassed, at the little black wrought-iron gate at the front entrance, and at that instant Dr. Grant had come swinging around the corner on his way to his own house, where they were to meet later that night, after dusk had fallen.

The greetings had been awkward, the second-year fellow sensing the current of Dr. Grant's disapproval. In bed that night, Walter (she had finally grown used to his Christian name) had asked her how she knew young Mr. Hansbury.

"We happened to be walking out at the same time. We were talking about electrons."

"You didn't look as if you were talking about electrons."

"Well, we were. What else would we be talking about?"

"He looked as if he wanted to fuck you." Walter used those words with her, *fuck* and *spunk* and *prick*. They had shocked her at first, but she soon grew to appreciate their earthiness, their total absence of hypocritical Victorian euphemism. *My prick is up you, child,* Walter would say, with his lugubrious bedroom grin, and who could refute this fact? What point was it to pretend away man's basic carnal urges, to deny the existence of such vital elements of the human body and the use to which they were put?

"Oh, for God's sake, Walter. You're not *jealous*."

"You shouldn't encourage them. Someone will find out about us."

"I'm not encouraging anyone. Except you, of course." She smiled.

Walter rose from the sheets and lit his pipe from a packet of matches on the bureau. "I fail to see how you could lead a man to your lodging house door without having encouraged some hope of reward, child."

She had soothed him back to bed, but a new note had entered the air between them, and after that afternoon in late February, Walter insisted that she leave the institute every day by the rear door and meet him in the alley, from which they would walk directly to his house. If she happened to be late, the walk took place in a frigid silence; and the more frigid the silence, the more immediate and forceful were Walter's requirements once inside. His staff seemed to recognize his moods. One look in the hallway, and the maid and housekeeper melted away downstairs, leaving free the sitting room at the back, the study, the conservatory, until Walter rang the bell for dinner.

Having never had a lover before, Violet presumed this was natural, that Walter's need for frequent copulation—for copulation in quantity and variety and sometimes bruising intensity, for copulation at an instant's notice—demonstrated the flattering largeness of his regard for her. When, in the middle of the afternoon, he locked the laboratory door and lifted her skirts and tailed her over a workbench, Violet felt powerful, irresistible, so uniquely and magnificently alluring that even the great Dr. Walter Grant could not rein in his animal desire for her. In his ownership of her flesh, she felt her ownership of his massive masculine will. Of, in consequence, his heart.

In April, as the watery English sun ducked around fistfuls of showers, Violet helped Walter put the finishing touches on a paper he was delivering at a conference in Brussels. The task nearly defeated her. His handwriting was impossible, his spelling atrocious, his equations riddled with the careless errors—positives and negatives unceremoniously reversed, variables switched without explanation, basic arithmetic ignored—of a man accustomed to larger thoughts. As a reward for her diligence, he included her among the small group of Devonshire fellows making the journey across the channel.

He treated her with impeccable professional indifference during the day, as any other colleague. No one could possibly have suspected that the serious and dowdily dressed Miss Schuyler crept to Dr. Grant's nearby suite once the hotel hallways were clear at night, that he stripped away her dowdy clothes and her professional indifference and instructed her in the finer points of fellatio as he sat on the edge of the bed and scribbled notes on the text of his prepared remarks.

The result of all this hard work was a resounding triumph. Walter delivered his paper with great verve to an enthusiastic reception. Violet sat at his feet, incandescent with pride as she watched him speak, in full command of the stage, displaying the array of equations and drawings she had prepared so carefully for him. At the dinner afterward, he had been deluged with company, and Violet had stolen off directly after dessert to wait for the coast to clear, to slip into his suite and congratulate him more privately, when all his well-wishers had left and there was only the two of them, Walter and Violet.

Around eleven o'clock, the footsteps and voices began to die down outside her door, and Violet gathered her anticipation about her and left the room.

But when she turned the lock and ducked through Walter's door, she saw no sign of him.

Well, it was hardly surprising, after such a victory. No doubt he had been delayed in cordial argument with some officious rival and would be up shortly. Tomorrow morning she and Walter were leaving for a week's holiday, in some discreet Alpine resort of which Violet had never heard. He would want to say good-bye to his scientific friends, to perhaps share a last drink. She took off her clothes and hung them in the wardrobe and readied herself for the night.

But the minutes had ticked by, and still Violet waited in Walter's bed, counting the repeats in the floral wallpaper by the streak of brown light from the crack in the curtains, dozing off only to jolt back awake, until the door had at last squeaked open at three o'clock in the morning. She pretended to be sleeping. Walter went to the bathroom and opened the tap in the tub, and after he had bathed and brushed his teeth, he slipped into the sheets beside her.

"Are you awake, child?" he asked gently.

She didn't reply, but when morning arrived, and after Walter's reassuring body had found hers in the early spring sunshine, she bent her forehead into his damp shoulder and told him that despite the diligent applications of vinegar each time they were together, she thought she might be pregnant.

Vivian

Monday morning! Now, I don't know about you, but I've always relished the idea of a new week, and never more than when it contained the prospect of a Doctor Paul ringing my doorbell right smack at the beginning.

But first. Work. And even work had its charms today! I whistled my way up the Lexington Avenue subway and sang my way through the brass-framed revolving doors into the musty lobby of the *Metropolitan* building on Forty-ninth Street. My great-aunt Violet lurked somewhere in the holy sanctity of the archives here. I was sure of it! And I would find her!

"Good morning, Agatha!" I trilled to the receptionist, the instant the elevator doors staggered open on the eleventh floor.

"Miss Schuyler," she said, in that charming voice of hers, somewhere between a rasp and a mutter. She didn't so much as raise her shellacked gray head from her magazine, which, by the way, was not the *Metropolitan*, not even close, unless you took a big black permanent marker and scrawled *Metro* over the *Cosmo*. She took a long draw of her cigarette and—again, without looking, the modern miracle of her!—tipped it into the ashtray just before a long crumb tumbled from the end.

And this was the storied magazine's face to visitors.

The switchboard rang as I swished past the desk. "*Metropolitan!*" Agatha snapped, like an accusation of manslaughter.

But don't you worry. Things got better as I went along, past the industrious typing pool (to which, thank God and Gogo, I had leapfrogged membership), past secretaries with scarlet nails and towering nests of hair, past secretaries with bitten nails and limp heads of hair, past office doors and distracted editors and clench-jawed columnists pecking wit at typewriters, until I reached my own humble corner and humbler desk, of which the only redeeming features were its convenient proximity to the office of Edmund Tibbs, managing editor, and its exclusion from the incessant clacking of the typing pool.

I dropped my pocketbook into the bottom desk drawer and headed to the kitchenette.

Tibby hadn't been kidding around about sugar, no cream. He liked a single teaspoon of the white stuff, not a grain more, and it had better be hot and it had better be brimming, and if so much as a precious drop spilled over the edge and into the saucer below, I would make it up in my own crimson blood: with sugar, no cream.

Still, regardless of that anomaly before heading into Doctor Paul's bedroom Saturday night, I was not of the trembly-handy tribe, and this Monday morning, as every morning, I delivered Tibby his medicine intact and stood before his desk, smiling my best smile, curving my best hip, even though I knew for a fact that Tibby liked his coffee black and sweet and his chromosomes strictly XY.

He winced at the first sip, but he always did.

"Good morning, Mr. Tibbs," I said.

"Miss Schuyler."

"Is there anything I can do for you this morning? Any facts to check?"

If looks could growl. "Check your desk."

"Right away, Mr. Tibbs."

I turned heel smartly and checked said desk, where two new articles had found their way into the wire tray that controlled my fact-checking inflow. Yes, I was a fact-checker. That was my official duty, anyway; Tibby's coffee was for free and for the understanding that a year or two of perfectly delivered joe might lead to bigger and better things.

Not that fact-checking constituted a minor patch of sand on the sunny *Metropolitan* beach. No no no. Our writers were brilliant word-smiths, elegant stylists, provocative storytellers, but they rarely let an in-convenient fact get in the way of a good *exposez-vous*. My job was to check these baser impulses—note the double meaning—and level the *Metropolitan*'s chances of a messy libel lawsuit from an embarrassed husband, a shamed politician, a misbehaving starlet.

And as it turned out, I had a truffle pig's nose for a rotten fact. Jocular reference to a Napoleonic princess giving birth to an heir and a spare? Hardly apropos, when Consuelo Vanderbilt bitterly coined the term in 1895. Andover graduate claims he gave Jack Kennedy a concussion at the Choate game in 1934? Must have occurred in an alternative universe in which pigs took wing and Andover played Choate that season.

This particular Monday morning, however, I was having an itty-bitty problem with the fact-checking, at least of the sort that I was being paid so unhandsomely to do. As I stood in the *Metropolitan*'s private li-brary, poring over an encyclopedia entry for P. G. Wodehouse, my eyes kept darting to the volume that contained the Max Planck Institute in Berlin, Germany, known in imperial bygones as the Kaiser Wilhelm Institut.

And a few minutes later, as I made notes about varieties of Indian tea versus those from China, I closed my eyes quite out of the blue and re-called how my fingers had traced along Doctor Paul's interesting clavicle on Saturday night, how he had turned me onto my belly and stretched me long and wide and bit my shoulder very gently . . .

"Vivs! There you are."

"Gogo. You shouldn't sneak up on a girl."

She turned me around. "Why, you're flushed! Do you have a fever? Can I get you some water?"

"No, honey. Just a passing whatever. You're looking particularly perfect this morning."

"Do you think so?" She fluffed her pale hair and leaned forward, woman to woman. "He's coming today, Vivs."

"Who's coming? Your honey bun?"

"Yes!" Gogo darted a look around my shoulder, grabbed my hand, and made like a bandit for the corner of the library. "I didn't want to say anything. I had just about given up on him."

"What, Mr. Perfect? I thought you were madly in love."

"We were. I thought we were. And then . . . well, you know what it's like. That feeling when he's losing interest." She sighed.

"But you've had new flowers on your desk every week."

"Most weeks."

"And . . . and you've gone out on dates every Saturday night."

"*Most* Saturday nights."

"And he moved to New York to be with you, didn't he? After all your reckless passion over the summer?"

Now the blush. "Well, I don't know about reckless passion . . ."

I chucked her flawless chin. "You were madly in love. Admit it."

"Madly, Vivs." She took my hands. "He's the handsomest, smartest, kindest, most gentlemanly—"

"Et cetera, et cetera, ne plus ultra, to the ends of terra firma—"

"Aw, Vivs. You know I wasn't any good at Latin."

I smiled and squeezed her hands. "Look at your shining eyes. He's a lucky man, this Mr. Perfect."

"His name is David, Vivs. *Da-vid.*" She said it slowly, as if I might not have heard the handle before.

"David Perfect." I waved my hand. "So why the doubt? Surely Mr. David Perfect wants to make you Mrs. David Perfect? Who better for the job than the loveliest girl in the history of Bryn Mawr College, Hepburn included?"

"Hardly."

"And the sweetest."

"Oh, Vivs. You're too much." Bubbly bubbles of laughter. "I know I was silly to doubt him; he's not the kind of man who would ever lead a girl on. I think he must have been distracted with his new job. You know how demanding his job can be."

I ransacked the old vault, trying to locate some mention of Mr. David Perfect's mode of employment amid the endless reels of Gogo's pleasant background chatter while I was checking my facts. But. Look. I couldn't even remember the man's first name without prompting. What chance did his career have? I considered the possibilities: lawyer, banker, broker, doctor.

Ha, ha. Doctor. Wouldn't that be funny.

"I know," I said. "So terribly, awfully demanding, that job of his."

"You see? And I was right. Listen to me, Vivs." Conspiratorial whisper. "He rang me up last night."

"He didn't!"

"He did! He wants to have lunch with me today. He has something very important to tell me, he says." She crushed my wrists with the force of her glee. "*Very important.* I just know he's going to propose, Vivs! How do I look?" Elegant twirl.

I rubbed my grateful wrists. "You look the same as always. Which is to say, no working candles for miles around."

She angled her million-dollar cheekbones to the light, just so. "You do say the funniest things, Vivs. What about my dress?"

I surveyed the kelly-greenness of it. "Makes your eyes look like emeralds and your curves look like honeydews. He'll want to marry you twice."

She sank into a nearby chair, no small feat for a chair as old and rackety as that one, and propped her flawless chin on her flawless fingers. "Oh, Vivs, I'm so happy. You don't know what it's like being me."

"What, infinitely gorgeous and adorable? Having men fall at your feet, like so many mosquitoes in spraying season?"

"Having men fall at your feet, yes, and then a few weeks later . . ." Melancholy. "Drifting away."

"Now, Gogo . . ."

"You know. They stop calling. The flowers stop arriving. No more notes, no more chocolates and dinners at 21. Every time, Vivian. Just as I was getting my hopes up, just as I was thinking, Oh, he's the one, we'll get married in June and have a dozen babies and a big white house in Darien with a big white oak tree out front and a swing on it . . ." She put her hands together and stared at the fingers. "I was starting to think there was something wrong with me."

I knelt at her feet and put my hands on her knees. "Honey. There's nothing wrong with you, okay? There's everything right with you. You are the finest person I know, Gogo Lightfoot. You are. You are true and solid gold, and if this Mr. David Perfect gives you the runaround, why, I'll punch his lights out."

"Oh, don't do that, Vivs!"

"You see what I mean?" I folded her hands between mine. "Solid gold."

Now. We'll pause a minute right here, because my conscience—such as it is—is stabbing me. Time to disabuse you of your notions. I can't go on any longer without telling you the whole truth and nothing but the truth, even if you despise me for it.

Because you *should* despise me for it.

Sweet Margaux Lightfoot, the dearest girl in the world, that adorable little scrap of feminine virtue you see above, with the emerald eyes and the honeydew curves and the eagerly twitching womb . . . well, I became friends with her for one reason, and one reason alone: I wanted a job at the *Metropolitan*.

You see? Flat-out despicable, aren't I?

I courted her like the most ardent suitor, starting in February of our junior year at Bryn Mawr. I became her best friend overnight. I held her hands and started her drinking when Suitor Number Eight faded back into the worm-eaten woodwork from whence he came; I kept her from drinking too much at the Penn mixer and losing her priceless virginity to a pockmarked fresher from a little house on the prairie. I went with her to the movies and shopping, I helped her study for her final exams. I did all this because I knew her father was S. Barnard Lightfoot III, owner and publisher of the *Metropolitan*, and there was no other grand journalistic institution in Manhattan—which is to say, the world—I more ardently wished to conquer than the malicious slick-sleek monthly *Metropolitan*, inscrutable cartoons and all.

As you can see, it worked like a charm.

But somewhere along the line, something happened I hadn't planned for: I actually started to like her. A sort of pinprick admiration, just in passing, that expanded outward as pinpricks will do.

Yes. Yes. I know it. You wouldn't think she's my type. She couldn't be less like Pepper, for example, and in her virgin modesty she bears a passing resemblance to Tiny. But she's just so . . .

Sweet.

Honestly, unaffectedly, unabashedly sweet. And I really did want to punch out the lights of Suitor Number Eight. I thought he was passing up the deal of a lifetime. Gogo would make a beautiful, loyal wife. Plop a husband at her breakfast table and a baby on her hip, and she would bloom kazoom into a nurturing mother, a thorough homemaker, a patiently charming hostess to every deadly friend and colleague Suitor Number Eight could drag home comatose from the executive boardroom. All the things, in short, that I would not.

Well, except the loyal part. I *am* loyal. I'll grant myself that.

So when Gogo had come home from a four-week graduation holiday in Los Angeles last July, bubbling over with enthusiasm for Disneyland and for Suitor Number Ten (we shall not mention Nine), I was delighted for her. He did sound like the real deal. They wrote all summer long. He came to visit her in New York. No, he was moving to New York! Actually moving here, supposedly for work, but really because he wanted to be with *her*, Margaux Lightfoot, which could mean only love and marriage and the baby carriage at last for the deserving Gogo. An MRS degree awarded with highest honors.

"You are the best, best friend in the whole world, Vivs," she said, looking into my eyes with her watery own, believing in my innocence so profoundly that I almost believed in it myself.

All right. I hugged her. I dare anyone to resist hugging Gogo when she looked at you like that, like a koala bear lost and found again. "I want every detail. I want to know exactly how he asks. Bended knee, the works. And nobody sees the ring before I do, Gogo. Not even your father."

She gurgled into my hair. "I promise. Oh! That reminds me!"

"What?" I asked innocently. Hopefully.

She pulled back and wagged her finger near my nose. "You have your own details to spill, Miss Femme Fatale. Tell me about Saturday!"

"I can't now, Gogo. It's a long story, and I have to—you know—W-O-R-K. Did you happen to speak to your little old father about my little old research?"

Guilty. "Not yet. I was thinking . . . well, it might be easier to ask him after lunch. You know, when I tell him the good news."

As I said before, not the bravest fusilier in the firing line, our Gogo. Still. "Not a bad plan, I guess."

"And then I can join you in there, and you can tell me all about Mr. Saturday while you're doing your research! It's perfect!"

"Gogo, dearest, that's the thing about a job, you're supposed to be actually doing it when you're at work." Actually, I wasn't quite sure *what* Gogo was supposed to be doing at the *Metropolitan*, at least in an official capacity. I think she was some sort of secretary to her father, but in the natural course of things, the real secretary did all the work, and Gogo simply wandered about the office, wondering how to type, shedding sunshine like a golden tabby kitten, causing even Tibby's eagle face to soften on occasion. Our mascot. Every magazine needs a mascot. It brings us together in times of trial. I stood up and tugged her with me. "And speaking of which, I have some facts to check. Go do whatever it is you do, and bring Mr. David Perfect by my desk before you leave."

"On approval?"

"Absolutely. He has to pass the Vivian test before he's allowed to ask my Gogo to marry him."

"And if he doesn't pass?" She actually looked worried. Heartbroken, even.

I patted her cheek. "Don't worry. The test is rigged. You'll be married in June, and I'll be your maid of honor."

The arms flung around me. "I love you, Vivs!"

"I love you, too, Gogo."

Because, really, what else could you say to that?

SO I CHEATED. How was I supposed to wait until after lunch before resuming my search for Aunt Violet's past? I cleared my fact-checking box by eleven o'clock, and rather than dance triumphantly into Tibby's office to ask for more work, I headed back into the *Metropolitan*'s private library to see what I could see. Oh, the library wasn't the archives, but I knew how to lift its stones to reveal the crawlies underneath.

I started where I'd left off on Saturday, with **GRANT, Walter, Ph.D.** Something about that encyclopedia entry tickled at the old nostrils, my truffle pig nose for rotten goods. You had the bare facts, clear and competent, but there was always the story behind them, the real story, contained in letters lost or burnt and official records moldering in official archives. So which one was the telling fact? The one that disguised the truth?

I ran my fingers over the unromantic type. "Physical chemist, an earlier colleague of Ernest Rutherford before a professional dispute caused a rift between the two, chair of the Devonshire Institute for Physical Chemistry (Oxford), and finally a fellow at the Kaiser Wilhelm Institut für Physikalische Chemie und Elektrochemie in Berlin, Germany, in the years before his death . . ."

Chair of the Devonshire Institute. Fellow at the Kaiser Wilhelm.

My nose twitched. Ah. Yes. But.

Why would a man at the height of his career give up a chairmanship of an Oxford University institute—*Oxford*, mind you!—running the whole works, directing research, his own secretary, his own name on the door, subordinates up the kowtow, to become a mere fellow at an institute in a foreign country? An Englishman, for God's sake. Everyone knew the English were allergic to foreigners, and Germans in particular.

And all this directly after his marriage to my aunt Violet.

Had she convinced him to do it? Did she have a lover already, and want to follow him to Berlin?

Or something else?

I laid my fingers on the page and closed my eyes. The trouble was, I didn't know either of them. I didn't know what they were like. I needed something else, some insight into their characters. Something personal. If only Grandfather or Grandmother were still alive. Or even Aunt Christina.

Now. I did have Aunt Violet's suitcase. But I didn't have the key to its lock, and, furthermore, said lock might possibly accidentally have proved rustily resistant to the prodding of a skillful hairpin. Should said skillful hairpin have been applied to said rusty lock, say, last night before bedkins.

"Vivian! There you are!"

I detached my claws from the ceiling and dropped back to earth. "Haven't I warned you about sneaking up on a girl?"

Gogo's eyes sparkled high. Oh, she had it all over, like a case of the chicken pox. "He's here, Vivian! Come and meet him!"

Mr. David Perfect. I had forgotten about him already.

"Righty-o," I said. "Let me just put this encyclopedia back on the shelf."

She took me by the hand and dragged me out the door. My head was still roiling with Grants and Violets and chairmanships and rusty locks. I thought, I should probably fix my lipstick, straighten my hair; he'll practically be my *brother*, for God's sake, and then we turned the corner and there he towered, Mr. David Perfect, tall of height, sturdy of shoulder, sun-streaked of hair.

Doctor Paul.

Violet

Violet had expected Walter to react with shock and perhaps anger at the news of her possible pregnancy, but instead he was matter-of-fact. "Oh, the devil," he said, propping himself against the white pillows and lighting his pipe. "What a damned nuisance. I suppose you'll have to wait until we get back from Gstaad before having it taken care of."

"Taken care of?"

"I can give you the name of a doctor. Discreet chap, very safe."

His meaning dawned on her. "Get rid of it, do you mean?"

"Yes, of course." He cast her a sidelong glance. "For God's sake, child. What else were you thinking?"

She sat up and pulled the sheet to the center of her chest. "Well, I hadn't . . . I hadn't thought about it at all . . . It's only a possibility."

Walter set down the pipe. "How many days are you late?"

"Three or four, I think. Perhaps five." It was actually eight.

"But you're never late."

"It might be anything. The strain of travel."

Walter swore softly and rose from the bed. He was still as trim as ever, wiry and elegant. He sucked on his pipe and looked out the window. "You can't possibly be thinking of bringing another creature into this over-crowded world, child. It's immoral."

"I didn't say that."

"Obviously, you haven't been douching properly."

"I don't think it's exactly foolproof. I've been reading pamphlets on the subject. I should have kept track of dates, too. We should have been more careful."

Walter swore again, even more softly, into the window glass. He took in a withering breath and turned to face her, and a gentle smile had appeared in the center of his beard. "Well, it's just conjecture at the moment, isn't it? Don't give it another thought until we're back home."

She promised she wouldn't, but when every morning failed to bring the expected signs, when Walter looked at her with raised brows every time she returned from the lavatory, the conjecture expanded like a gas to fill the entire room, the entire universe of interaction between them. It was early April, and their Alpine village was still packed with snow, glittering and dripping off the eaves in the afternoon sun, an unutterably romantic landscape, but Walter made love to her only twice that entire week, and those times grudgingly, wordlessly, hardly touching her except where it was essential, as if her body and its possibilities disgusted him. He came to bed long after she had already retired, and she became accustomed to the sound of his bathing, his ritual cleansing before he would join her in the lavender-scented sheets.

"Right," he said, the morning after their return to Oxford, after she had rushed to the bathroom upon waking and returned, miserable and perspiring, to the bed. "You'll have to see Dr. Winslow, that's all. He's got rooms in George Street. He'll set you up directly."

"Walter, you're not serious. It's so soon."

"The sooner the better. You'll be back to normal in a week."

"You must let me think. You must let me decide for myself."

He took her by the shoulders. "That's the trouble. You can't think right now. You're not rational. Are you actually thinking of having this *thing,* this baby? Giving up everything you've worked for? You'd have to leave the Devonshire, of course. You'd spend your days attached to some incontinent howling infant instead of putting that extraordinary brain of yours to its proper use. And the scandal, my God! You're my student. It would bring me down, Violet. It would ruin me."

Violet opened her mouth to say that it wasn't quite true, they could marry and have the baby respectably, they could find a nanny and she could perhaps still carry on her work at the institute, they could find a way, for God's sake, but she managed to clamp her lips down on the words and burst into tears instead.

Walter took her in his arms and drew her into the bed with him. "There, now, child. You see? You're not yourself at all. Already this alien clump of cells has addled your orderly little mind. Nature's way, I suppose." He shook his head in sorrow. "Let me handle all this for you. Let me ring up Winslow, set up the appointment. I'll take perfect care of you, and things can go on just as before. Haven't things been wonderful since we began together? Haven't I advanced your every interest? Are we not two beings of the very same mind?"

She snuffled a *yes.*

"Then you must trust me, Violet. I do know what's best."

Walter laid her back in the pillows and removed her nightgown, almost as if everything were normal again, as if her female organs had not betrayed them both, and the next afternoon called her into his office and handed her a slip of paper. He was smiling kindly. "Winslow will see you tomorrow morning at ten o'clock. You can take a taxi to my house directly after. Don't worry about the bill; everything's to be sent to me."

Vivian

They say time is supposed to lengthen when you're in shock, that your body shuts itself down, but I felt the opposite. I felt as if the seconds were racing by, sharp with unnecessary detail, the molecules of air pinging separately and rapidly against me. I heard Gogo introduce us, Dr. David Paul Salisbury, Miss Vivian Schuyler, and the way her voice tip-tilted the *Schuyler* as if she were making a private little joke. I saw Doctor Paul's neat gray courting suit, his blue-sky tie, the individual locks of his damp hair brushed back from his face. I counted each tiny black lick of flame around Doctor Paul's pupils as his eyes opened wide to take me in.

"You again," I whispered.

"Vivs." His eyes were dark; his face was pale. "You're Vivs. Holy Christ."

Gogo had danced off to find her coat and say good-bye to her father. I snatched Doctor Paul's hand and hauled him to the library and closed the door.

"What the hell do you think you're doing here? Proposing to *Gogo*?"

Shock. "I'm not proposing to her!"

"She thinks you are!"

He grabbed his hair and turned away. "God, no. Vivian, you can't think—"

"You're Suitor Number Ten. You're Gogo's Mr. Perfect. *You.*" I backed up a step, stumbled over the chair that Gogo had vacated earlier, and crumpled into the seat. I stared at his gray-suited back, the delicate wisps of hair at the base of his neck. The neck I had kissed Saturday night, the back I had gripped with my fingers for dear life.

I was going to hell.

On the other hand, so was he.

"*You*! You lying old son of a . . . of a dog of a . . . two-timing . . . *rat*! What am I, your bit on the side? Your afternoon snack? I'm supposed to be the mistress of my friend's husband?"

"Husband!" He spun around. "Her *husband*? God, no. I was going to . . . Today, I was going to tell her it wasn't working, that she was a dear girl but I—"

"You were going to break things off." My head was pounding fury. My tongue was so dry I could hardly speak.

"Yes. What else?"

"You tell me."

He found the table edge with his fingernails. "Vivian, you can't think there would ever be anyone else. Not after Saturday night."

"What about Saturday night?"

"Don't tell me you didn't feel it, too. Do not, Vivian, do *not* tell me that wasn't the best thing that's ever happened to you. To me. To us, together."

"You are mighty confident for a two-timing rat."

"I know what happened with us, Vivian. I know what that was, because I know it was always missing before. And you know it, too."

Something buckled and collapsed, deep in my chest, some object I didn't even realize I owned. I thought, *Only in New York.* A classic New York coincidence, all of us marbles rolling together in our box, the way the old gal sitting next to you at the luncheonette turns out to have grown up in the apartment right smack next to yours. The law of big numbers. You bring home a precious gift from the post office and you fall at last, at last, you peel off your leathery old skin and fall so hard in a leap of pure and uncharacteristic faith, and the bastard turns out to be practically engaged to your boss's daughter. To the one girl in the world who tolerates you, the one girl who doesn't think you're out to hunt down her man with your acquisitive Schuyler claws.

I stood up. "Nothing happened with us. You are not going to break Gogo's heart."

He didn't move.

"*Loose ends*. Sweet little Gogo was your loose end."

He whispered, white-faced: "You're killing me, Vivian."

"You are going to march out of this room and take Gogo to lunch, and you are not going to break her heart."

"What the hell does that mean?"

"What does that *mean*? She's expecting a ring, you idiot, you son of a bitch, and you were planning to say thanks for the memories, but I'm in love with your friend? Do you know what that would do to her?"

To Gogo. To her delight, like a fizzy pink cloud around her head.

To me. To my career. My beloved battered desk in a *Metropolitan* corner, my box full of rotten facts, my ambitions poured daily into a coffee cup, sugar, no cream.

"You *cannot* be suggesting that I propose to her!"

I clenched my hands. "No. But you're not . . . You can't—"

"Can't what, Vivian? What can't I do?" His eyes weren't dark anymore; they were incandescent blue, lighter than light, alive enough to burn.

Indeed. What couldn't he do? What should he do? For once, I couldn't think. Something messy had spilled in my brain, short-circuiting the orderly hum of logic. I had lain naked in bed with this man, I had taken him inside me, I had known every inch of him. Except this inch, the Gogo inch, the most important inch of all. Gogo and Doctor Paul. I couldn't bear it.

"Just have lunch," I said. "Tell her how sweet she is."

"I can't believe you're saying this."

"Believe it."

"Vivian, I'm in love with you."

My hands. Cold.

"No, you're not. We spent twelve hours together. We had a little fun."

"Don't tell me what I'm feeling or not feeling. Don't tell me that was just a little fun. Margaux is a sweet girl, a wonderful girl, but it wouldn't be fair to her, it wouldn't be right to continue things with her after—"

"If you break her heart, Paul Salisbury, I'll never speak to you again. *Never.*"

As if the air shattered into pieces. We stood in a vacuum, Doctor Paul and I, staring at each other, unable to breathe. *Never speak to you again.* It had the weight of a death sentence.

"Go. Go to lunch."

"We will discuss this later."

"Take her to lunch, Paul."

The door crashed open. Gogo. "Oh, my goodness! Everyone thought you'd run off together!"

I turned, shiny-bright as a counterfeit new penny. "I was only administering the Vivian test."

"Ooh!" She gazed at my Doctor Paul with a look of such tremulous and unadulterated adoration, I had to glance away. "Did he pass?"

I stepped forward and took her hand, and I hooked it over Doctor Paul's strong and competent right arm, the arm that saved the lives of dying children, the arm that had stripped away my old leathery skin and held me in place while his body filled mine.

"I'll let you know."

I STAYED in the library after they left. I didn't want to think about the two of them sharing an intimate table at 21 or the Peninsula, leaning into each other, Doctor Paul telling beautiful Gogo how sweet she was, as I had instructed. The bottle of chilled wine—champagne, perhaps. The trout meunière, the new potatoes gleaming with butter. A salad to cleanse the palate. Dessert: something chocolate. Gogo loved chocolate. *Gogo, I'm sorry I haven't been attentive lately. I've been busy. It isn't you. You're a sweet girl, a darling girl. The perfect emerald-eyed girl. Look at your heart face, your blistering blondness. As good as gold.* He takes her hand. She blushes, she's so happy, she's so in love with the handsome young doctor sitting across the table.

I trudged through the stacks. I followed every possible lead, I scoured the index of every book the *Metropolitan* owned on the subjects of chemistry and physics (for the record, there were three) but I could find no mention of Violet Grant. Even the paragraphs devoted to Dr. Walter Grant never once referred to her. She was invisible. If it weren't for her wedding announcement in the *Times*, she might never have existed.

I closed my last hope and reshelved it next to the Einstein biography. I checked my watch. One-forty-five. Gogo and Doctor Paul would be back from lunch any minute.

Time to secure a strategic alliance.

I straightened out my snug little suit, girded my sleek little loins, and prowled like a lioness into Tibby's office.

He was delighted to see me, as ever. "Make it quick, Miss Schuyler. I'm busy."

I came to a dramatic stop before his desk, placed my manicured fingertips on the august battered wood, and leaned forward. A shame he wouldn't appreciate the view. "I have a story," I said.

The skeptical eyebrow. "A story."

"A humdinger, Mr. Tibbs. Murder, sex, high society."

"Been done a million times."

"It never gets old."

He acknowledged this truth with a minute twitch of his lips and a lowering of the skeptical eyebrow. He set down his black Cross fountain pen next to the blotter—a gentleman of the old school, Edmund Tibbs—and leaned back in his chair. "Pitch me."

I swung myself into the leather armchair facing him and crossed my legs. Unlike most of the editors at the *Metropolitan*, Tibby didn't smoke, and I drew in a good clean breath of leather and ink before I began.

"It all starts with a suitcase, Mr. Tibbs. A suitcase sent to my apartment last Saturday from Zurich, Switzerland, containing the effects of my great-aunt, Violet Schuyler, who was last seen in Berlin in the summer of 1914."

Pause, for effect.

"Go on," said Tibby.

"It turns out that Aunt Violet left home in 1911 to study as an atomic physicist at Oxford. She married her professor, the head of a prestigious institute, and they moved to Berlin, where he was found in his apartment, murdered, just before the First World War broke out."

"Who murdered him?"

I raised my finger. "That, you see, is the mystery. No one was ever found guilty. But Aunt Violet disappeared with her lover into that hot July night, and I, Mr. Tibbs"—I stabbed my finger into the wooden armrest—"I intend to find out what happened."

Tibby knit his hands together over his professorial waistcoat. "And you plan to do this how?"

"First, I want access to the *Metropolitan* archives."

"Continue."

"Second, I happen to have the contents of Aunt Violet's suitcase."

"Which are?"

My brave finger crumpled against the armrest. "I haven't opened it yet."

"Why not?"

"The lock's a little rusty."

No one held a silence like Tibby. His pale eyes examined the pores of my forehead, the whites of my eyes, the tenor of my thoughts. "Fair enough. Continue."

Damn it all, my palms were damp. I prided myself on my dry palms. I opened my hands a crack to let the healing air inside. "I will proceed with my research based on the information I discover in the suitcase."

"Who was her lover?"

"Her lover?"

"Violet's lover. Who was he?"

"I don't know. You perceive they would have kept the affair secret."

"May I humbly suggest, Miss Schuyler, that the name of the lover might prove a logical fact with which to anchor your research—"

The heart soared. "Absolutely, Mr. Tibbs. The highest priority."

"—if I were to commission this story. Which I am not."

The heart crashed. "You're not? But you just said—"

"I *would* suggest, Miss Schuyler, *if* I were to commission. The conditional tense."

"Why not, for God's sake?"

Tibby picked up his pen and dipped it into an antique ink pot of purple-tinted glass. "Because, Miss Schuyler, you're a fact-checker, not a writer."

"I can write. I can write this story."

"Nevertheless. I need you to check facts, not invent them."

I bolted to my feet. "You're making a mistake."

"No, I'm not."

"This is a good story, Mr. Tibbs. A great story, and I'm the only one who can write it. I'm the only one in this office who can find out what happened, the only person anywhere."

"Except this Violet herself."

"Dead, we can safely presume. Or she would have turned up by now."

He turned to the paper before him and began scratching with his pen. "Go back to work, Miss Schuyler. I believe you'll find a few new items in your box."

I put my fingers back on the desk, right before his paper and his scribbling black enamel. My gold Hermès bracelet made a satisfying clink against the wood, trumping effortlessly the prestige of the Cross pen. "I'm going to do this story, whether you commission it or not. I'm going to find out what happened to Violet, I'm going to write the best damned article this magazine has ever seen. And you will be damned well *begging* me for it by the time I'm done."

I didn't wait for a reply. I turned back toward the door from whence I prowled and flung it open. Just before I slammed it shut in a skull-rattling crash, I heard Tibby's voice growl out behind me.

"Now, that's the proper spirit, Miss Schuyler."

Violet

E ven now, when Violet thinks of Dr. Winslow's surgery in George Street—which she tries not to do, which she has striven valiantly to obliterate from her memory—she is seized with mortal terror.

It wasn't that Dr. Winslow was cruel. On the contrary, he smiled at her warmly when she entered the surgery, shook her hand with cordial strength, settled her in a chair, and asked her the most intimate questions with such ease and matter-of-factness that all trace of Violet's embarrassment dissolved within minutes.

Dr. Winslow made notes in his leather book, nodding at her answers. When he had finished, he closed the book and met her gaze. He was a youngish man, perhaps in his middle thirties, with waving brown hair that had been brushed back scrupulously from his face, and large brown eyes that reminded Violet of her aunt Martha's loyal Great Dane. "Now, then, Miss Schuyler, I suspect from what you tell me that you are, indeed, with child. Do you have any objection to a physical examination to confirm the pregnancy? We can also draw blood to be absolutely sure, though the results may take a few days."

"A physical examination will be sufficient, I'm sure," she said, and he had shown her into a small room to the side and left her to take off her skirt and drawers but not her stockings and girdle, to lie on the hard bed and stare at the white ceiling and wait for his return.

Dr. Winslow's fingers were warm and brief and professional. She felt them with detachment. "Well, Miss Schuyler," he said, drawing back, "it seems you are expectant. The cervix is fully thickened, which indicates a length of gestation of at least seven weeks. I am given to understand that the pregnancy is not, however, entirely welcome?"

"No," she whispered, still staring at the ceiling.

She heard the scrape of his chair, the rush of water at the tap as he washed his hands. "You are free to dress yourself, Miss Schuyler. I shall wait on you in the other room to discuss the case."

When she returned to the chair before Dr. Winslow's desk, a steaming cup of tea was waiting for her. "I took the liberty of adding cream and sugar," he said, with another of his easy smiles.

"Thank you." She sipped.

"Now, Miss Schuyler. If you wish to terminate this pregnancy, I will undertake the procedure. But allow me to observe that you present a unique exception to the usual sort of patient who enters my surgery with such an objective in mind."

"Do I? In what way?"

The doctor leaned back in his chair and bent his fingers together. "She is often young and unwed, as you are, but her circumstances are entirely different. She may belong to a lower class of society, without much prospect for advancement. She may have parents to whom she cannot confess her condition, she may be a prostitute, she may be a married woman with several children already. She may have been seduced and abandoned, or in poor health, or for any number of reasons unable to bear and care for a child. I am always reluctant to perform a termination, which, apart from the considerable physical risks, is both illegal and a moral dilemma of the heaviest sort, and which would cause the end of my career if it were formally known to the various authorities."

"Then why?" Violet whispered.

"Because I fear the consequences for the patient if I do not, and have come to the conclusion that, in these wretched cases, the procedure is the lesser of many unspeakable evils, despite the risk to the patient. Some may not agree with me, and I quite understand. The burden is a heavy one, and I bear it in full knowledge of what I do—that is, the cutting short of a nascent, if unrealized, human life, for which I shall answer one day to God."

He paused in this speech, staring for a moment at the brown leather notebook before him. The sun was shifting, just beginning to illuminate the window glass behind him, and it cast an odd and unearthly glow about the fringes of his brown hair.

Violet, whose breath had lodged deep in her chest as he began to speak, felt her ribs sink downward as the air left her lungs.

"I cannot look into your heart, Miss Schuyler, but I urge you to think through the matter fully before you make the decision. You cannot conceive the desperation in the faces of my patients who do undertake this procedure. If you're not desperate, if you're not certain this is the only course, you have every right to consider this matter very carefully indeed before going forward. Consider the alternatives before you. Consider the risk of infection, of hemorrhage, of future difficulty in conceiving and carrying to term."

He paused again. Violet watched the tiny motes of dust circle around his illuminated head.

"On the other hand," he went on, "if you're quite certain you cannot continue this pregnancy, I can perform the procedure right now. As Dr. Grant ordered me, over the telephone." A slight ironic weight pressed down on the word *ordered*.

"He will be very angry if I don't."

"I fail to see how Dr. Grant's anger should affect your decision, one way or another, Miss Schuyler. You strike me as a woman of considerable strength and intellect."

Considerable strength and intellect. The words revolved in her head.

The room was very quiet, situated at the rear of the building, and Violet could hear her own heartbeat in her ear, measured and certain and fearless, quite capable of feeding the other heartbeat that fluttered unheard somewhere inside her, the result of her heedless union with Walter, her thoughtless faith in him.

She rose from her chair. "Thank you, Dr. Winslow. You've been so helpful. I will of course let you know my decision."

The taxi was waiting for her outside, as Walter had promised, but she paid it off with her own money and walked instead. She returned not to Walter's house but to her own rooms, which gave off a dusty air of disuse as she let herself in with her key. She looked about the tiny sitting room with its two threadbare chairs, its round rocking-legged table, its gas ring topped by a battered teapot. Her own rooms, paid for with her own stipend from the institute, which of course was only a gift in Walter's keeping.

Walter arrived at half past six, shown up by the landlady, who left them alone with a discreet click of the door. "What the devil are you doing?" he asked, in a blaze.

"I've decided not to get rid of the baby. Would you like some tea?"

The argument had lasted half an hour, but Violet had not budged. She would have the baby, she would make a living somehow, she could sell her watch if she had to. She had a brain and she would use it, she would find a way, even if it meant leaving the institute. Walter told her she was a fool, he would have nothing to do with it, she was ruining herself and him, she was bringing another unneeded child into an overpopulated world, she had no sense of responsibility to her fellow man.

"What are you thinking, Violet? Becoming a *mother*? You, of all women." His scorn was so huge, Violet could have reached out and grabbed a fistful of it.

"I'll find a way. I've always found a way," she said. "I am, after all, a woman of considerable strength and intellect."

"You're a fool."

He left in an arctic rage at eight o'clock, and Violet ate a supper of canned soup and went to bed. Only then did she begin to shake, in little tremors at first, and then violently, as if her whole body were overtaken by terror. She crawled to her trunk and put on her warmest woolen cardigan and climbed back into bed, and still she could not get warm, she could not banish the cold.

Vivian

When I arrived back at 52 Christopher Street at seven o'clock that evening, delicatessen pastrami in hand, a man was sitting on the stoop by the door. He was still wearing his gray courting suit, his blue-sky necktie that matched his eyes. The cool October evening ruffled his hair affectionately.

He rose at the sight of me. "You're late."

"I can explain." I walked past him and fit my key into the lock.

"Wait, Vivian. You have to listen to me."

"I don't have to do anything, Dr. Salisbury. I'm busy."

His hand appeared out of nowhere to rest atop mine on the knob. "Please, Vivian. Let me explain. Let me in, just for a moment."

It crushed me, the sight of that hand. And I had planned to be so strong.

"I won't change my mind."

"I know. I just need you to hear me out."

How was it possible I could be in love with a man's knuckles?

"All right," I said. "For a moment."

The stairwell was cold and smelled like vomit. I kept my breath shallow as I climbed upward, listening for the guilty beat of Doctor Paul's footsteps behind me. He didn't say a word, and neither did I.

I opened the door to the wholesome sight of Sally lounging at the table, smoke floating from her fingers, wearing a short red kimono and conspicuously nothing else. "What's with the suitcase?" she asked, not looking up.

I set down the pastrami sandwich and snatched the suitcase away. "None of your business."

"You cranky thing. Cigarette?" She looked up and saw Doctor Paul. Her hands went frantically to the ends of the kimono, seeking additional silk that wasn't there. "Jiminy Cricket. Who's the blonde?"

"This is Dr. David Salisbury. Dr. Salisbury, this is my esteemed roommate, Sally Finch. She's from Arizona."

"Utah."

"One of those places."

Sally stuck out her hand. "Pleased to meet you, Dr. David Salisbury."

"Likewise. It's Paul, actually. Only my pops calls me David."

"Paul." She gave up on the kimono and reached for the Lucky Strikes. "I'm Sally. Smoke?"

He patted his jacket pocket and kept his eyes faithfully on her face. "I've got my own, thanks. I hope we're not disturbing you."

"Not a lick." She looked at me. "Would you two like a little privacy? I can skip out."

"No, thanks, Sally. We'll just be a few minutes." I picked up the suitcase, crossed to my bedroom, and heaved the old leather on the bed. "Come along, Doctor, dear."

I'd been counting on Sally being out this evening—what were the odds, really?—but this would do nicely. My bedroom contained no other human perch except the bed, and that was already occupied by Aunt Violet's suitcase. Doctor Paul stood uncomfortably next to the opposite wall, arms crossed, face flushed pink. As well it should.

I crossed my own arms. "Proceed."

"You aren't going to make this easy, are you?"

"Why should I? You can light a cigarette if you like."

He sighed and reached into his pocket. I liked his cigarette case, plain silver, not even engraved. In my world, you monogrammed everything. The missing stamp of ownership seemed a modest touch. Not that I wanted to count Doctor Paul's virtues at the moment.

He held out the case to me. I shook my head. He lit himself up and leaned against the wall, right next to the vivid blue and tangled arms of my favorite Matisse print.

The room was too warm. I took off my jacket and tossed it on top of Aunt Violet's suitcase. "What did you say to Gogo?"

"What did she tell you?"

"She didn't tell me anything. She never came back to the office."

He swore softly. "I was kind, Vivian. I tried so hard to be kind."

"Did you break things off?"

"Christ, Vivian. What else could I do? I couldn't be dishonest."

I slid down the wall and sat with my knees pressed against my forehead. I saw her face before they left for lunch, her tremulous adoration. "Oh, God. Poor Gogo."

"Vivian—"

"Leave. Just leave."

"Vivian, you're laboring under a complete misapprehension. I don't know where Margaux got this absurd notion that I wanted to marry her—"

"Two guesses."

"I did not lead her on, Vivian. We went on a few dates, that's all."

I looked up. I knew my eyes were red, and I didn't care. "You had an affair last summer! You moved to New York to be with her!"

"Not true. We had some fun—"

"Oh, fun again."

"Your word, remember? Only this time that's all it was. She was with her family. I was staying with friends. I took her out to dinner, to the beach. It was nothing."

"Did you kiss her?"

He found the ashtray on the footstool that served as my nightstand. "Once or twice."

"Anything more?"

"Maybe a little." He picked up the ashtray and concentrated on tapping his cigarette just so.

"She says you were madly in love. On the hook."

"Well, I'm sorry for that. I thought it was a little lighthearted vacation flirtation. I liked her tremendously; she's a sweet girl."

"A beautiful girl."

"All right, yes. She's beautiful. What of it?"

"You moved to New York."

"Vivian, I'd already accepted the offer here. She had nothing to do with it."

"But you picked right up where you left off."

"Vivian, it wasn't serious. I swear it wasn't. We dated, that's all. I hardly knew anyone else in the city. How was I supposed to know I'd meet *you* a few weeks later?" He finished the cigarette and started another. I reached over before he closed the case and took one. He lit me up in silence, and I saw how drawn he looked, how shattered.

"It was serious to her," I said.

"Well, I was beginning to realize that. I tried to draw away. I didn't want to hurt her, Vivian."

Well, it fit, didn't it? And I couldn't blame him. He'd done nothing wrong, really, except he'd failed to fall in love with a girl; and whose fault was that? He hadn't failed willfully. He hadn't failed with cruel intent. It was just the breaks. I sat down on the corner of the bed, next to Aunt Violet's suitcase, with my back toward Paul. The old mattress sagged beneath me. The cigarette burned quietly between my fingers, and I stared at the wall, which Pepper had helped me paint a cheerful daffodil yellow the very day I'd moved in.

"Could you open the window?" I asked.

The wood scraped obediently behind me. A rush of cool air swirled against my blouse. I felt the mattress sink behind me, and I closed my eyes as Paul's hand touched my shoulder. "I was going to break things off anyway, Vivian. It was inevitable. I should have done it sooner, but I hated to hurt her like that. I regret deeply that she's hurt, that I hurt her, but what could I do? Lie to her instead?"

"She would have been perfect for you."

"No, she wouldn't. That's not the marriage I want. Yes, you're right, she's sweet and beautiful. She'll make someone a wonderful wife, but not me."

"Why not?"

His sigh blew against my neck. "Vivian, she's not *you*. I don't mean to be cruel, but she bored me. We never talked about anything important. In the months I knew her, we didn't share a fraction of what you and I shared in a single hour on Saturday. She doesn't think about things. She takes everything as it is. I don't know what it is, really. A sense of curiosity, maybe? I couldn't have told you, I didn't even know what was lacking until you came up behind me in that post office line. I didn't know what was possible."

His hand came around my ribs to rest on my stomach. I was vain enough to let it stay.

"Let me in, Vivian," he said. "Please. Let me in again. Let me know you."

I took a last pull on my cigarette and reached to crush it out. The brief separation chilled my spine. "And if you don't like what you learn?"

"Doesn't matter. It's you, that's all."

How did he do that? *It's you, that's all.* It's you, Vivian, and whatever is inside you, whatever beauty or corruption, whatever virtue or vice, I must love.

What could I say to that? There was no answer in the world.

"Let me make you happy, Vivian."

"I *am* happy."

"Happier, then." He plucked at the buttons on my blouse. "Tell me. What do you do at that magazine of yours?"

"I check facts. When I grow up, I want to write articles, features, the ones right there on the front cover, with my byline underneath in thick letters."

"Sounds very Vivian-like. I can't wait to read them. In the meantime, here's a fact you can check." He kissed the hollow where my neck and shoulder met. My skin shook at the familiarity of his lips. I loved the mintiness of his shampoo, the scrubbed warmth of him. I closed my eyes.

Fine, then. I was no saint. Why nail myself to the cross when Doctor Paul was right here, my Doctor Paul, ready to love me, taking nothing away from Gogo that had never really been hers to begin with?

I took Doctor Paul's willing hand and moved it to my willing breast.

At which point, as if God himself were delivering me a thunderbolt upside the head to adjust my moral philosophy, a knock shook the hollow panel of my bedroom door.

"*Shh.*" Doctor Paul moved the suitcase to the floor and laid me back on the bed. The startled mattress groaned out beneath us.

"What is it?" I gasped.

Sally's voice. "Telephone for you!"

Doctor Paul, growling in my ear: "Tell her you'll call back."

"I'll call back!"

Lips on my breast. "Tomorrow."

"Tomorrow!"

Footsteps. Silence. I put my hands to Doctor Paul's lapels and struggled him out of his unnecessary jacket. He was smiling, light with relief. He threw the jacket on the floor and cradled my face and kissed me.

Sally again. Bored and urgent. "Vivian! It's your friend Gogo. She says it's important."

Gogo.

My hands froze in Doctor Paul's hair.

"Vivian, no. Call her back. She'll be fine. She's stronger than you think."

Just like that, in a blink of the eternal eye, Doctor Paul's weight atop me was intolerable. I scrabbled at his chest and pushed him up.

"Vivian—"

But I was already buttoning up my guilty blouse, already straightening my telltale hair. I threw open the door and ran to the telephone.

"Gogo."

"Oh, Vivs." Her tears were flooding so fast, they nearly ran down the telephone line to wet my hand.

"Gogo, what happened?"

"He said . . ." Hiccup. "He said . . ." Hiccup.

"He didn't propose?"

"No! He said . . ." Hiccup.

I lowered myself into the chair and rested my cheek against my arm. My skin still returned the imprint of Paul's lips; the tips of my breasts still tingled without remorse. Nerves, hormones: they had no conscience. I looked out the window and wanted to throw myself into the courtyard. "Oh, Gogo. Oh, sweetie pie."

"What's wrong with me, Vivs? Why doesn't anyone want to marry me?"

I heard Doctor Paul's words in my head. "Oh, honey, because they're idiots. They think they want something else, but they're wrong. They want something exciting, and they don't understand that—"

"I'm not exciting?"

"You *are* exciting. To the right man. The right man will come along, Gogo. A smart, wonderful man who—"

"Are you crying, too, Vivs?"

"Yes, Gogo. I'm crying, too. I'm so sorry. So . . . God, so sorry." I looked up, and there was Doctor Paul, leaning against the door frame, arms folded, shirt untucked. His face had gone all heavy and confounded. My bed hovered in the tiny Manhattan space behind him.

"The worst—" Hiccup. "The worst of it was that he was so nice."

"Nice."

"He was so k—" Hiccup. "Kind. He kept telling me how much he cared for me, how much he wanted me to be happy. I thought . . . I thought he'd pull out the ring any minute. And then lunch was over, and we got up, and . . . He kissed my cheek, Vivs. My cheek!" Flooding anew. "And then I realized what he meant. Happy! How could I ever be happy without him?"

My eyes shot a stream of gamma rays straight through the frontal bone of Doctor Paul's skull. "Gogo, let me come to you. You shouldn't be alone."

"I'm not alone. I have Rufus."

"Jesus, Gogo. Your teddy bear is not enough. You need a martini. You need five martinis. You need—"

"Vivs, stop."

"You need to be taken out and gotten thoroughly drunk, and then we'll—"

"Vivs, stop. I'm not like you. I just need—" Sniff. "I just need a good cry, that's all. I'll be fine. I really will."

"Forgive me, but your strategy doesn't seem to be working. You should try mine."

Gurgle. "Oh, Vivs. I do love you."

I turned away from Doctor Paul's elegantly poised body and watched my finger travel along the smooth dark plastic of the telephone, the spiraling cord, the little twin buttons that could sever this excruciating connection in an instant. I whispered: "I love you, too, Gogo."

"Good night, Vivs."

"Good night, sweetiest of pies. Feel better."

The line clicked. I hung up the receiver with both hands and stared at that damned apparatus, that instrument of divine retribution, waiting for Doctor Paul to speak first, because I surely to God could not. I surely to God could not say what I had to say.

A coffee cup clattered before me, black and hot and smelling strongly of cheap brandy. "From the sound of Gogo's voice, I thought I might just get a pot going," said Sally.

"Always prepared." I sipped. The coffee-to-brandy ratio was just about where I needed it. Which is to say, six of one, half a dozen of the other.

"And now," Sally went on, with a long red kimono stretch, "I think I'll just slink on back to my cave and give you two a little privacy. There's more brandy in the cupboard if you need it. Enchanted to meet you, Dr. Salisbury."

"Pleasure."

I waited until the bedroom door closed. "She's wrecked. We wrecked her."

"*I* wrecked her. You have nothing to do with it. It's on my conscience, Vivian, not yours."

"Gallant to the last."

"This is not the last."

I shook my head. "I'm afraid it is."

"Will you look at me, at least?"

I turned. He'd pushed himself away from the door frame and stood on his own two feet. His eyes were wide and desperate.

"I can't, Paul. I can't do this. I'm not perfect, God knows, I'm no angel. But I can't do this to her. I will sink like a stone if I do. I will be beyond human hope."

"You're not doing anything to her. It's my fault. I'm the one who led her on."

"You didn't lead her on. It's just Gogo. She's . . . she's romantic. But that doesn't change anything. In fact, it makes things worse. If she saw us together, if she knew . . ."

Doctor Paul was shaking his head. "So we'll wait a bit. We'll give her a week or two—"

"No. Never."

"A month. Two months. Whatever it takes. We'll be as quiet as mice."

"Never, never."

"You're not serious. She'll understand, Vivian. She's a beautiful girl. She'll find someone else in no time."

"You don't understand. Not ever, do you hear me? Do you not understand a single thing about women? If she were to fall madly in love and marry and have a dozen kids, and if you and I were to start an affair when we were sixty, it would still not be okay. It just wouldn't."

He stood still and stricken, about ten feet away. The shadow from the lamp made his cheeks hollow.

"And there's my job," I said. "Lightfoot will fire me faster than a Soviet rocket."

"Your *job?*"

"My gig, my career. A writer at the *Metropolitan*. It's all I ever wanted from life."

"Vivian, there are other magazines. Look at you. The most dazzling woman in Manhattan. They'll be clamoring for you. You are sitting there, Vivian, and throwing away our happiness with your two hands."

"For God's sake. Listen to yourself. It's Monday. When you woke up Saturday morning you didn't even know I existed."

"Saturday morning I was a different man."

"Oh, lose the melodrama. This is not Saturday night at the Met. People don't just fall in love in a minute and a half."

"It was twelve hours. Plenty of time for a quick study like me."

"You're a quick *something*, I'll give you that."

Without warning, he whipped around and slammed his fist into the door frame.

I jumped to my feet. "What the hell was that?"

"You *can't*, Vivian. You can't just send me away. You can't pretend this never happened." He spoke into the plaster next to his fingers.

"I'm a Schuyler, kiddo. Watch and learn."

"I don't understand. I cannot comprehend why you're doing this."

I whispered: "Yes, you can."

Here's the thing about New York, the thing I love most: there is no such substance as silence. If you stop talking, and he stops talking, the city takes over for you. A siren forms a distant parabola of sound. A door slams. The old couple in 4A argues over who will answer the telephone. The young lovers in 2C reach an animalistic climax. A million other lives play out on your doorstep, and not one of them gives a damn about your little problems. Life goes on and on and on.

Without looking at me, Doctor Paul detached himself from the wall and picked up his jacket from my bedroom floor. He shrugged it over his shoulders and shook out his cuffs. I stared at him: handsome of face, straightforward of shoulders, sunshine of hair.

He paused with his hand on the doorknob. The entry bulb shone on the back of his neck. "One more thing. As a practical matter, after what happened Saturday night. Do you mind telling me the date of your last menstruation?"

"You sound like a doctor."

"Imagine that."

I fingered the wrapper on the pastrami sandwich. "Three weeks ago. We should be safe."

"You're never safe. So will you let me know? If we're not."

"Of course. But I'm not worried. I wouldn't have . . . I mean, I would have made you . . . I'm not that reckless."

He opened the door. "I'm not giving up, Vivian. I'm as stubborn as you are. If I have to wait until we're sixty."

"Trust me, Doctor. I'm not worth it."

The back of his head swung back and forth in the doorway.

"Trust me, Vivian. You are."

Violet

The day after Violet's visit to Dr. Winslow, she dressed and walked to the institute, and no one stopped her, no one told her she was no longer welcome. She did not see Walter all day, in fact.

She spoke with the other fellows, she sat and worked on the equations from her latest round of experiments. At five o'clock she left and picked up dinner from a cookshop and took it home, though the smell made her queasy, and as she forced it down she thought she had better humble herself and write to Christina. Perhaps something could be worked out. She would not return to New York in shame—*pregnant!* of all the sordid and predictable female defeats!—no, she could never do that, but Christina had always supported her. Christina had a streak of adventure, had secretly longed to commit some grievous impropriety and live in freedom thereafter. Perhaps Christina would come and help her with the baby, and they could live a wonderful bohemian existence, the three of them. Like a modern novel, like something Olive Schreiner might write.

Except that Christina now had a husband and a brand-new baby of her own, a respectable existence, stamped and approved with the Schuyler seal.

She washed her plate and cup and changed into her nightgown and her soft cashmere-lined dressing gown, a relic from her brief young-ladyhood. She added coals to her little fire and settled herself in the nearby chair with the latest *Proceedings*.

She must have dozed off, because a gentle knock startled her into alertness. "Come in," she said.

The door cracked open. "Miss Schuyler, Dr. Grant is waiting downstairs for you. Shall I allow him up?" said her landlady. On her face was an expression of compassion that made Violet want to weep with gratitude.

"Yes, thank you." She stood up and straightened her robe, straightened her hair. She wished she had a sword to buckle to her waist, a set of chain mail to cover her body.

Walter swept into the room with his usual assurance. He took off his hat and placed it on the table and turned to her, smiling. "Good evening, Violet. I've come to apologize."

"Indeed."

He walked up fearlessly and took her hands. His eyes were warm and blue. "How are you, child? Are you well?"

"Don't call me that."

"I was wrong, I was quite wrong. You have every right to be angry." He took up her hands and kissed them, and his beard scratched its familiar scratch against her skin. "I'm sorry, Violet."

"Very well. You're sorry. I accept your apology."

"Sit down, child." He drew on her hands.

Violet paused, resisting, and then allowed herself to be lowered into the armchair she had just left. "What is it?" she asked, placing her hands in her lap.

Walter sat down on the stool next to the fire. "I think we should marry, Violet."

"*What?*"

"We should marry. It's the sensible thing, the obvious solution to our little dilemma. We suit each other in every way."

His words whirled past her ears. *Marry*. "You, Walter? But I thought . . . I never thought . . . You don't believe in it. You told me so. Marriage is an artificial institution, it denies the essential independence of . . . of . . ." She could not remember the exact words, but their meaning was etched in her brain. After all, she hadn't disagreed with it. She had believed it, too, with all her heart.

He shook his head and took her hands again. "Ordinary marriage, child, between ordinary people. But ours will be a different sort of marriage, won't it? We'll have a new model, a marriage of equals, of like minds united in respect for the fundamental independence of the other. We won't be constrained by the rigid and hypocritical morality of the previous age. We shall place no restrictions on the freedom of the other person to pursue whatever interests give him or her happiness and pleasure."

Violet looked into Walter's face: at his eyes, alight with sincerity. "What are you saying, Walter? Tell me plainly."

"That I was wrong to tell you to visit Dr. Winslow. I engaged with you knowingly in the act of creation, I accepted that risk, and it is your right to handle the matter as your conscience dictates."

"And you don't mind?" Violet's throat strained with disbelief. "You'll agree to . . . to raise the baby with me?"

"If that's what you wish, Violet." He paused. "I admit, in all honesty, that I would have chosen differently. But I am a man of honor. If you must have this baby, then you shall do it by my side. As my wife, since society demands it, but with my assurance of partnership in any case."

Violet couldn't speak; she couldn't collect her thoughts. The reversal was so swift and unexpected, she felt almost sick.

Walter wanted to marry her. The brilliant Dr. Walter Grant, who had lived half a century without a wife, wanted to marry *her*, Violet Schuyler.

"What are you thinking, child?" He kissed her hands again. "Do you need time to consider?"

"Yes," she said. Her eyes were wet. "That is, no, I don't need time to consider. I'll marry you, Walter. You don't mind, really?"

He pulled her into her arms. "I don't mind."

They were married two weeks later, as soon as Christina could be summoned by cable (Violet's parents refused to acknowledge the telegram) and carried by liner across the ocean to attend the small civil ceremony in the town hall of Oxford, attended by a few colleagues from the Devonshire and by Walter's stern-faced secretary. Violet wore a tidy blue suit and an unfashionably small hat, and a bell tolled from some nearby church as they left the building. The April air smelled of damp grass and new flowers.

After an elegant wedding breakfast at the Randolph Hotel, Christina returned to her husband and baby in New York, and Walter and Violet left for a short honeymoon in Paris, staying at the Crillon and visiting the Louvre and Versailles, where the extraordinary gardens were fully abloom with spring. Violet walked with Walter down the Hall of Mirrors and marveled at their infinite reflections, husband and wife, repeated into eternity, united by the child nestled invisibly within, united by the great ideas and great works to come. She looped her arm through Walter's and squeezed him to her ribs.

They dined sumptuously each evening. Walter took no notice of her frequent exits to the lavatory, her fussy appetite, her visceral distaste for wine and for the strong-smelling tobacco in his pipe. He did, however, insist on her having tea every afternoon, which he served her himself in the privacy of their hotel sitting room, shooing her playfully away as he measured her leaves and added her cream and sugar. He made her drink every drop.

When they arrived back at Oxford, Violet's things had been packed and moved into Walter's house, where they sat in brown boxes surrounded by uniformed removal men, who were rolling up rugs and tucking away vases. "What's this?" she asked, rotating about in confusion.

"Surprise, dear child." He took her in his arms and kissed her nose. "I've been offered a position at the new Kaiser Wilhelm in Berlin. It's all arranged. You've got your own place, too, I absolutely insisted, as the first condition of my employment."

"But . . . but the baby!"

"Don't worry about the baby," he said, and indeed, a week after their arrival in Berlin, Violet saw the first spot of blood on her drawers, and by the end of the next day she had miscarried in quiet anguish, attended by a sympathetic German physician.

Walter stopped making her tea after that. He waited a considerate six weeks before approaching her in bed, and when he did, he first opened up a box of custom-made sheepskin condoms from a chemist on Charlot-tenstrasse.

"No more careless mistakes, child," he said, smiling.

Vivian

When the metallic crash of the front door had finished echoing up the stairs, I rose from the chair, stumbled to my bedroom, and lifted Aunt Violet's suitcase back on the bed.

My eyes had dried out. If I'd wanted numbness, I had it now: a thick blanket of it, covering my ears and fingers and heart. My mind, however, was clear and scissor-sharp. Ready for business again. Thank God. No more messy spills to impair the old intellect.

This time I reached for the clasp and hairpin with determination. I had a story to write. I had a job to do.

Now, don't be shocked, but I wasn't wholly unfamiliar with the science of picking a lock. Friends in high places, the usual. I closed my eyes and poked among the tumblers as delicately as a new mother with a Q-tip, and all for nothing: the metal parts were stuck fast, beyond the might of a human hairpin. Round one, the lock.

I rapped said hairpin against the jagged opening, which seemed, in my present mood, to be leering at me, in a bare-toothed, rusty way I found insulting.

"All right, then, Violet Grant. My stubborn little Houdini," I said. "You've left me no choice."

I rose to my feet and made for the under-sink cabinet in the kitchen.

Under a tactical bombardment of WD-40, the tumblers surrendered and the edges of the valise released with a musty sigh of defeat. I opened them wide.

The contents had been packed with an eerie tidiness. Violet herself, or some modern official who had found the valise in a forgotten corner and searched for some clue to its provenance? Given the state of the lock, I guessed the former.

Clothes first, and not many. Maybe you didn't need them, when you ran away with your lover. I lifted them out, one by one. I'd thought they went in for lace and frills in those days, but these threads were simple, sturdy cottons and linens in summer colors, except for one in blue gossamer that looked as if it were made of clouds. I shook it out. Creases, marks. And was that a grass stain on the back?

Why, Aunt Violet. You naughty, naughty girl.

A cardigan followed, a practical knit, belted at the waist. I lifted it to my nose. Just wool and dust, no sign of human habitation. What had Violet smelled like? Lysol and laboratories, probably. That acrid scent of acids in beakers. All of it gone now, lost to time and Zurich cupboards.

Underthings! Long and tipped with a bit of lace, at least. This was more like it. I could perceive the allure of these drawers, mysterious in their lengthy modesty, especially when topped by the corset that unfolded in my hands. I rounded my lips into a soundless whistle of appreciation. She'd had a tiny waist, Aunt Violet, as she gallivanted about with her atoms and molecules. No wonder she'd snagged the eyeballs of this eminent Dr. Grant. He could have spanned her with his hands if he wanted.

Which, obviously, he had.

I reached inside. There were no more clothes: just books and papers and a soft felt bag filled with tantalizing bumps. I loosened the drawstring and spilled out the contents onto the bedspread.

Jewelry. A pair of gold bracelets, wide as handcuffs, monogrammed *W* on one and *G* on the other. An amethyst brooch. A necklace made of aquamarine flowers: pretty, really, if dainty jewelry was your narcotic of choice.

Then. A watch. A plain gold watch, unadorned except for the engraving at the back:

To Violet
from her sister Christina
1911
"Why, then the world's mine oyster
which I with sword will open."

A little chill stirred at the base of my neck, as if someone had blown on it. I turned the watch back over and opened the case. At seven-oh-three in the morning or evening, some day in late July or perhaps early August of 1914, this watch had ticked its last tock. If I rubbed my fingers against it, I might still feel Violet's touch, her slender scientific hands winding it up. Checking the time. Sliding it into her pocket. She must have dropped her valise in a hurry, if she'd left this watch inside. She must have meant to come back for it.

Why hadn't she?

I laid the watch atop the blue gossamer dress with the grass stains and pulled out the remaining contents of the valise.

Great guns.

Travel papers. For the love of Peter, Paul, and Mary. *Travel papers.*

I snatched them up. The one on top was Violet's, a photograph pasted to a thick sheet written in gothic German script, and there she was. Just like that.

Violet Grant.

Her exquisite black-and-white photograph stared sightlessly at me through melting huge eyes. Scientist? More like a Gibson girl who'd lost her tint, a girl to adorn chocolate boxes and Coca-Cola advertisements, not at all the kind of girl who bent over microscopes and singed her hair on Bunsen burners. How could this darling creature be Violet? Scientific Violet, married Violet. Adulterous Violet.

I smudged my thumbs around the edge of her image and examined her pointed chin, her wide cheekbones. Her eyes. Now, that was better. I knew those eyes. I wielded them myself to great effect.

She existed. She had stood before that camera with her alluring eyes and her adorable heart-shaped face. She was a person. Name: Violet Schuyler Grant. Verheiratet. Geburtsdatum, 10 November 1891. Geburtsort, New York City, New York, U.S.A. Every fact in order. Nothing I didn't already know, really.

But the others. I hadn't known there were others, plural.

Americans. Jane Johnson Mortimer de Saint-Honoré, divorced, born 15 July 1878 in Rapid City, Iowa: Now, who the sweet social ladder was *she*?

And Henry Johnson Mortimer, born 9 August 1894. I turned that one over. Jane's son? He regarded the camera with profound gravity and too much dark hair atop his narrow face. I held him next to Jane and gasped.

The broad was beautiful.

She beheld the camera as if it were her dearest friend, and I mean *dearest* in the bedroom sense. You could not mistake that look. It ricocheted down the generations. It belonged to a different half-lidded category of allurement altogether from the huge gaze of Violet Grant, weightless with innocence, void of corruption. Whoever she was, whatever she was, this Mrs. Jane Johnson de Saint-Honoré was eminently corruptible. She knew the heat of a luxurious bed or two, if you'll pardon my bard.

And judging by Henry Mortimer's date of birth, she knew it early.

I spread the papers out before me. One, two, three. Violet, Jane, Henry.

But Henry was only nineteen years old in July 1914. Surely this couldn't be Violet's lover, the one she'd murdered her husband for. Not this grave dark-haired boy traveling with his come-hither mumsy. Youth aside, he didn't look like the kind of kid who inspired a grand passion. Or even a petit passion. He looked like the kind of kid who inspired a grand yawn of ennui. Trust me, I knew the type. They flocked to me in their heat-seeking dozens.

Where had Violet picked them up, and why?

And where was the lover in all this?

I flipped through the leather-bound books that remained on the bed, searching for something else. Anything. A name, a postcard.

The books must have been Violet's scientific journals. They were filled with drawings and equations, inscrutable alphas and deltas that were decidedly Greek to me. Still. I liked her handwriting, quick and masculine. Rather like mine.

But the last book wasn't the same. Here the scrawl took a different slant, a thicker brush, smaller letters. The ink was still rich and black. The cover was stamped in gold: 1912. I turned to the back, and a folded piece of paper fell out, scattering dried rose petals over the bedspread. I collected them gently in my hand and unfolded the paper.

proclaimed the engraved monogram at the top, marking it Violet's, but this was a different handwriting altogether:

Ah! So Violet is a romantic after all
I have kissed each one to last you until I return
Lionel

The pulse in my neck took a flying leap off a vertical gulp.

Lionel. Oh, my bright twinkling stars. *Lionel.*

Violet's lover.

He was real. He had held a pen in his hand and written these words. This story handed down through discreet channels, this secret shame of the secretly shameless Schuylers, this tragic Berlin affair: it had happened. I'd found Violet's husband, and now I knew her lover.

His name was Lionel.

I opened my hands and looked again at the petals. I picked one and held it to my lips.

After half a century, it had lost its scent and its velvet texture, but a little color still held on, a half-remembered dream of scarlet. *I have kissed each one to last you until I return.* Elvis Aaron Presley, give me strength. *Kissed each one.* Kissed each petal for you, Violet, and when I say petal, you know whereof I metaphor.

Who could blame Violet? If this Lionel appeared in the room right now before me, I'd have him kissing my roses before you could say *voulez-vous.*

I returned the petal to my palm and looked adoringly at the pile nestled there. The faded little dears. I imagined them sitting there in Violet's ecru stationery all these years, beneath her gossamer dress and her underclothes, inside the journal labeled 1912: so many layers to shield them from the brutal half century that followed their secret Lionel-lipped benediction, the modern world of muddy trenches and nuclear bombs, of rock and roll and Norman Mailer and the Duchess of Argyll.

I poured them back into the note and folded it with care. Like eggs in a nest, like my own private little secret with Aunt Violet. I opened the book to slip them safely back inside, and as I did so, a single and rather surprising word jumped out from one of the pages.

Jumped at me not because it was unfamiliar, necessarily, but because it clashed with such contemporary force against the chivalry of Lionel's rose-petal kisses.

fuck

. . .

I PAUSED, notebook in one hand and petals in the other. I set the note on the bed, and then I flipped back through the pages of the book, intensely curious, trying to find the word again. Because. What was it doing there?

Neither word nor book belonged to Violet or Lionel; even to my untrained eyes, the handwriting here was distinct from both the love note and the scientific notebooks. It was a journal of some kind—the dates were printed in a tiny typeface at the top of each page—and when I stopped to read an entry, my breath caught. I slid to the floor, braced my back against the bedpost, and clutched the leather in my hand.

Once I was accustomed to the archaic shape of the letters, the near-illegibility of the hurried italic lines, it didn't take me long to figure out who had authored them. I read on in horrified fascination, wanting to stop, unable to stop.

I had once happened upon a gruesome street corner on Park Avenue one shiny spring day, where a taxi had so thoroughly obliterated a pedestrian that you couldn't see if this former human being had been male or female, young or old, except for the graceful high-heeled shoe tossed into the center median, in the middle of a bed of orange and yellow tulips, with a foot still stuffed inside. I had tried to look away from that shoe, just as I did from this journal, and yet my eyes kept going back, as if they needed to know every detail, to normalize this abnormality into insignificance.

By the time I reached the end of May, I felt physically sick. I gathered the shards of my moral composure and shut the book with a leathery snap.

"Great guns," I whispered to the ceiling. "Dr. Walter Grant. You filthy beast."

Violet, 1912

Violet cannot recall the exact moment she realized Walter was sleeping with other women. *Sleeping:* that's the wrong word. He was fucking other women, and then returning home to their marital bedroom, to bathe and change and sometimes to fuck her, too, and then fall asleep snoring in their iron-framed bed in the luxurious flat on Kronenstrasse.

There was no sudden epiphany. The suspicion crept up on her, inch by inch, nudged along by minute clues and conjectures. A woman's eyes, laughing knowingly at her at some dinner party, before turning away. A hint of perfume on Walter's linens, before the maid had a chance to launder. Lise's sympathetic face. The memory of Walter's smooth acceptance of her suspicions of pregnancy, and his practiced solution to the dilemma, his prior acquaintance with Dr. Winslow. All the evidence supported her hypothesis, that Walter was unfaithful, habitually and casually unfaithful. She began, with a curious dispassion, to imagine him with other women: what they would look like, where he would meet them. This other world of his, in which she played no part.

So the immediate encounter with Walter's infidelity came more as a shock than a surprise.

When they first moved to Berlin, and after Violet had recovered—physically, at least—from the miscarriage, she went to parties with her husband. She considered it part of her duty, since she was so unwifely in other regards: endless troglodyte hours spent in the basement of the institute, rumpled unfashionable clothes, housekeeping left entirely to the housekeeper, equations scrawled on napkins, conversation dominated by the technical, face screwed all too often in unreachable concentration. That summer and autumn, as a kind of restitution, she forced herself to depart her cramped office by six o'clock to accompany Walter to dinner parties, music parties, opera and ballet, soirées and balls, enduring them chiefly by sitting quietly near a window and contemplating the progress, or lack of it, she had made in her laboratory or her notebooks.

At one such evening, held at the Baroness von Schrager's magnificent flat near the Reichstag, knotted up and frustrated by a particularly inconclusive experiment that day, she had allowed herself to drink a glass or two of champagne and to be led into dancing. The results astonished her. Gentleman after unaccountable gentleman had walked up and asked her for the next waltz, and she had complied, even laughing a little, enjoying the new sensation of being sought after and admired.

After the fifth or sixth dance, she recalled the hour and went looking for Walter. She had found him easily, in a small sitting room at the back of the flat, his tailcoat flung over a chair, his formal black trousers about his knees, his white buttocks clenching steadily as he immersed himself in the backside of a small dark-haired matron dressed in emerald green. The woman was bent over a French escritoire: Directoire, Violet noted, though not a particularly fine example. Her ring-crusted knuckles curled about the opposite edge; her breasts and her pearls dangled together heavily from her unfastened bodice. At each thrust, she called out *Mein Gott!* in a voice so feral, she did not detect the sound of Violet's entry into the room.

Walter did, however. He turned his red and passion-bloated face in his wife's direction, registering surprise; but instead of desisting, he merely offered Violet an apologetic shrug and continued his work. Through the open door, the Baroness von Schrager's orchestra played heedless Schubert.

Violet, frozen, misted with champagne, pictured herself lifting the statue of a curving bronze Aphrodite from the shelf nearby and dropping it over Walter's head.

She did not, however. Instead, she backed away and closed the door with a numb hand. She found herself a taxi and went to bed, thinking that she had dreamed all this before, that this new picture in her head was exactly as she had imagined it. This shock she felt, it was recognition.

The next morning, she found Walter lying next to her in bed, in remorseless slumber. Over breakfast, he reminded her that their marriage was a modern one, a new model of partnership, in which they placed no restrictions on the freedom of the other person to pursue whatever interests gave him or her happiness and pleasure. He had brought her to Berlin with him, he had given her her place at the institute; she had everything she wanted, and all because of his untiring efforts on her behalf, his unflagging ambition for her. She understood that, of course?

She did.

He reached across the breakfast table and squeezed her hand, where it lay next to her steaming coffee. He was so very glad he had married her, the only woman in the world he could have made his wife, always first in his heart. She was no narrow-minded bourgeois. She was clear-headed and scientific, thank God; she understood men were subject to physical urges from time to time, simple transactions of the body, but she, Violet, was his wife. He would always support and encourage her interests, as long as she supported and encouraged his. She understood that, too, of course?

Violet picked up her coffee, drank it scalding hot, and said that of course she understood.

After all, a mutual pursuit of happiness was the foundation of a marriage of equals.

PART TWO

Since there's no help, come let us kiss and part;
Nay, I have done, you get no more out of me
And I am glad, yea glad with all my heart
That thus so cleanly I myself can free;
Shake hands forever, cancel all our vows,
And when we meet at any time again,
Be it not seen in either of our brows
That we one jot of former love retain.

Now at the last gasp of love's latest breath,
When, his pulse failing, passion speechless lies,
When faith is kneeling by his bed of death,
And innocence is closing up his eyes,
Now if thou wouldst, when all have given him over,
From death to life thou mightst him yet recover.

—Michael Drayton (1563–1631)

Vivian

I walked into the *Metropolitan* lobby Tuesday morning with considerably less *joie de travailler* than I had danced through the day before, but I wasn't about to let anyone know it.

"Good morning, Agatha! Where on earth have you been hiding that feathered comb? It sets off your hair to perfection." I kissed the tips of my fingers.

She moved her nail file from ring finger to pinkie. "Mr. Lightfoot wants to see you." Like a sentence of lethal injection.

"Why, thank you, Agatha. I'll just drop my pocketbook and briefcase at my desk and be with him—"

"*Now*, he says." She snapped her Wrigley's, set down the nail file, and picked up her magazine.

I leaned over her desk. "Agatha, you have such a way with words. Why aren't you writing for the magazine, that's what I've always wondered."

"Get lost," she said.

"You see? Concise, to the point." I gave my briefcase a joyous little swing as I set off down the corridor to the hallowed Lightfoot wing. "Brevity is the soul of rudeness, my mother always says."

Outside Mr. Lightfoot's double doors, Gogo's desk overflowed with silver-framed photos and crystal candy dishes. The only item missing was Gogo herself. His lordship's secretary looked up from her own Spartan empire on the left-hand side, dressed impeccably in neutral colors, lipstick immaculate, eyelashes extravagant. "Miss Schuyler. I'll just announce you."

She picked up the Lightfoot Hotline and murmured a few words. I swallowed back a gum wad of anxiety and shifted my pocketbook to the same hand as my briefcase.

The secretary rose in hourglass splendor from her desk and opened the right-hand door. "You can go in, Miss Schuyler."

I sallied forth with hips swinging. "Good morning, Mr. Lightfoot. What a charming way to start the day. We should do this more often."

He looked up from the starched pages of *The Wall Street Journal*, spread like a rectangle of sanity atop the liquid brown of his desk, and removed his reading glasses, the better to strip me naked with.

Now. A word about S. Barnard Lightfoot III. He had three houses and four ex-wives, and the only thing he loved more than first editions and hourglass secretaries was his daughter, Margaux. (Of S. Barnard Lightfoot IV, the less said the merrier.) Having, as I've said, an agreeable waist-to-hip ratio myself, I'd found myself on the receiving end of a Lightfoot proposition within a week of my employment here at the *Metropolitan*. I'd refused it gracefully, no feelings hurt, no careers destroyed, and I hadn't entered the inner sanctum since.

So. Here I stood, the day after Gogo's heartbreak, two days after waking up in Suitor Number Ten's coveted bed. The timing was suspicious, to say the damnedest.

"Miss Schuyler." Those famous pale eyes did an ankle-to-bosom evaluation, weighted arithmetically to the bosom. Mr. Lightfoot had a face that recalled Bath sandstone, grandly proportioned and always lightly tanned, as if he'd just stepped off a Mediterranean liner accompanied by twenty steamer trunks filled with cigars, tailcoats, and hair oil. Actually, I liked him. He made no bones about who he was and what he wanted.

He was a man I could deal with. "Please sit. I suppose you know why you're here."

I dropped into the chair and set my briefcase on the floor. "I can't imagine. My sins are so numerous."

"My daughter is home in bed today. I expect she'll be out all week."

"Poor Gogo. She told me about it last night. It's awful. How is she? Is there anything I can do?"

He flipped open a silver case on his desk and withdrew a cigarette, which he lit in a single experienced strike of a gold Zippo lighter. "You can tell me the nature of your relationship with Dr. Salisbury."

"I'm sorry, I don't—"

"I understand you had a heated conversation with him in the library, before he took my daughter out to lunch and broke her heart."

Pale eyes could be so piercing.

"Ah, your network of spies at work again. Do you mind if I smoke, Mr. Lightfoot?"

That, at least, got a twitch of eyebrow out of him. He nudged at the silver box. "Be my guest, Miss Schuyler."

I rose and took a cigarette, and then I leaned forward so he could light me up. I settled back in my chair. It was a modern number, low-slung, designed to lull the sitter with an excess of ergonomic comfort. Also to hold him in place a good foot or two lower than the boss. "I'll be candid, Mr. Lightfoot, if I may speak in confidence."

"Please do."

"I am acquainted with Dr. Salisbury. We met over the weekend. I didn't realize he was Suitor Number Ten."

"Suitor Number Ten?"

I waved my smoky hand. "Gogo and I are close, as you know."

"Not close enough, evidently."

"No, no, Mr. Lightfoot. You've got it all wrong. If I'd known who Dr. Salisbury was, I'd never have . . ." A flutter of the fingers.

"Hmm." He considered. "May I ask what occurred between you?"

"You may not."

"I see."

"Yes, I expect you do. However, once he walked into the office yesterday and I put one and one together into three, if you take my meaning, I told him it was off. That *I* was off. I am very fond of Gogo, Mr. Lightfoot, and I would never indulge myself at her expense." I looked at him straight and true, piercing eye for piercing eye.

"By God," he said. "Then why did he break things off with her after all?"

And here we are again, Vivian and her shortcomings. If you weren't well disposed to me before, you're really going to despise me now. I'm sorry, but it can't be helped. I am who I am. And that Tuesday morning, in contrast to Monday, I had nothing to lose. I had no more Doctor Paul. I had a suitcase full of unsolved Violet and Lionel. I had a promise to keep to myself, a resolution to guard and protect against human weakness.

So here's what I said next.

"Because he's in love with me, Mr. Lightfoot. Passionately in love."

"After a single weekend?"

I shrugged modestly. Lightfoot's eyes dropped back to my bosom.

"I can't explain it, sir. I suppose the heart has its reasons. As you can imagine, the confrontation was taxing for us both." I dragged hard on my cigarette and stared out the window to Lightfoot's private terrace, thick with potted chrysanthemums. "He refused to give me up. He says he'll keep trying until he's sixty."

"I see. And what do you intend to do about it?"

I turned bravely back to him. "Well, I have my career, don't I? I suppose I'll just have to throw myself into my work at the *Metropolitan* and hope for the best. Hope it can distract me from all this."

Lightfoot twiddled his thumbs. He lifted his cigarette. He blew out a sizable cloud and tipped the ash into a handsome glass tray. He pushed it toward me.

"Thank you." I leaned over and did the necessary.

"Admirable sentiments, Miss Schuyler," he said. "Of course, I stand ready to support you in any way I can."

"I appreciate the gesture, sir. I do so happen to have a bit of research I'm working on, in my spare time. An exposé, of a sort."

"Do you, now?"

"Yes. A fifty-year-old murder mystery. High-society wife murders husband, disappears into the German countryside with lover. If the *Metropolitan* is interested in that kind of thing."

"Have you spoken to Tibby about this?"

I extended my crossed legs, fatale-style. "I'm afraid Mr. Tibbs doesn't possess quite so much eagerness to support my noble intentions, sir."

"I can speak to him."

"I'd appreciate that, sir. It would certainly keep me busy. Keep my mind off personal matters for some time." I brushed at my skirt. "I might need a little help from the *Metropolitan* archives."

"They are at your disposal, of course. I'll tell my secretary to give you a key."

I nearly swallowed my cigarette. "That would be very helpful, Mr. Lightfoot. I'd be most appreciative."

"Hmm." He dropped his smoke in the ashtray and rose from his desk. I took the hint and unwound my legs.

"I'm glad we had this talk, Miss Schuyler." Lightfoot came around the desk and motioned me ahead of him. "I think we've come to an excellent understanding, don't you?"

"It's so lovely to be understood."

His hand appeared on the doorknob in front of me. His voice dropped an octave. "All in one weekend, *hmm?* Dr. Salisbury must have been favorably impressed."

"It's a mistake I don't mean to repeat, sir," I said. *"Ever."*

"I see." He opened the door for me and extended his other hand. "Good day, Miss Schuyler."

I shook his hand. "Good day, Mr. Lightfoot."

. . .

I STRODE down the corridor, away from the Lightfoot wing. My eyeballs began to sting just as I reached my desk. I placed my briefcase on the floor and my pocketbook in the bottom drawer. Tibby's head poked out from his office. His bark followed with considerable bite. "Where the hell is my coffee, Miss Schuyler?"

"In a moment, Mr. Tibbs."

I found the bathroom just in time. I locked myself in the far stall, the one nobody used because the latch always stuck and made your nail varish chip. I sat on the seat and folded six squares of toilet tissue and cried silently into them, careful not to smudge my mascara, blotting as I went so no one would ever, ever suspect.

BY THE TIME I'd delivered Tibby's coffee black, no sugar, everything was arranged except his willing cooperation. His unwilling cooperation, I had in spades.

He gulped his coffee straight before he began. At the second bob of his throat, I realized I'd forgotten the sugar. He didn't seem to notice. "Your work has been reassigned to one of the junior writers," he said, investing the sentence with as much irony as it could legally bear. "I will expect a full draft of this article on my desk within a week."

"That won't be possible. I have a tremendous amount of research to do. This is a big story, Tibby. Big big big."

He flinched. "Two weeks."

"I believe Mr. Lightfoot wants me to do the job as thoroughly as possible."

"Three. Or I hand in my resignation."

I held out my hand and gave him a blinding smile. "Done."

When I returned to my desk, the key to the hallowed *Metropolitan* archives lay in a plain white envelope on my desk. I kissed it and danced to the elevator, taking care to wave Agatha a cheery farewell as I passed her desk.

Now, let's be clear: the *Metropolitan* archives did not exist, officially speaking. I don't even remember how I first heard about them. They were like a myth handed down, somewhere between the third Scotch and the fifth martini, in a hushed and reverent whisper obscured by a miasma of tobacco smoke. Gogo once told me they were located on the nineteenth floor of the building, behind a door marked FURNITURE REPOSITORY, but I doubt she would have recalled this small indiscretion the next morning. All I knew was that I needed those archives, because wherever the story of Walter and Violet and Lionel existed, it was not in the official library, the biographies, the encyclopedias, the *New York Times*.

It existed in the drawing rooms and bedrooms of 1914 Germany, where it would have caused a delicious scandal that summer; and if the affair had made its way to 1964 Manhattan at all, it would be contained in the gossipy correspondence of those who dined on it.

Like, for example, that sent by the *Metropolitan* correspondent in Berlin to his editor back in New York.

I know. I like the way my brain works, too.

But first. You had to appreciate the sight that stretched before you, as you used your private key to open up the battered metal door on the nineteenth floor marked FURNITURE REPOSITORY. I know I did. Rows and rows of wooden filing cabinets, covered with the thinnest layer of dust, just for atmosphere. The single bare bulb hanging from the center of the ceiling, looking as if Edison himself had installed it. That dark and musty flavor of the same million-billion particles of air rubbing against one another for weeks on end. I sighed it all in and out. The splendors of the world lay in wait.

It occurred to me, as I made my way to the first filing cabinet, as I touched it with my index finger as I might touch the Ark of the Covenant, that Lightfoot hadn't imposed any conditions on my visit here. No vow of secrecy, no injunction on copying or removing or destroying as

I saw fit. Maybe all that was implicit in the granting of the key itself. I was the inner circle now; I was the archives. You did not befoul your own bed.

I rolled open the first drawer. Secret the archives might be, but they were arranged impeccably by date and office, in crisp manila folders rarely exposed to the horrors of oxidation. I pulled out the first, just for the sake of curiosity. Paris office, 1888. From the Baroness Pauline Marie Plessis de Meaux to Mr. S. Barnard Lightfoot, written in French, deeply apologetic that she had not written since last month, but she had been *très, très occupée* with the redecoration of her salon, and the races at Deauville had been divine, divine, and please would he remember that these little notices were to be kept strictly confidential? Her dear husband would not be pleased, and perhaps not her friends, either.

As I said. The splendors of the world.

Still. Work to be done. I put the baroness back where she belonged and dragged my greedy fingers along the cabinets until I came to the year 1914, which in fact filled two separate filing cabinets, so great was the flood of information pouring into S. Barnard Lightfoot Jr.'s mailbox in that tumultuous year. (Lightfoot *père* had died happily of asphyxiation between his mistress's breasts in the summer of 1905, as everyone knew.) I flipped past tantalizing folders for Paris, Rome, London, Shanghai, Tokyo, and finally came upon one marked BERLIN, JAN–MAR.

I drew it out.

Now. Here's the trouble turning a curious animal like me loose in an archive like this, with no clear idea what I was looking for, and no clue where it might be. I picked up the first item—a cablegram, as it happened—and while I meant simply to scan the thing over for the names Violet, Walter, Grant, or Lionel, I was immediately sucked into contemplation of the word *fellatio*. And my goodness! What a parade of scandal could be contained in a single cablegram! Who was this Lolo, and why would she (or, equally, he) risk all with the photographic evidence the *Metropolitan*'s Berlin correspondent evidently now had in hand?

NO SMOKING read a small brass sign above the reading table, where I carried my chosen files. Normally, I enjoyed a good smoke as I browsed through a comfortable stack of scandal of an afternoon, but this time I didn't notice the absence, because the Berlin of 1914 was my kind of town.

Spent all night at the Bluebird, spilled out at dawn (and I do mean spilled), wrote the correspondent on March 11. *Witnessed at least three acts of adultery between midnight and three, and heard from my dear General X that the Kaiser and Kaiserin are quarreling again. Plus ça change. The cabaret was excellent. Lolo as Dido, or perhaps Dido as Lolo: one can no longer distinguish between history and reality after the absinthe goes in the punch.*

Then in April: *The anarchists have taken over my favorite café on Unter den Linden this week, and we are forced to abandon our post for the less hospitable reaches of the Café des Westerns, sweating, sick, and hot as Brooke had it. Oh, damn, I know it!*

By now, the small of my back was aching, and so were my eyes: the *Metropolitan's* Berlin correspondent appeared to have written most of his letters while drunk on absinthe or something else, not that I could blame him. I rose from my chair, stretched, and reached for my pocketbook.

The windows of the archive were concealed by thick yellowing blinds and stuck shut by strata of old paint, but I persevered until a few inches of chilled October air could be coaxed from the bottom sash and into the room, laced with automobile exhaust and the arrhythmic staccato of taxi horns. *Pace* brass-plated prohibitions, I lit a cigarette and watched the traffic crawl below, the hatted hoards stream along the pavement in their dozens. Lunchtime.

What was Doctor Paul having for lunch today? Something quick and cheap from the hospital automat? A sandwich from home? Or was he too busy for lunch at all?

I thought, *I could still turn back.* I could walk out of this room and lock the door up tight, and I could swish down the elevator and out into the bristling New York sidewalk. I could rattle down the IRT to Saint Vincent's Hospital and ask for Dr. David Paul Salisbury and tell him I'd made a terrible mistake, I couldn't live without him, could we start over and forget Gogo, forget Violet and Lionel, forget the whole damned world, because the problems of two people didn't amount to a hill of beans in this . . .

Ah, pardon me. Wrong movie.

I stubbed out my cigarette and got back to work, and I must have done the right thing, because on the first letter of the next file folder, dated May 21, 1914, the *Metropolitan's* intrepid Berlin correspondent sandwiched the following between a military review in the Tiergarten and scandal in the ballet de corps of the Berlin Opera:

At the Bluebird last night, and only just recovered. First off, saw the Countess de Saint-Honoré (née Jane Johnson of Rapid City, if one's feeling sufficiently ungenerous to recall that inconvenient fact, which it seems most ladies of her acquaintance are, at least behind her lovely back). In excellent looks, as ever. She arrived in tandem with a young man of perhaps eighteen or twenty: her son, I presume, since word has it she intends him to study amongst the eminent brains at the Kaiser Wilhelm. (Either that, or she hopes to add a German title to her collection. One suspects the latter, but on the other hand, what doting mother could resist the temptation of tossing her young prodigy under the very noses of Herr Einstein and Dr. Grant?)

Gathump gathump, went my heart.

Our story begins at the Bluebird café.

Violet, 1914

They dine at a café along Unter den Linden, Violet and her husband and Lionel Richardson, amid a high-pitched atmosphere of cigarettes and roasting meat and rattling dishes. Walter calls imperiously for two bottles of Margaux. "The fatted calf," he says, laying aside the menu, "for the prodigal student."

"Hardly prodigal, though I appreciate the gesture." Lionel lights himself a cigarette and leans back in his chair. The frail wood seems too small for him; the room seems too small for him. His shoulders strain against his jacket, too full of life and muscle to be contained by so fine a sheet of gray wool.

"You left the virtuous labor of my laboratory for the British Army. Subduing the innocents in South Africa, I believe." Walter smiles and takes his pipe from the inside pocket of his jacket.

"Colonial subjects in revolt."

"Precisely."

Lionel throws back his dark head and laughs. The electric lights flash along the ridges of his throat. "Still a Marxist, I see. I suppose it comes with the territory, as you Americans say, Mrs. Grant. Isn't that right?" He turns to Violet, and his eyes crinkle in a silent laugh.

She fingers the bowl of her wineglass. "Of course Walter is a socialist.

We are all socialists, aren't we? All forward-thinking people must be. It's the natural progression of history."

"Oh, quite. I can't fault you there." He blows out another slow stream of smoke and winks at her, and she thinks that it's not fair, not a bit. No just Nature should have bestowed so many physical gifts on a single man, while the rest huddle about their urban café tables in thin-shouldered, narrow-faced obscurity. He reclines like a lion before her, or rather a particularly robust panther, with his dark sleek hair and watchful gray eyes, his easy muscular grace, his air of patient vitality. When she switched on the lights in the laboratory two hours ago, she nearly staggered in shock. Had she really shared a darkened room with such a predatory creature? As if she were a mouse curled up with a cat for the night.

"There's no point in arguing with him, my dear," says Walter. "One cannot expect the son of a British peer to welcome the revolution with hands outstretched to lift up the downtrodden."

"Third son. Of no account whatever, really. I should be marching with sickle in hand this instant." Lionel's charming lopsided mouth maintains its smile. He looks directly at Violet, as if daring her to challenge him on the subject of primogeniture.

Walter laughs and refills Violet's glass. "Beware Captain Richardson's charm, child. He may be a pretty fellow, but he's not the sort of man to allow women careers in the sciences."

"Perish the thought. Should never allow my wife near the laboratory. Primitive brute of the worst sort." Richardson's white teeth bare themselves at Violet. "Barbaric, on good authority."

"You deferred to me perfectly well during the experiment."

"Oh, that's quite another matter. I'm perfectly civilized with other men's wives."

"But not your own?"

"I'm not married, Mrs. Grant. I speak hypothetically."

Violet tilts forward. "I don't envy this hypothetical wife of yours. She sounds more like a vassal. I don't suppose you'd allow her a single thought of her own. A life's work of her own."

"Naturally. I'd expect *I* would be her life's work. And a damned tedious project it is, too. I shouldn't wish it on anyone, which is why I remain obstinately unshackled." He reaches for his wineglass, cigarette still planted between his index and middle fingers, and inspects the bowl against the light from the sputtering yellow-tinged candle at the center of the table. Three deep lines extend from the corner of his squinting right eye, interrupting the marvelously even flow of his skin. The red-dark wine stills obediently before his gaze.

"I don't believe you. Surely you're not opposed to the rights of women."

"I suppose it depends on the woman. *You* seem perfectly capable of making rational decisions, Mrs. Grant, but I shudder to think of the state of the British nation if any of the chattering canaries in my mother's drawing room were allowed the vote. An absolute balls-up within a generation, wouldn't you agree?"

"It depends on which way they voted."

"Then you don't mind how idiotic the rationalization, so long as the poor fools vote for your side?" Lionel sighs and sets down the glass without drinking.

"But that's not the point. There are plenty of idiotic *men* already voting. The point is that a fair vote, a just vote, must extend to everyone who's subject to the government in question, whether stupid or blind or poor or self-interested. Equality must be enshrined in the franchise itself, otherwise those in power can decide who *does* have the vote, as arbitrarily as they like . . ."

"Stop, stop!" Lionel waves both hands, causing a ribbon of smoke to undulate between them. "You go too far, Mrs. Grant, with all this talk of franchises and equality. As a frivolous and frankly apolitical chap, I won't stand for it. You see?" He turns to Walter, smiling again. "I warned you what would come of your feminist sympathies. I suppose you talk suffrage and the proletariat over your pillow at night. *Propagande par le fait,* isn't that it?"

Walter rumbles a low laugh and covers Violet's hand with his. "As you see, I have fashioned my ideal mate. A fortuitous turn of the stars, the day she marched into my office and demanded a place at the Devonshire."

Lionel's warm eyes tilt back to Violet. "I can rather picture it."

Violet pictures it. She looks down now at the quiet hand covering hers, and the swamp of gratitude floods her again. She is understood; she is accepted. She lifts her thumb to sidle against his: Walter's thumb, his hand, his whip-thin body that—for all its sins—is her bulwark against the Schuylers, against the cuts and slights of her fellow scientists at Oxford and now in Berlin, against the primitive barbarism of men like Lionel Richardson.

Lionel Richardson, whose left eyebrow is now raised, having caught the minute caress of Violet's thumb against Walter's. "My felicitations."

"Thank you," says Walter.

"And how long are you married? I'm useless with dates."

"Two years."

Lionel stubs out his cigarette. The charming smile has returned, curling around the wide edges of his mouth. He seems to have twice as many teeth as ordinary men, lined up like gleaming white soldiers at the parting of his lips. "Dare one hope for the pitter-patter of little scientific feet?"

Walter's hand drops away, leaving Violet exposed. She doesn't wear a wedding ring—both she and Walter agreed that it was a loathsome symbol, a relic—and by the up-and-down flicker of Lionel's gray eyes she knows he's registered the absence. His question rotates in her mind, *pitter-patter of little scientific feet,* his panther smile, and Violet looks down at the smooth grain of the table before her while her belly rotates in sympathy. She waits for Walter to say something, but he remains silent at her side. She wonders what expression sits on his face, and whether Lionel is reading him, too.

"I beg your pardon. Have I put my foot in it?" says Lionel quietly, and then: "Ah! Here's our dinner at last."

The waiter departs, and Lionel switches topics effortlessly. He draws in Walter with a reminiscence of old Oxford days here, a shared joke there, an earnest diversion into the results of Walter's current experiments. At the shift in tone, Violet lifts her head from her *boeuf en daube*, her potatoes Lyonnaise, and inserts herself bluntly. She is convinced that Rutherford is right about his neutrons, and Walter is wrong.

"Child, you defend this theoretical particle as if it were your own creation," Walter says, smiling.

"Because it exists, and you refuse to acknowledge it."

Lionel whistles low. "There's a chap for you. Sponsors his wife's experiments, though he doesn't believe her theory."

"It's a legitimate line of inquiry," says Walter, "though wrongheaded."

"As opposed to imagining that electrons and protons can be packed into the atomic nucleus together without bursting it apart . . ." Violet launches passionately into her argument, waving her fork in a way that would cause the entire Schuyler matriarchy to expire of shame, arranging her peas to illustrate her point. She doesn't notice that Walter is clearing his throat, that Lionel has uncrossed his long legs and shifted in his chair, until an actual shadow crosses the neat clusters of legumes on her plate.

Violet glances upward, and her sentence dangles half finished and forgotten in the smoke.

"I beg your pardon. Am I interrupting something *dreadfully* important?"

Days later, years later, when Violet has immersed herself in an entirely different world peopled with entirely different characters, when her memories of Berlin have settled into a sequence of emotions and impressions and crisis, she will still recall the precise shade of the Comtesse de Saint-Honoré's blue silk dress as she stood silhouetted against a blurring backdrop of black-and-white waiters and attentive faces.

She will still picture the exact slant of the elbow-length sleeves against the pale skin, the angle at which the neckline caresses the bosom, the height of the gathered hair underneath a jaunty tip-tilted confection of a blue hat. She will recall the angle of those black-lashed violet eyes, the thick piano-key ivory of the skin, the pools of color along the velvety arch of the cheekbones.

Most of all, Violet will know the smile: a slow and confident widening of a too-abundant mouth. This woman is something more than beautiful, something alchemical, an unstable mixture of rare elements bound together by nerve and charm. *Am I interrupting something dreadfully important?* she asks, with the ironic warmth of a woman who knows in her bones that she is always the most important object in the room.

Am I interrupting something: pronounced in a distinct American accent, not quite like Violet's own. The drawling sophistication of her words slips around the flatness of her vowels.

The men rise in tandem. "Not at all," says Walter.

"Why, *Lionel*," says the intruder, with an arch surprise that might or might not be feigned, "is that you?"

Of course this woman knows Lionel Richardson. They are made for each other, hungry predator and luscious prey. Or perhaps it is the other way around?

"Comtesse." Lionel's delight is not feigned at all. He takes her gloved hand and kisses it rapturously. "Imagine you in Berlin in May. Saint-Germaine must be hung with mourning."

"Ha. I'm sure Paris is glad to see the last of me. But you! Aren't you supposed to be galloping about the Transvaal with saber flashing?" She keeps her hand safe within his grip and does something with her eyes, some dip or flutter, unspeakably flirtatious.

Lionel taps his leg. "Invalided for the summer. This barmy old knee of mine. I'm to see some surgical specialist on Wednesday, who's meant to fix everything up, or at least knock off the clicking for me."

"How boring for you."

"And you, my dear? Specialists? Business, perhaps? Surely not shopping."

She laughs. "No, no. How could you possibly think I'm so frivolous? I'm here for Henry, of course." She slides her hand away from Lionel's grasp at last and loops it around the elbow of the grave young man at her side.

Walter intrudes. "Look here, Richardson. Do you mean to introduce your charming friend, or not?"

"What a wretch I am. I thought you must know one another. My dear, I have here none other than the renowned physicist Dr. Walter Grant and his accomplished and rather argumentative wife, Violet Grant. Dr. and Mrs. Grant, the Comtesse de Saint-Honoré, whom I believe needs no introduction, and her son, Henry Mortimer." Lionel steps back a single pace and extends his hand, palm outward, as if offering up young Mr. Mortimer and the comtesse for the private amusement of Violet and Walter.

The Comtesse de Saint-Honoré holds out her hand and extends her smile to dazzling proportions. "But I know Dr. Grant already. He's the very reason I'm here."

Violet watches her husband take the comtesse's kid-gloved hand and shake it. A flush overtakes the skin of his cheeks, the tip of his nose: a flush she knows well. "Of course, of course. I recall the name. Henry Mortimer, of course. The young fellow who wishes to be a physicist."

"Not just any young fellow, Dr. Grant. My son is brilliant, an acknowledged genius, and yet I had no reply at all to my repeated applications on his behalf."

Walter glances at the boy. "He is only sixteen, is he not, madame?"

"Nineteen. Nearly twenty. But you've seen the letters of introduction I sent you, haven't you? He's *just* back from Princeton, graduated six days ago with the highest possible marks in mathematics, the youngest boy ever to do it. I want him to study with *you*, Dr. Grant. No one else will do."

The comtesse's flat American vowels ring with authority. Violet looks at Henry Mortimer, who should be languishing with humiliation in the blue-silk shadow of his mother's ferocity, but he only stands there with a patient expression, as if he's heard it all before. He's a tall boy, rather handsome, with a thatch of dark hair brushed back from his high pale forehead, and a pair of solemn eyes fixed toward the wall beyond Lionel Richardson's sturdy right shoulder. His navy blue suit hangs a little loosely on his skeletal frame, held up by the pristine round-edged Eton collar that strangles his neck. Violet knows a few Mortimers, or once did. A Boston family, severely Brahmin, not the sort to breed with flat-voweled professional beauties, and certainly not to divorce them afterward. But then, Violet doesn't follow scandal very closely.

All at once Violet becomes conscious of the silence teetering in the space between them, the absolute rock-stillness of Walter's body next to her. She looks back at the Comtesse de Saint-Honoré, whose bright eyes haven't waved a millimeter from Walter's stricken face.

Lionel's laugh fractures the impasse. "Ah! That's the marvelous thing about American women. You're never in any doubt where you stand, are you?"

The comtesse laughs, too. "I'm awfully sorry. Was I too direct? Perhaps you might offer us a seat, Dr. Grant, and I'll promise to be on my best behavior."

"Of course, of course." Walter lifts his hand and gestures with relief for the waiter. Chairs are brought, another bottle of wine called for in Lionel's flawless German. Violet crams herself into the corner, making room for Henry's lanky adolescent shoulders. He glances at the clusters of dainty green peas on her plate.

"Oxygen?" he asks quietly.

Violet lets out a breath she hardly knew she was holding. "Yes, oxygen."

She glances up, sensing observation, and finds Lionel Richardson watching them both with his patient gray eyes.

. . .

VIOLET WAITS until Walter joins her in the bedroom before making her decision. She is already in bed, a book in her lap; the evening is warm, and for the first time since September she wears a summer night-gown, white cotton trimmed with a token bit of lace at the neck and sleeves. She dislikes the itchiness of lace against her skin, the sense of delicate entrapment.

Walter comes from the bathroom in his thick flannel pajamas, smelling of soap and tooth powder. He bathes every night before bed, no matter how late the hour, and again in the morning when he wakes up, bracketing his sleep with cleanliness. Ordinarily Violet is irritated by this ritual, the way she's forced to wait for his attention in the evening, and she resents the lemony dampness of his skin when he climbs at last into bed beside her. Tonight, for some reason, she welcomes it.

"I think you should take him on," she says.

Walter is swinging his legs under the covers. "What's that?"

"The boy, Henry Mortimer. I think you should take him on."

"Do you?"

"Yes. I think he's brilliant. I think you should give him a chance."

"Hmm."

Violet turns on her side to face him. He has already switched off the lamp on his side of the bed; hers still casts out a gentle incandescent glow. Their Berlin flat is large and quite modern, quite up-to-date, fully wired for electricity and telephone, piping-hot water delivered with casual abundance to every bathroom. There are brand-new Victrola gramophones in the study and here in the bedroom. Violet feels the outline of the electric light along her body and sets the book on the nightstand.

"What did you think of them?" she asks. "The comtesse and her son."

"I shall take the matter under consideration." He turns his head to look at her. His eyes are crinkled at the corners, wry or amused. "And you, child? What did you think of my surprise this afternoon?"

171

"What surprise?"

"Young Richardson."

"He's not so young. He's older than I am."

"Ah, but you're very, very young, aren't you, child? Not much older than Mr. Mortimer."

"I am *several* years older than Mr. Mortimer."

"Did you find him handsome?"

"What, the boy?"

Walter laughs. "No. Richardson."

"I suppose so. Not really."

Another laugh. "Which is it?"

"Well, he's not conventionally handsome, is he? Not an Adonis." Violet closes her eyes and pictures a silken black head.

"He was quite the most extraordinary student I ever had. Excepting you, of course, little child." He pulls away abruptly and rises from the bed.

Violet watches him pad across the bare wooden floorboards to the Victrola and sift through the recordings piled up beside the machine. "How so?"

"He murdered his stepfather when he was fifteen."

Violet starts upward. The blanket falls away from her chest. "What?"

"Oh, it wasn't cold-blooded. His parents divorced when he was quite young—the old earl was a vicious chap, there's the aristocracy for you—and the mother picked another blackguard for her second husband, as these silly women do. Regular beatings, according to the evidence. Bloody threats and knifepoint arguments." Walter holds up a black disc and examines the label. "And one day Lionel had had enough. Picked up a gun of some sort and shot the old fellow through the heart. The court ruled it was self-defense, but of course none of the other universities would have him. I had to fight like blazes to bring him in."

"Good God." Violet's pulse bangs against the skin of her neck. She recalls Lionel's measured movements, his thick arms, his predatory grace. His silvery gray eyes, vivid in her memory. "Why did you? Bring him in?"

"He's ferociously intelligent. And not a rote thinker at all; he has a way of looking at every problem in a new way. An original way. Often wrong, of course, but sometimes startlingly right." Walter lays a black disc upon the Victrola's plate and turns the switch. He bends over to place the needle just so. "And yet he was absolutely conventional in his habits. Rode to bloody hounds all winter, boxing and shooting and every last thing. Built like a prizefighter, as you saw. I expect he votes Conservative."

"Good God."

Walter laughs. "Don't be afraid, child. It was years ago. He's a soldier now. Gets all that barbarism out of his system by legitimate means."

The opening notes of the Pastorale explore the room in scratches and pops. Violet's muscles clench in response, her arms and legs and jaws, her heart. As if to bolt. She forces herself to breathe. "I suppose I'm not surprised. I know his sort."

"He's not a bad chap. Only unenlightened."

"Did you hear what he said?" Violet deepens her voice into a mocking English cadence. *"I'd expect I would be her life's work.* I wanted to smack him."

Her husband turns to lean against the dresser and folds his arms across his chest. His teeth flash yellow-white in the glow of Violet's lamp. "He might have liked that."

"Brute," she whispers.

"Ah, child." Walter, smiling, approaches the bed and opens the night-stand drawer, where his tissue-thin made-to-order sheepskin condoms wait in their ivory case. The violins swell into a tinny chorus through the Victrola's curving horn. "All men are brutes."

Vivian

Gogo was already wearing her carnation polka-dot pajamas when I arrived for visiting hours at a quarter to seven, or maybe she'd never dressed to begin with. Her eyes were rabbity pink, and her long hair was wrapped up in an improbably cheerful green-and-yellow Hermès headscarf.

"You look like an Easter egg." I kissed her cheeks.

She managed a giggle. "I've eaten nothing but chocolate all day. I even drank chocolate. Mummy calls it her cure."

"Mummy should know," I said. Gogo lived with her mother, the original Mrs. S. Barnard Lightfoot III, who had about as much luck with her next two husbands as she had with her first. She was now engaged to an aging bon vivant who was probably homosexual. Hope springeth eternal, as the gentle rain from heaven.

Or maybe that was mercy. Droppeth.

"Poor Mummy. Do you think it runs in the family?" Gogo didn't wait for an answer, but took me by the hand and led me past fluffy pastel furniture and Mummy's antique doll collection until we arrived at her bedroom, decorated abundantly in Early American Princess.

"It's just possible." I sat down delicately on my usual gingham armchair while Gogo threw herself on her usual tissue-strewn bed. "You know, this is all feeling strangely familiar."

Gogo clutched Rufus to her chest and stared at the ceiling. "It's different this time, Vivs. I really loved him. I really did."

"He's a handsome one, that's for sure. A shiny specimen. Naturally you're snowed. But—"

"It wasn't just that. It was the way he looked at me, Vivs. As if he understood me. As if he could see past all *this*"—she waved a hand dismissively up and down her fashion-plate figure—"and saw everything inside. Do you know what it was like?"

"I can't imagine."

She turned her head to look at me. Her eyes were brimming with teary goodness. "Like the way you look at me. As if I'm a human being."

"Oh, honey." I leaned forward and propped my elbows on the mattress. "How can you be the way you are, Gogo? The way you trust people. The way you see the beauty in everything. I don't understand you, not a bit."

"Yes, you do. I'm not complicated, like you are. I'm as simple as simple can be. All I want is someone to love me, a family to take care of, a house to fill up. The way things were when I was a little girl. I . . ." Her eyes filled anew. "That's it, isn't it? I'm boring."

"You're not boring."

"I wish I were more like you, Vivs. I wish I had your . . . I don't know what it is. That spirit of yours. You're so modern and brave."

"I'm not brave at all. Brash, maybe."

"Yes, you *are* brave." She took my hand and pulled me onto the bed next to her and put her polka-dot arms around me. She smelled like Johnson's baby powder, pink and perfect. "Can I tell you a secret?"

"You can tell me anything."

"The moment I knew I was in love with him."

I breathed carefully around the knot of building pressure in my chest.

I found it helped to dig my fingernails into my palms, as hard as I could bear.

She went on in her soft voice: "It was at the end of vacation. He was going home in a few days. We went out to dinner and drinks and I had . . . well, I had a little too much champagne. I guess he did, too."

"That's my girl."

"And we went back to my room—Mummy was still out with Gilbert—and we . . . we were kissing and . . . things . . . and I decided I would do it. I would . . . you know . . . with him."

There was no breathing now. I was suffocating on the hard knot lodged in my lungs, I was sinking irretrievably into the squish of Gogo's mattress.

Gogo was stroking my arm. Her fingers found the skin beneath the elbow-length sleeves of my black-and-white checked jacket, my snug little wonder of a female business suit. "So we took off our clothes and we were on the bed and . . . well, it felt so good, Vivs, the way he touched me. Really, really good. Is that bad of me?"

"No. It's not bad of you."

"Because Mummy always said . . ." She hesitated. "But it felt *so* good, Vivs. He was so gentle. And we were about to . . . you know . . . and I told him . . . I told him I'd never done this before. And he . . . he . . . Oh, Vivs."

"What did he do, honey?" I whispered. My eyes were watering from the cut of my fingernails into my palms. My body was too hot in its wool suit and silk stockings. I toed off my shoes and let them tumble to the fluffy pink carpet. "Did he hurt you?"

She moved us both with her sigh. "He stopped."

"He stopped."

"He stopped. He said we should wait. He said it should be special, my first time. Well, I told him that it *was* special, that it was, you know, perfect. I told him I really wanted to do it. And I did! I really did! But he said no, we should wait." She made a sad little giggle, a brokenhearted noise.

"I thought that meant he wanted to wait until we were married. That it was a sign, you know, that the reason I'd always been disappointed, the reason I'd been saving myself all this time, was for him."

"You'd think."

"Anyway, that was when I knew it was real. That he was a true gentleman and I loved him."

"Of course it was."

"Do you think it was wrong of me? Going to bed with him like that?"

I withdrew my claws from my palms and curled my fingers around hers. "No, Gogo. You were in love with him. You wanted to show him. There's nothing wrong with that."

"I thought he loved me. I really did. Why else would he stop like that?"

Why, indeed.

I stared across the room at the gigantic antique dollhouse against the wall, a relic of Victorian girlhood, flawless in every gingerbread detail. It had been Gogo's mother's dollhouse, and she had given it to Gogo for her eighth birthday. Gogo once told me that she, Gogo, wanted to put it away in storage somewhere—she was twenty-two years old, for heaven's sake—but she didn't want to hurt her mother's feelings. She had been reclining on this very bed at the time, staring at the ceiling, dressed in a white nightie and fluffy white slippers, which she propped up against the wall, one slender ankle twined around the other. She'd just wait until she got married, she said, and give it to her own daughter. She'd name her daughter Vivian, she said, and then the little girl would be just like me.

Well, in that case, her little girl might not have much to do with dollhouses, I'd pointed out. Gogo had laughed and said yes, but she'd play with it anyway, just to humor her mummy.

I wondered, sometimes, if Gogo didn't understand me better than anyone.

"Can you stay with me tonight?" Gogo asked.

"I'm sorry, hon. I have a lot of work to do. I'm working on a gig for the magazine."

"The one you told me about on the telephone?"

"That's the one." I swallowed and went on. "You know what? I found out today that Aunt Violet knew all the most eminent physicists of her time. They were all there together at this scientific institute in Berlin, the Kaiser Wilhelm Institut, before the war. Einstein was there. Max Planck. Otto Hahn and Lise Meitner. They used to get together at Planck's house for musical evenings, after they left the laboratory for the day. Einstein played the violin."

"Einstein. Really."

"Can you imagine? All those brilliant minds in one place. A real bash."

"Like college all over again. Don't you miss college, Vivs? We had such laughs. Do you remember that time we stayed up late, talking about that book, what was it . . . the heiress whose husband had to take her name, except his family wouldn't let him . . ."

"*Cecilia.* Fanny Burney."

"I liked that book." She picked at her pajamas. "Sometimes I wish we didn't have to grow up like this. Daddy used to say that to me, all the time, you know that?" She deepened her voice into the Lightfoot growl. "*Don't grow up, sweetie. Stay just the way you are.* And he was dead right, wasn't he, like he always is. Being a grown-up is the pits."

I gave her hands a little squeeze and sat up. "I should really be going."

"Do you have to?"

"Yes, I really do. I brought a couple of biographies with me. Einstein and Meitner. I'll read them tonight."

She padded after me through the ghostly Easter-egg rooms of her mother's apartment. I found my pocketbook and briefcase in the hall and turned around to hug her good-bye. "You'll be all right, won't you? I can stay if you want."

"I'll be fine. Daddy's calling every half hour."

"Good. I'll call you at bedtime."

Gogo's blue eyes went round. "Oh, Vivs, I completely forgot! I'm such a selfish little thing. Your boy, the one you met over the weekend. I never even asked about him!"

I picked up my briefcase. "Oh, it was nothing, really. I woke up Monday and realized I could live without him. End of story. Fun while it lasted."

"Really, Vivs?" Her soulful look, searching me out.

"Really, Gogo."

She shook her head. "Gosh, Vivs. I wish I could be you."

That one, I had no answer for.

A LETTER in the mail slot. I almost didn't open it, I almost chucked it into the bin right there in the vestibule, but I am who I am. A curious animal.

I read it at the table in the living room. I tend to get too sentimental in the bedroom. Too much like Gogo.

> Dear Vivian,
>
> I'm writing this between surgeries, so excuse my haste. I just wanted to let you know that I'm thinking of you all the time, you're like a low and constant hum at the back of my brain, even when I'm working, and when I have a moment to myself with a cup of coffee, you rise up and stand before me in electric Vivian color with that smile on your face, the one that got me in the chest right from the start. I try not to waste a second, so I pick some scene from the weekend—the coffee shop, or the library, or when we stood in front

of the Balto statue in the park and read the inscription together, and you wouldn't look at me afterward, and I knew you were crying. Well, that brave old dog made me tear up, too, just so you know. I try not to think about what happened afterward, at my apartment. How perfect it was. I'm saving that for when I'm really down.

Not giving up, Vivian. Ever.

Yours,
Paul

Oh, Jesus. Oh, my ever-loving Christ.

Here's what I would do: I would think about Gogo and Doctor Paul in that Los Angeles hotel bed together. I would think about Gogo naked and him naked, and fuse the two images into one entwined whole, and the nausea that followed this thought would work like a reverse Pavlovian response, until every time I remembered Doctor Paul, I'd feel that same curl of nausea. I would be cured.

A little fun, he'd said. A few kisses, maybe a little more.

Liar, liar. Pants on fire.

I crumpled the letter into a ball and tossed it into the basket. I thought about making dinner, but I wasn't hungry, still had that ball of nausea in my stomach, so instead I carried my briefcase into my bedroom and changed into my favorite blue-stripe pajamas. I took out the Einstein biography, propped myself on the pillow, and focused my eyes on the dry words before me.

Violet, 1914

Violet has only to survey the interior of the Plancks' comfortable electric-lit music room to remind herself how much she owes to Walter.

Of course, Walter himself is not present this evening. But Herr Planck is there, mixing drinks in the corner, and Otto Hahn and his wife, and Lise Meitner. Herr Einstein already sits in his favorite chair, listening intently to his violin, adjusting the strings. Isn't it worth any personal humiliation, any number of dark-haired beauties copulating with your husband atop an antique French escritoire, to be creating music shoulder-to-shoulder with Einstein himself?

Next to her, Henry Mortimer's serious gray eyes are shining with the afterglow of the day's work in the laboratory. "I've read all Dr. Grant's articles, of course, but it's astonishing, isn't it? Like looking inside the actual atomic nucleus."

"It isn't, though. Not really. You're only seeing the results of one proton colliding with another." They are sitting on the piano bench. Violet opens up her leather satchel and takes out a few sheets of music, the Bach and the Dvořák, as they had agreed. Her movements are brusque and efficient; she has done this so many times before, and she wants to communicate that fact to Mr. Mortimer, that the sheer wonder of scientific discovery grays quickly into the drudgery of endless repetition, getting nowhere in particular, persevering out of sheer goat-headed stubbornness.

As she has.

"Exactly. The most beautiful thing I've ever seen." Henry holds up the bow of his violin. "A billion atoms form the tip of this bow, and I've seen the collision of a single component of a single nucleus. It's the heart of matter, the beating heart."

"You'll grow accustomed to it."

Henry twirls his bow around his thumb and forefinger. His hands are long and patrician, the nails neatly trimmed into razor crescents at the tips. He tilts his head, watching her with his quiet eyes, his ancient composure. "I only want you to know how much I appreciate your taking me on this summer, Mrs. Grant."

Violet skims her hand along the top of her satchel and turns to Henry. He must look a great deal like his father, she thinks, because there's very little of the Comtesse de Saint-Honoré in his narrow face, in his small mouth and grave eyes. Only the lashes recall his mother, thick and excessive, a bristle of black around the lighter gray of his irises. He sits there twiddling his violin bow, looking at her expectantly, a thick curl of his overlong hair drooping into his forehead.

"In the end, it was my husband's decision," she says.

"Well, I appreciate it. It's the most tremendous opportunity. I—"

"Here you are, Frau Grant. Are you sure you'll only have water?" Herr Planck stands kindly before her, every eminent inch of him, offering her a crystal tumbler.

"Yes, thank you. Just water." She takes it from him.

"I'm sorry your husband couldn't be with us tonight."

How she hates that look of sympathy. "I'm afraid he had another engagement. And Walter would rather listen than play, I'm afraid."

There is the briefest of awkward silences, as everybody looks away, except Henry, who lifts his violin to his chin and plays a few notes.

"Shall we start with the Bach?" says Lise cheerfully.

Dear Lise. How might Violet's life be different, if there had been an English Lise Meitner at the Devonshire Institute? Like her, Lise has fought for her place at the institute. Unlike her, Lise has the encouragement and financial support of her intellectual Viennese parents, and she remains unmarried. She works with Otto Hahn in the basement of the chemistry building, patiently discovering the isotopes of various radioactive elements. At present they are investigating thorium. What does Frau Hahn think of this arrangement? Violet can't imagine, because Lise is an attractive woman, dark-haired and large-eyed, and a distinct air of kinship fizzles between her and Herr Hahn.

Violet turns to the piano keys behind her, and Henry rises to his feet, violin still at his chin, and makes his way to an unoccupied chair. Henry has all the notes by memory; Violet has never seen him study a sheet of music.

They start with the Bach. In its elegant symmetry, its intricate phrases, the Violet of laboratory and matrimony soon dissolves. She's been playing with her colleagues for months now, and sometimes it's the only thing keeping her alive, the only thing keeping her whole, this music in which she creates and participates, free from Walter's sharp eyes and his neatly clipped fingers stroking his neatly clipped beard as he reads over her latest laboratory notes, her frustrating lack of progress. The last movement ends, and a sweet silence arrests the air of Max Planck's music room. Beyond the windows, the summer night is falling at last.

A maid arrives with tiny glasses of schnapps. This time Violet accepts one and sips it delicately. Otto and Lise are laughing together at some miscue in the second movement. A few yards away, Herr Einstein's thick, dark head is bent over his violin. Violet takes another sip, another, sets down her empty glass, and approaches him.

"Good evening, Herr Einstein," she says, possibly the bravest act of her life. She has played Bach with him for months, and still she hasn't spoken with him like this, eye to eye with the brilliant Einstein, whose 1905 paper still ricochets like revolutionary gunfire about the halls of physics. His line of inquiry lies as far apart from Violet's as the infinite from the minute, but oh, the breathtaking audacity of his thought! The brash overturning of the static Newtonian universe!

"Frau Grant." He sets aside his glass of schnapps and stands politely.

"Oh, don't bother. I only wanted to thank you for your note this morning. You were very kind to answer me so quickly."

His bristling black mustache lifts in a smile, and it transforms his face, which usually hangs below his large dark downturned eyes in an expression of natural dole. Violet knows he has a troubled marriage; his wife, rarely seen, is said to be quitting Berlin for Zurich with the children. Perhaps she's already left. Walter says Einstein has a mistress, his own cousin: *You see, my dear? Beasts, all of us.* But Violet walks past Einstein's handsome drooping face daily, and she thinks perhaps he has more in common with her than with Walter.

"You asked an excellent question, Frau Grant," Einstein says. "I hope my answer was intelligible."

"The handwriting or the equations?" Violet laughs, or rather the schnapps laughs for her, God bless it.

"Both!" He laughs with her.

"I'm only teasing. Your handwriting was no trouble. I transcribe all my husband's work, and his writing is much worse, believe me." Violet speaks without thinking, and gets her just deserts: a look of compassion.

"I'm sorry Dr. Grant couldn't be with us tonight," Herr Einstein says awkwardly.

"Oh, he doesn't miss us a bit. He's at a party in Leipzigerstrasse, very glamorous, loads of courtiers and officials."

"And my mother." Henry ranges up alongside. His bow dangles from his fingers. "No fashionable party would be complete without her."

"At least you have each other, then." Einstein looks between the two of them and smiles vaguely.

Violet feels a little pink. She opens her mouth to reply, but Herr Planck is already calling them to order for the Dvořák.

Afterward, as they're gathering their music, Violet tries to think of some excuse to approach him again. The room is full of happy chatter, of the exuberant good feeling created from the chemical reaction between music and schnapps. Einstein is speaking to Lise, both of them smiling. Violet gathers herself and steps forward.

Herr Planck's hand falls on her shoulder. "My dear, there's a gentleman here for you and young Mr. Mortimer."

She turns. "A gentleman?"

Planck steps aside.

Lionel Richardson. Dressed in formal blacks, a silk hat dangling from one hand, a cane dangling from the opposite elbow, silvery-gray eyes gazing quietly at them. His mighty soldier's torso overflows the doorway.

"There you are," he says.

"Yes, here we are." Violet looks at him quizzically. Her hand moves unconsciously to her neck, to conceal the startled jump of her pulse. "Why are you here?"

The happy chatter dies away. Everyone turns to take in the sight of Lionel, brimming with outdoor energy, covered in night air and glamour. He leans against the door frame and crosses his arms. "To escort you home, of course. You and Henry."

"Escort us home?"

"There's a devil of a business in the streets tonight. The usual sort of Saturday revelry, I suppose, but hardly the sort of environment for a gently bred young lady and a chap of Mr. Mortimer's tender years." He tosses a smile at Henry.

Violet's hands close around her leather satchel. "I am quite capable—"

"I'm sure you are, but I promised Madame de Saint-Honoré that I would see to her son's safety personally."

"I see." Violet's pulse calms. Behind her, the scientists have resumed talking, resolutely ignoring the two of them. She turns to Herr Planck and speaks in German. "Are we quite finished here, then?"

"Yes, yes! Go on, before it becomes late."

"Well said, Herr Planck." Lionel pushes himself away from the door frame and holds out his hand. "Have you a coat?"

"No."

Henry draws next to her. "This is quite unnecessary, sir. We'd have been all right on our own."

"No doubt, no doubt. But mothers will worry, won't they?" Lionel winks at Henry, a soldier's conspiratorial wink, man to man. Henry seems to read something in this wink. He straightens his shoulders and picks up his violin case.

"Ready, then, Mrs. Grant?" says Lionel.

"Yes, quite ready." Violet says good-bye to the others, an especially warm handshake with Einstein, a kiss on the cheek from Lise. Her friends, she tells herself, and the word *friends* is so alien and thrilling, it tingles her bones with possibility.

Outside, the early June air is still warm, the sky still retaining a faint purple glow from the departed twilight. Distant shouts carry around the buildings, distant laughter, distant tinkling of music. Berlin is enjoying itself this evening, in all the usual ways. A motor-taxi waits at the curb, rumbling with impatience, and Lionel opens the door for them.

"I am quite happy walking," says Violet.

"But I am not." Lionel holds up his cane. "My operation was only a week ago, and strictly speaking I'm not supposed to be up at all."

Violet slides into the rear seat after Henry, and Lionel shuts the door behind them and swings into the front, next to the driver. "Französische-strasse, *bitte*," he says quietly.

"Don't you have crutches?" she asks.

"Yes, I do."

The taxi jerks away from the curb, into the swarming melee of Berlin traffic. After the somnolence of Oxford, Violet can't quite get used to the way the automobiles and carts and delivery wagons crowd the streets of the energetic German capital, even at ten o'clock at night on the first Saturday in June. She looks out the window at the sidewalk. A café swims past her eyes, wriggling with people, students in shabby brown suits and prostitutes in bright silks. They are all so happy, so full of purpose even while lounging about a café, smoking and drinking. Violet thinks of her dark laboratory, her green-white fireworks of atomic energy, the minute scale of her life's work.

"How was the party?" she asks. "I hope we haven't ruined your evening."

"Not at all. The party was full of German officials in a frenzy of enjoyment, if you can picture it. They're all about to head off for their summer amusements, the lucky ones, at any rate."

"I'm sorry to have torn you away."

"They can spare me, I assure you. Tell me, Mr. Mortimer, how you're enjoying your summer *this* far."

"Very much, sir. I assisted Mrs. Grant with her scintillations today. The most extraordinary thing I've ever seen."

Lionel laughs aloud. "Yes, I remember it well. I used to be Dr. Grant's assistant, a few years ago, before Mrs. Grant swept in and stole his heart away."

"*Were* you?"

"Hasn't your mother told you anything? Yes, I was the first man to count those little flashes of light." He pauses. He hasn't replaced his hat, and his sleek black hair curves in a perfect arc against the blue darkness around them. He tilts his face back toward them. "Do you know what amazed me most? All that space."

"Yes." Henry leans forward eagerly.

Lionel holds up his hand. In the yellow-gray flash of a passing streetlamp, it seems unnaturally large, shadow-rugged, each finger thick with strength. "You see? That this apparently solid and immutable flesh, that everything around us, is only empty space. Empty space, with a few lonely bits of electrical energy spinning about inside. That only one particle from the radium in perhaps ten thousand actually finds a nucleus to collide with. The rest simply stream along unseen, unknowing even, right through the damned gold foil."

"Astonishing, isn't it?" Violet stares at Lionel's hand.

He lowers his hand and turns to gaze out his own window. They are hurtling down Unter den Linden, a lamplit blur of cafés and people and ambitious new hotels. "I found it rather terrifying, in fact. Knowing this solid world around us is as insubstantial as a dream. Realizing the vast emptiness surrounding every bloody speck of matter in the universe."

Without warning, the taxicab staggers to a throaty halt before a woman in a floating red silk gown, who dances with abandon in the middle of the street. Her eyes are closed to the astonished traffic around her. The streetlamps gleam like oil on her writhing bare arms.

"Mein Gott," mutters the driver. He steers the taxi cautiously around the dancer. As the automobile slides past, she opens her eyes and gazes into the rear window, directly at Violet. She taps the glass with a long lacquered finger, throws back her head and laughs, and then she's gone, disappeared into the tangle of lights and traffic behind them.

"Ah, Berlin," says Lionel.

"A friend of yours, perhaps?" Violet thinks of the woman's low neckline, her heavy unbound breasts like pendula beneath clouds of red silk. The mockery of that laugh.

"Not that I can recall," says Lionel blandly.

The car turns down Französischestrasse and pulls up before a splendid block of apartments, rising perhaps sixteen floors in an extravagant explosion of stonework. Lionel springs out of the taxi, pivots gracefully about his cane, and opens the door for Henry. "I'll just be a moment," he says to Violet.

Henry looks over his shoulder. "Good night, Mrs. Grant."

"Good night, Mr. Mortimer. Thank you for your assistance."

Violet stares ahead at the back of the driver's head. Französische-strasse is much quieter than Unter den Linden, a residential street, no café in sight. The sultry smell of petrol exhaust curls around her nose; the seat rumbles gently beneath her dress.

The door opens. Lionel slides in next to her and leans forward to address the driver. "Kronenstrasse. Number sixteen, isn't that right, Mrs. Grant?"

"Yes. But you don't need to take me there."

"Nonsense. It's on my way."

"Back to your party, I suppose."

He lays his cane over his legs. "I suppose so."

Kronenstrasse isn't far away, but the minutes and seconds stretch out to occupy the viscous silence between them. Violet looks out her window to avoid the sight of Lionel, though she feels him anyway, a great edifice looming perhaps eighteen inches away, so close she can touch him, so close she can feel his heat like a hot coal glowing at her side, she can feel the pitch of his chest as he breathes, the angle of the cloth seat under his weight.

The traffic has come to an ominous full stop in Friedrichstrasse; Lionel swears softly and cranes his head to see what the matter is. The movement of his body causes his cane to brush Violet's thigh. "It's hopeless," he says. "Do you mind walking?"

"Do you?" She nods at his leg.

He shrugs. "It's only a block or two."

Lionel gets out and pays the driver and holds out his hand for Violet. Neither of them are wearing gloves. Lionel's palm is warm and dry and strong beneath hers, his thumb firm where it crosses her fingers. She climbs out of the taxi and draws her hand away. "Thank you."

They walk without speaking. Violet listens to the cadence of his stride along the sidewalk, the delicate chuff of the cane alongside the sturdier clacks of his shoes. His limp is almost indistinguishable, as if the cane itself is only a gentlemanly pose.

They reach Violet's apartment building. She stops and half turns toward him, wanting him to go, wanting him to stay a few more minutes, an hour, a night, a year. He stands just outside the circle of light from the entrance foyer, and she cannot see his expression properly. But there is something hesitant in the way he stands and gazes down at her: something expectant, or perhaps indecisive.

Say good night, Violet.

Lionel clears his throat. "Shall I see you up?"

"That's not necessary."

His face moves in the darkness, and she knows he's smiling. "Doesn't a chap deserve a drink for all his hard work? Besides, I'm curious to see the apartment of the eminent Dr. Grant and his wife. Radium lying about the bric-a-brac and all that."

"Nothing like that. Walter's very particular. What about your party?"

"Bother the party." He's still smiling. A pair of headlamps flashes along his face, his daring eyes, his strong jaw, the curve of one ear. His shirt-points are terribly white against his neck.

Violet succumbs.

"All right, then. Come along."

Vivian

No one throws a party like Mums, I'll give her that. I arrived long before the fashionable hour in order to have first pop at the champagne, and I was rewarded for my early-birdness with the usual worm.

"Christ, Vivian," said Dad, reaching for his cigar. "Do you know what we used to do to women who dressed like that?"

I kissed both cheeks. "Married them?"

"And what have you done with your eyes? You look like a cat."

"That's the idea."

"Now, now, Charles." Mums took my shoulders and gave me a twirl. "I think she looks just adorable. Doesn't she look adorable, Pepper?"

"Not nearly enough bosom," said Pepper.

Mums stepped back with her critical eye, and by critical I mean slice 'em and dice 'em and serve 'em for elevenses. "Yes. Yes, I see what you mean," she said, and without further ado took the edge of my neckline with both hands and yanked it down a good two inches. My father made a strangled noise and headed for the bar.

Pepper nodded. "That should do the trick."

"Do what trick?"

"Never you mind," said Mums. "Have some champagne."

It didn't take a truffle-pig nose to detect the presence of a few suspicious truffles lying about the old Schuyler aerie, but I wasn't the girl to look a gift bubbly in the bubbles. I poured myself a heaping tablespoon and dragged Pepper out on the terrace for a smoke and a grilling.

"What was that about?" Once the preliminaries had been performed.

Pepper made busy with her cigarette. "What was what about?"

"The Marilyn makeover just now. You want I should dye my little old hair and speak all Babykins, too?" I did a fair impression.

"Not bad. Not bad at all."

"Pepper."

She zipped her lips.

"You *cannot* be plotting with Mums, Pepper. You can't do that to me. I need someone on my side."

"Try Dadums. Your bosom gives him the vapors. He'll be happy to help."

"He'll be passed out by nine o'clock."

"Oh, right. Well, who needs the big lug, anyway?" Champagne, smoke. "Is it cold out here, or is it just my dress?"

"Speaking of bosom."

"I wasn't going to let you steal the show, was I?" She linked arms and dragged me to the edge of the terrace. "You see? This is what I mean by sisterly solidarity. The Schuyler girls, on top of the world. Look at that park, Vivian. Do you ever get tired of a view like that?"

I gazed down at the bumpy dark rectangle of Central Park, the sharp and twinkling edges of the towers around it. No, you could not ever get tired of a view like this. You could never ever get tired of Manhattan.

Pepper squeezed my arm. "How's Violet these days?"

"Playing violin with Einstein. I can't figure her out."

Pepper turned around and propped herself against a planter filled with purpling cabbage. "How so?"

"How she could live with him. Her husband, I mean. She had to have known what he was like. Why did she put up with it?"

Pepper laughed. "Oh, listen to you. *Why did she put up with it?* Why do any of them put up with it? Mums, Dadums. I think the secret to marriage is just old-fashioned tolerance."

"Tolerance of lovers?"

"Tolerance of whatever your husband's sins. Or vice versa. Obviously Mr. Pepper Schuyler would have to put up with a few."

"You make it sound so tempting."

She nodded to the glowing terrace doors. "Everyone makes their own bed, Vivian. Everyone makes their own bargain. Anyway, Violet didn't put up with it in the end, did she?"

"No, something set her off at last. I just wish I could find out what it was."

Pepper leaned her head back and let the Manhattan moon bathe her face. Her beauty was so sudden and sharp, it stunned me. She crossed her long legs at the glittery ankle straps. "You'll let me know when you do."

"Girls! What are you doing, shivering out here like this?"

We turned in tandem.

"Cousin Lily!" I ran up to her as fast as my skittering heels would allow and pressed kisses to both her sweet little cheeks. She beamed back at me, the old darling, just before Pepper grabbed her for equal treatment.

"I don't know how you can stand it," she said. "Look at you in your little dresses."

"Look at you in yours."

"You like it? Your aunt Julie took me shopping this week."

"Say no more," said Pepper.

I took Lily's right arm and Pepper took her left, and together we jiggled champagne, cigarettes, and cousin back into the living room, where Lily's husband, Nick Greenwald, was locked in stiff conversation with Dad. He cast her a look as we entered, a look containing an entire quarter century of shared spousal amusement, and my toes ached.

Confession. I'd had an itty-bitty girlhood crush on Nick Greenwald when I was just beginning to have such thoughts. Well, goodness, he was a war hero! And handsome and exceptionally tall, and with that irresistible air of the forbidden about him, being half Jewish and therefore Not Quite One of Us, as Mums put it. *Not quite one of us, is he,* she would say, making her eyebrow do that thing of hers, that insolent right angle, while she stubbed her cigarette viciously into the tray. I would think, *Thank Jehovah and all the prophets for that.* He and Lily were like a bulwark, knit together at every stitch against the pick pick pick of implicit Schuyler disapproval. I marveled at them. Lily was my aunt Christina's daughter. After Christina died, she and Nick had raised her younger sister, Kiki, along with five children of their own, two of them born after the war. Maybe that was where the crush started. I'd been twelve years old, and there was tall Nick cradling Baby Number Five against his shoulder with the delicate reverence he might lavish on a Fabergé egg (I still remembered Mums's disapproval, her sneering *Forty-three years old and she lets herself get pregnant again*) and who couldn't fall a little in love with that?

Nick Greenwald was in his fifties now, so was Lily, and his brown hair was sprinkled with gray, his hazel eyes crinkled deeply at the corners, but he still had it. Especially standing next to old Dadums, who only had *it* if *it* were a gut rounded out with too many cocktails and a face sagging downward with too much pick pick pick. Maybe that's why Mums resented Nick. He stood up so well to scrutiny. He loved his wife. He loved his kids. He was too damned happy.

The living room was trickling full now. Pepper fled to the bar for a refill. I started to follow her, but Lily's arm tightened around mine. "Hold on. Before you flutter away, you bird of paradise, I have something for you."

"A present? For little old me?"

"Little old you. Come sit down."

My dress wasn't made for sitting, but with a wee trifle of leg crossing I made myself decent. Lily eased herself next to me in the sinuous athletic style of a woman who kept herself busy, which Lily did. Apart from her husband and her merry band, she swam daily—I'd tried and failed to keep up with her at the Colony Club pool one morning—and wrote. Wrote for real money, actual checks made out in her name. Mostly articles about New England history, that kind of thing, but rumor had it she'd been short-listed for the Pulitzer one year for her book about the hurricane of 1938. She'd doled out generous helpings of advice to me over the years, not that I'd followed more than a few green peas of it, but she persevered because she was Lily and she'd give you the food off her own plate if you needed it, the brassiere off her back.

She propped her elbow atop the back of the settee and gave me the old conspiratorial smile. "How are you, Vivian? How's the *Metropolitan*? How's old Tibby?"

"He likes his coffee black and sweet. But I have a plan." I tapped my temple.

Laugh laugh. "I knew you would. Now, listen up. Julie had lunch with us this past week and told me you were poking into the old stories about Aunt Violet."

The heart leapt. "I might be."

She patted her pocketbook, a sleek blue wedge that matched her sleek blue dress, and which must also have been picked out for her by said Aunt Julie during the aforementioned shopping expedition, for among Lily Greenwald's many virtues was not, how shall I put it, the eye of style. "Then I might just have her letters to my mother tucked away in here."

The heart crashed into the moon. I itched my fingers at her. "*Ooh. Ooh.* You always were my favorite cousin."

"Now, now. Wait a moment, you greedy thing." She laid a protective hand over the pocketbook. "I also received a fascinating telephone call from your mother later that day—she's looking at us right this second, as a matter of fact, now don't look so alarmed—asking me whether I possessed any such letters—"

"That Mums."

"—and if I did, could I please burn them down to ash and then dispose permanently of the ash itself, at my earliest convenience."

"And you told her to get lost?"

She assumed an angelic aspect. "I would never use those words, Vivian. I just told her that I had no idea where any such letters might be. Which was true, to a point."

"Which point was that?"

"I mean I had no idea which box they were in. We put all my mother's old letters in boxes after she died. A storage closet in the apartment building. I didn't have the heart to go through them all at the time, and then . . . well, we had Nick Junior right away, and got so busy. Anyway."

A shadow cast across our conspiratorial laps. I looked up and smiled.

"Mums. I was just telling Cousin Lily how lovely she looks tonight. Doesn't she look lovely in that shade of blue? It brings out her eyes."

"Lovely. Vivian, my sweet, you need to mingle."

"Why do I need to mingle?"

The lips pursed. "Because that's how you meet people, dear. When I was your age, I had already been engaged three times—"

"The lucky dears," I said.

"Now, Vivian. Your mother's right. You shouldn't spend your Saturday night all tucked up in the corner with your old cousin Lily." Lily rose to her feet and held out her hand for me. "Come with me, and I'll have Nick Junior introduce you to his friends."

Mums's face went all hallelujah, as good as a facelift. "That's so dear of you, Lily. She only seems to be interested in the most unsuitable young men."

"Well, now," said Lily. "I'd be disappointed if she weren't. Distraction," she whispered to me as we drew away. "I learned that trick as a mother myself. Anyway, I'll slip you the letters before I go. There aren't many, to be honest, so I hope you can get something useful from them. But be warned: your mother doesn't want any of this to come to light."

"This I already know."

Lily stopped and turned around to face me. "No. I mean she really doesn't want this. So you need to decide, Vivian Schuyler, if the prey is worth the hunt."

"Meaning?"

"Meaning you may find yourself on the outside of the cozy Schuyler circle if you find Violet's corpse and dig it up for a public viewing. And trust me"—she glanced at her husband with a wistful old smile—"that's no place for the faint of heart."

NOW. I don't know if you could exactly call me and Nicholson Greenwald Jr. kissing cousins. I mean, we'd only kissed once. Well, twice. But we had a zing, he and I, if you know what I mean, and my poor wounded little heart revived just a smidgen at the way his handsome old scoundrelly face lit to blazes at the sight of me.

"Nick Junior, you handsome old scoundrel." I bussed him soundly on the cheek, right there in front of his friends, and slapped a little mustard on the *Junior*. "How many hearts have you broken this week?"

"Aw, Vivian. Always busting my chops." He slipped his hand down my back to give the old derrière a friendly warning squeeze. "Boys, this is my cousin Vivian Schuyler. Proceed at your own risk."

I extended my hand to the handsomest and tilted my cat eyes to a welcoming angle. "Enchanted."

"Damn it, Vivian. Will you go easy on the poor fellas?" said Nick Junior.

Oh, Cousin Nick. Bless you. Not tonight.

Well, I was human, wasn't I? I'd taken a blow, a nasty witch of a blow to the solar plexus, and nothing soothes the battered solar plexus like a nice reassuring Epsom salt bath of male admiration. I had them fetching my drinks. I had them laughing at my jokes. I had them on the beaches, I had them on the landing grounds, I had them in the fields and in the streets. And great God almighty, it felt good. It felt reckless and self-indulgent, the old Vivian, the one who didn't care. Triumphant Vivian, back on top.

Somewhere in the middle of my fourth glass of champagne, Pepper found me. She fluttered her fingers. "Hello, boys."

"Boys, this is my sister Pepper," I said.

Chorus of approval.

"Tell me why they call you Pepper," said one strapping lad, a little quicker on the wit than his mates.

"Because I'm that bad."

"Aw, Pepper," said poor Nick Junior. "That's not true. Tell them why."

She shrugged. "Not on your life."

"Vivian?"

I zipped my lips. "Code of sisterly honor."

"You two." He threw up his hands. "And they wonder why I don't go to more of these nice little family get-togethers."

Pepper leaned into me. "This is perfect. They're eating out of your hand."

"Perfect for what?"

"Never you mind. Here."

She nudged me. I looked down. A small packet of envelopes lay in her hand.

"The letters from Cousin Lily?"

"You betcha, dollface. Don't read them all in one place." She unfastened my pocketbook and slipped the envelopes in between the lipstick tubes.

"Counselors! Sidebar's concluded," said the handsomest, snapping his fingers.

Pepper turned her chin over her luminous bare shoulder and gave him the old up-and-down. "Permission to approach the bench?"

Before the lucky young man could reply, Mums butted in between our conspiratorial shoulders.

"Excuse me," she said.

And that, my dears, is the point at which I should have known. I should have recognized that tone of voice, that note of almost weepy triumph.

But what could I have done?

She had planned all this with the skill of a master strategist. Ludendorff had nothing on Mums. She had probably invited the Greenwalds, had probably encouraged Nick Junior to bring his attentive friends, had forged an alliance with Pepper, had filled me with champagne. She had placed every pawn in its proper square before introducing the knight to the board, armor shining.

You had to hand it to Mums.

She spoke near my ear, in her butteriest voice. "Vivian, dearest. We have a special guest I'd like you to entertain for me tonight."

I turned.

Mums's eyes glittered as fearlessly as the Schuyler crystal. In one hand she held a drink and cigarette, and in the other she held a smiling Doctor Paul. She withdrew her arm and patted the back of his shoulder in a proprietary mother-of-the-bride way. "I think you've met already, isn't that right, Vivian?"

I turned to my sister. "Bad girl, Pepper. Very. Bad. Girl."

Violet

B y the time the lift clangs to a stop at the ninth floor, Violet's face
is hot with shame. The attendant stares directly ahead, not meeting her eyes, and she wants to scream, *He's not my lover! Who brings
a lover home to her own married flat?* But it's her own fault. If Lionel were
some innocent acquaintance, she would be talking and laughing with him
as they walked across the foyer and went up the lift. There would not be
this guilty silence, this tense expectancy, this flush on Violet's cheeks.

The attendant opens the grille. *"Danke,"* says Violet clearly.

The lift opens up directly to their apartment, which covers the entire
floor. Walter's family made a fortune in pottery a hundred years ago, and
the evidence of that wealth lies everywhere: the elegant rented address in
Kronenstrasse, the marble entry, the black-and-white housekeeper who
takes their coats and hats and asks Violet if she and her guest will be taking refreshment.

"Thank you, Hilda, but we'll only be a few minutes," says Violet in
German.

She leads Lionel past the grand drawing room and into a smaller sitting room off the study, where Walter keeps a liquor cabinet. Lionel's cane
clicks rhythmically behind her on the polished parquet floor.

"Cozy little place you've got here."

"Walter likes to entertain."

"And you don't?"

She opens the liquor cabinet. "What would you like? We've got just about everything, I think."

"Brandy will do."

She finds the brandy and the snifter, and though she pours with extreme care, the bottle still clinks against the edge of the glass, betraying the slight shake in her hands. She sets down the bottle and lifts the glass between her palms to warm the brandy.

"An expert, I see."

"My father used to drink brandy. Well, I suppose he still does. When I wanted to ask for a favor, I started him off with a glass of his favorite."

"An excellent strategy. Did it work?"

Violet hands him the glass and watches as he takes a sip. "Occasionally. Please sit. I don't want your surgeon to come after me, shaking his fist."

"You first, Mrs. Grant."

Violet lowers herself into one end of the sofa. Lionel takes a chair, exhaling just a fraction as the weight draws off his left knee. He extends the leg in a rigid line across the rug before him, nearly touching Violet's crossed ankles.

Violet curls her fingers together in her lap. The lamplight is kind to Lionel, softening his face, so that the pronounced jut of his soldier's cheekbones mellows into something more elegant. He reclines his large body, staring somewhere to Violet's left, quite at home in Walter's favorite chair. The brandy revolves drunkenly in his palm.

Violet is terrible at small talk. She waits for Lionel to speak first.

He lifts the glass and sips. "What sort of favors?"

"I beg your pardon?"

"From your father. What sort of favors did you ask?"

"My freedom, mostly. To go to college, to go to Oxford afterward. To study chemistry instead of English or history."

"Nothing wrong with English or history."

"There's nothing wrong with chemistry, either, unless you're a seventeen-year-old girl just out of school whose sole purpose in life is to marry well and make brilliant conversation at dinner parties."

"But you weren't that girl."

"No, not at all."

He smiles and leans forward. His eyes smile at her, too, reflecting the color of the brandy in his glass. "Good. You're better this way. Anyway, if you *had* done the conventional thing, you wouldn't be here now."

Violet springs to her feet and goes to the window. "And wouldn't that be a shame."

"I'd be devastated."

Sexual attraction. Violet knows what it is; she knows she's feeling it now, that she's felt it from the moment he prowled into the middle of her dark laboratory room ten days ago. Why not? Lionel Richardson is a strapping, healthy specimen of a man, an animal in its prime, manifestly ready to mate. She would be made of stone if the chemistry of her body did not respond to the proximity of his.

But what should she do about it?

Outside the window, night has fallen like a cloak over the streets of Berlin, but Berlin hasn't noticed. Violet can't hear the revelry, but she knows it's there: people laughing and drinking and smoking, in the cafés along Unter den Linden and in the grand apartments around the Tiergarten. In one of those apartments, her husband is laughing and drinking and smoking, talking with his friends, politicians and generals and minor German royalty, professional American divorcées like the Comtesse de Saint-Honoré. Committing adultery in his heart, and perhaps in actual deed. Probably not even perhaps. Parties are Walter's favorite hunting ground, after all: the prey is well-groomed, is relaxed and daring with drink. Possibly, at this very instant, Walter is with another woman.

"Have I offended you, Mrs. Grant?"

She turns to face him. "Of course not. I know it was only one of your jokes. Have you finished your brandy? You must be desperate to get back to your party."

He hasn't finished his brandy; he's hardly touched it. He's only toying with it, back and forth between his hands. "I'm not, in fact. I think you're much more interesting than another damned party."

"I'm not, actually."

"You are. You're fascinating. Do you know what I love most about you?"

"I can't imagine. We hardly know each other."

He taps the wide bowl of the snifter with one finger. "Among other things, that I could pull out a sheet of paper and a pencil and sit here and talk all night with you about bloody atoms, and it would be the most interesting and illuminating conversation I've had in years."

Violet laughs drily. "Then why did you leave the institute in the first place, all those years ago, and join the Army? Of all things."

"Ah." He leans back in the chair and watches her with a speculative expression. "Funnily enough."

"Was it something to do with Walter?"

In a swift and unexpected movement, Lionel lifts the brandy to his lips and swallows it all. Violet watches in astonishment as his throat works, as his white-tipped fingers grip the bowl.

"I know he can be difficult," Violet says quietly.

Lionel sets the glass on the table and rises to his feet. "Listen, Mrs. Grant—"

"Violet," says some other woman, not her at all.

"Violet." He lingers over the vowels. His teeth gleam briefly at her. "I'm not going to tell you the story. You're loyal to him; I can see that. I believe I rather admire that about you. Add it to the list in my head, number thirty-seven: *Violet is loyal as the devil.* But if I may be unpardonably bold, I suggest you ask yourself just how well Dr. Grant returns your loyalty."

Violet's fingers curl around the window frame. In his evening dress, Lionel looks even larger than before: the black tailcoat stretches across his bulky shoulders, his rifle-bearing soldier's shoulders; the white waistcoat swoops below his thick chest to button trimly at his waist. There are no shades of gray to Lionel. "Walter has his own brand of loyalty."

"Mostly to himself, I imagine." Lionel raises his hand and taps the starched white board of his shirtfront. "I have many faults, Violet, God knows. But I know what loyalty is, and what it isn't."

"Yes, I suppose you would."

Lionel's hand drops away. He reaches inside his waistcoat pocket and draws out a slim gold watch. "I don't mean to vilify the chap, of course. Many sterling qualities and all that. I was in absolute awe of his intellect, back at the institute."

"Yes, we all were."

Lionel looks up. "I say. Would you mind if I took a peek in his study?"

THE STUDY is cool and dark, having been protected from the sunshine all afternoon by a set of thick green damask curtains. Violet flicks on a lamp with nervous fingers, feeling like a child stealing a midnight peek at the Christmas presents.

"Ah, that's it." Lionel sticks his hand in his pocket and limps along one wall. "Exactly as I pictured. The antique Persian rug—Tabriz, isn't it? The bookshelves with their glass fronts, all locked up, of course. Are those his notebooks?"

"Yes. He arranges them by subject and then by date."

"Does he let you have the keys?"

"Of course he does." Violet leans against the wall and watches him as he moves about, running his finger along the glass, lifting aside one damask curtain to glance at the street below. "That is, he's told me where he keeps them, in case he needs something retrieved."

Lionel laughs. "He was always such a suspicious chap. Rivals lurking around every corner, twirling their mustaches, working to undermine him."

"Occasionally he's right."

"Do you ever read them? His notebooks, I mean." Lionel passes his thumb along the edge of the green-shaded lamp on the desk and pulls the little chain at the corner. A gentle glow pools atop the immaculate baize surface.

"Not really. I have my own line of inquiry now."

"Yes, you do. You're looking for this mysterious neutron."

"*Elusive* neutron." Because of the brandy, she allows herself a sigh.

"For what it's worth, I think the theory makes a great deal of sense. You can't have all those extra electrons crammed into the nucleus itself, and nothing else explains the neutral electric charge. Number of protons must equal number of electrons."

"Walter would say it's a made-up particle, the neutron. That we've made up its existence to fit the facts of the case, the atomic weight being twice the number of protons in the nucleus. A convenience."

"That doesn't mean it's not there. Isn't as if we've seen and felt a bloody electron, either, but we know it exists. You see? Aren't you marvelous. I could talk like this for hours with you. I could sit with you and count damned flashing particles for the rest of my life."

"Don't talk nonsense." But she blushes and turns her head, watching him from the peripheral limits of her vision.

Lionel lowers himself into the chair and sends her a devilish look. "Rather handsome, this. All sorts of possibilities come to mind."

"I suppose you used to play pranks on your headmasters."

He leans back, passing his face into shadow. "When I could. How are you enjoying Berlin, Violet?"

She shifts her feet. "I don't pay much attention to Berlin. I'm too busy with my work."

"What's this? No play at all?" He shakes his head and *tsks*. "Doesn't your husband take you out?"

"He knows I'm not interested in that sort of thing. Parties and endless chatter with people who don't understand."

"I suppose it's useful for him, though. Getting to know all these important chaps, having his path smoothed. Do you think he misses the English race at all?" Lionel folds his fingers together across his middle and twiddles his thumbs.

"Oh, there's plenty of English people around. But Walter's a cosmopolitan. He loves meeting people from other countries. I'm no help at all to him in that regard, I'm afraid. He sometimes brings them here for dinner parties, and of course I do my best, but they're all so . . ." She drifts off, unable to account for the stream of unguarded words. It's the darkness, perhaps, or the conspiratorial nature of what they're doing, meeting like this in Walter's private study. Or the way Lionel sits back in Walter's chair, his gray eyes charcoal with understanding. Easy to confess her thoughts, her failings.

"Of course it's a bloody nuisance for you. All those stiff Prussian fellows. We had a dinner a year or so ago, a regimental dinner, to which we invited a few visiting German colonels. Frightfully clever and all that, but they *would* say the most outspoken things." He smiles. "I nearly challenged my opposite number to a duel by the end of it. Whereas he probably wondered why I kept going on about the weather."

"And yet you've been very outspoken tonight."

"Only to you." He lifts himself forward and dribbles his fingers on the desktop. "Were you awfully uncomfortable, then? Who was there?"

"Oh, von this and von that. I don't recall. That's part of my problem, you see: I can't keep names straight, and I can't pretend interest in someone who doesn't interest me."

"Yes, that's number thirty-eight."

"Number thirty-eight?"

"On my list. *Violet cannot tell a lie.* Do you mind if I smoke?"

"Not at all."

Lionel takes a cigarette case and lighter from the inside pocket of his tailcoat. The silk lining gleams in the yellow light from the lamp. Violet looks down and listens to the snap of the metal case, the scratch of the lighter. "There was only one interesting fellow. The nephew of that old general, the one who laid siege to Paris in the seventies."

"Oh, von Moltke, you mean? By God, was he there? I'd have given a hundred pounds to meet him."

"Yes, he was there. I didn't mind talking to him. He actually talked to me as if I were a human being, instead of a . . ."

Lionel smiles again. "A terribly attractive woman?"

Violet has always viewed with contempt her shallow pretty-prettiness, her large blue eyes and chestnut hair and rosebud mouth, far better suited to chocolate boxes and Coca-Cola advertisements than laboratories. She despises the way it makes her seem younger than she already is, the way it makes men stare at her mouth as she speaks, not listening to her words. Not that she imagines herself a great beauty. If she were really beautiful, beautiful like the Comtesse de Saint-Honoré, formidably beautiful, powerfully beautiful, it would be easier. People obeyed the comtesse; people rose and fell according to her whim. People respected that sort of beauty, imperfect though it was. It was like a being unto itself, an idol to be worshipped, mythic. Violet's beauty—her prettiness, she reminds herself, for that's what it is, a very conventional combination of features to which the human animal was trained to respond—diminishes her.

She's not stupid. She knows that Walter, human animal that he is, was at least as attracted to her face as her mind, and that she wouldn't have achieved her present arrangement without her large blue eyes and her full bosom. But perhaps she would have achieved more. Perhaps she'd still be in Oxford, part of a larger team, making actual progress, instead of exiled here in Berlin carrying out her experiments almost by herself.

She certainly wouldn't be standing here in this well-appointed study in Kronenstrasse, with the likes of Lionel Richardson sizing up her charms and her willingness to share them, inviting her to tell him *Yes, please, kiss me senseless, never mind my husband and my life's work, my everything.* Her wanting desperately to say *yes,* wanting desperately to be kissed senseless, and the force of that wanting carrying through the air like a wave of alpha particles, exploding in tiny green-white pings against the solid atomic nucleus of Lionel Richardson.

The smell of Lionel's cigarette wafts past her nose. "Have I been too bold? Are you going to send me away?" he asks, in an amused voice.

"No, of course not. You're only flirting. It's what you do."

"What if I'm not just flirting?"

Violet stares at the desktop, at Lionel's fingers spread apart like the legs of a spider.

"Do you know, this is a magnificent damned desk," says Lionel. He flattens his palms and smoothes them across the surface. "The same one he had at the institute?"

"No, that's in his office now. But they're much the same, I suppose."

"He keeps it very tidy, as ever."

"Everything in its place."

Lionel rises from his chair and switches off the desk lamp. He picks up his cane, which was leaning against the edge of the desk, and makes his way in Violet's direction.

She concentrates on her breathing as he approaches, on maintaining her clinical detachment. His heavy dark hair, his heavy dark eyes: they are simply features, objects offered up for her observation. The neat white triangles of his bow tie, lying snug against his throat: an aspect of dress.

"I've never met anyone like you, Violet. You've been on my mind constantly. I've been looking out for you everywhere, whenever your damned husband appears in the room. Wanting to speak to you, to get to the bottom of you."

He stands far too close. Violet holds her ground and stares at the hollow of his throat. "Well, you've done that now, haven't you? Are you satisfied?"

Lionel reaches around her to stub out his cigarette in the ashtray behind her.

"No, Violet. I'm not satisfied at all."

. . .

VIOLET IS STILL AWAKE when the bedroom door creaks open and Walter's footsteps pad across the rug to the bathroom. She stares at the ceiling and listens to the rush of the faucet, the quiet bumps and clicks as he removes his clothing, discards his linen, hangs his jacket and trousers in the wardrobe. He will be thorough, she knows, taking care with every crease. His hands will pass along the sleek wool, just to be sure.

A year seems to pass before the damp lemony smell reaches her nostrils, before the bed sags under Walter's weight and the light switches off beyond her closed eyelids.

"Are you awake, child?"

"Hmm?" Stirring. Bleary.

"I believe I smelled cigarettes in my study, when I came in. Or was it my imagination?"

She rolls her head and blinks her eyes open. *"Hmm?* Oh, that was Lionel. He fetched us back from the office. Henry Mortimer and me."

"Yes, I recall Jane sending him off to find her boy. I suppose you asked him for a drink?"

"A glass of brandy. His knee was hurting him."

"Did you fuck him, too?" Walter's tone remains companionable, mildly curious, as if he were asking her what she ate for dinner.

"What? No, of course not. Don't be ridiculous." Her heart smacks against the sheets.

"You can't hide it from me, you know."

"Oh, for God's sake, Walter. Of course I haven't. Where do you get these ideas? I've hardly met him. He had a drink, that's all. We talked for a bit. He smoked a cigarette in your precious study." She rolls over, turning her back to him.

"Child, I quite understand the attraction. He's a fine sleek animal. He had any number of women back at Oxford, to my certain knowledge."

"Well, he hasn't had *me*. I dislike him more than ever, in fact." Her eyes are closed again; she is thinking of Lionel's lips, so close to her own in the shadowed corner of the study. His massive shoulder brushing hers, as he reached to stub out his cigarette. The intimate scent of his shaving soap disarming the pungency of the tobacco. All this, she had resisted. She had turned away from his imminent kiss, from the willing energy of his nearby arms. The injustice of Walter's accusation slips neatly between her ribs.

"I will find out, Violet. I could find out right now. I could tell if he's been inside you. Shall I?"

Violet says nothing. She waits for the expected sound of his footsteps, for the whir of the Victrola's plate and the scratch of the needle, because that's the sort of thing that would amuse Walter: confirming his wife's infidelity by the very act of enjoying her himself.

But her husband only laughs and settles himself into the mattress.

"Good night, child."

Vivian

Don't ask me how I ended up alone in a taxi with Doctor Paul, headed downtown. Ask my mother, who had made sure I was good and liquored up before she executed her master stroke. I looked down at the pocketbook in my lap, full of Violet's letters to my aunt Christina. The champagne whirlpool in my head refused to stop swirling. What was it about champagne? I should have stuck to vodka.

"Sneaky," I said. "Miserable, devious, underhanded rapscallion. That's you."

"I don't know what you mean." He was perfectly sober, damn him. "Your mother called me up at the hospital, out of the blue, and asked me to a party. Begged me, really. I rearranged my schedule. It would have been rude to refuse when she went to such trouble."

"You are so smug."

"I am."

"What if Gogo had been there, *hmm*? What then?"

Hesitation. "I didn't think she would."

"Oh, really?" I looked up at his profile in the streetlights. "How could you be so sure?"

"I called her yesterday, to see how she was doing."

Gogo hadn't mentioned this little fact. I curled my fingers around my pocketbook. "Good. I'm glad you did."

"Believe it or not, Vivian, I want to do the right thing here."

"Do you, now?" I turned to the window and watched all the pretty lights dance by. "You didn't tell me you nearly slept with her, back in Los Angeles."

His body was heavy and still next to mine. "No, I didn't. I'm not in the habit of revealing women's secrets, Vivian. I figured if she wanted you to know the details, she'd tell you herself."

"Convenient for you."

"Twist it how you like. It was Margaux I was trying to protect, not myself. I don't kiss and tell."

How many glasses had I drunk after Mums pitched Doctor Paul in my direction? Enough to make it stop hurting for a minute or two. But the hurting had started up again, and now here I was, drunk as could be, right smack next to the source of my hurt, because he had to go back to the hospital and I lived a few blocks away, and it was perfect, Vivian, perfect! A kiss on each cheek from Mums, a chuck on the arm from Dad, and off we went. If only the pretty lights would stop dancing like that. "All right. If you like. But it does put a new spin on things."

"What do you mean?"

"I mean, you went to bed with her."

"I didn't go to bed with her. All right, I was going to, we'd had a fun evening, she was sending out all the signals. Maybe I had a little too much to drink, maybe she did. It was a warm evening. It just . . . it started happening. She took the lead. I had no idea she was a virgin. I stopped when she told me." His voice was flatter than flat.

"So she said. Very gentlemanly of you."

"What the hell does that mean? It didn't happen, Vivian. I didn't let it happen. I don't take advantage of drunk virgins."

"Salisbury." I shook my head. "Tell me something. Without naming names. Without giving numbers. Is this something you do a lot?"

"What, sex?" At the instant he said the word *sex*, God flicked his fingers, the taxi lurched sideways, and I spilled into Doctor Paul's lap.

Lady Luck, she had me by the oysters tonight.

I picked myself up with drunken dignity. "It's all easy for you, isn't it? They fall for you, you sleep with them. You put on your honorable act, but you're really not, are you? You take what's offered."

"All right, I'm no innocent. That has nothing to do with us."

"Yes, it does." I was trying to find my logic here, so bear with me. "It has to do with sincerity."

"You doubt my *sincerity* with you?"

"Well, yes. You lied about what happened with Gogo—"

"I didn't lie about it. I just didn't tell you about it. It was private, for God's sake, it was Margaux's business. I didn't tell a soul. And anyway, the whole thing should show you that I'm capable of controlling myself. We were drunk, she was ready to go, and I stopped it. I don't know if you know much about men, Vivian, but that's not easy to do. Especially when the lady's that willing." His voice wasn't flat anymore. It rose and fell and stabbed at me.

"Well, I don't know if you know much about women, Casanova, but as far as Gogo's concerned, you might as well have finished what you started."

"But I didn't!"

"I mean as far as she's concerned. She was naked on that bed with you. She gave it all up to you. And you made her think you were doing the honorable thing by not taking the prize."

"I was. A cad would have kept on going regardless."

"Well, she thought the opposite. She thought you were so overwhelmed by her innocence, you were saving it for the wedding night."

Finally, a goddamned red light. The taxi slammed to a halt. Twenty-third Street. The radio was scratching urgently about a murder in the West Side, a street gang thing. Oddly, the pretty lights didn't stop twirling. The taxi seemed to be still moving, even though it had demonstrably stopped.

"Nothing to say to that, have you?"

"I'm sorry she misunderstood. I was damned if I did and damned if I didn't, I guess. Probably I shouldn't have gone in the room with her to begin with, but I did, I made that mistake, and I'm sorry. The point is, it's the past. It's what I was before I met you."

I shook my head, side to side, against the sticky leather seat of the taxi. "It's not in the past. You can't just say, well, none of that matters anymore because I'm in love."

"Listen to you, Vivian. For God's sake. Have I made a single peep about the men you've been with before me? We're just the same. We're not lily-white. I understood that, I didn't give a damn, I didn't need to ask. I understood you."

I lifted my heavy head. "If you had, Doctor Paul, if you'd asked even once, you'd have known that I slept with one man. One. That professor, three years ago."

The taxi thrust forward again. Doctor Paul grabbed the door handle. "Is that so."

"That's so."

"Why?"

"Because I have this little problem, you see, that you obviously don't share. I have a little problem getting attached to the men I sleep with. So. There it is. Not quite as daring as you thought, am I?"

He tried to take my hand. I snatched it away. We bumped on down Fifth Avenue. I thought about what Mums had said, taking me aside when I went to her bedroom to pick up my coat. *Don't hate me. I asked around a bit. It turns out Uncle Leo's younger brother knew him at Princeton. He was at the top of his class, Vivian. And dear old Oscar on the hospital board says he's the most promising young surgeon they've got, he's just naturally gifted, and so good with the children. He's perfect, honey. Perfect.* I'd thought to myself, she must have it bad, he must have really bamboozled her, if she didn't care about his family and his scholarship and his obscure San Francisco roots. Did she know about the gambling father yet?

"Vivian," Doctor Paul said, over Mums's voice in my head, "listen for a minute. Do you know what happened the other day? Margaux's father came to the hospital."

"You don't say. S. Barnard Lightfoot III himself?" I whistled sloppily.

"Himself. He sat down and offered me a million dollars to marry Margaux."

"Oh, for the love of Pete."

"You don't believe me?"

"A million dollars? To marry Gogo?"

But even as I said the words, I felt that whoosh in my chest, that sudden vacuum of vital strength that meant I *did* believe him, I knew this was exactly the kind of thing Lightfoot would do, arrogant and big-balled and not to be denied. Not to be outbid by a third party, in any currency.

"You don't have to believe me, I suppose. It shocked the hell out of me, that's for certain. That doesn't mean it's not true."

Possibly I would vomit now. I stared at the cab ceiling and tried to breathe slowly.

"A million fat ones. That's a lot of bread, young stud. You must have impressed him."

"Half on our engagement, half on our wedding day, he said. Our own apartment on Park when we had our first child."

"Classic six?"

"Seven."

"Not playing around, is he? When's the wedding?"

"What the hell does that mean? I told him no."

"But you must have been tempted. A million dollars." I lifted my hand and rubbed together my thumb and forefinger.

"Vivian. Stop it."

"So why are you telling me about it?"

"To show you that I'm sincere."

"All you're showing me, Salisbury, is that you're willing to make yourself intimate with a pretty girl and break her heart afterward. That you'll do anything, you'll turn down a million dollars to avoid making good on what you did to Gogo."

"For the last time, I didn't sleep with her."

I turned to him and shouted, "For the last time, it doesn't matter! It's how she feels!"

"What are you saying, Vivian? What do you want? Just tell me what you want and I'll give it to you."

What do I want. A simple question.

I fingered my pocketbook, considered the envelopes tucked inside. "Funny little coincidence. As it happens, I had a conference with S. Barnard Lightfoot myself on Tuesday morning. He as good as told me that if I backed off with you, he'd give me carte blanche at the *Metropolitan* for my story on Violet. He'd make my career."

"What did you say?"

"What do you think I said? I said yes."

Somehow, we'd reached my apartment building. Doctor Paul sprang out, opened my door, and handed me out. He reached in his pocket and shoved a couple of dollar bills through the passenger window.

"You're not coming in," I said.

"You're not going in alone, the state you're in."

I knew right away I wasn't going to win this battle. I let him fish my keys out of my pocketbook. "What's with all the envelopes?" he asked.

"Violet's letters to my aunt."

"But that's tremendous! Why didn't you tell me?"

I didn't answer. I swept past him and climbed the stairs. I won't say I didn't appreciate the steadying hand he put to the small of my back. I was stumbling a little, not at my best. When we reached my apartment, I had to run to the bathroom. He was still there when I came out, tall and imposing in his overcoat. "Don't you have a hospital to inhabit somewhere?" I asked.

"Not for an hour or so."

"Just my luck."

He walked to the kitchen, found a miraculous tumbler in a cabinet, and poured a glass of water from the tap. "Here. You'll thank me in the morning."

I drank obediently.

He said softly, "You're so absolute, Vivian. So ardent, inside that crisp shell of yours. You come on like Ava Gardner . . . no, that's not it. Like Hepburn, Katharine Hepburn, like there's nothing you wouldn't dare. But in the end, when the chips are down, when everyone pairs off at midnight, you shy away. You can't stand the nakedness, can you?"

"I can stand it, all right. I'm just particular. Nothing wrong with that."

"Your parents must have done some number on you. Or that professor. Tender Vivian. What did they do to you?"

I crashed the tumbler onto the tabletop, hard and loud, to shout down the sudden pain in my ribs. "Oh, you're shrinking my head now, are you? Look, I just think you should try doing the right thing for once. You know the rules. You broke it, you bought it?"

"I didn't break Margaux."

"I beg to differ."

He took the empty glass and poured another one. His face was somber as an abandoned puppy. "You're drunk. You don't even know what you're saying."

"You just don't want to hear what I'm saying. I'm offering you a chance to make amends. To do what's right for someone else for a change. Not just to suit yourself."

He watched as I drank my water. Without realizing it, I had retreated a few paces. In another step or two, I'd have my slinky low-cut back to my bedroom door. Nowhere to go. He moved forward one square.

"What are you afraid of, Vivian?"

"I'm not afraid of anything."

Another square. "Look at you. Your eyes. You are scared to death,

Vivian Schuyler. I can tell, because for what I suspect is the first time in your life, you're not making the littlest bit of sense. Tell the man you love to marry your best friend, will you? To *marry* her? When he loves you instead? You must really want me safely out of reach, don't you?"

I opened my mouth to tell him he was an arrogant son of a gun and I didn't love him. But the damned old throat clammed up on me. Well, I'm not made of stone! He was standing right there, right there, breathing down the bridge of my nose with his promising lips, staring down the marrow of my bones with his blue-scrubbed Paul Newman eyes. Who was I to say I didn't love the very darling dickens out of him?

I took a step backward instead.

"Margaux's a big girl, Vivian. She doesn't need you to take care of her. She has lots of people to do that. She's got a father who'll spend a million bucks to buy her a husband. She'll be just fine. The thing I want to know is, who takes care of Vivian?"

I wet my lips. My back was touching the door now. I let the water glass slide to the floor with a bump. "Vivian takes care of Vivian."

"If you don't mind my saying so, she's letting herself slip a bit at the moment." He laid one hand against the door, next to my hair. "I'd think of hiring her an assistant, if I were you."

"Then it's a good thing you're not me."

"I'm close enough. You're stuck in my head, Vivian. My blood. I can't shake you." With his other hand, he found my palm and kissed it, like a goddamned romantic movie, like a man who didn't know what was good for him.

I leaned back against my bedroom door.

"So who takes care of you, Doctor Paul?"

"You do."

Violet

The party in the Comtesse de Saint-Honoré's splendid flat in Französischestrasse reaches its riotous zenith just after one o'clock in the morning. By then, the butler has long since given up answering the door, and any unfortunate latecomer is forced to wedge his own path from the packed entry hall to the dining room, where the table and chairs have been pushed back and the enormous tiger-striped rug rolled up for dancing, to the cavernous drawing room, where champagne circulates by the bottle and people lean out the windows, trailing smoke.

Through the walls, the music jingles and jingles, a bouncy ragtime tune Violet recognizes by sound but not by name. She stands by a wall in the library, cradling a glass of champagne between her palms and staring up at a wall of books. The flat has been rented at an exorbitant price from a newly rich family of Prussian industrialists, away in Monte Carlo for the duration of the summer, and if the titles of their books are any indication, they would be delighted by the use to which their rooms have been put. Violet has already opened one door to reveal a half-dressed woman straddling a man atop a precarious French chair; when she stole into the library a few moments ago, she surprised another couple on the sofa in the final throes of concourse. (Not her own husband, thank God.) The comtesse's friends have followed her here to Berlin, and are making the most of her champagne and her ragtime and her plentiful rooms.

Violet waited calmly while the couple straightened their clothes and left the room in fits of giggles, and now she is blessedly alone with the German translations of de Sade and Casanova.

Violet has read de Sade, in the original French. Walter gave her the book soon after they began their affair; she was too reserved, he said, too inhibited, and needed shocking. As if carrying on a clandestine sexual relationship with her decades-older professor, with the renowned Dr. Grant, hadn't been shocking enough already for a Fifth Avenue debutante from a sedate Knickerbocker family.

Violet reaches out her hand and runs her finger along the spine. Walter is somewhere in that merry cloud of noise, smoking his pungent pipe. The comtesse drew him away at the moment of their arrival, there was someone she must introduce him to, *Oh, my dear Mrs. Grant, you don't mind my borrowing your husband for just a short, short minute?*

No, Violet had not minded.

A faint squeak of hinges announces a newcomer, and an instant later Violet hears the heaviness of Lionel Richardson's voice from the doorway: "I thought I'd find you here."

He was looking for her. She extinguishes the thought at once and keeps her gaze trained to the shelves before her, her head canted at the same two o'clock angle to read the titles. She presses her fingers into her champagne glass and says, "It wasn't much of a stretch, was it? Did you expect to find me dancing ragtime?"

He doesn't reply. His footsteps cross the room in authoritative clicks of his well-polished shoes, until he arrives directly behind her, so close she can feel the warmth of his body through his clothing and hers, she can smell his cigarettes and the familiar flavor of his shaving soap beneath, the *I, Lionel* to which her nerves are now attuned. The tip of his chin, she judges, is within an inch of the crown of her head, and he's gazing up at the books, matching her own line of vision.

"Wholesome," he says, amused.

"The Prussians are the worst. The strict ones always are."

"Don't I know it." He moves away, toward one of the giant twelve-paned sash windows, which he opens a few inches. He takes a plain silver case from his jacket pocket and opens it to reveal a neat line of white-papered cigarettes. He doesn't offer her one; he knows she doesn't smoke.

"What are you drinking?" She nods at his glass.

"Whiskey, in fact. A fine old single-malt Scotch whiskey, hiding amongst the cognac and champagne and schnapps. Would you believe it?" He lifts his glass to her and takes a drink. "Why are you here, Violet? It was the devil of a shock to see you waltz in on your husband's arm. Not your sort of go at all, is it?"

"I don't know. Restless, I suppose. I came home early from the lab and . . ." She lets her voice drift off, leaving it all unsaid: the limpid June air outside, fragrant with promise; Walter, straightening his tie in the mirror and looking at her in surprise, the alarmed sort of surprise. The alternative rising before her eyes, the waiting for him to return, waiting and waiting, pretending to sleep, the late-night click of the door and the rush of the bath water, the old lemony dampness again as he slides noise-lessly into the bed beside her. She had accepted their routine long ago. It was part of his job, Walter told her. Part of his job, to discuss ideas into the night, to make connections with the right people. All part of the process of scientific collaboration.

But tonight she had yearned to go out, too. To meet and connect, to collaborate in the promising June air.

Except that she was not collaborating, after all, was she? She was hiding away in the study with her champagne, listening to distant ragtime while Walter talked and smiled somewhere inside the music, his trim beard parting for his laugh.

"It's that sort of evening, isn't it?" Lionel lights his cigarette in a rapid flare. The study is dusky and still, lit by a single lamp next to the sofa on which the previous couple had been so joyfully collaborating, disturbed only by the gaiety behind the wall and the occasional shout or blast of horn from the street outside, four stories down. "Anything could happen."

Violet swallows the rest of her champagne and sets the glass on an empty patch of shelf. She has always disliked gloves, and the bowl is smudged with her fingerprints, making her think, rather absurdly, of detective novels. "That's a rather melodramatic thought, coming from you."

"What can I say? I'm a romantic at heart, beneath all my carefully cultivated cynicism. Hence the cavalry, rather than a foot regiment."

"Yes, Walter said something like that, the evening we met. That he couldn't quite make you out."

"And you? Have you made me out yet?"

"No. Other than that you're what you said you were that first night, a barbarian."

He laughs. "Not a civilized socialist, like you and Walter? I admit it freely. Though of course I understand your point of view, far better than you understand mine."

Violet turns to him, bracing her fingers against the shelf behind her. She's wearing her best dress, one given to her by Walter a month or two ago, fashionably narrow and high-waisted, a gossamer amethyst purple that suits her pale skin and dark auburn hair. A silver band sparkles around her ribs, just below her breasts, and her shoes are silvery, too. The effect, she suspects, is one of ethereal virginity. She looks now at Lionel Richardson, leaning his laconic body against the windowsill, cigarette dangling between his fingers, lowball glass glinting at his side, eyes regarding her thoughtfully, and wishes she had something like what the Comtesse de Saint-Honoré is wearing tonight: a red silk dress the same color as wine in candlelight, cut low across her bosom, baring her shoulders. "I don't think that's true at all," she says.

"Of course you don't." He uncrosses his legs and tilts his head toward the window. "Do you know what they're shouting about, out there?"

"No."

"The Hapsburg heir was assassinated yesterday, in Serbia. Shot with his wife in their motorcar, on a state visit."

"How dreadful."

"You needn't pretend with me. I'm sure you're crowing inside. Down with the ancient empires, isn't it? They had it coming." He slips his hand through the opening in the window and knocks the ash from his cigarette onto the sidewalk below.

"That's not true. I deplore any sort of violence."

"Ah. Not a Bolshevik, then? Not quite so far as that."

"Not at all. I believe it will all evolve naturally, the equality of man and the just distribution of property. I don't think we need a revolution."

"I don't know about that," Lionel says. His face begins to take on weight, as if the air has grown heavy upon him. "Men want to fight, don't they? We've gone a hundred years without a general European war. England, Germany, France. They're like horses at the hunt, milling about, waiting for the first hound to scent. Then bloody mayhem."

"That's nonsense. We're far too rational to fall into that trap again. The workers will never agree to fight."

"Won't they? We're all nationalists, deep down, Violet. Your average German hates a Slav far more than he hates his factory foreman, and vice versa. It's human instinct."

Violet thrusts herself away from the shelves. "Anyway, it's all theoretical, isn't it? There's no reason to fight."

"They'll find something eventually."

"War is never inevitable."

"Eventually, it is. Maybe not tonight, maybe not this year. But eventually."

"God, I thought *I* was a pessimist." The champagne is hitting her brain now, making her fidgety and dreamlike all at once. She circles the room. "Why are we even discussing this? War."

"I don't know. Don't mind me. Whenever this sort of thing happens, these international crises, Agadir and all that, I get in a funk. Wondering if this is it, if this is the spark that sets everything ablaze." He stubs out his cigarette against the windowsill and lifts his glass.

Violet picks up a small Chinese vase and turns it over in her hands. Her blood is beating pleasantly, her nerves alive and tingling. She has done her best to avoid Lionel Richardson since the night in Walter's study, to avoid this odd understanding that runs like an electromagnetic current between them whenever they collide: at dinner parties in her flat, at Herr Planck's musical evenings, in the halls of the Kaiser Wilhelm Institut. This unexpected intersection of their orbits (or perhaps it *is* expected, perhaps she has planned it like this) together in this room, without Walter or the Comtesse de Saint-Honoré or Henry Mortimer or anyone else, feels rare and precious, not to be handled roughly, not to be taken for granted. "I suppose it's your job, to wonder about war," she says. "I suppose you'd be the first in the fight."

"Naturally. I'm a soldier, aren't I?"

"Yes, you are. You enjoy it, don't you? Fighting and killing."

"No, I don't enjoy it. But I don't mind it, if that's what you mean. It's elemental. It slices right through all the rubbish, it erases your thoughts, it erases everything else but the essential struggle. You're never closer to nature than when you're out hunting, when you're nothing but an animal yourself. Better and purer than your civilized self."

"You don't have a civilized self."

"Yes, I do. Look at me now, quite calm and under control, while you stand right there, a few feet away from me, and the light glows against your skin. Turning you to gold. I don't think there's any higher proof of the power of civilization, that I'm not kissing you senseless."

Violet stares at the vase in her hands, the intersecting whorls of virgin blue and white, the soft bleeding of color at the edges, the curve that shapes itself perfectly beneath her palm. At the edge of her vision, Lionel stands waiting by the window. She doesn't look at his face, but she imagines, in absolute clarity, the expression it wears now: eyes silver and watchful beneath the furrows of his patient forehead. The predatory angle of his cheekbones, perfectly still.

"How is your knee?" she asks, still staring at the vase.

He turns to the window and braces his hands against the sill. "Splendid. These German surgeons are the wonder of the world. I should have headed home a week ago."

"Perhaps you *should* head home. Go back to England, to your regiment. Killing things."

"Do you really mean that?"

Violet cannot say *yes*. She cannot tell an outright lie. She puts the vase down and wanders to the other side of the room. "You could always take up with the comtesse."

"I understand she's otherwise occupied."

"I'm sure there's room for one more. She strikes me as the accommodating sort."

"Don't, Violet."

Her palms are damp. She presses them against the side of her dress. Why doesn't she just leave? Why can't she say good evening and walk back through the door? Or—a better question perhaps, more to the point—why can't she simply give in and lie secretly down on the sofa with Lionel Richardson and lose herself, as everyone else in Berlin loses themselves? Is it some vestige of loyalty to Walter himself, some superstitious reluctance to profane her marriage vows? Or the more practical fear of discovery and its consequences?

Or something else, something worse: the hypothesis, still unproven, that if she laid herself on the sofa in Lionel Richardson's embrace, she would never rise again.

"Don't what?" she asks mechanically, because anything is better than this screaming silence between them.

"Don't pretend this is something simple, between us."

"Of course it's not simple. My husband is a friend of yours. That's what I mean. You're much better off with someone like the comtesse. It suits you."

"As it happens, I have already had that honor, and we didn't suit at all."

Violet feels his words like a bad fall: one moment jogging comfortably along, a little breathless, and the next landing shocked against the pavement without any breath at all. "Oh? When was this?" she asks lightly, fingering the edge of the sofa as if his answer means nothing at all.

"A year or two ago, when I was on leave in London, right after her latest divorce."

"But you're still friends."

"Why not? That's what happens when things are simple, you see. You meet, you flirt, you engage in a spot of fucking to pass the excruciating bloody time, to forget yourself for a single godforsaken moment. You head back to your regiment when your leave is over." He takes the Berlin evening deeply into his lungs and turns around. "I'm not at all certain I could remain friends with you afterward."

"There won't *be* an afterward with us."

"No, you're right about that. If I had you, I wouldn't let you go."

"Then we had better not start at all."

"No, we'd better not." He picks up his glass, examines the remains against the light, and tilts it up to his mouth. "Your husband has invited me along to Wittenberg with you."

"Oh? What did you say?"

He takes out another cigarette and lights it swiftly. "I said *yes*, of course. Fresh air, sunshine, tennis in abundance. Who could refuse?"

"I won't go. I'll stay here in Berlin. I'll tell him I want to keep working."

"Look at you. You're dead frightened, aren't you?"

"What about your regiment? I suppose they need you."

"Let me worry about my regiment."

She grips the sofa edge and pictures Wittenberg, the charming villa

Walter has rented for the month of July, the sky and the clean water and the pungent sunshine. She pictures Lionel dropped in the center of this bucolic idyll, dazzling in tennis whites, shedding restless energy into the shimmering air. "He's your friend, Lionel. Don't do this."

"Ah, loyal Violet. I can't imagine what the good doctor has done to earn this violent fidelity of yours. Still, I suppose I've only to wait. The chap's twenty-eight years older than you—"

"Thirty."

"Thirty, of course. But anything might happen at that age. A heart attack, a fall, an accidental poisoning, that sort of thing. I'm a patient man."

"I wish you wouldn't joke."

"God *damn* it, Violet." Lionel springs from the window and tosses his empty glass into the empty fireplace. The shattering crystal makes her jump. He follows the sound to the mantel and curls his hands around the edge, on either side of his bowed head. "I wish to God I *were* joking."

A peal of laughter trills through the walls, unnervingly close, perhaps just outside the closed library door. Lionel doesn't move. The smoke trails delicately from the cigarette in his right hand, winding around his ear.

Violet whispers, "Perhaps you should just leave Berlin altogether."

"If I could leave, Violet, I would. Believe me."

Another burst of laughter, which clarifies suddenly as the library door swings open. Violet turns in a jolt. The Comtesse de Saint-Honoré illuminates the room, resplendent in red silk, her chin tilted back to expose her long neck.

"Oh!" she exclaims, looking first at Violet and then at Lionel, who now stands facing the room, one arm still slung on the mantel, one ankle crossed before the other, smiling mysteriously. "There you are! We were looking for you."

Only then does Violet notice her husband standing next to the comtesse. His necktie has come unraveled, and his elbow forms a convenient nook for her arm.

"Violet, my dear," he says. "Have you been hiding yourself away all this time?"

"You know I dislike parties."

"Yes, I wondered why you insisted on coming." He glances at Lionel and takes a drink from the glass that dangles from his other hand. "But I see you haven't suffered alone."

Lionel shrugs his broad shoulders. "We were discussing this wretched tragedy in Sarajevo."

"Shocking affair," says Walter.

"Why, what's happened in Sarajevo?" asks the comtesse.

"Oh, only the assassination of the Austrian heir and his wife," says Lionel. "Nothing for the ladies to bother themselves about."

Violet boils over. She opens her mouth to object, but the comtesse's gravelly laughter already crowds the air.

"Oh, really, Lionel. You're impossible. But poor Sophie. I really am upset. I met her in Vienna last year. She was charming, not a snob at all, as these Austrian aristocrats usually are. What happened?"

"Shot in their motorcar on a state visit. Some damned Serbian nationalist, I'm sure. Not that the Hapsburgs are fit to govern a village sheep run any longer, but what the devil good does regicide do? Only provokes Austria to kick them with booted heel." Lionel tosses the end of his cigarette into the fireplace, amid the shards of his whiskey.

"No doubt the diplomats will sort it all out," says Walter blandly.

The silence in the room contrasts with the merriment outside, as if the four of them are attending some secret rite in the middle of a wedding feast. Lionel drums his fingers against the mantel and trades inscrutable glances with the comtesse.

She turns to Violet. "My dear, do come along with me. I've got so many people to introduce you to. You don't know what a divine novelty you are."

Violet protests, but the Comtesse de Saint-Honoré takes her arm. "It's not that hard, really. They're all good and tight. Quite harmless. Just put one word in front of the other."

Later, after Violet has made the rounds with the comtesse, has met a thousand cosmopolitan drunks and become silly herself with champagne and ragtime and male admiration, she lies sprawled on the sofa in the library while Jane strokes her hair. Neither Walter nor Lionel can be found.

"You've got to sleep here tonight, I guess," says Jane. "There's nobody respectable to see you home."

"There was nobody respectable here to begin with." The gentle stroke of Jane's fingers, the rustle of red silk as she moves her arm, is lulling Violet to sleep.

"What a bad influence I am. But I can't help it, you know. It's how I'm made; I've given up trying to reform. I just like it."

"Like what? Having parties? Having affairs?"

"Yes, all of it. There's nothing more exciting than a new lover, or the chance of one. I'm addicted to it. You should try it yourself. Or I suppose you already have, when you started with Walter." She giggles softly. She's matched champagne with Violet that evening, glass for glass. "So try it again."

"No, I won't." Violet yawns. "I can't."

"Yes, you can. Why not? Lionel's dotty for you."

"I'm married."

Jane laughs outright and gives Violet a squeeze with her other arm. "What does that mean anymore? I've been married three times already."

"I don't know how you managed all that. Where did you find the time?"

"I started early, of course. That's the trick, start early. I ran away with my first husband when I was only fifteen. He was twenty-seven and a beast, but he was rich enough, the richest man in Rapid City, and I had to get away. Out of the house." Her fingers find a few stray ends of Violet's hair and rub them together.

"I don't suppose I can argue with that."

"I divorced him the year after that. That nice old judge awarded me plenty of money, once he saw the photographs. Always get evidence, Violet, that's my advice."

"I'll try to remember that."

"No, I really mean it. The deck is stacked against us, you know. I have no patience for women who won't look after themselves. I suppose that's why women don't like me very much."

"Don't they?"

"Well, I don't guess *I'd* like me, if I were them. No, they're right. I'm not one of them, I'm the enemy. You see, I don't need all this business about cuddles and fidelity and love everlasting. I don't believe in it. I like flirting; I like making love. I don't mind sleeping with someone's husband, if the opportunity arises. Why should I? It's just a physical transaction that gives pleasure on both sides, if it's done right. I've never understood why women make such a fuss about . . ." She waves her hand. "Well, all of it. Love and babies."

"But you've had three husbands. And a child."

The sofa cushions move beneath Violet's shoulders. Both of Jane's hands insert themselves in Violet's hair to gather up the waves and lift them from her neck. "Do you wear it loose at night, or do you braid it?"

"Loose. I can't be bothered."

Jane begins to braid Violet's hair. Violet closes her eyes. The little tugs and twists of Jane's manicured fingers electrify her scalp; Jane's exotic perfume drifts against the haze of champagne surrounding her brain. She loves the unfamiliar female intimacy of lying here, listening to Jane's secrets while Jane braids her hair.

"Listen, Violet. I love three things: money, myself, and my son. Not in that order. I'd do anything for them, especially Henry."

"That's all? Not your family? Any of your husbands?" She searches for something else, some other possible object for Jane's worship, and hazards—of all things—"God?"

"God?" Jane laughs mightily. "Really? What about Him? He's done nothing for me, I can tell you. I've done it all by myself, tooth and nail. I don't see why *He* should get any credit. And you don't, either, I'll bet. That's why I like you, Violet. I don't like many women, but I like you." She's finished the braid. She wraps her fingers around the paintbrush end and gives it a gentle pull.

"Are you sleeping with my husband?" Violet asks drowsily.

"Would you be angry if I were? Would you even care?"

Violet doesn't reply. She doesn't know how.

Jane pulls the braid apart and combs it out with her fingers. Violet opens her eyes. The apartment is quiet now, the guests shooed away, the servants in the scullery with the acres of glassware. It must be past four o'clock in the morning.

"You have the loveliest hair, Violet. I'll bet Walter loves your hair."

Violet stares up at the creamy library ceiling, and her mind turns back to another sofa and another ceiling, another body pressed against hers on an Oxford winter afternoon.

"Yes, he does. Walter loves my hair."

Vivian

November! They say time flies when you're having a tawdry affair.

"Lionel arrived in her life on the same day as this Jane Johnson," I said. "Don't you think that's a funny coincidence?"

"Hmm," said the man lying next to me, meaning, *I'm half asleep and I've no idea what you've just said, but even while semi-conscious I know better than to ignore you, Vivian Schuyler.*

I nudged his ribs. "Violet and Lionel."

"Violet. Sweetheart." He turned his face into my neck and went still.

"Just listen to this. It's in the second letter, dated May twenty-first: *'The most extraordinary character walked into my laboratory yesterday, an old student of Walter's. His name is Lionel Richardson and he's some sort of soldier, about six feet tall with one of those large and brutal bodies, like something you might see on safari, thickly muscled, with straight black hair. He's rather alarming to sit next to; one feels as if one will be swallowed up at any instant. We took him to a café later, where we were accosted by an American woman who wants Walter to take her son into the laboratory for the summer. The son, by the way, is not yet twenty. Altogether an extraordinary evening.'* Amazing, isn't it? And he sounds like a dreamboat."

"Mmm."

"And I checked it against the *Metropolitan* archives, and it's the same day as the correspondent mentioned seeing the Comtesse de Saint-Honoré—that's Jane, she's a real husband-hunter—with her son at the Bluebird café." I leaned my head back in the pillow and sighed to charm the angels. "It's the best feeling in the world, isn't it? When your research fits together like that, and all of a sudden you realize these were real people, living real lives, and . . . Are you listening?"

This time, no sound at all emerged from Doctor Paul's body, which lay heavy and slack against mine, one arm thrown across my middle. And really, who could blame him? His shift last night was supposed to end at ten o'clock, and I'd gone to the hospital to meet him there, but no—some sort of emergency surgery, a kid hit by a car—he would be out in an hour, in another hour, and at about midnight I'd realized that the huddled couple at the other corner of the antiseptic waiting room must be the child's parents, because they kept lifting their reddened eyes hopefully to the door whenever it moved, and the man's hand was locked so hard with the woman's that the bones of his knuckles shone white through his skin. I had sat there in a cold lump, no idea what to do. Couldn't just walk up to them and say, *Hello there, dearies, I'm Dr. Salisbury's lover, and I can assure you those clever old hands can perform all kinds of miracles,* or even *I know Dr. Salisbury personally, and he's the best new resident surgeon in years, and if anyone can save your darling angel, he will.*

And just as I'd made up my mind to do just that—the second greeting, not the first—the door had opened and Doctor Paul himself walked through in his stained blue scrubs, and from the weight of grief on his face I knew the news was as bad as news could be. I had felt an instant compulsion to run to him, to toss my cashmere arms around him and give him the unrestrained Vivian, but he didn't even see me. He walked right past my crossed and shapely legs and pulled up a chair next to the parents. He took the woman's hand like a sandwich between his own, and I thought, *Oh my God, oh my sweet twinkling stars, I love you so much, I can't even breathe, I think my heart just stopped, somebody save me.*

When I brought him back to my apartment an hour later, I'd thought he would want to go right to sleep, maybe accept a little comfort of the strictly platonic sort—look, a girl could take a rain check once in a while, in a good cause—but instead he threw me into the bedroom and engaged me like a lion, like a beast of the wild, in such a speechless frenzy of erotic energy that I, Vivian Schuyler, could hardly keep up. And I thought, as he lay sleeping and senseless the next instant, trusting and comatose along the length of my back, well, that makes sense, doesn't it? To combat death with life. To fight back.

I lifted my other hand and ran it through Doctor Paul's too-long sunshine hair, darkening at the roots now as November took its toll on all of us. Morning nudged through the cracks in the blinds. I needed my coffee and cigarette, but I couldn't dislodge my poor dear doctor, could I? I reached for Violet's gold watch, where it sat always on my nightstand, and wiped the glass with my thumb. Perpetual seven-oh-three. When time stopped for Violet and Lionel.

I said quietly, so I wouldn't wake him: "I still don't know when they began their affair. She mentions seeing him at a party at Jane's apartment and that he's recovering from an operation. And then he turns up in Wittenberg, where she and Walter rent a villa every summer. But it seems as if the more she likes him, the less she writes about him."

I looked down at Doctor Paul's head, tucked into my neck like a child's, and touched the delicate tip of his ear with my finger. "I guess I can understand that."

A plaintive gurgle emerged from my belly. I strained my neck to place a kiss on Doctor Paul's peaceful head and then detached myself, limb by limb, from the tangle we'd gotten ourselves into. I tucked the bedclothes back around him, found my robe, and picked my way through the strewn clothes into the living room.

No sign of Sally. Surprise, surprise. I started the coffee going and rummaged in the icebox. If the mingled scents of bacon and Yuban couldn't rouse my sleeping stallion, nothing could. I whipped the eggs to a proper froth and started a batch of toast, and I was just jabbing the fork in the toaster when a pair of arms came around my waist and a pair of lips collided with my temple.

"You again," I said.

"Like a bad penny. That smells fantastic. Are you sharing?"

"I might, if you're a good boy and find the plates."

He didn't move. He'd put his pants back on but not his shirt. I felt his heart beat between my shoulders. I reached to flip the bacon on the back burner.

He said, "I'm sorry about last night."

"Nothing to be sorry about."

"Are you . . . ?" Cleared the old throat. "I wasn't too . . . ?"

"Doctor. This is Vivian, remember? I'll let you know when I'm not enjoying myself."

"*Mmm.*" Another kiss.

He was making me right at home in his skin-scented middle. Ready to let the bacon burn and the eggs scramble themselves. "*Mmm* yourself," I said.

"So. Another thing."

"There's more?"

"Last night. In my primal haste."

"*Hmm.* Yes. We forgot a little something, didn't we?"

"A big something. My fault. I'm sorry, Vivian, I was just so . . . God, it was such hell yesterday . . . and there you were . . . I wasn't thinking straight . . ."

"I know. My fault, too. Heat of the moment." I peeled myself from his arms and poured a cup of coffee. "Here. My magic beans will make you all better."

"I *do* feel better. It's you I'm thinking about." Sip. Soulful, worried eyes. "How close are you?"

"Close. Not too close, I think." Pretty damned hair's-breadth close.

"Jesus. It won't happen again, I promise." He stretched out his not-coffee hand and stroked my tumbled locks. "Or there's the Pill."

"So I've heard."

"I do know this doctor. He could get you a prescription."

"Do you, now. Might be a good idea. If we're planning to make a habit of this."

I tried not to grin. I really did. So did he. But.

He said: "Thank you for last night. You saved me. You do know that."

"Anytime. And I do mean anytime."

He leaned forward and kissed the strands between his fingers. "I love this hair of yours."

Look, now. A man holds your hair in his hands and kisses it, the man who made love to you last night, and I dare you not to wrap your hands around his sweet skull and kiss him silly, until you're crashing into the icebox together, spilling hot coffee everywhere, giggling and groaning, all choked up with mutual worship. And then he stops suddenly and crushes you into his bones—your robe's come undone by now, naturally, and your bare skin attaches to his bare skin—and says, "It's been magic. This month with you, it's been heaven," and what the hell are you supposed to say to that?

"Yes."

"I just . . . Almighty God, Vivian, I love you so much. I just need you to know that. When I fall short of you. Give you less than you deserve. I love you, you can't imagine. You're the world to me." He said it violently, into that hair of mine he said he loved. In another second, he'd be proposing.

"Great guns," I said. "I think the bacon's burning."

DID I MENTION today was a Wednesday? Well. Today was a Wednesday, and what with all the bacon and the shenanigans, I slunk like an alley cat into the *Metropolitan* offices well past my usual hour of lateness. And I am not, as you may have noticed, the world's earliest alley cat to begin with.

But. I had lateness privileges now! Everyone knew I was now among Lightfoot's chosen. Even Agatha did no more than snap her Wrigley's at me as I waved my cheeriest and whipped around the corner before Gogo could triangulate my position from her radar station outside her father's office.

"Hello there, Vivs!"

Gogo was perched atop my desk, right smack between the telephone and the empty fact-checking box, gams crossed, topmost footsie bounce bounce bouncing. Her face wore a brilliant pink smile.

She knows.

Gathump gathump, went the old heart. I swung my briefcase into place. "Hello there, honey. What's cooking?"

Who told her? Where did she see us?

"You are. You're cooking. Look at that dress! And your hair. It's all . . ." She motioned.

I coughed. "New style." The Salon Doctor Paul Deluxe. "You like?"

"*Mmm.* I want one just like it."

"Wouldn't suit you at all, dearest. So. What are you up to this morning? Don't you have some advertisers to charm?" My heart was slowing from a gallop to a trot. There was not a drop of guile in Gogo. If she knew about Doctor Paul, she wouldn't go about confronting me all sideways like this. She would come at me straight, with bathtubs of tears and that lost-koala expression that did me in, every time.

Gogo laughed. "Not today. I'm doing the decorations for Agatha's anniversary party, and then I'm going shopping for a new dress."

"Nothing beats shopping to heal a broken heart."

A bit of sparkle in the eyes. "Absolutely."

Doctor Paul had been right about Gogo. After a week or so of despair, she'd begun to bounce back nicely. She'd returned to work, the smile had reappeared on her face from time to time, the old sunshine had begun to beam out from her baby blues. Maybe she was stronger than I thought. Maybe I was in the clear.

It didn't make me feel any less squalid as I stood before her, though.

I could meet her eyes. Just. But I couldn't return to girly intimacy with her, I couldn't lean forward across her bed and share secrets. What if she could see right through my eyes and periscope downward to the guilty depths of my hippocampus? What if she could see the memory of Doctor Paul and yours truly, locked together on a sofa, against a wall, atop a kitchen counter, asleep in his bed in a Gordian knot of perfect accord?

She took my hand. "Come with me. I miss you, Vivs. You've been working so hard."

"I miss you, too, Gogo. But I can't come with you this afternoon. Some of us have a real job, you know."

"Then come tonight to Daddy's place. Please? We're having dinner together. I want you to be there, Vivs. I asked Daddy. He said it was a wonderful idea. He wants you there, too." A bit of the old lost koala to the eyes, a bit of plaintive quiver to the voice.

Dinner with Lightfoot. The chest quaked. Did he know something? He couldn't confront me with his own daughter right there, could he?

I could proclaim I was already engaged this evening. But what had Paul said this morning, as we rushed down the stairs together, all tardy-faced and laughing? He couldn't get away until midnight. He'd meet me at my place. So. I couldn't say I wasn't free.

Unless I lied.

I couldn't lie to Gogo. I know, I know. Everyone says that once you involve yourself in the Big Lie, the little lies line up behind like ducklings, until they just paddle effortlessly out of your mouth, one by one, sometimes two at a time. Not the case with me. Instead, since I began playing alley cats with Doctor Paul, I knew an unstoppable compulsion to accord myself with scrupulous honesty everywhere else. As if that could somehow atone.

I squeezed her hand. "I can make it. What time?"

"Seven o'clock sharp." She popped off my desk and gave me a sticky pink kiss. "Don't be late!"

BACK IN THE STACKS. I loved the stacks. They suited my newfound need to hide myself in obscurity, among people who no longer existed. The truth was, though, I'd reached a bit of a dead end, as I told Tibby when he walked in without warning through the Furniture Repository door at—I checked my watch—one o'clock in the afternoon.

"Miss Schuyler. How is your research progressing?"

I looked up the patrician line of his nose. "The truth is, I've reached a bit of a dead end."

"It happens."

"Would you like to sit down?"

"No. I came to tell you that you're wanted downstairs. Miss Brown's fortieth anniversary party. Everyone's required to attend."

"Miss Brown?"

"Our receptionist, Miss Schuyler. Miss Brown? Miss *Agatha* Brown?"

"Oh! Agatha! Forty years, is it?" I whistled. "Certainly, a party's in order. Knees up, I say."

"Indeed."

I leaned back in my chair and crossed the shapely legs. "And you haven't got better things to do than to come and fetch me personally?"

"I'm the only one with a key."

"Now, now, Mr. Tibbs. I can tell when a man wants to have a private word with me." I motioned to the other chair, which, in fairness to Tibby, might or might not remain intact under the weight of human hindquarters. "Do sit."

His professorial vest squeezed out a sigh. He sat. "You've exceeded your three weeks. As I'm sure you're aware."

"It's been a little rougher seas than I imagined at the outset."

"Where are you now?"

"Well." I looked down at the letters before me, the stack of biographies, the folder from the *Metropolitan* archives marked BERLIN 1914. "I have Violet's letters home. There aren't many, and they're all to her sister Christina, who evidently wasn't privy to her innermost thoughts, if you know what I mean. I know she met this Lionel Richardson in May of 1914, and he stayed with them at their summer villa in Wittenberg, along with Jane and her son. It seems the whole crowd from the institute joined them at the end. Einstein, even. Einstein!"

"All this, with war in the air? Wouldn't that be aiding and abetting the enemy?"

"Walter seems to have been the cosmopolitan sort. And anyway, the war took everyone by surprise. As you know. But I suspect Violet and Lionel began their affair there in Wittenberg, because here"—I pointed to the next-to-last letter—"Violet stops mentioning him at all. And then, poof, there's nothing, not a single letter, except for this." I picked up the final missive, a postcard, and handed it to Tibby.

"Having a lovely excursion. All well. Will write more soon. Violet.'" He looked up. "I see what you mean."

"But look at the date on the postmark. July twenty-sixth. That's *before* Walter was supposedly murdered in their flat in Berlin. So obviously they, the two of them, the three of them, Lionel and Walter and Violet, they all left Wittenberg for some reason. The question is why. Possibly because the political situation was worsening, but from all I've read, the final declaration of war came as a shock. It wasn't until the mobilization order went out that people, the man on the street I mean, believed they were actually going to fight. I suppose the shrinks would call it denial. Everyone thought that civilization would prevail."

Tibby took his reading glasses out of his pocket and squinted. "I can't read the name of the town on the postmark."

"Neither can I. It's too smudged. But I'll tell you one thing: it's not Berlin."

He removed his glasses. "Are the archives any help?"

"They might be, if there were any correspondence from Berlin after July twenty-fifth, when Austria declared war on Serbia and set the whole thing going. I suppose everyone was leaving the country by then."

"*Hmm.*"

"Why '*hmm*'?"

"Because it's odd. Because you'd think there would be a flood of chatter. Any good journalist would stay until the bitter end." He looked back at the rows of wooden cabinets. "Have you looked in the confidential files?"

"The what?"

"The confidential files. The ones containing particularly sensitive information. The real dirt, as they say."

I climbed to the tippy-tips of my four-inch heels. "WHAT DID YOU SAY? NOBODY TOLD ME THERE WERE CONFIDENTIAL DAMNED FILES!"

Oh, he smiled at me, old Tibby, with the patience of a governess instructing her charge. He fished around in his tweed jacket pocket, produced a set of keys, and dangled one in front of me. "Someone is telling you now."

Violet

The villa in Wittenberg is seething with guests, the way Walter likes it. Jane and Henry have joined them, and Lionel Richardson, who goes out shooting with Walter every morning. Violet never realized Walter knew how to shoot, she presumed that sort of thing went against his principles, but off he goes, shotgun slung under his tweedy arm, like an English squire, while Henry and Violet retire to the makeshift laboratory in the carriage house and Jane lies in bed, writing letters. Lise and Albert Einstein and Otto Hahn and his wife are expected later tonight in Hahn's automobile; they telephoned from Treuenbrietzen at four o'clock to say that they had been delayed by a number of unlucky flats and would probably miss dinner.

In the meantime, a pair of German officials have come to dinner, and Jane is acting as hostess. If the arrangement seems odd, nobody appears to notice. Violet, sitting in nominal wifely state at the opposite end of the table, the quiet end, is happy to let Jane direct the conversation from Walter's left hand, flirting first with one German official and then the other, while Violet answers stilted questions from the officials' wives and passes the salt. Jane has ordered candles instead of the harsh electric lights, and the scent of burning wax reminds Violet of childhood, when she would peer through the doorway and watch her parents host their long and ponderous dinner parties.

"But surely it won't come to war," says Jane, sounding more amused than alarmed.

Herr von Karlow throws a nervous glance at Lionel. "Nobody wants war, of course, madame. It is simply a matter of obligations."

"Obligations." Jane laughs. "Surely, Herr von Karlow, you can't possibly suggest that Germany would allow herself to be dragged into defending Austria from the colossal threat of poor little Serbia?"

Lionel has finished his duck and now calmly plucks a plum from the display at the center of the table. He lifts his knife to slip out the pit. "But it isn't just poor little Serbia, is it? Russia will rush in to defend her fellow Slavs from Austria's outrage. That's the point. Serbia can defy Austria because she counts on Russia, and Austria can defy Russia because she counts on Germany. A neat little arrangement, which is supposed to keep everyone from fighting at all." He cuts the plum into slices and pops one into his mouth.

"Russia should not interfere in Austria's affairs," says Herr von Karlow, pale-faced. "Austria has every right to avenge the murder of her prince."

"Well said." Lionel eats another section of plum. "And I have every confidence that Austria will do all in her considerable power to ensure that other nations are not dragged into such a local dispute. Because if Russia goes to war, then France must mobilize in her defense, and then all Europe comes to Armageddon."

His easy words bring the table to stillness. Someone's knife clinks musically against a Meissen plate. Violet looks out the window, where the air is still light and hazy, the sunset still hours away. The green lawn lies at peace beneath a pale blue sky; beyond the cluster of linden trees, Violet can just see the corner of the tennis court. A lugubrious hot summer: how could war possibly interrupt it?

The other German speaks up. "Naturally Germany should deplore a general war."

"Naturally," says Lionel.

DUSK SETTLES SWEETLY. Violet has stolen away to the laboratory after dessert—something is nudging the edge of her mind, some beginning of an idea that will not let her rest—and when she steps at last through the French doors to the terrace, the air is flat and indigo-quiet, scented with cigarettes and with the jasmine that grows in a neat row along the side of the house.

A faint noise drifts into her right ear, a male noise, a chuckle perhaps. She knows it belongs to Lionel. She cannot resist turning her head, and she sees him at once: a midnight shadow tucked against the lindens, feet crossed at the ankles while he speaks to the solid height and heft of Herr von Karlow. The smoke from their cigarettes whorls ghostlike in the darkness.

She hears other sounds, too. She hears Jane's light laughter from the lounge chairs at the opposite end of the terrace, where she sits with Walter every evening.

"Mrs. Grant. I was growing alarmed."

Violet spins and crashes into the shoulder of Herr Schulmann.

"I beg your pardon. I didn't mean to startle you," he says, in his perfect English. Over tea that afternoon, Jane told her that Herr Schulmann attended school at Harrow and university at Cambridge, that he was once engaged to an Englishwoman, though it had ended unhappily. How Jane has discovered these facts, Violet can't imagine; it's as if she pulled them from some all-knowing ether, beyond the reach of Violet's senses.

"Not at all." Violet's Schuyler upbringing takes over, as it's meant to do in such moments. She asks if he would like a drink, if he would like to sit down. The butler has already wheeled out the after-dinner trolley, an abundant arrangement of crystal decanters and cigarettes and coffee and petits fours. Can she offer him something?

He holds up his glass. "I am already sufficiently supplied, thank you. But you have nothing. May I fetch you a glass?"

They wander to the trolley. Herr Shulmann is drinking port, which he pronounces excellent; Violet, for want of imagination, allows him to pour her a glass. They come to rest on the low wall at the edge of the terrace, where the jasmine brushes Violet's bare arm.

"I've never met a more unusual hostess," says Herr Shulmann. "You disappear and reappear as if borne by fairies."

Violet laughs. Her head is still sparkling a little from the excitement of discovery on her page of equations, from the low chuckle of Lionel's nearby throat. "Not fairies at all, I'm afraid. I was in the laboratory."

"Most wives would be visiting the nursery at this hour."

"Dr. Grant and I have a different sort of progeny."

"Indeed." Herr Schulmann looks at his hands and rolls the sharp-edged bowl of his glass back and forth between his fingers, which are long and polished. He is a government official of some sort, Herr Schulmann, though Violet can't remember what he does. "I suppose it's much the same with me. My work is my child, or more properly Germany, and I love her with the same passion as I might love my own daughter, if I had one."

"Yes, I understand."

He looks up. He's not a handsome man—his face is narrow, his hair thin—but the light from the house is kind to him, erasing the tiny pits in his skin, giving his eyes a liquid warmth. He fastens those eyes on her earnestly. "You are American, Mrs. Grant, though your husband is English. Are you a patriot?"

"I am not, I'm afraid. I find myself frustrated by these rivalries between nations."

"As do I. As do I." Herr Schulmann rises from the wall, strides to the trolley, and pours himself another glass with a shaking hand. He returns to her, sweeping up his black tails as he replaces himself in his seat. "All this talk of war tonight. You must understand, Mrs. Grant, that

Germany does not want war. But we're encircled, encroached upon." He makes a motion with his hands. "France on the one side, Russia and the Balkans on the other. Spain begins to align herself against us." He drinks. "And there is Britain."

"Britain hasn't committed herself, has she?" Violet peers through her memory, which traps equations and chemical formulae in perfect detail, but cannot always recall the current political map of Europe.

"Not publicly. But there is an understanding with France, that Britain will follow her into war if declared. And *if* war is declared, Mrs. Grant, *if* we teeter into this abyss, Germany will be beset on both sides. France to her west, Russia to her east. And she would fight with all her strength. She would fight to the end."

"Pardon me, Herr Schulmann, but you appall me. All war appalls me. It is barbaric, the most brutal means of solving differences between nations. Men will be killed, men with wives and mothers and children. Hearts will break, and for what?"

Herr Schulmann's hand reaches out unexpectedly to enclose her own, over her glass of port. "I agree, Mrs. Grant. I am not belligerent. I despise the very thought of war."

Violet's breath thins to a wisp in her chest. The giddiness of the laboratory has fled her; she is aware of Lionel's laconic figure among the lindens, of the strength of passion in Herr Schulmann's gaze. "Then why do you speak of it as inevitable?"

For an instant, Herr Schulmann glances at the moon-shadowed trees, where Lionel and Herr von Karlow are still speaking. "Because there are those in the government, those in the military especially, who welcome war. Who believe that a decisive battle is the only way for Germany to rid herself of this encirclement. Who are convinced that an early war, before our enemies gain any further strength, is to be brought forward on any pretext." Herr Schulmann finishes his port, sets down the glass, and reaches into his pocket for a cigarette. "Do you mind, Mrs. Grant?"

"Not at all." Despite the warm air, Violet's hands are cold. She finishes her own port and watches Herr Schulmann's elegantly nervous fingers as he shakes a cigarette from its gold case and strikes a match against the stone. The flame sends a lurid shadow chasing across his face. Nearby, the Comtesse de Saint-Honoré's laugh pirouettes in the twilight air. Walter has pulled his chair closer to Jane's, and his elbows rest attentively on his thighs as he leans toward her. Violet takes in all these details, all these filaments of her life, woven together in some audacious new pattern that snatches her breath with its possibilities.

"I disagree with my colleagues, Mrs. Grant," says Herr Schulmann, with another quick glance at the lindens, from which Herr von Karlow's voice rises with growing urgency. "I think a general war would be disastrous for Germany, for Europe, and for humanity. But mine is a lonely voice."

"I am very sorry to hear that."

"No man is more loyal to Germany than I am, Mrs. Grant. I only wish I might save her from herself." He looks at her again, his gaze pressing into hers, as if he's trying to explain something vital.

"I wish you can, Herr Schulmann," Violet says. She lays her palms against her dress. Von Karlow's voice rises angrily to her left, and a second later his feet strike hard on the terrace steps. He passes them both in a gust of startled air. "I wish you can."

VIOLET FINDS LIONEL in his usual spot, among the rose trellises. Night has enclosed the garden, and she feels her way along, scraping her fingers against the thorns, until she catches the scent of Lionel's cigarette and stops, waiting for his shadow to detach from the darkness.

His hand reaches her first, drawing her next to him. "There you are."

"I'm sorry. The Germans left; I had to see them off."

"My fault, I'm afraid." He laughs softly, and she can see him now, the whites of his shirt and tie finding the moonlight at last. Something brushes her cheek. "I've plucked you a rose, if only to annoy you."

She reaches up and takes it from his fingers. "The poor thing."

"Either way, it will wither and die."

"Like your everlasting regard?"

"Well, there it is, anyway." He thrusts one hand in his pocket and leans against the trellis, mindless of thorns. "Yours to keep. You can always dry it and place it between the leaves of your diary."

"I don't have a diary. Not for personal things, anyway. I have my scientific journals."

"Yes, of course. What a pair we'll make for the historians of the future. Not a scrap of personal sentiment left behind to incriminate us."

"We've done nothing criminal." The air is cool among the roses, but Violet is flushed and warm. Her dress itches against her skin. She takes a step back, away from Lionel.

"No, we haven't. Not yet." The faint orange end of his cigarette moves up to his lips, flares, and moves away. He waits, as always, for Violet to speak next, to say the words that will set everything into motion.

"What did you say to poor von Karlow?" asks Violet. "He was very angry."

Lionel shrugs. "He wanted me to admit that the Allies were in the wrong, that poor old Germany was persecuted and encircled. *Einkreisung*, the old word. He's not entirely wrong, that's the devil of it."

Violet tears a leaf from the stem of her rose.

"And you, Violet? What were you discussing so intently with our good Herr Schulmann?"

"The same thing, I suppose, except that he doesn't want war. He was almost pleading with me, as if I could do something about it." She allows a bitter laugh. "I, an American scientist, married to an Englishman, with no interest whatsoever in politics."

Lionel straightens. "What did he say, exactly?"

"I don't remember exactly. That he wished he could save Germany from herself, or something like that."

"Did he?" Lionel exhales a slow stream of smoke and drops his spent cigarette into the paving stone, soft with lichen. He moves his foot to crush out the last of the glow. "That's good of him."

Lionel's body rests a very few inches away, electric with life, blood racing and cells dividing. Here and present before her, with a vital force that might grasp Violet by the shoulders and shake her awake.

"Will there really be a war, Lionel? It doesn't seem possible."

"I don't know, Violet."

"Can't you do something? Your father, somebody."

He laughs drily. "I'm flattered. You must have an extraordinary faith in me."

"I do. You can do anything. You . . . you're that sort of person. Nothing's impossible with you." The rose is denuded of leaves. Violet wraps her fingers around the stem and stares at the hole in the darkness where Lionel leans against the trellis.

An automobile engine grinds faintly from the road. Violet knows it might be Lise and Albert and the Hahns arriving at last, hot and weary with travel, but she cannot make her heavy limbs move. She cannot free herself from this rose-scented cocoon she shares with Lionel.

"Violet." Lionel's body shifts. His hand touches her hair, pulls a few strands from the loose knot at the nape of her neck. He bends his head and kisses them. "I'm falling in love with you."

"Don't." She puts her hand on his arm, intending to detach him, but her fingers in their weakness only rest there on his smooth black sleeve, examining the bony curve of his elbow. Lionel's sleeve, Lionel's elbow, Lionel's peppermint shaving soap and his warm brandy-scented breath.

"Let me kiss you, Violet. Just once."

"No. He'll know, Lionel."

"How can he know?"

"He'll smell you on me. He'll see it in my eyes."

"The devil he will. And what if he does? It's only a kiss."

"You don't know him."

"He doesn't deserve you. He doesn't deserve *this*, your loyalty." Lionel holds her hair against his lips. His other hand is somewhere between them, ready to strike, ready to touch her if she lets him. "You think you need him, Violet, but you don't. You can stand on your own. You're strong, you're the strongest woman I know, and you've made yourself his hand-maiden because he's convinced you, God knows how, that he created you."

"And now you want me to be *your* handmaiden."

"No, I don't." He pulls away. His face lies in dark fragments before her: a line of cheekbone, a glint of forehead, an unstoppable eye fixed on hers. "Listen to me, Violet. I want more than this. I want to lie next to you at night and worship you. I want to watch you by day and see what you're capable of, you astonishing woman, you bloody beautiful thing. I want to count every scintillation of you."

"For a month or two, anyway."

"Why not?" His voice is stone. "Why not, if it amuses us both?"

"I don't want to be amused."

He releases her hair and steps back. "Well, neither do I. God help me."

An insect hums past Violet's ear. There is the crackle of gravel from the driveway, the voices raised in welcome. "I should go."

"Go, then."

"You're angry."

"By God, I am. I'm furious. You've made me helpless. I'm nothing but a damned bystander. Watching and waiting." He throws his fist into the trellis with a crash, causing a pair of birds to scuttle upward from the roses.

Violet gasps.

"I'm sorry," he says.

"Don't be. They're only roses."

Lionel turns away. "Go, Violet. Go to your guests."

"I can't leave you like this."

"And what else do you propose?"

Jane's laugh rises up from the front of the house, and Walter's low chuckle. Violet's palm hurts. She looks down and sees the rose crushed in her fist, and what must be its tiny thorns piercing her skin. Lionel's back lies before her, his arm braced against the trellis, his black head tucked under a speck of moonlight.

Well, Violet? What else do you propose?

Violet pulls the petals away from the stem in a clump and does something she has never imagined doing, on a whim she cannot begin to fathom. She scatters the petals one by one over Lionel's granite shoulders.

"Say good night to me," she whispers.

"Good night, Violet."

Violet slips under his arm and stands in front of him. She stretches on her toes and puts her hand on his cheek.

Lionel's kiss is delicate, as if he's afraid of her touch, as if he doesn't trust himself with her. Violet expects something wholly exotic, Lionel's brand-new taste and smell and the feel of his lips, but in that first instant of contact he reminds her shockingly of Walter, warm-skinned, round-lipped, pungent with tobacco and masculine spirits.

And then she deepens the kiss and it falls apart, this image of Walter, because Lionel's chin is smooth-shaved, his cheeks are sleek against her fingers, his mouth moves so gently it hurts her chest. He touches her hair, her back. His body is wide and strong across her breast. She stops, holding her lips around his, and her shoulders begin to quiver.

"*Shh.*" Lionel strokes her neck. "*Shh.*"

Vivian

You can imagine the festive spirit with which I entered the *Metropolitan* conference room five minutes later, knowing that those confidential files were waiting for me upstairs.

Tibby had insisted. All right. Tibby had actually locked his hand around my arm and refused to relinquish the key until I agreed to attend Agatha's anniversary party. "If I have to eat cake, you have to eat cake," he said, and in the end it was this promise of implied solidarity that moved me to go along. I needed a friend, didn't I?

Gogo was there, beaming. Gogo had known Agatha since she was a baby. In fact, Gogo had probably decorated the birthday room herself. The place was unrecognizable. Festooned with bunting, chock-a-block with hearts and sparkling forties, overflowing with refreshments and a cake of Agatha-like proportions. The honored lady stood there herself in the center of the sitting area, pursed of lip, gimlet of eye, pointy paper hat balanced atop her pointy shellacked head.

"Congratulations." I lunged in to kiss the exact center of her leftmost patch of rouge. "Forty years of service! I'd never have guessed a day over thirty-eight."

Gogo was filling paper cups with champagne. "I'm going to cry in a minute. Remember when you spanked my bottom for rearranging all the pens in the storage closet?"

"Spanked it good," said Agatha with satisfaction. "You were just two and a half."

"Well done, Mary Poppins," I said.

Oh, the warm feelings packed into that room! Editors, writers, secretaries, even the typing pool, all guzzling down Lightfoot champagne and eyeing that cake like crocodiles at a zebra convention. That cake! Some zealous confectioner had created a three-dimensional chocolate-frosted telephone, with *Congratulations Agatha!* trailing in swirly icing letters from the receiver earpiece, and *Forty Years of Service!* shouting from the mouthpiece. How we were going to cut it up, I had no idea.

Within minutes, a dozen empty champagne bottles had piled up on the service tray, the ashtrays were overflowing, and the mood was turning fractious. "I think we'd better start the cake," I whispered to Gogo.

"Not yet. Daddy wants to say a few words."

"Mr. Lightfoot?" I owned myself shocked. S. Barnard had never made an appearance at any of the birthdays, engagements, anniversaries we occasionally moved ourselves to celebrate in the office. Word had it he only attended the *Metropolitan* Christmas party for a single ceremonial half hour, before departing by limousine for parts unknown but roundly suspected. "Why?"

"Oh, they've known each other forever."

The room went silent as she spoke, so the word *forever* floated out cheerfully above our heads. I looked to the door, where Mr. Lightfoot stood in his elegant pin-striped charcoals, a royal purple handkerchief showing in a neat triangle from his breast pocket. A distinct air of martini wafted through the nimbus of cigarette smoke, suggesting lunch at his club with the *Metropolitan*'s largest advertiser.

"Miss Brown!" he said. He walked up to her, snatched her talons, and kissed each cheek pouch.

Someone coughed. I believe it was Tibby.

Mr. Lightfoot turned to face the assembled minions. One hand still held Agatha's. Gogo pressed a paper cup of champagne into the other.

"Let me tell you about Miss Brown," he said.

I measured the distance to the door. Too far.

Agatha was smiling a foundation-cracking smile, her lips stretched so wide that the scarlet had thinned out to fuchsia.

"I first met Miss Brown thirty-nine years ago. I was just out of Philips Exeter, working at my father's magazine the summer before I started Harvard. I had never seen anyone like her. Gorgeous face, shining blond hair. Tits like torpedoes, out to here"—he motioned extravagantly with his champagne hand—"and an ass to match."

No one made a sound. The word *ass* echoed its way around the room, nearly setting the champagne bottles to rattling. I could just see Gogo's pink face at my periphery.

"She was every young man's dream." Mr. Lightfoot exhaled the memory and drank down his bubbly in a single large-throated gulp. He turned to Agatha and gestured wide, as if he were presenting her to the Queen of England. "And now. Just look at her!"

I looked obediently at Agatha's shellacked head and paper hat and wide smile. I looked at the cherry-red tip of Lightfoot's nose. I looked, for lack of anything better, at the enormous chocolate telephone in the center of the conference table: *Congratulations Agatha! Forty Years of Service!*

A furious and rapid clapping exploded the stunned silence. "Brava!" said Gogo. "Brava, Agatha! Hear, hear!"

"Hear, hear!" we murmured in chorus, and all at once, there wasn't enough champagne in the world.

BY THE TIME we filed out of the conference room, I was far too tight to sit down with the precious confidential files upstairs. "I've changed my mind," I said to Gogo. "I'll go shopping with you after all. Just let me have a word with Tibby."

I called Doctor Paul first, from the telephone in the library, taking a chance he was between surgeries. He came on the line right away. "Vivian! Where are you?"

"In the library. The *Metropolitan* library. I miss you, Doctor."

"I miss you, too." Bemused, maybe. "Are you all right? You sound a bit—"

"Tipsy? Yes, I am. Champagne and cake in the office today. It's the receptionist's forty-year anniversary with the magazine."

"Must have been some party."

"That doesn't begin to cover it. Listen. I'm going shopping with Gogo this afternoon."

"What? Why?"

"Don't be so alarmed. I can't just drop her, you know. She'll wonder what's going on."

He said something under his breath. "Are you going to say anything to her?"

"About us, you mean? Of course not. Not yet. Why?" I doodled with the cord. I was feeling loose and champagney, not particularly worried about anything, even Gogo's wounded heart, which seemed to be healing nicely anyway. "Do you want me to tell her?"

"I guess not. Not if you don't want to."

"All right. I won't. But I think you're right. I think she's bouncing back. Our bouncing baby Gogo."

"Good. Good for her. I'm glad."

I kissed the mouthpiece noisily. "I'll see you tonight?"

"I'll be late, I'm afraid. No rest for the weary."

"That's why I gave you the key."

We said good-bye. Before I left, I went upstairs with Tibby's super-secret key and unlocked the super-secret file cabinet, and what I found there made my tipsy jaw swing as low as a sweet chariot.

I packed up the folders and put them in my briefcase. Which was, strictly speaking, forbidden, but when did that ever stop me?

Violet

Violet's first rebellion occurred at the age of eleven, when, in the natural course of things, she was sent out of the nursery schoolroom on the third floor of the Schuyler town house on Sixty-third Street to attend a proper girls' academy.

Her mother had expected her to matriculate at Miss Porter's School, where she herself had learned her copperplate handwriting, her English literature, her ladylike arts, her code of disciplined female conformity, but Violet had studied the course schedule with horror. She had already taught herself the essentials of algebra, startling the family governess, and had read most of the works listed on the curriculum. What she wanted was Latin and Greek, like her brothers, and advanced mathematics. And chemistry, and naturally German. So many of the great scientists were German these days.

But rebellion never did arise easily in Violet. Smiles came her way when she was obedient and good; frowns and disapproval and exclusion came when she was not. For nights she wept in her bed, locked in struggle with herself. She must be bad, thoroughly bad, for wanting these things, and yet when she considered the misery of imprisonment in Miss Porter's School, pretending to be like all the other girls, while her brothers sent careless letters home from Saint Paul's describing this athletic triumph or that eminent instructor, she wanted to scream into her pillow. She did scream into her pillow.

A week before Violet's departure for Farmingham, after Mrs. Schuyler and the housekeeper had already begun to count her linens and line her shiny new trunk with lavender-scented paper, Violet had walked into her father's study and told him that she wanted to attend the Haddam Young Women's Academy instead, a new school where young ladies were subject to a rigorous academic schedule in preparation for college, and where the chemistry laboratory in particular was as well-equipped as that at Saint Paul's.

She would never forget the way her father's warm smile of welcome had cooled and frozen, the way her ribs had ached at the sight of his hard eyes. But Violet had made her decision, she had crossed her Rubicon, and the pain of standing her ground before her father's disapproval was now nothing to the pain of going back across the river to strand herself in the desolation of her old life. So she stood her ground, she went to Haddam, but though the ache had faded it had never really gone away; it settled for years around her lungs and heart like a dark hole that could not be filled.

This was the consequence of rebellion, the price that must be paid for crossing the invisible line.

As Violet lies wobbly against Lionel's chest in the rose-scented summer evening, she can't decide what terrifies her so: the act of betraying Walter, or the unknown territory that lies beyond.

Or perhaps, she thinks, listening to Lionel's reassuring heart beat into her ear through the stiffness of his shirtfront, this is not terror but anticipation.

"*Shh,*" he says again, and his fingers rise from her neck into the tiny strands of hair that have escaped from the careful knot at her nape. The action is soothing, a gesture not of sexual suggestion but of reassurance, of acceptance, and Violet closes her eyes, which are useless anyway in the darkness. Lionel's body seeps warmth into hers, filling the void around her heart and lungs, and the shock under her skin smooths away into quietude.

He speaks into her hair. "Violet. Is it really you?"

"Yes."

"*My* Violet."

From any other man, those words would sound possessive, but in Lionel's voice they lack the necessary dominion. He is neither stern nor fierce. He's stating a fact, that Violet and Lionel are one, that they have been held together by invisible sutures since he walked into her laboratory room and sat sharing her burden in the darkness; or perhaps even before, in some unseen laboratory of fate. He might as well say *Your Lionel*. His other arm wraps around her waist, fastening her against him. She can't escape now, even if she wanted to.

"Isn't it a joke," he says. "The greatest damned joke in the world. Why *you*, Violet? Of all women. I don't understand it."

"It had to be someone."

"No. It could only be you."

Violet's blood is stirring now, propelled by the solid promise of Lionel's body against hers, by the precious architecture of his bone and sinew beneath her arms and cheek and breast. Beneath the smooth black wool of his formal tailcoat, beneath his white shirtfront and sharp bowtie, lies Lionel. She listens to his heart beating, the proof of him, and tilts her face upward.

"You'll kill me," he whispers, but he kisses her anyway, less gently than before, cupping the curve of her skull with his hand. He leans back against the trellis, bringing her with him, mindless of thorns, still kissing her, and Violet is gone, gone. Above them, dislodged by the weight of Lionel's body, a ripened rose scatters its petals into her hair.

"Let's go," she says, between damp kisses. "Let's go tonight. We'll go back to Berlin in your motor."

Lionel lifts his mouth away. "Go?"

"Yes, go. How can I stay, after this?"

Lionel is still, except for the heavy rise and fall of his chest. "Tonight," he says at last.

"Yes, tonight. I can't sleep another night next to him, not now."

"I thought he slept with Jane."

Violet's face grows warm. "No, he . . . he usually comes in around midnight."

Lionel doesn't move, but Violet can feel the hardening of his limbs around hers. "I see."

"It isn't like that. He hasn't touched me, Lionel. Not since Berlin. He's in love with her."

"Christ."

"That's what I meant. Let's go tonight, there's nothing to stop us, you have your motor. I'll pack a few things, I'll leave a note." She presses her mouth into his, mad urgent kisses. "Let's go."

"Violet." His hands close around her upper arms. He sets her back. "Wait. I can't, not tonight. I've got . . . There's a matter or two."

"I don't understand."

He pushes her away and takes a few long strides down the arbor.

"What do you mean, Lionel?" Her voice is rising in pitch; she pushes it down. "How can we stay? How can you make love to me and then send me back to *his* room, to *his* bed—"

"I haven't made love to you, have I? We've kissed, that's all."

That's all. The warm evening air ripples around Violet's ears. She feels as if she's falling, except that the beaten path remains solid beneath her feet, the roses hang motionless next to her cheek. She longs to reach out and grasp the wooden slats of the trellis. Instead she says, coldly: "I see. Then I suppose I should thank you for your time and wish you a pleasant evening."

"Violet."

She smoothes the floating chiffon layers of her dress. "It's good of you, of course, to be strong for the both of us—"

"Stop it, Violet." He turns. "I'm thinking, that's all. I wasn't expecting this, not tonight. I've got to think."

"Think, by all means."

He steps back and pulls her against him. "Violet, for God's sake. It isn't as simple as you imagine. You're talking about leaving your husband, you're talking about . . . What, exactly? Leaving your place at the institute? What will you do?"

"I'll find a place elsewhere. I'll find something. The point is to leave. The point is to get away from him."

"And me?"

"You can do what you like," she says defiantly.

He breathes into her hair, her forehead. "No, I can't. Where you go, I'll follow, I've got no choice anymore. But for God's sake, Violet . . ."

Violet's chest begins to move again, to take the heavy air back into her lungs. "I'll find something for us. I'll ask Planck and Einstein to write letters for me. I know they will. We can go to England—"

"For God's sake, not tonight." He kisses her forehead. "Please. Not tonight. Give me that, won't you? A day or two, that's all."

"Why?"

"A day or two, that's all."

"Is it . . . is it all this . . . Austria and Serbia . . ." She tries again to picture the map of Europe, the tangled and meandering borders, the crosshatch railways, the red lines of disputed frontiers. This murdered Archduke: what was his name? What right had he to determine her life, the lives of millions? Surely it would come to nothing. She whispers: "Do you have to report to your regiment?"

"*Shh.* Go back to the house now, Violet. Wait for me. Trust me, do you hear?" His hand finds hers and squeezes her fingers. "Look at me."

"I can hardly see you."

"Do you trust me, Violet?"

"Yes, I trust you."

"Good." Another squeeze, a long kiss, and he releases her hand. "Go back to the house. Be ready for me, do you hear?"

"Yes." Her fingers find his cheeks, his strong neck, his shoulders scattered with petals.

"And Violet?"

"Yes."

He seizes her close and whispers in her ear. "Don't let him touch you."

"No, never. Never again."

"Good. If he touches you now, by God, I'll kill him."

WHEN VIOLET arrives in the room she shares with Walter, she's relieved to find it empty. She looks in the mirror at her flushed face, the scarlet petals in her hair. She plucks them out, one by one. As she confessed to Lionel, she keeps no diary; instead she tucks the petals into a folded sheet of stationery and places them in her drawer, among her underthings.

Violet takes off her clothes and returns to the enormous cheval glass in the bedroom. She now looks no different than before. Her face has composed itself, her skin is even, her lips innocently pink. Only her breasts give her away, puckered like raisins at the tips, despite the turgid warmth of the bedroom air.

A door slams distantly, making her start. She washes her face and teeth; she changes into a long and shapeless nightgown and crawls into bed, to the furthest possible corner, and switches off the lamp. Her last thought is that she's too giddy to close her eyes, too elated for sleep.

She wakes when Walter enters, some untold time later, not because of the sound of his entrance but because of the impatient energy that bursts into the room with him. He strides about, silent and coiled, bathing and changing in a thick cloud of brandy. When he enters the bed, he reaches for her, for the first time since leaving Berlin, even though her back is turned and her body is quite still.

Violet's skin shrivels away from his touch, but she doesn't move. She imagines herself a stone, though her heart thuds beneath Walter's searching hand.

"Violet." His voice falls downward on the last syllable, like a warning. He turns her on her stomach.

"Stop it, Walter," she mutters.

His fingers scrape against her legs, lifting her nightgown.

"No," she says, more clearly, pushing against him, thrashing to lift herself, but his body lies like a rope atop hers, forcing her chest and face into the pillows.

His hands grip her legs. He's too strong, there's no fighting him, her limbs can find no purchase in the soft mattress. He hisses in her ear: "Lie still, child."

"Walter, I'm . . . I'm poorly," she gasps. "My poorliness."

His body suspends above her.

"It . . . it started this evening, just after dinner." Violet lies clenched, dragging for air, praying Walter does not put his hand between her legs to demand the nonexistent proof. She can feel him panting atop her, smell the brandy as it seeps from his mouth. Is he counting up the weeks? Does he remember? Is he too drunk? Does he notice the rhythm of her female calendar at all anymore?

Walter swears in her ear and falls away.

Violet lies limp, unable even to shake. When Walter's pants subside into regularity, she curls herself into a slow ball at the edge of the bed and stares at the wall with eyes that will not close.

Vivian

B y the time I'd finished shopping with Gogo and dragged myself up the sour-smelling stairs to my apartment, I was sober enough to study the *Metropolitan* files at length. What I didn't have was time. I had to dress and head back uptown to the Lightfoot mansion on Seventieth and Park.

I tried calling Aunt Julie, but there was no answer. I called Cousin Lily instead.

"You've been holding out on me," I said.

"I have not. Is this about Violet?"

Tap tap tap went my suspicious finger. Sniff sniff sniff went my . . . well, you know about my nose. "Ha! You *are* holding out. Otherwise those two sentences would have gone in reverse order."

"Vivian, why would I hold out on you? I'm on your side." So guileless.

"Because it has to do with your own mother."

"Trust me, Vivian. In the annals of my mother's crimes, this is nothing."

"Alrighty, then. Why did one Christina Schuyler Dane write to one S. Barnard Lightfoot, Junior, in the fall of 1914 and ask him to purge any mention of Violet Grant in the magazine's records?"

An extensive pause. "That, I don't know. Did he?"

"Not exactly. It all just went under lock and key. But what were *you* thinking about?" In the background behind her, I heard a faint drawn-out *Maa-maa* from Baby Number Five. (No longer a baby, I need hardly add, but a somewhat imperious young lady on the verge of adolescence.) In the foreground, there was hemming and hawing.

"Lily," I said darkly.

"I might have another letter for you."

"Might? Or have?"

Maa-maa! Like a singsong goat. Closer now. Would Doctor Paul want five children? I hoped not. On the other hand, he'd look as adorable as Nick Greenwald did, holding the little cherubs against his shoulder.

"In a moment, honey. *Have* a letter. You see, you finally got me looking through Mother's old letters, which, being Mother, she kept strictly organized by sender. I thought you had all of them, and then . . . well, I don't know if she misfiled it on purpose or by accident. Probably on purpose, knowing her."

"And?"

"*Weellll.*" The word stretched doubtfully. "I think you'd better see for yourself."

"You read it?"

"Of course I *read* it, Vivian. I do have *some* curiosity left. Can I bring it by your office tomorrow?"

"Better yet. I'm heading uptown in half an hour. I'll stop by your apartment on the way."

"That's perfect. Vivian?"

I was already standing, telephone cord stretched to the limit. The cells of my skin were fairly popping with eagerness. "What, Cousin Lily?"

"You might want to read those lock-and-key files, if you haven't already."

· · ·

WELL, of course I read them. You don't think I'd let a little thing like lipstick get in the way of my curiosity, do you? I read in front of the mirror, I read as I was fastening my stockings, I read as I was pulling the fat curlers from my hair and fluffing everything in place. I read mostly about the breathless diplomatic maneuvering into war, about the hourly frissons of schadenfreude as the American correspondent watched Europe teeter above the chasm. And then, on July 30, sandwiched between Russian mobilization and frantic British attempts to intercede:

> *In response to your cable about the Grant affair, I haven't the foggiest, that is to say, it's pretty clear what happened but they'll never be able to catch the perpetrators or prove anything at all. They say all the scientists are mute about it. Einstein himself was with them in Wittenberg a week ago, and won't say a thing. Clearly the wife has run off with the lover, but they're being protected somehow, no one will let slip an unofficial word about it, let alone an official one, there's hardly anything in the papers with all the war talk. It's the quietest scandal I ever heard, which means it must be something very delicious indeed, especially since our old friend the Comtesse de S.H. is an interested party, by which I mean she was intimate with Dr. Grant and making no attempt to disguise the affair. I would ask her about it, but she's left town as well. Soon I shall be utterly on my own, with only Germans to speak to, and they're all war and no play at the moment.*

I glanced at the clock. Half an hour until I was expected uptown, and I still had to retrieve Violet's letter from Lily.

I put the letter back in its folder, and it occurred to me, as I retrieved my coat and hat and pocketbook from the careless dump by the entry, that it might be a good thing I had a strong stomach.

. . .

THE STOMACH in question wasn't holding up well as I traveled from the Greenwalds' elegant ten-room apartment in Gramercy Park to the Light-foot mansion on East Seventieth Street, but it wasn't the fault of Aunt Violet's letter to her sister. Fate had given me the lurchiest of lurchy cab drivers, a hunched-over monosyllabic stick of a man who evidently thought I was auditioning him for the Daytona 500.

I, of all people, should have know better. Never, ever climb into a New York City taxi and tell the cabbie to step on it.

Well, I was late! I hadn't counted on Five-O wanting to tell me all about the fifth-grade Thanksgiving feast at Nightingale-Bamford (for the record, she had been an Indian), or on Nick Junior turning up at a quarter to seven and scolding me for my performance at the Schuyler drinkies a month ago: *They're still wiping the lipstick off my cheek, Vivs. Six of them asked for your number! I'm never living it down.*

So by the time Lily had shooed everyone off and called down for the doorman to find me a taxi, I had only five minutes to travel fifty city blocks on a Thursday evening. So: *Step on it,* I told the driver, and the next instant I found myself pinned to the seat by the gravitational force of the resulting acceleration, clutching my pocketbook to my stomach like a life belt on the *Titanic.* By the time we reached Thirty-fourth Street, we'd driven up on the sidewalk twice and possibly taken out a parking meter.

It wasn't until a red light forced us to a growling stop near Grand Central Terminal that I could unclench my hand from the door handle and open up Violet's letter. (What? Me, wait until I got home? You know better.) By now I was accustomed to her handwriting; I knew it like my own. I held the paper next to the window, where the glow of a streetlamp illuminated the words just enough, and read:

My dear Christina, I am leaving Walter . . .

Lurch went the taxi, and *thump* went Vivian against the seat. I righted myself and strained to hold the letter back up against the window, but the flashes of passing light weren't quite enough to reveal the page.

. . . leaving Walter . . .

What was the date? What was the date? I hadn't even checked. The date might make all the difference. If she'd left him first, and he'd come after her and threatened her—I knew Walter by now, I knew he had his pride, I knew he wasn't just going to let his wife depart his control without a fight—and then the murder had taken place. Or if she'd murdered him and left him, all in the same bold stroke.

And where was Lionel Richardson in all this? *Who* was Lionel Richardson?

On we raced, up Park Avenue, into a ribbon of green lights. The engine was cranking now, grinding out speed in a triumphant roar. We hit a bump, and the wheels left the pavement for a weightless instant. My stomach remained suspended for considerably longer. I was going to die, and Violet's letter with me.

I peeked over the top of the seat and saw the light turn red. The engine screamed, the taxi leapt ahead, and before I could ask God for mercy on my sin-scorched soul, we whipped around the corner of Seventieth Street and banged to a stop in front of the cool limestone face of the Lightfoot mansion.

I climbed out the door and onto the sidewalk. I maybe might have been a teensy bit shaky. Violet's letter was clenched in my hand, my pocketbook tucked under my arm. I opened it and found a few crisp dollar bills somewhere inside. I looked at my watch, and saw it was seven-oh-three. If I'd climbed into a helicopter at Gramercy Park, we couldn't have made it any faster.

I shoved the dollar bills through the window. "Thanks for the thrill, buddy. You might want to check those tires."

I rang the Lightfoot doorbell. Just as the butler arrived—yes, the Lightfoots had goddamned Jeeves answering the door—I remembered Violet's letter.

"Good evening, Miss Schuyler," said Jeeves. (No, I didn't know his real name.)

"Just a moment, please." I straightened out the paper in my hands. There was no date at the top. I hunted back in my pocketbook and found the envelope.

Jeeves cleared his tactful throat. "They're expecting you in the drawing room, Miss Schuyler."

"One moment." I found the postmark and stepped into the radiant entry hall. Berlin, it said. 25 JULI 1914. So had Violet written the letter on July 25, or had she written it earlier and only posted it on the twenty-fifth?

Jeeves was handing me skillfully out of my coat. "The drawing room, Miss Schuyler," he said, with a little more vim. "Up the stairs and to the left."

"Yes, I know. Thank you." I folded the paper back into the envelope and stuffed it into my pocketbook. The hall smelled of orchids. As I raced up the curving stairs to the drawing room, a new and entirely different thought reared its curious head among my snapping synapses.

That hat on the hat stand. Where had I seen it before?

I reached the top of the stairs and turned left, and just as I passed through the open doorway into the monumental Lightfoot drawing room, my snapping synapses shot back an answer.

But by that time the owner of the hat was already standing white-faced before me, with his hand surrounding that of the gleaming Gogo. And lo! S. Barnard Lightfoot himself, fully recovered from the afternoon's festivities in the *Metropolitan* conference room, was rising from his armchair and holding out his triumphant hand to me while his polished face smiled and smiled.

"Why, there you are, Miss Schuyler," he said. "You're just in time to raise a glass to the happy couple."

Violet

At breakfast, there's no sign of Lionel Richardson. The coffee is brought in, the sweet rolls and fruit, Walter's very English eggs and kidneys, and at every swing of the door behind her, Violet clenches the muscles of her abdomen and stops her head from turning.

"Lionel?" Jane covers a yawn with her long-fingered hand. "I saw him go off in his motor last night, just before I went to bed."

"What a shame," says Lise Meitner. "I had wanted to share some good results with him."

Violet speaks in German. "What sort of results?"

"He and I had the most interesting discussion about alpha radiation before you left Berlin." Lise leans forward over her plate. The coffee steams untouched by her elbow. "The problem of the heterogeneous patterns. Herr Hahn and I have managed to isolate a very pure sample of thorium that . . ."

Jane clinks her fork against her plate. "No secrets!"

"There's no secret, Mama," says Henry. "They're only speaking about work."

Violet says, "I'm sorry, Jane. It's just easier in German, that's all."

"*Hmm.*" Jane's gaze meets hers. Her eyes are bright and well-rested, her skin petal-of-rose, making Violet conscious of her own hollow strain, the listless knot with which she bound her hair this morning, before Walter had stirred. How she covered her alien limbs in an old dress and went outside, hoping to meet with fresh air and perhaps Lionel, but the morning air was already sticky and Lionel had not appeared.

Jane takes in the history of Violet's morning with her purple-bright eyes. She lifts her eyebrows and looks around the rest of the table. At the other end, Walter mutely sips his tea, shielded by a week-old English newspaper. Herr Einstein sits between the Hahns, drinking milky coffee and eating black bread, mournful and preoccupied, his dark pomaded hair absorbing the morning light.

Jane steeples her fingers and says, "I have a terrific idea. Let's go on a picnic."

"MOTHER LOVES PICNICS," says Henry Mortimer, in an apologetic tone, and as Violet finishes her fourth deviled egg, washed down with ice-cold champagne, she's hardly in a position to disagree. She hasn't begun to plumb the depth of cured meats and pickled vegetables, delicate sandwiches and exotic fruits, fragrant cheeses and chiffon desserts laid out upon the picnic cloth before her.

Picnic cloth. In fact, there are three picnic cloths, spread beneath the lindens on the hillside to accommodate them all without crowding. Violet reclines her long legs along the side of one; Henry sits to her right and Lise Meitner to her left. They've been discussing thorium, and possible explanations for why the measurements of alpha radiation in Lise and Otto's latest experiments continue stubbornly to present themselves in a heterogeneous pattern, when everyone knows—everyone has *accepted*, anyway; certainty isn't a commodity in which the chemists of the Kaiser Wilhelm Institut regularly trade—that each radioactive isotope emits particles with its own precise signature. Henry's remark comes *a propos* of nothing, during a pause in the discussion; Violet's brain, which she has concentrated fiercely on the subject of thorium radiation, has begun to wander, and Lise has slipped into a familiar meditative trance.

"It was a good idea, this picnic," Violet says. Both she and Henry speak in German, in courtesy to Lise, whose English is good but not quite fluent. "I'm glad we have someone here capable of organizing these things so well. I'm hopeless."

"The perfect day for it." Lise shakes off her reverie and stretches her arms high above her head. The sun, finding the holes between the leaves, strikes her dark hair in tiny dapples. "I find it's always useful to think outside the laboratory from time to time. There's nothing like fresh air when one has an intractable problem."

Violet glances at Lise. She's gazing into the distance, her feet with their sensible half boots crossed at the ankles, her skirt draped correctly over her legs. A ladylike woman, Lise Meitner, raised in an orderly intellectual household in Vienna. Has she ever been in love? Working all day in her laboratory with Herr Hahn: did she ever wish for something more than professional friendship between them? If she did, it's too late now. Otto and his wife sit side by side on the second picnic cloth, his head bent solicitously next to her smiling face, perhaps sharing a joke, perhaps asking her what picnic delicacy he can select for her. Herr Einstein reclines on his back next to them with his hands knit across his stomach, staring through the leaves at the hazy sky.

"If you don't mind," Lise says, "I think I'll go for a walk. The countryside is so beautiful here."

"Not at all."

Lise stands and shakes the crumbs from her skirts. She is strong and fit and sturdy, silhouetted by the white July sun. She pins her hat atop her neat waves of hair and says gravely, "Herr Mortimer, would you care to accompany me? Perhaps you help tease me out of this dilemma of mine."

Henry's eyes widen into moons, as if he's found a ten-mark note in some forgotten pocket. He scrambles to his feet. "I'd be delighted."

Violet leans back on her elbows and watches Lise and Henry stride out of the shade and into the heavy sunshine. At her back, she feels the presence of the third picnic cloth, occupied by Walter and Jane in a tête-à-tête even more tangibly intimate than that of the Hahns.

She has worked perseveringly to banish the thought of Walter from her head. She hasn't looked in his direction all morning, not during the walk through the grass to Jane's chosen picnic spot, not during the un-loading of the baskets and the spreading of the cloths, not during the picnic itself. One or twice the sight of his uncovered gray head, his light summer suit, crossed her vision, and her belly went sick, her clear head felt dizzy. She hears him now, his voice lifting into laughter, and her throat clots with rage.

A hand falls on her shoulder. Violet leaps to her feet, spilling cham-pagne and deviled egg, but it's only the Comtesse de Saint-Honoré. Her beautiful face is lit by the sun, and her expression is serious. "Would you walk with me, Violet? We haven't had a nice chat in ever so long."

Not since Berlin.

"Of course." Violet finds her hat.

Even in the shelter of the trees, the air is hot; out in the full throb of sunshine, Violet's skin scorches under the thin and wilted linen of her dress. Her hair sticks unpleasantly to her neck and temples. Beside her, Jane's cool composure seems to exist in a separate season altogether.

Jane's arm loops through hers. She carries a parasol, as if they're walk-ing along some graveled path in the Tiergarten. "What heat! It reminds me of the summers back home."

"Really? You look as if it doesn't bother you at all."

"Well, I was born to it, I guess. Among other things. Tell me, Violet, how are you and Lionel getting along these days?"

Violet's throat closes. She makes a dismissive noise and tries to shrug.

"Oh, I don't mean to pry! You see, I have a little problem of my own at the moment, and its name is your husband."

"You seem to be getting along very well."

"Too well. I've held him off as best I can, but . . ." She shrugs. "Well, he isn't the kind of man who's used to hearing the word *no*, if you know what I mean, and I think you do."

"I don't understand. I thought you and he . . . I thought he . . ."

Jane turned a curious expression toward her. "What, that we were lovers? I wouldn't do that to you, Violet. He's still your husband, and I like you. I told you that, didn't I? I've done all I could to keep him going without it, for Henry's sake, but last night . . . Well, we had a bit of a struggle. Had to take some stern measures, if you follow me, and while I've managed to smooth his poor little feathers this morning . . ."

Violet speaks slowly. "Do you mean to say that all this time—"

"Why, Violet! I do believe I'm insulted. Did you think I'd go to bed with him under your roof? I do have my code, you know, rickety as it is."

Violet's mind has ceased grasping. Ahead of them, the grass stands motionless, golden-brown tips pointed to the pale sky. The air is full of it, the stifling smell of hot summer grass. *His poor little feathers,* Jane said, so dismissive, so careless. "Well, you don't need to bother. I mean, you're quite free to . . . to indulge him. I don't mind."

"Yes, that's what I was getting at, just now. Whether it would make things easier for everyone. But you see . . ." Jane gives her parasol a spin. "I've been thinking."

"Yes."

"You see, I brought Henry to Berlin to study with Dr. Walter Grant, but I don't believe he's the one. I think you are."

"Me?"

"Yes, you. You're doing all the work, the experiments, in that desperate little basement of yours in Berlin, in the laboratory you've set up here. Writing the articles. Don't think I don't notice. You're the one on the cutting edge, you and the others. You're the ones who give a damn about bringing in Henry. Walter, from what I can see, he's gotten old. He's given everything up, except to look in and criticize from time to time. He doesn't give a damn for anyone anymore, except himself. And frankly"—another swirl of the parasol, another squeeze of the arm—"I don't particularly like him. Not that I let that stand in my way, everything else being equal, but if there's no use in it, why give myself the bother?"

A pair of sparrows wings by, swooping unexpectedly close. Violet hears the flutter of feathers, the slight impact as a wingtip brushes the Comtesse de Saint-Honoré's white lace parasol.

"Or so I asked myself, last night," Jane adds softly.

"Jane," says Violet. "I have a favor to ask you."

NOT UNTIL after the lunch has been packed away does Violet find an opportunity to approach Herr Einstein. The Hahns have taken a walk with Jane and Walter; Lise and Henry have returned and fallen into an animated discussion, in which the squares of the picnic cloth serve as spaces on the periodic table; and Einstein sits alone under an apple tree, examining a blade of grass.

"Like Newton," Violet says, nodding at the tiny green apples above.

Einstein looks at her and smiles. "I am honored. Please sit, Frau Grant." He motions to the grass next to him.

"I'm not disturbing you, I hope."

"I only wish you were. I seem unable to concentrate today."

Violet kneels into the grass. "I'm sorry to hear that. Did you sleep well?"

"Not badly." He grasps the blade between the thumb and forefinger of each hand and splits it delicately apart. "To be perfectly honest, Frau Grant, I am concerned about you."

"Me."

"You are unhappy."

Violet does not reply.

"I'm sorry. Am I too familiar?" he asks.

"No. I'm grateful for your concern."

"And is it misplaced?"

The white sun burns through the leaves of the apple tree from its zenith overhead. In a tiny channel between Violet's stays and her skin, just to the right of her spine, a drop of perspiration trickles downward to disappear into the waistband of her drawers. The air is laden with ripe grass and fruit, toasting quietly in the still summer heat.

"I don't know how to answer that," she says.

Einstein continues to shred his blade of grass into fibers of minute width. "I have been thinking about the question you posed me, several weeks ago, just before one of Herr Planck's little gatherings. Do you remember it?"

"I do."

"You have an insightful imagination, Frau Grant. I took the liberty of looking into your latest article for the *Journal*. What a tedious task you have set yourself, and yet you cut no corners. Your observations were extensive, and your conclusions thorough."

"I think it's fair to say, Herr Einstein, that the task is not one I've set for myself. I have another line of inquiry I've been pursuing . . ." Violet catches her breath. In the distance, she can see Walter and Jane and the Hahns walking against a golden-green hillside. The Hahns have stepped ahead, and Jane's arm is linked with Walter's beneath the shelter of her parasol. Violet can't distinguish any details, but she recognizes Walter's elastic stride, his confident movement, his body like a whip.

"Yes, Frau Grant?" His gentle eyes are upon her face. "What sort of inquiry?"

She looks at him. "I want to break apart the atomic nucleus and see what's inside."

"Ah. Like your countryman Rutherford."

"Not my countryman. I'm American, you remember."

"But your husband is English." Though he's speaking in German, he says the word *English* in its native pronunciation, with great precision.

"I am not my husband."

"*Hmm.* Yes." He opens his palm and lets the fibers of grass drift to the hot carpet beneath their legs. A bottle of sweating lemonade sits next to his knee; he lifts and drinks. "Frau Grant, I would not have accepted your invitation to stay here this week, without the hope to find a private moment with you."

"Yes?"

Herr Einstein is watching the progress of the walkers against the hill. A rare breath of wind stirs the wild hair at the back of his head. "I want to make clear, Frau Grant, absolutely clear, that I stand ready to write a letter of recommendation on your behalf, should you find yourself in need of one."

Violet blinks her eyes and looks down at her ringless hands, spread wide across the limp fabric of her linen dress. Her underarms are prickling, her heart beats relief into her chest.

"Frau Grant?"

She looks up and smiles into his somber face. "Herr Einstein, forgive me, but that is exactly why I asked you to stay."

WAIT FOR ME, Lionel said, *trust me,* but Violet knows she can't sleep another night in the villa. The afternoon deepens, and still no automobile growls up the long drive from the road. She must act for herself.

She enters the warm acid-scented quiet of the laboratory and packs her notes; the apparatuses and materials she must leave behind. As she leaves, she stands at the door and casts her gaze about: the clean surfaces, the singular motes of circling dust. In the center of the room sits the black box with its scintillation screen, its aperture, its chamber lined with lead.

VIOLET BATHES and dresses for dinner. No sign yet of Lionel; he has disappeared into the thick Prussian summer. Through the plaster walls comes the clatter of pots and china, the distinct high laugh of the down-stairs maid.

Walter arrives as she's sitting in the slipper chair, buckling her shoes. He's still dressed in his summer linen suit, wrinkled from heat. "How are you feeling?" he asks, unbuttoning his jacket.

She straightens and says coldly: "Well enough."

"Excellent." He smiles, a slow and straight-edged smile in the middle of his neat beard. "I say, I was rather surprised when I happened to see the linens this morning."

"*Happened* to see the linens."

"You lied to me."

"I had to tell you something, didn't I? You weren't going to stop otherwise."

"You shouldn't have provoked me."

"I don't recall provoking you."

"*Hmm.*" He walks across the room, removing his cuff links as he goes, and drops them into the silver tray on his chest of drawers. "You do have an astonishingly handsome figure, child. I believe your bosom is a degree or two fuller than when I first met you in Oxford. More womanly. Don't you think?"

"I was only nineteen then. I suppose it's possible."

He removes his jacket and waistcoat and hangs them in the wardrobe. "No, I'm quite certain. I can picture you clearly, lying on my sofa like a newly opened peach. Those months afterward. Do you remember them?"

"Yes, of course."

"I took excellent care of you, do you agree?"

"You were attentive, if that's what you mean." Violet folds her hands behind her back, so Walter can't see how her hands are shaking.

"Of course I was. My God, what a fresh young child you were. En-trancing. To take a girl for the first time, it's the greatest joy a man knows. And you were as innocent as a newborn. I could think of nothing else."

Trousers, shirt, drawers. Violet stands by the wall with her hands pinned to her back, watching her husband undress, willing herself not to look at her own wardrobe, in which her battered leather valise sits, packed and ready.

"Yes, I was very young, wasn't I?" she says clearly.

He is naked and monstrously erect. He walks back to the chest of drawers and finds his pipe and his tin of tobacco. "Do you have anything to tell me, Violet?"

Violet curves her fingernails into her palms. But her face is cool and without shame as she replies: "I kissed him."

Walter, unhurried, strikes a match and lights his pipe. He turns and leans one elbow atop the bureau, sucking carefully to start the flow of smoke into his lungs, one loving hand cupping the bowl. His gray hair, ordinarily in perfect order, has come disheveled, and the electric light casts his lean body into a relief so stark as to be emaciated. He blows out a long cloud of smoke and smiles. "Is that all?"

"It was a lovely kiss. A tremendous kiss."

"I hope you're not hiding something from me, Violet."

Violet rises from the chair, walks to the dressing table, and picks up the little pot of lip rouge she owns but rarely uses. "If there's one thing I cannot abide about you, Walter, it's your hypocrisy."

"*My* hypocrisy. And what do you think of a wife, Violet, who fucks another man and then refuses concourse to her own husband? Her husband who's done everything for her."

"I'd say she was in love, for the first time in her life."

Walter's image appears suddenly in the mirror, like an apparition, eyes narrowed and blazing. His hands close about her arms. The pipe nearly burns her skin. "You are an ungrateful idiot," he says, between his teeth.

"Go away, Walter."

"Do you think Richardson will stand by you? Do you think he loves you?"

"I know he loves me."

"Do you know how many women he had in Oxford?"

Violet's teeth cut into her lower lip. "Not as many as you, I'm sure."

"He's already left, you know. Packed his bags and left. Since he had what he wanted."

Violet's cup of rage runs over. In a swift jolt, she breaks one arm free of Walter's enclosing hand and jams her elbow into his ribs.

He grunts and falls back. The pipe drops to the floor. Violet flies to the bathroom, where Walter's things have been laid out already by the maid: soap, brush, towel, scissors, the razor he uses to create the crisp borders of his beard. She grasps the straightedge, flicks out the blade, and whirls around just as Walter invades the doorway.

He halts respectfully at the sight of the razor. "Violet, really. Don't be melodramatic."

"I will if I have to."

"I'm your husband, Violet. I have your interests at heart. Richardson is a scoundrel."

He stands before her, wiry and watchful, smiling and aroused, muscles flexing gently. There is a curious light in his eyes, a primal excitement.

What a fool she was. What a fool, to think that Lionel was the predator of which she must beware. She has never felt more hunted than this moment.

Walter takes a step toward her. "Put down the razor, Violet. Don't be ridiculous. Would I ever hurt you?"

"You tried, last night."

"Because you refused me. After all I've done for you, Violet."

"Am I not allowed a choice? I thought we had a *partnership*. A marriage of equal minds."

Walter's fingers twitch. "You can't lie with Richardson in the grass like a whore, and deny your own husband in his bed. That is a fact, Violet, the bedrock of our agreement. Did I ever neglect you, whatever my other adventures?"

"I see. Then it's all right if I take lovers, as long as I let you have me, too? Perhaps we should all get in bed together. Wouldn't that be daring and modern!" The metal razor warms in her hand, light and agile. She wonders why Walter doesn't simply turn around and leave her alone.

"Violet, my dear. You're being ridiculous. Put down the razor."

"You cannot touch me, Walter. Never again."

"Trust me, child. Put down the razor. You're overwrought."

"I am not—"

But Walter strikes in a flash, knocking the razor from her hand. He pins her hands neatly behind her back and forces her from the bathroom. She struggles against him, but his hold on her is expert, perfectly placed to lever her across the bedroom, as if he's done this sort of thing before. He turns her over the bed and places his knuckles in the small of her back, atop her kidneys. He smells of sweat.

"You're a brute." She locks her legs together, but he inserts his knee exactly in the center of her thighs and forces her open.

"You do not *refuse* me, Violet." Walter's breath invades her ear, and she braces herself, shuts her eyes and mouth, shuts down every sensation and thought in her body so she will live through the next two minutes.

Because of this, because she's concentrating so hard on severing her mind from the workings of Walter's brusque hands, she doesn't hear the knock on the door, the rattle of the locked knob. She hardly notices the crash of wood as a booted foot forces it open.

Then Walter is gone: his hands, his heavy body, his sweaty breath. Shouts, thumps. A hard grunt. With effort, Violet pushes herself up and turns around, bracing herself on the mattress.

Walter lies on the floor. Lionel stands above him, rumpled and unshaven, rubbing his fist. "Christ, Violet." He turns and pulls her against him. He is as thick as a pillar, as solid as a tree. "I'm sorry, Christ, I'm sorry, I'm sorry. Did he hurt you?"

"Not . . . not yet."

"I'm sorry. Christ. What an idiot. I'm sorry."

"Is he dead? Is he dead?" Violet shoves her nose into his scratchy tweeds, full of outdoors and automobiles and Lionel. Her nerves jump, her head spins.

"Dead? No, damn him. If I'd had my revolver he would be."

She pushes away and stumbles over Walter's body to the wardrobe. "Is your motor outside?"

"Yes, but—"

"Take me to Berlin."

"Violet, wait—"

"Now, Lionel. Before he wakes up." She finds the valise and yanks it out from behind her dresses with a spring of her electric muscles. Her brain is a blur, coalesced around a single overriding thought: flight. "For God's sake."

"We can't just leave . . ."

She drags the valise across the floor and drops it at Lionel's feet and takes his jacket into her fists. She stares up at him to communicate the desperation in her babble of words. "We can. We can. We can. Jane will take care of everything. Take me to Berlin, Lionel. Now. We can. We can."

Lionel's hands find her elbows. His brow is worried, his cheekbones pink with a sunburn that disappears under the new prickles of his beard. The skin around his eyes is heavy with exhaustion.

He looks down at Walter and back at Violet. She wants to touch his face, but her fingers have stiffened around Lionel's lapels, the only way she can hold herself still, and she doesn't dare open them.

Lionel releases her elbows and pries her hands from his jacket. He keeps one firmly in his palm and reaches down for her valise.

"Right, then. Berlin."

Vivian

Anyway. I'm not going to bore you with a long and self-indulgent description of the scene that followed, there in the orchid-scented Lightfoot mansion that fine November evening, a week before Thanksgiving. I'm sure you can imagine it for yourself. To be honest, I don't even remember most of the details.

Not that I dragged myself through dinner in a trance. No siree. No no no. Not Vivian Schuyler. I was the life of the damned party. You should have seen me! You'd have been so proud. The way I kissed Gogo's cheek and hailed Doctor Paul with a vigorous congratulatory handshake; the way I exclaimed over the height and breadth and brilliance of the engagement rock that perched precariously atop Gogo's slender finger. The way I turned to Lightfoot and began to flirt as I'd never flirted before. Nothing vulgar, mind you. Just the *nulli secundus* of elegant flattery, the ne plus ultra of sparkling admiration. I knew how to pirouette along that slender line without losing my balance.

I'd learned it from a master, after all. I out-Mumsied Mums herself at dinner tonight.

Oh, and what a dinner! Lightfoot had pulled out all the stops for his treasured daughter. The crispiest champagne, the meltiest foie gras. Tournedos in perfect meaty circles, served with a dollop of creamy

Béarnaise. I don't remember the trimmings. I think there was a salad. Waldorf. A fine Bordeaux, really top-drawer. As I ate, I watched the sparkle of Gogo's finger while it went about its business. (I couldn't meet her face, not yet.) Knowing Doctor Paul's salary as I did, I imagined Lightfoot had selected Gogo's engagement ring with the same consummate deliberation as he had selected the fiancé himself, and I wondered whether the cost had been subtracted from the half-million-dollar engagement bounty. Whether the money had changed hands yet, or whether Doctor Paul would have to wait for his cold hard cash until the announcement actually appeared in the *New York Times*.

Oh. Doctor Paul! You're probably wondering about him. Well, he didn't say much. His face never quite regained its color, though he ate heartily enough for three fiancés. I watched his strong throat move as he drank his champagne (I couldn't quite meet his gaze, either) and his capable surgeon's hands as he dissected his filet. A splendid animal, Doctor Paul. A prime specimen to fertilize the Lightfoot breeding stock. Worth every penny.

Well, that was lovely, I said, after the last graceful bite of *bombe glacée*, but I really must head home. Work tomorrow, you know! Bright and early!

The gentlemen rose. I felt Doctor Paul's pleading eyes like an attractor beam from an enemy starship. But I slid right over his gaze, skated right past his desperate ocular apology with a laugh and a *Now, you two behave yourselves tonight, you crazy kids, you're not married yet!* I kissed Gogo again and told her she'd better make me her maid of honor, or else.

Then. *May I kiss the groom?* I daringly asked, and Gogo laughed and said you'd better do it quick, before I get started, I might never want to stop, just look at him! Laugh laugh. Oh, how we laughed.

I leaned in and laid one on Doctor Paul's terrified cheek, a big fat see-if-I-care to Mr. S. Barnard Lightfoot III. And then I . . .

Well, damn. Here I am, going on like this, after I promised not to indulge myself.

Anyway. Et cetera, et cetera. Good-bye, good-bye. You get the idea. The Lightfoot door slammed behind me, leaving me in the dark void between two pale streetlights, and I trudged down Seventieth Street to Lexington Avenue and two blocks to the subway entrance. I didn't want to take a taxi. I wanted the rattle of New York around me, I wanted stink and strangers and the sour dank air of the IRT clutching me to its bosom. I wanted hustle and bustle. I wanted to know that millions of lives were playing out on my doorstep, and not one of them gave a damn about my little problems.

I took the local train down to Union Square and trudged the beaten path west by southwest. The air had hardened, and a flake or two blurred past me to disappear into the rotten gray pavement. I thought, how magical, the first glimpse of snow. By March I would be sick of it, but here in this November instant those tiny flakes swirled with the unspeakable purity of a divine gift.

The storefronts were all closed and barricaded in metal. I passed fruit stands and bookstores, dry cleaners and travel agents. The snow was picking up, filling the air. I felt it ping the back of my throat as I breathed. I turned the corner of Bleecker and Christopher Street, where the crowd at the Apple Tree was just getting started. A man in a thick black overcoat stood against the lamppost just outside, smoking a cigarette, staring at the snow. I might have passed him right by, if the light from one of the windows hadn't fallen on his face just so.

I stopped. Took a few more steps. Stopped and turned.

"Didn't know you smoked, Mr. Tibbs," I said quietly.

He looked startled, and yet wearily not. As if he couldn't be bothered to feel any surprise at the sight of me. He took an awkward puff and blew it into the street. "I don't."

I glanced at the wide-open entrance to the Apple Tree, and back to Tibby. "Need a drink?"

He finished the cigarette and dropped it on the sidewalk, where he crushed it with his heel. "Sure do."

By the smell of him, as we walked the block or two to my apartment building, this wouldn't be his first drink of the evening. Possibly not his second, either, but who was I to judge? I unlocked the door and left him to follow me upstairs.

"Obviously we don't pay you enough," he said, when he walked through the door. He took in the disheveled living room, the half-dressed roommate asleep on the sofa, the half-full bottle of Smirnoff on the table.

I slung my coat and hat on the hall stand and stalked into the kitchen for glasses. "Make yourself at home."

When I turned to face him, mission accomplished, he had taken my advice and hung up his overcoat. He sat now in my usual chair, eyeing the vodka wistfully. A distant pink neon sign flashed like a heartbeat on his cheek. I took the opposite chair, set down the glasses, and poured the vodka. *"Salut,"* I said.

"Salut."

I finished first, but it was a close call. I opened my pocketbook and found my cigarettes. "Smoke? Or another drink?"

"Both."

I lit him up and then me, and I refilled the glasses. "I should warn you. In about an hour, a man's going to burst into this room and enact a melodrama. You're welcome to stay. But I thought I should give you the choice."

Tibby was right, he wasn't a smoker. Something in the unfamiliar way he held the cigarette between his forefinger and thumb, the tremor of trepidation as he lifted it to his mouth. He raised his glass with a relieved expression. A poison he recognized. "Do I know this man?"

"He's Gogo's brand-new fiancé. You heard it here first."

"I see."

"As I said." I tipped my vodka at him and polished it off with bees-wax. "Melodrama."

Tibby sat back in his chair. I pushed an ashtray at him. He let his half-finished cigarette drop gratefully inside. "How's the article going?"

"Jesus. I forgot." I opened my pocketbook and drew out Violet's letter, Violet's letter that had seemed so vital a few hours ago.

From the sofa, Sally made a startled noise and sat up. One breast fell out of her robe, and then—as an afterthought—the other. She belted herself back up without haste. "Who the hell is he?" she asked, wide awake.

Without lifting my head: "Sally, Mr. Edmund Tibbs, editor extraordinaire, takes his coffee black, with sugar. Tibby, Sally." I waved my hand.

She stood up. "Enchanted. I'm going to bed."

Tibby reached for the vodka bottle. "First thing tomorrow, I'm going to recommend you for a raise."

I looked up awestruck from my letter. "Tibby, this is *it*. I think this is *it*."

Tibby did the slow blink. "Is what?"

"Look at this." I handed over Violet's letter.

He pulled his reading glasses out of his waistcoat pocket and said aloud, in a voice that slurred only once or twice: "*My dear Christina, I am leaving Walter at last. I don't mean to surprise you, but there it is. He has always been selfish and unfaithful, but I could live with that; now he's turned brutal, and I have fallen in love with another man. Lionel Richardson. You remember I've written about him. We're off to Berlin tonight, as soon as we can slip away. I shall stop at the flat for a few things, but I hope never to see or speak to Walter again, unless the divorce process requires it. I have all the grounds in the world, or at least I will once I've reached the flat and find what I'm looking for. I hope you're not disappointed in me. I hope I may count on you to give evidence if necessary. I know I've made a dreadful mistake. I expect the family would disown me, if they hadn't already done so years ago. I shall write again when I can. Your loving sister, Violet. Postscript. All well. Terrible scene in Wittenberg. Have just reached Berlin with Lionel. Will post this immediately.*"

Tibby pulled off his glasses and looked at me. "There's no date."

"It's postmarked July twenty-sixth."

"Assuming she did as she said and posted the letter right away . . ."

"She never intended to murder her husband. He must have followed her and confronted her at the flat in Berlin, and then . . ." I shrugged.

The telephone let loose.

"Aren't you going to answer that?" asked Tibby.

"Why bother? It's just Gogo. I know what she's going to say. She wants to tell me how happy she is, how it's been a whirlwind the last week or two, he just called her up out of the blue and said he'd made a terrible, terrible mistake. She's been dying to tell me but he swore her to secrecy. For some reason. And now she wants to spill every detail. Proposal, ring, kiss, the works." I pulled out another cigarette.

The shrilling stopped. Tibby sat absolutely still, no mean feat for a man in his condition. I knew he was watching my profile. Me, I watched the ashtray. The smoke drifting from my fingers.

I could face Doctor Paul. Probably would face Doctor Paul in short order. But I could not face Gogo, even and especially the telephone Gogo, crackling her joy down the copper wire from the Lightfoot mansion to my sordid squalor.

"All right," said Tibby. "But then why did Violet flee? If she killed Walter in self-defense. She was a scientist. A rational thinker. She would have stayed to clear her name. She wouldn't have simply run off and disappeared." He held out the letter.

I laid the paper flat on the table. The old ink stared back at me, the hasty scribble of a woman in love. My eyes fastened on the words *Terrible scene*. What did that mean? "Because of the war?" I offered.

"She was an American. She wasn't in any danger."

I looked up. "But not Lionel. Lionel was English. An officer in the British Army."

A distant crash made the walls tremble. The front door.

"That was quick." I folded up Violet's letter and put it away in my pocketbook. I lifted my cigarette and gave Tibby an assessing look. He was already on his unsteady feet, putting on his overcoat.

"What's the rush?" I said. "Make yourself at home."

"I thought I might be a little *de trop*." He aimed for dry, but it came out all wet.

"Oh, you would be very much *de trop*. Deliciously, perfectly *de trop*. Do you mind taking off your shirt for me?"

"I do." A touch of huff.

"Well, the jacket and waistcoat, at least." I stood up and unbuttoned him. "We could loosen the tie a bit. Ruffle your hair."

Thump thump went the stairs. Those feet, they were not kidding around.

Asked Tibby: "He's not a large man, is he?"

"Well, he's not small. But I don't think he's violent. And even if he were, he's a doctor. Do no harm, you know the rest. He'd have an ethical obligation to put you back together again afterward."

Tibby released his necktie with a sigh and draped it over the sofa arm like a good sport.

"How immensely reassuring," he said, slurring each *s*.

Violet

They are flying down the road, while the sun sinks to the left in a pale hot sky. The air rushes against Violet's face. Lionel drives in silence, gripping the steering wheel with ungloved hands.

Violet stares straight ahead, through the dust and the insect smears to the empty road before them. She's still wearing her blue gossamer evening dress, and her hair is pinned up, pulling impatiently in the draft. She reaches up and removes the pins, one by one, and shakes her hair free.

"Good," says Lionel, "I love your hair," and without warning Violet's teeth begin to rattle, her chest heaves. She gasps for breath and clenches her fingers around the door frame, the cloth-covered edge of the seat, anything solid at all.

Lionel hits the brakes and swerves to the side. "Oh, damn. Oh, Christ." He hauls her against him, and she lets herself go, heaving and sobbing into his tweed jacket. "I'm sorry. I should have taken you with me. The bloody bastard. The dirty fucking bastard."

DUSK DROPS QUIETLY behind the surge of the engine. There's no moon yet, and Lionel switches on the headlamps. Violet's eyes grow heavy, her head lolls against the rumbling seat. Lionel's jacket covers her shoulders, smelling of him, soap, and wind and smoke.

WHEN VIOLET WAKES, the world is silent and tilted. She lifts her head. There is only a scrap of moon, just enough to see by. The motorcar rests on the shoulder of the road, sloping ever so slightly toward a field dotted with shapeless black cows. A shadow of trees looms a few yards away. Next to her, Lionel is fast asleep, his exhausted head tucked at an acute angle into the crevice between his seat and the door frame.

The night is still warm. Violet reaches for Lionel's shoulders and tugs gently. He resists, muttering something in his chest, and then gives way into her lap.

She strokes his hair and stares at the silver meadow. The cows are motionless; perhaps they're not cows at all, but stumps or bushes or bales of sun-ripened hay. Lionel's breath warms her lap. She loves his heavy weight, his hair like mink beneath her hand.

LIONEL JOLTS AWAKE an hour later, nearly falling off the seat. Violet draws him back, rolling him a little, so his face turns up toward her, his black hair gilt with silver, his eyes like mirrors. They watch each other warily.

"It wasn't a dream," says Lionel.

"No." Violet strokes his hair. "It wasn't a dream."

She knows it's up to her, that Lionel will make no move unless she asks him. Is he like that with all women, or just her? She touches his forehead, his sunburnt cheek. With one finger she worries the tiny stubs of his beard.

"No time to shave," he says.

"No." Violet plucks at the buttons of his waistcoat. She spreads it open and rests her hand on his ribs, counting the slow rises of his breath, the inner thud of his heartbeat beneath his phosphorescent shirt. The living Lionel.

As if this is the signal he's been waiting for, Lionel reaches for her with both arms and buries himself in her neck, her breast, her warm belly.

HE CLASPS her afterward for ages, far longer than the frantic conjoining itself. Violet's forehead presses his cheek; her legs straddle his lap. She feels his imprint everywhere on her body, stamping out everything else, Walter and Wittenberg, Oxford and Gstaad, the young woman in emerald silk.

Neither speaks. The shared culmination came too rushed and hard, too premature on both sides; they are still dressed, still strangers to each other's secrets. Violet's drawers and stockings lie next to them on the battered cloth seat; Lionel's hands are fisted around the blue gossamer that bunches about her waist and hips. His head lolls back on the seat top, eyes wide to the sky.

Violet touches the damp hair at his temple. "If you ask me if I'm all right, I'll throttle you."

He laughs. "And here I was simply assuming you felt the same as I did."

"Which is?"

"Which is better than I've ever felt in my life."

Violet rests against his chest, brimming with Lionel, too heavy to move, while he strokes her legs with his thumbs. Something rustles in the trees nearby; an owl hoots softly. The fragrant evening air lies still in her lungs. At last she disengages to collapse into the seat. Lionel helps her straighten her dress. He opens the door and goes around to the back and returns with a blanket, which he spreads under the small stand of trees near the pasture fence.

"Come with me," he says, and lifts her from the seat.

Beneath the trees, Lionel removes her dress and underthings and opens her to the moonlight. "My God," he whispers, and he kisses her sleek newborn skin in awe, he makes love to her again with a slow reverence that settles into her marrow.

Later, he wraps them both in the blanket and they watch the stars, too alive to sleep. Violet's hand curls around Lionel's bare shoulder, so much larger than Walter's, thick with inelegant muscle. She thinks of Walter's crumpled body on the floor of the bedroom, defeated at a stroke.

"Tell me about your stepfather," she says.

He doesn't answer. Violet detaches herself from his arms and walks naked to the automobile. Lionel's gaze casts across her skin like a ray of moonlight, following her. His cigarette case sits in the pocket of his discarded jacket; she takes it out and returns to the blanket in the trees, where she feeds him a smoke and lights it herself.

"All right," he says, when she has tucked herself back in the blanket. "I suppose you've a right to know. You *should* know."

"Not if you can't speak of it."

"Well, I haven't, have I? Not since I gave evidence." He breathes out a slow cloud of smoke. "How much do you know?"

"That he was a brute. That he was brutal to your mother, and you shot him."

"Brutal. Yes. He beat her regularly, when he wasn't out with some mistress or another. A chap of the old school. I don't know why she took it; I suppose she figured that having divorced an earl to marry him, she couldn't go back. She had too much pride. So she stayed. My sister was born a year or two later . . ."

"Your *sister?*"

"Charlotte. You'll love her; she's like me, only eleven years old and far nicer."

For this casual glimpse of a shared future, Violet pinches him. He pinches her back.

"Anyway, Charlotte was born, and a few weeks later a woman turned up at the door, pregnant, by my stepfather she claimed. Mother went hysterical. The old man was out; I picked the lock on his desk and gave the woman a hundred pounds and sent her off."

"Good Lord."

"He came home at one o'clock in the morning. I heard them fighting in their room. I heard him hitting her. I tried putting my face in the pillow, but it didn't help. The servants had locked themselves in their rooms by then; they always did when the fighting started. I expect they were just as scared of him as we were."

Lionel pauses to smoke, tipping the ash into the grass beside them. "Then Charlotte started crying—Mother was nursing her herself, you see, so she had a little bassinet in their room. I don't know if you've heard a baby cry, a newborn, but you can't ignore it. You hear it in your gut."

Violet burrows herself closer into him, not wanting to hear the rest, desperate to hear the rest. "No, I haven't. Not in many years."

"Well, I had to do something, didn't I? I went to his study and picked the lock on the desk again, the drawer where he kept his revolver. I went back upstairs and opened the door. He was . . . well, he had her over the bed, just like you were this afternoon when I walked in, and she was crying and bloody, and the baby was crying. I told him if he touched her again, I'd kill him."

"What did he say?"

"He laughed and said he'd like to see me try. And he grabbed my mother's hair and jerked it back and told her to look at her little boy with his gun—he was very drunk, I could see that, and I didn't care—and I shot him. I shot him twice." Lionel grinds out his cigarette and rests his arm in the grass, palm upward. "I didn't mean to kill him, actually. I was aiming for his shoulders."

"You did the right thing. The only thing."

"Did I? I could have rung for a constable. I could have made one of the servants come out."

"He might have killed her in the meantime. And you were a boy, you were scared."

"Anyway," he says, "I made sure Mother was all right—she was in shock, of course, so I laid her in the bed and put a blanket over her. I wrapped up the baby and ran upstairs with her, to the nanny's room, and told her to ring for the police and a doctor, that I'd shot her master. The rest is a bit of a blur, I'm afraid."

"How old were you, at the time?"

"Fourteen."

"So you're only twenty-five," she says in wonder, touching his chest.

"And you're only twenty-two, and yet we've both lived longer than most people, haven't we? We're as old as Methuselah."

"Walter always called me a child."

"He was as wrong about that as everything else." Lionel's hand finds her hair. "When I came into your room and saw you, the two of you, I went blind, Violet. I wanted to kill him. I don't know why I didn't."

"Because you couldn't. You've grown up, you knew he had no power over you."

Lionel turns on his side and lifts the blanket away. "Let me look at you, Violet. Let me see you, the moonlight on you."

She sees the tears in his eyes. She lifts her arms and takes him to her breast. "We'll be old together now."

"Yes," he says. "Nothing can touch us, can it?"

Vivian

At least he had the grace to knock, instead of using his key.

I was still tying the belt on my robe, still pulling the bobby pins from my hair, which I scattered on the floor as I went. I unlocked the dead bolt and pulled open the door. "Well, hello! Look who's come to apologize for getting engaged to my dear old friend."

Doctor Paul looked me up and down. He had undone the buttons of his overcoat, and underneath he was still dressed in his betrothal suit, every flawless crease of it, trim and tidy except for his sunshine hair, which had been raked through a few too many times, and his chest, which was moving rapidly. He took off his hat. "You've been drinking?"

I turned away and sauntered to the table. I picked up the vodka bottle and gave it a healthy jiggle. "Still a bit left, if you want it. Although I suppose you can afford your own liquor now. Half a million smackeroos! And more to come! That's a lot of money for a regular kid from San Francisco. I can't blame you for taking the dough and the blonde."

His hand was on the door frame. "May I come in?"

"You might as well."

He stepped forward. I was weak enough to steal another peek. Well, wouldn't you? In the harshness of the bare entry bulb, his face was still pallid with shock and gleaming damp. Even his lips look exhausted, drained of blood. He reached inside the pocket of his overcoat and pulled out his cigarette case, but instead of opening it, he fiddled the plain silver around his fingers. "Look, I'm not asking you to forgive me—"

"You won't be disappointed, then."

"I know what I did was unforgivable. I knew it when I did it. I guess I thought I could just wait until . . . until I'd fixed everything, and then—"

"And then we could live happily ever after on Lightfoot's money and Gogo's heartbreak? What a brilliant plan. Devious, even." I clapped my hands. "I applaud you."

"Listen to me, Vivian . . ."

The sound of his voice hurt me. *Listen to me, Vivian,* said my mother, when my eleven-year-old self encountered her half dressed on the library sofa with a man not my Dadums. *Listen to me, Vivian,* said my professor, pale and naked on a cold February afternoon, except for a sagging Trojan and another girl's lipstick.

Why did I ever listen? Why did I ever crack myself open enough to allow the slightest whiff of sentiment inside? With sentiment arrived pain, they were twins, inseparable, didn't I know that already?

I said: "Believe me, I understand. The allure of riches for the scholar-ship boy. Always had your nose pressed against the glass, watching us, didn't you? I mean, you'd have some money eventually, a nice well-padded life at the country club, but that's the thing about medicine, they make you work for it—"

"What a bitch you can be, Vivian. What a goddamned snob." He said it without rancor, as if he knew why I said those things, why I needed to hurt him back. He opened up the cigarette case and took one out. "So you think I wanted the money, did you?"

I let myself tumble onto the sofa and retracted my legs under my robe like a turtle. I couldn't look at him straight. I couldn't look at his sym-metry, his lovely body in its thick herringbone overcoat, because if I did I'd remember how he looked without it. How just this morning, that body had huddled with mine in the tiny shower cubicle, had kissed me with its bacon-and-coffee mouth, had soaped me all over, inspecting each knob and spindle of me, describing its tip-top healthy-pink condition and its scientific Latin name. How he had wrapped me in a towel and laid me on the bed and kissed his way down my backbone, identifying each vertebra, and I'd thought how handy it was to have a doctor for your lover, you were really in the best of hands.

And now. This. Like your heart had been carved from your rib cage with a scalpel.

I said, "I admit, money was the logical conclusion. Don't tell me it was true love after all?"

"No, it was the money, all right." He lit the cigarette and raised it to his mouth. "A week ago I got a little package in the mail. I won't tell you what was inside. Pops had gotten himself in deep at a casino in Vegas."

"You don't say. How deep?"

"Just over three hundred."

"Dollars?"

"Thousand."

All right, my toes went a little cold. Even if he *were* lying, that was a lot of bread to be tossing around so casually in a ramshackle Village apartment. "Well. So what were you planning to do with the other two hundred?"

"You don't believe me."

I held up my hands. "Look, whatever you say. Your pops had debts, Lightfoot had a deal you couldn't refuse. I mean, who am I to stand in your way?"

Doctor Paul picked up the vodka bottle from the center of the table and threw it against the opposite wall. I didn't even jump.

"You have no idea, do you? No idea what it's like to have no money, no way on God's earth to beg, borrow, or steal it. No idea what it's like to have no choice. No idea what it's like to sit there and stare at the bare walls and realize you've got to do something, and whatever you do, it's the wrong thing. You could take some money, propose to a girl, and break her heart later, and in so doing lose the love of the single most breathtaking woman you've ever met, the love of your lonely godforsaken life. Or you could let your father get his fingers and nuts cut off by the Vegas racket . . ."

"Oh, come on. You could have called the police."

He turned to me. His pale head shook back and forth. "You are such an innocent, Vivian. Call the police. This is the Vegas racket, baby. You don't even want to know what they do after they cut off his nuts. And do you know what they do when they're all done? They hand the body over to the police for a decent burial in the Hoover Dam, that's what they do."

My chest had stopped moving. "You could have told me. I could have helped," I whispered.

"And do what? Could you have come up with three hundred thousand dollars in unmarked bills within forty-eight hours?"

I shook my head.

The door to my bedroom squeaked open. Tibby appeared, all tousled up, made to order. "Everything all right here?"

Doctor Paul swung like a bat. "Who the hell is this?"

"A friend."

Without a word, Doctor Paul took in Tibby's gaping buttons, his ruffled hair, his absent necktie. He turned back to me, and his face was stone. Tibby's strip of marigold Brooks Brothers silk screamed from the arm of the sofa, next to my toes. I took the ends of my robe and drew them closer together.

"I see," he said. "You've never heard that revenge is best served cold?"

"Patience is not my favorite virtue."

"All right." He found his hat and put it on. "Like I said, I didn't expect you to forgive me. God knows I won't forgive myself. I just wanted to explain things a little."

"Well, thanks for the explanation. It's all pretty clear now." I made no move from the sofa. I couldn't. My bones had turned into iron.

The telephone shrilled again. I could have sworn the ring sounded more urgent this time. Doctor Paul glanced at it.

"Ignore," I said.

We stood there, eyeing each other, while Gogo trilled eagerly through the cigarette haze.

"I meant everything I said, Vivian. This morning. Every day since I've known you." He spoke as if Tibby weren't there, standing half dressed in my bedroom entrance, where Paul himself had stood so often, and with even fewer clothes. He turned to the door and stopped. His hat tilted back, as if he were reading his next lines on the ceiling. "If you ever need me for anything, Vivian, just let me know. I know you don't agree with what I did. I'm sorry. I guess I'm not as honorable as your kind of people, when the chips are down. When I see my dad's ear in a box, wrapped in Kleenex. But just so you know, I'd do the same thing for your sake. I'd make a deal with fucking Khrushchev, if I had to. I'd do it a hundred times over."

He left, shutting the door gently behind him.

Tibby was already shrugging clumsily into his old-fashioned waist-coat and jacket. "You know what I think?"

I settled my forehead into my palm. "I can only imagine."

He picked up his marigold necktie from the sofa and went to the scrap of mirror hanging near the door. "I think you've been barking up the wrong tree. I don't think Violet is the key to all this. I think it's Lionel."

"Lionel?"

His arms were moving in sloppy jerks. "Ah, women. You're seduced by the affair itself, the evolution of adultery, the climax. Why she did it. When she did it. Every last loving pornographic detail."

I thought of Dr. Grant's handwritten diary and winced.

Tibby turned. The knot wasn't perfect, but you had to be impressed he could arrange a necktie at all. "But think a moment. Does it really matter what happened in that Berlin apartment? She met another man. Her husband was a brute. She killed him—"

"We don't know that for certain."

"Vivian, the facts of the case are obvious enough. That story is always the same, everywhere, every time. It's boring, frankly. What matters—what always matters, Vivian—is what happened after the crisis. Why they disappeared. Where they went. That's the real mystery. That's what we don't know. That's what gives this story zing."

"Zing? We're talking about real people here, Tibby."

"You're talking about real people. I'm talking about a magazine story. I need a hook, I need an angle, I need a man biting a dog. *Zing.* And for zing, you need to find Lionel Richardson. The English lover, the man she killed her husband for, the man in whose hands she placed herself afterward. He's where the mystery begins and ends."

"But Violet is the one—"

"She's the one you care about, obviously. She's your aunt. But Lionel's the one who matters, historically speaking. The one who would have left the most tracks. Who was he? What sort of man? Why did Violet disappear after running away with him? He was a soldier, Vivian. An officer in the British Army. If he managed to get safely across the border, there must be some record of him. Desertion, at the very least, and some sort of official investigation into his whereabouts."

Christ. Of course. Hadn't I said the same thing, in no less a monument than the New York Public Library, to Doctor Paul himself?

It's much easier to find out about the men.

He might not turn up in an encyclopedia, Lionel Richardson. But he must exist somewhere.

"Lionel." I fingered the ends of my robe. "I'd probably have to fly to England to do that."

Tibby took his overcoat off the stand and levered himself inside. He squashed his hat on top of his disreputable head.

"I think that's the idea, Vivian. Don't you?"

When he left, I rose from the sofa and rummaged through the kitchen until I found the brush and dustpan. I knelt on the floor and swept up the vodka shards, every last one, and let the whole glittering mess slide into the garbage can. I found a dishcloth and wiped down the wall and the floorboards, until there was no sign that anything had occurred there at all.

At which point. The telephone rang again, like it meant business this time.

Sally's voice floated out from the other bedroom. "Could you answer the goddamned phone, Vivs?" A few more obscenities trailed behind. I'll spare you the color.

I laid my hand on the receiver. No point in hiding any longer, was there?

"All right, Gogo," I said. "Give it to me straight."

But it wasn't Gogo, after all. It was Mums, exasperated, telling me to hurry on up to Lenox Hill Hospital, because Aunt Julie had fallen down the stairs of her Park Avenue duplex and into a coma.

Violet

They reach the outskirts of Berlin just before dawn. Violet lifts her head from Lionel's shoulder to see the pinkening rooftops, the transparency of air. "What day is it?" she asks. "I've lost count."

"The twenty-fifth of July. Serbia's reply to Austria is due today."

"What does that mean?"

"Unless Serbia intends to grovel at Austria's feet, I suppose it means war."

But his tone is light. He drives down the empty streets, confident of the route, whistling softly. It takes Violet a moment to recognize the tune. "Stop that," she says, laughing. "You'll have us arrested."

He breaks into his booming rich baritone, echoing from the stones. *Send him victorious, happy and glorious . . .*

"Lionel, you're an idiot."

But he doesn't stop, and Violet sits up. *Oh, say, can you see, by the dawn's early light . . .* she sings defiantly into the morning.

Lionel lifts his voice. *Confound their politics, frustrate their knavish tricks . . .*

. . . Whose broad stripes and bright stars . . .

. . . God save the King!

They duel all the way past the Reichstag, along the empty Potsdamer

Platz, laughing and singing to raise the dead, until Violet's throat aches a happy ache. *Nothing can touch us.* The automobile turns the corner of Kronenstrasse, and a bolt of golden-orange sunrise hits the windscreen. Lionel parks the car along the curb, just outside Violet's apartment building. "I'll go up with you."

"You shouldn't. The attendants will notice."

"Let them notice. Let them see the way I look at you." He reaches in the back for her valise. "I don't want to be without you, not for a minute."

"Well, then."

He jumps around the front of the car and helps her out. Together they walk through the door, they nod at the sleepy doorman. Lionel's hand grips hers. His jacket lies about her shoulders. The attendant in the lift, a man Violet doesn't recognize, keeps his eyes trained on the silk-lined ceiling and sees no evil.

Violet's heart pounds as the numbers tick upward. The machinery clangs to a stop; the attendant opens the door and the grille. A musty smell floods around her: the scent of abandonment. All of the servants have gone with them to Wittenberg.

Lionel tugs her hand. "Come along, then."

There isn't much to pack; Violet only wants enough to get by until she can find new things, a new life. She picks a couple of old dresses from the wardrobe, a woolen cardigan she bought that autumn in Oxford. She folds them carefully atop her notebooks and underthings from Wittenberg, the jewelry from Walter she plans to sell. Lionel waits in the doorway, watching her, his arms folded.

She snaps the valise shut. Lionel steps forward and takes it from her. "Is that all?"

"No. There's something else."

Lionel follows her to the study. She selects a book from one of the shelves, opens it, and takes a small key from the hollowed-out center. Lionel examines the spine and snorts. "*The Hound of the Baskervilles.* How clever."

Violet unlocks the glass shelves near the desk and flips through Walter's journals until she finds the one she wants.

Lionel props himself on the desk and watches her lazily. His arms are crossed against the bottom of his ribs. The valise sits next to him, atop Walter's empty green leather blotter. "What's that?" he asks.

"Nothing. Just to satisfy my curiosity." She tucks the journal into the valise and snaps it shut.

He holds out his hand. "Shall I?"

She hands Walter's key to him. He slips it into its hollowed-out nest of Conan Doyle and slides the book back into the slot on the library shelf. He turns to her and smiles. "Let's go."

"Where to, exactly?"

"I thought we'd go to my hotel. Clean up and have breakfast. Do you object?" He picks up the valise and holds out his other hand for her.

She takes it. "Not at all."

THE STAFF at the Adlon is far too polite to notice their disheveled appearance, the road dust and the faint whiff of petrol. It might be Lionel's confidence, the way he strides up to the desk with Violet's hand indisputably enclosed within his elbow, and asks for his key.

"My luggage is in the motor out front," he says in German. "The Daimler. Could you have it sent up immediately." More command than question.

"Yes, Herr Richardson."

They cross the marble lobby toward the multitude of lifts. "Did they save your room for you, all this time?" asks Violet.

"I should hope so. I paid in advance for the entire summer."

The lift whisks them upward. Lionel still carries Violet's valise, as if he doesn't trust it to any other hands. She curls her hand around his arm and wonders if he's brought any other women into this elevator. Jane,

THE SECRET LIFE OF VIOLET GRANT

perhaps, or some woman from a party, some wealthy baroness or an official's bored wife. To her horror, she hears herself asking him.

Lionel twists his hand to knit her fingers with his. "No, Violet."

"I'm sorry. It's not my business, is it?"

"Christ. Of course it is."

They reach his room, a comfortable corner suite with a double-doored entrance. "I wanted something comfortable, as I was staying all summer," says Lionel, standing back to allow her through.

The room is beautiful, furnished elegantly in pinks and greens, a large sitting room and a bedroom door to the right. The early sunlight gushes through the tall windows. Lionel sets the valise on a desk and turns to her, smiling, rubbing his unshaven cheek. "Bath first, don't you think?"

They bathe together in the luxurious enamel tub, surrounded by steam and a weightless translucency of sunlight. Violet lathers his chest an inch thick; she fills her hands with suds and lavishes him all over, his arms and legs and privates, his toes and ears and the sharp tip of his nose. "Now you're all clean," she says, "clean and bright and lovely."

"And scruffy." He touches his chin.

"Clean and bright and lovely and scruffy."

Lionel turns her around, against his oaken chest. He unpins her hair and washes it with gentle movements of his strong fingers. He rinses it clean. When the water cools, he wraps her in a towel and takes her to bed.

VIOLET LOVES the way she and Lionel make love: his exuberant movements, the impish way he tickles her and nudges unexpected parts of her body into wakefulness; the snatches of delighted laughter, the luxurious stopping and lingering. She loves the morning beauty of his body, his black hair and golden skin, his burly strength, the way the light curves around his shoulders as she rolls him over for more. The way he looks at her, as if he's about to swallow her whole, and then he does.

Now he clasps both her hands, now he tightens his fingers and dares her to look away. Now she finishes with a violent cry, under his naked stare, his tender pummeling, and a moment later she finishes him, too. They lie joined and senseless in the sunlit bed. He keeps his palms locked with her palms, his fever skin pressed into her fever skin, his body safe inside hers as long as he possibly can.

VIOLET WAKES to the sound of splashing water. Through the open wedge of the bathroom door, she sees Lionel standing before the sink, beautifully naked, brute-boned and muscular, shaving his face with efficient strokes of his razor. She stretches pleasurably, enthralled by the intimacy of this domestic act. He catches her gaze in the mirror and smiles. "Awake at last?"

"It can't be that long, can it?"

"Three hours, sleepyhead. It's past ten o'clock." He finishes, cleans the blade, pats his face dry with a towel. "I've ordered breakfast. It should be up any minute."

"Good. I'm awfully hungry."

"You should be." He hangs the towel on the rack and emerges from the bathroom to sit next to her on the tousled bed. His black hair has been sleeked back from his face with a wet comb. He rests his hand on her hip. "I've been thinking."

"Oh, don't do *that*."

"What we should do next."

She smiles and wiggles her toes. "I have a few ideas."

But Lionel doesn't laugh. "We have to leave Berlin, Violet. As soon as possible. You know we can't stay."

"No, of course not." She rolls onto her back and stares at the ceiling. Her body is loose and heavy from the warm bath, from Lionel's lovemaking, and the soft feather-scented nap afterward. "I shall have to divorce Walter."

"The sooner the better, I think."

"As soon as I can speak to a lawyer."

"Well, you've plenty of grounds. But we'll have to do it in London. We'll have to leave, in any case; I daresay they'll be expelling us shortly, if the situation gets any touchier. Or worse, interning us." He pauses. "What are you thinking, Violet?"

"I was thinking that I should probably apply to Rutherford's laboratory, in Manchester. I suppose Walter has too much influence at the Devonshire; they'll never take me back."

"Actually, I imagine it's quite the opposite."

She turns her head to look at him. "The *opposite*?"

"I mean he's still in disgrace there, the last I heard."

Violet heaves herself up to a sitting position and holds the sheets illogically to her chest. "Disgrace? What do you mean? Are they angry because he left them for Berlin?"

The skin flexes below Lionel's right eye. He studies her for a moment, and says, "Do you mean you don't know? You've no idea?"

"About what?" She grips his bare knee. "About what, Lionel?"

"Violet, he was thrown out. You didn't know that? When you left. Someone had told the trustees about you, that he'd seduced you." His hand covers hers. "That you were with child by him."

Violet whispers: "Yes, I was. But nobody knew, except for me and Walter. Well, and . . ." She frowns. "But he wouldn't have said anything, would he? He couldn't, he would have been risking everything—"

"Who, Violet?"

"The doctor. The doctor Walter sent me to." She doesn't say, *To get rid of the baby.*

Lionel looks at her earnestly, as if he knows she's holding something back. But he's a gentleman, he doesn't ask. Instead he allows a patient pause and says: "Violet, Grant was thrown out. I know it beyond a doubt. I expect they only helped him with the Kaiser Wilhelm to keep things quiet."

She watches Lionel's face blankly, hollowed out, bewildered. "That's why he married me. That was their condition. Their dirty bargain."

"Not so dirty, I think. They were only trying to protect you."

"If they wanted to protect me, they should have kept me away from him." Violet stares at her hands, enclosed in Lionel's. They are not a lady's hands. They have been tried and tested in a chemical laboratory, and despite her youth there are tiny wrinkles about the knuckles, callouses about the pads of her fingers and thumbs. "I lost the baby anyway."

"I'm very sorry."

"You sound as if you mean that."

"I do. I gather you wanted it?"

Her eyes well. "Yes. Not at first, but later. And then it was gone."

Violet expects him to fill her ears with idiotic platitudes. *Well, we'll have one of our own,* or *Don't worry, darling, I'll give you all the babies you want.* She remembers lying in bed, with all that sterile white linen stuffed between her legs, and the doctor above her with his expression of professional sympathy. *Never fear, Frau Grant, you'll have another.* But she hadn't wanted another. She'd wanted this one, her baby.

Lionel's thumbs move, but he doesn't speak. She imagines what he's thinking, the obvious fact that Lionel and Violet have mated in utmost passion, entirely without restriction. No sheepskin condoms from Charlottenstrasse, no useless vinegar douches, no last-instant withdrawal or precarious tabulation of dates.

"Have you had any children?" she asks.

"No. God, no. I'm not . . . I've been careful."

"Except with me."

"Except with you." He doesn't move, doesn't look at her, doesn't demand her attention. He doesn't tell her why, of all women, she is his exception. He doesn't ask her any of the questions that must be burning in his head: why, for example, she and Walter didn't have another child. Whether she wants a child with him, Lionel.

Instead, he says, "Violet, in case I haven't made things clear. I do mean to marry you, if you'll have me."

"Yes."

"Yes, you understand, or yes, you'll have me?"

She looks back up at him. "Both."

"Good, then." He exhales. "In the interim, however, I suppose I should exercise a bit more caution. My fault. The heat of the moment and all that."

"Yes, of course." And Violet knows, in that moment, that she does not want to be careful. She wants to be thoroughly reckless. She wants the possibility of life, of some mark of permanence between them, some proof that she and Lionel once existed and were in love and lay joyfully together.

A knock sounds. *Zimmerservice,* calls a voice through the wood and plaster.

"Breakfast," says Lionel. "Thank God."

LIONEL HELPS HER DRESS; she buttons his waistcoat and manages, after several tries, to knot his necktie properly. "Not that I wouldn't rather spend the day shamelessly in bed with you," he says, picking up his hat, "but I've a few loose ends to tie up, if we're to leave tomorrow. You don't mind?"

"Not at all. I have to pay a visit to the laboratory. There won't be many people there, it's shutting up for August any day, but I want to gather my things and say good-bye."

"I'll drive you, then." He holds out his hand to her, and she takes it.

They drive in silence to Dahlem. Lionel keeps his hands on the wheel, his eyes on the road. Violet keeps to her side of the seat and crosses her hands in her lap. It's a fine day, hot and clear, and the patches of shade look unbearably inviting. "What sort of loose ends?" asks Violet.

"Oh, the usual." He changes gears with an expert thrust of his hand. "Bidding friends good-bye. Check in with Goschen on the war situation, see if there's any news from my regiment. Whether I'm being called back yet. And I've got to return the motor, of course."

Violet shuts her eyes and sees him in uniform, resplendent with khaki and shining leather. The image is so alien, and yet this is his life. His profession, the genuine Lionel. "Who's Goschen?"

"Sir Edward Goschen. The British ambassador in Berlin."

"As high as all that? What circles you move in."

"He's a friend of my father's. He's been splendidly useful since I arrived, introductions and smoothing channels and all that."

"Naturally." Violet looks to the side, where the buildings slide past Lionel's borrowed automobile, giving way to blocks of abundant summer green, as Berlin drifts into the suburbs.

"Darling, what's wrong?"

"Nothing," she says, as she might say to Walter, but then she remembers this isn't Walter. This is Lionel, and he might actually care what she thinks. "Nothing reasonable, anyway. I had a chilling sense of familiarity just now."

"What's that?"

"My parents were very good friends with the British ambassador in America."

"Were they, now? That would have been Bryce, wouldn't it? James Bryce."

"Yes."

"Well, I personally find the chap intolerable." The white new-built edifice of the institute rises up from the block ahead, lined with young trees. Lionel breezes through the empty intersection and slows the car.

Violet laughs. "So did I."

"You see, then?" The car rolls to a stop next to the curb. Lionel sets the brake and jumps out to open her door. "We're straight, aren't we, Violet? As you Americans say. We understand each other. You know I want you to be happy."

His eyes are a serious gray. Violet leans forward and kisses him good-bye, right there in the open, in front of the entrance to the institute. "I believe you."

"I'll come for you later to take you home. Back to the hotel, I mean, to pack up. Is four o'clock all right?"

To pack up. To leave with Lionel on the morning train out of Berlin, to run away with her lover. Or hadn't she already done that? Already given up everything and crossed the frontier.

"Four o'clock is fine," she says.

VIOLET CHECKS all the offices, but only Max Planck is still there at his desk. She can see him through the glass, his bowed head and lined face. His secretary's chair is empty. Violet pokes her head around the door. "Herr Planck?"

"Frau Grant. I thought you were in Wittenberg." He takes off his glasses, rises, and makes a gesture of welcome.

"I came back early. I . . . I regret to say that I've come to tender my resignation, such as it is." She holds out the ridiculous piece of paper, which relinquishes her title to a post that never really officially existed.

"I'm very sorry to hear that. Is there anything I can say to change your mind? I hope it's not this wretched situation in the Balkans." He braces his fingers against the edge of the desk. In the overbright electric light, his eyes are heavy and shadowed, his forehead lined.

"That's part of it, I suppose, but the real reason is that I've left Walter. I've left Dr. Grant. I thought I should tell you first; I don't intend to hide it." She says all this in a rush, as a single defiant sentence.

"I see." He looks down and fingers his glasses. "Thank you for telling me. May I be perfectly candid?"

"I hope you will."

He looks up again. "I'm overjoyed to hear it. I hope you'll let me know if there's anything at all I can do for you. Letters, recommendations, anything."

Violet curls her fingernails into her palms. It doesn't work; her eyes fill anyway. "Thank you, Herr Planck. I appreciate that tremendously. I'll write, of course, once I've settled what to do. I . . . I am deeply grateful for my time here at the institute."

"No more grateful than we were to have you." He holds out his hand. "I wish you all the happiness in the world, Frau Grant. I hope our paths meet again."

VIOLET FINDS her cramped office, her tiny desk. The space is hot and musty, smelling of rubber and old pencil shavings. Everything is in perfect order; she had already tied off her own loose ends before departing for Wittenberg. The office itself contains very little: no photographs, no personal items, only papers and journals and a few instruments. She opens a drawer and finds her familiar slide rule, the one she brought with her from New York, its paint faded from use. She fingers the worn wood and slips it in her jacket pocket, and when her hand withdraws, it holds the small leather-covered notebook from Walter's study. On the lower right corner, the number 1912 is stamped in gold.

She places the diary on the desk before her and closes her eyes.

Just open it. Just look.

She has no right. She's stolen it, Walter's private thoughts, to which he has every right. If she kept a diary, a personal journal of some kind, she would be outraged to find Walter reading it.

But the suspicion will not quiet. If she doesn't answer it now, she may never have another opportunity. And isn't this her affair, as well?

She places her fingers on the smooth leather and opens her eyes.

4 January. *Fucked V in my office (desk), then again at home. What a fine snug cunt she has, very supple and muscular, lovely clipping motion when she spends (not often).*

5 January. *Fucked V briskly on waking, went to laboratory in excellent humor. How she refreshes me, the eager young child. Argument with D—d on procedure for thorium isolation, the usual wrong-headed rubbish. Out to lunch. Looked for B—e at Crown, did not see her.*

6 January. *Crown again for lunch (curious about B—e—is she fucking someone?). Found her in kitchen. Old N-d suspicious apparently and sent her out for errands y'day when I arrived. Took her upstairs and had a glorious uprighter in linen cupboard—ha! She spent copiously. How I love her big fleshy thighs and bum, tho my current lech is for V and her childlike little cunt. No V this evening, experiment running late. Nearly returned to Crown for B—e but went home instead. Sent note to V to come to Norham Gardens when finished.*

7 January. *V arrived at ten o'clock last night, rather tired and listless, but after sweetened by brandy and kisses (kisses will warm up the coldest cunt) let me fuck her, a long voluptuous fuck as seconds are, resulting in spend for V. Arrived late at laboratory. D—d stormed into my office before lunch and said he'd had a note from a friend who saw me with V at Ritz at New Year. Assumed outraged aspect and told him he was an idiot. V busy all day but came by Nham Gdns after dark. Had her twice before midnight, very credibly, once from behind (waking her up), tho she would not spend. Slept like an anvil afterward, completely fucked out.*

Violet sets down the leather notebook. She is dizzy; there are actual spots appearing before her eyes, in between her brain and the black scribble of Walter's private thoughts. Another word, and she will vomit on the institute's sanitary linoleum floor.

"Frau Grant! Are you all right?"

Violet staggers to her feet, interposing herself between the door and Walter's diary, as if to shield the world from her disgrace.

"Quite all right, thank you."

It's one of the laboratory assistants, a young man with pale hair and earnest blue eyes. "You look white, Frau Grant. Quite ill."

"It's the heat, I suppose."

The young man hurries to the tiny window and struggles to open it. Violet opens her mouth to protest, but there's no voice inside, no will at all. She sinks to her seat and watches him heave at the sash, until the heat-swollen wood gives way at last and the glass jumps upward with a bang.

"Thank you," she says.

"Would you like a glass of water?"

"Yes, please."

When he returns with the water, she takes a small sip, and another. She is calmer now, her head clear. She remembers that night she came home late from the laboratory, when Walter was waiting for her. January the sixth, apparently; how strange that dates only become significant in hindsight. He was so coaxing and affectionate. He had a glass of brandy waiting for her, and a bit of cake. When he made love to her, so slowly and surely, she thought for the first time that she might actually be in love with him, that this must certainly be love: a man who waited for her with brandy and cake and made love with such amorous invention.

Violet rises and circles about her cage; she braces her hands on the window frame and breathes in the hot air from the courtyard. A little gust stirs her hair. She sits down and sips her water and opens the diary, flipping through the pages until she finds April.

This time her head is sharp. She's reading about some other girl, some poor deluded fool who thinks she's so very much more clever and sophisticated than she really is.

24 April. *Delivered paper to great success. Banquet followed, excellent wine. Went out afterward with H—n and F—y, fine time. F—y knew of decent house nearby, very pleasing girls, found a jolly fleshy hot-cunted one of perhaps seventeen and fucked her twice in an hour*

(feat not managed since first night with V, and before that not for a year at least—thus middle age!). Slept a little, had her again with some effort, returned to hotel at 3. V asleep.

25 April. *Woke with prick standing, by G-d. Lovely comfortable fuck, V delightfully accommodating. Managed an heroic spend. Afterward V told me she might be in a family way. The devil. Told her she should take care of it back in Oxford, she said she would not, the fool. Resolved not to try her again until condition is confirmed. There is no arguing with women in that state.*

Violet flips forward a few pages.

2 May. *V returned from Dr. W—w determined to keep child. No argument would move her, the wretch. Left in fury and went directly to Dr. W—w. What the devil had he said to her? I used very forceful language to make myself clear, that I might go to authorities if he did not convince V of necessity for taking care of things. He resisted passionately. D—n all doctors.*

3 May. *Devil in it. Message from D—d and trustees this morning. Met with them directly after lunch. That b—d Dr W—w has apparently told them all. Am to marry V and tender resignation; they will assist me in finding place on the Continent if I comply. Marriage!!!! D—n Dr W—w.*

4 May. *Went to see V last night. Secured her agreement, then hard and satisfying fuck on floor, tho she did not like it. Still in bad humor so went to Crown afterward but B—e out. D—n all women.*

Violet puts one hand to her hipbone. In the morning after Walter's proposal, she had found two large bruises, one on either side, from the repeated concussion against the hard wood. She remembers viewing them in the mirror with pride: the sacrifice she had made for Walter's pleasure.

8 May. Morning at Tuileries. Feeling rather better about V as wife. She is an excellent companion, helpful at work, no ill humors in bed as most women, has never once refused me except when poorly. In afternoon, made first pot of tea for V according to receipt. Watched her for any reaction; none. Resolved not to have her tonight, just in case.

Violet's head remains clear, so clear she can hear the deep thud of her heart as it smashes into her ribs.

11 May. Morning at Versailles, V very affectionate. Excellent dinner at hotel, tho V left twice to visit lavatory. V continued affectionate in evening, so managed short fuck before bed. Examined prick carefully afterward; nothing. Continuing tea with 2 additional grains.

Violet turns a few pages with her cold fingers, until she reaches Berlin.

18 May. Success!!!! V complained of pain in morning. Blood on sheets. Called doctor; confirmed miscarriage at five o'clock. V very low. Made her comfortable, poor thing. After dinner, went to Mme G——d's, had two bottles of champagne and fucked dear little P——e until she could not stand!! By good chance met General von M——e there on way out, made appointment for tomorrow aftern . . .

Violet closes the book. This is all she needs to know; to read any more would be little better than common espionage.

She places the notebook in her pocket, closes the window, and leaves the office.

Vivian

I hadn't set foot inside Lenox Hill Hospital since the day my nanny carried me out of it with my Baby Girl Schuyler tag still swinging from my ankle. I hadn't missed much, it seemed.

The feel of the place was familiar enough. God knew I'd spent more time in hospital waiting rooms (well, one in particular) in the past few weeks than in the rest of my twenty-two years combined. I sniffed the Lysol and floor wax, the bouquet garni of overcooked food and effluvia, and I'll be damned if my shameless glands didn't start churning out a Welcome Doctor Paul cocktail of desire. All this while I was hurrying down corridors and scrubbed blind alleys in a frantic hunt for my comatose great-aunt.

"Coma. There's Mums for you," said Pepper, when I screeched to a huff-a-puff halt in front of the door marked HADLEY. (Half my trouble at the reception downstairs was remembering which ex-husband had come last.) "She knocked her head on the way down, and she hasn't come out of it. The doctors are rather bored about it, really." But Pepper's face was long and grave. She looked like a different woman without her lipstick.

"Did she hurt anything else?" I tried to peer through the oblong window on the door.

"Ribs and things. They had to stitch up her forehead. She's not going to be happy about that."

"Nothing her plastic surgeon can't handle, I'm sure."

The door swung open, and my parents sallied forth. "Vivian! There you are at last!" Mums took me by the shoulders and burst into tears, as if Aunt Julie were her own mother instead of an in-law with whom she traded regular volleys across the DMZ of Madison Avenue.

I patted her back. "There, there. Everything will be all right."

"At least your legs are covered," said my father.

"Your concern for your aunt steals my breath. Speaking of which, how is she?"

"The same," sobbed Mums. "Just lying there. With that bandage."

A doctor detached himself from all the boys in white coats. He held a clipboard in one hand. Thanks to Doctor Paul, I knew how to read a chart (oh, you dirty thing, you thought we spent all our time in bed?) and I snatched it from him with professional aplomb.

"Hmm," said I, clicking a ballpoint pen thoughtfully, next to my ear. "You must be a little concerned about that blood pressure."

"I understand her blood pressure is normally elevated. We're keeping an eye on it." Was that amusement?

I pointed the pen at him. "Don't get sassy with me, young man."

"No, ma'am."

"Other than that, her vitals seem stable." I handed back the clipboard. "Why is she still unconscious?"

"It could be a number of things, but the most likely explanation is that the brain is simply healing itself. She sustained a concussion, a serious one, but we've found no sign of a depressed fracture or intracranial bleeding."

"What about fluid pressure?"

"A bit above what we'd like to see. We're monitoring it carefully."

"How many sutures in her forehead?"

"Twelve. Quite a gash, really, but superficial. She also broke three ribs, as you may have heard. When she wakes up, she'll be in a great deal of pain. I've prescribed something to help with that."

"Have you, now? She'll like that. Intravenous, of course?"

"Yes, ma'am."

"When can I see her?"

He gestured to the door. "Now, if you like. We've just finished checking her. Back in half an hour for further assessment."

I gave him the Vivian special. He'd earned it. "Excellent, Doctor . . ."

"Miller. James Miller."

"Dr. James Miller." I widened my smile. "I'm Vivian Schuyler. That will be all for now."

"Any time, Miss Schuyler," he said, meaning *any time you like, you just crook your little finger, ask for me by name, I'll be right there like Buck Rogers in hyperwarp.*

And that, I thought with satisfaction, would ensure my great-aunt Julie the finest care available at the Lenox Hill Hospital this dark November night. God knew, she would have done the same for me.

Only then did I become aware of the awestruck faces surrounding me. "What the hell was that?" said Pepper, as we filed into the room.

"Oh, just a delightful little trick known as flirting for favors," I said.

"Well, that much was obvious. I meant the intracranial jabberwocky and the fluid pressure. What sort of Greek is that?"

"Dear Pepper. Don't tell me you've never slept with a doctor before."

But I sobered up at once at the sight of Aunt Julie, just lying there (as Mums had promised) with that bandage. The room had been darkened, and the gauze glowed a dim white just above her left eyebrow, or what had been her left eyebrow, sculpted and spidery, before the doctors had shaved it. Poor Aunt Julie. She'd be appalled when she woke up and looked in the mirror. No makeup, her hair flat and matted against her skull, her fashionable clothes replaced with the indignity of a blue open-back hospital gown. No cosmetic barrier of any kind against the unkind eyes of the world around her. She didn't look old, exactly. Just tired.

I touched her forehead with my fingertips. "It's Vivian, Aunt Julie. Vivian's here. I've given your doctors a good grilling. They're going to take excellent care of you. Back on your feet in no time."

Not a whisper of a reaction, not a flicker.

"She's been like that for four hours now," whispered Pepper.

"Sleeping Beauty," I said. "You're like Sleeping Beauty, aren't you, Aunt Julie? I'll go round up a prince to kiss you. I'm sure you'll have plenty of volunteers."

Don't humor me, young lady. I could almost hear her say it.

IN THE WAITING ROOM, Mums had regained her composure and was handing Dad a cup of coffee. He accepted wearily. Mums turned and watched me settle in a chair like a horse to the knackers. "Where were you all this time, Vivian? We were trying to reach you for hours."

"I was at the Lightfoots' house. Dinner."

"Would you like a cup of coffee?"

"Yes, please."

She poured the coffee from the urn in the corner and gave it to me. I was surprised that she knew I liked it black. I took a sip. "It was an engagement dinner for Gogo, in fact. You'll never guess whom she's marrying."

Mums sat down next to me. "I can't imagine. Wasn't she seeing that nice young man, what was his name . . ."

"She's marrying Doctor Paul, Mums."

She plucked an invisible speck from her dress, next to the knee. *"Your Doctor Paul? From the post office?"*

"That's the one."

"I'm afraid I don't understand."

I drank my coffee and considered how much to tell her. "So sorry. I can't divulge the sordid details, Mums. Let's just say that if you and Mr.

Lightfoot had ever married, the two of you, you'd be living in the White House by now."

"I see." You could have cracked an egg on those two words.

"Well, you know how it is, Mums. You win some, you lose some." I stretched my arms above my head, coffee and all, and smothered a yawn in my throat.

"Is that so."

It occurred to me, as I absorbed the message in those three frigid words, which might best be summed up as Very Bad News for Mr. S. Barnard Lightfoot III, that maybe Mums wasn't such a bad sport after all.

A tiny smile elbowed its way past the wreckage of the past six hours to prop up the corner of my mouth. A *smile,* of all things. Horrors. Up with the coffee cup, on the pronto.

"Why are you laughing?" asked Mums.

I gave her a shove, shoulder to shoulder. "I was just thinking. You as First Lady."

AT TWO O'CLOCK in the morning, Dr. Miller walked into the waiting room. Our slumped bodies snapped to attention.

"Vivian Schuyler?" He looked at me. His face hung with fatigue, but he was smiling. "She's asking for you."

AUNT JULIE WAS PALE and blinking and smelled of medicine, but she was awake.

I brushed her hair away from her bandage. "Don't do that again, all right?"

"Goddamned stairs."

"What was that, Aunt Julie? I can't hear you. Something about watching your step next time?"

A raspy harrumph.

I smoothed my hand over her sheets, white and crisp as any good hotel. "How do you feel, Aunt Julie? Do you want more morphine?"

"Yes."

"Rephrase. Do you need more morphine?"

Her eyes were fluttering shut. Dr. Miller stepped forward with a penlight and did his thing.

"All right. I'm all right." Her voice was only the dry husk around the usual Aunt Julie snap and crackle.

"You should rest, Aunt Julie. You need to heal. We're just glad you're back with us."

She made an impatient movement of her chin. I couldn't blame her. I'd have done the same thing if she said that to me.

"Max," she said, or something like it.

"What's that?"

"Her. Vivian. I mean Violet."

I leaned in. "What did you say?"

"Violet."

My heart delivered a few hard smacks against the wall of my chest. I stroked Aunt Julie's hair with my fingers, nice and slow. I counted to three, and I said: "What about Violet?"

"Max. Maxwell."

Dr. Miller, soothing voice: "I know you mean well, Miss Schuyler, but we really shouldn't encourage her to talk just now. She's not thinking clearly anyway. It's probably just nonsense."

Only I, simpatico, could have caught the flash of indignation in Aunt Julie's eyes.

"Never mind, Aunt Julie. You can tell me later." I leaned forward, making busy with the tucking and the stroking, and as I brushed past her ear I said: "Maxwell who?"

Aunt Julie's pale and cracked lips moved: "Institute. Paris."

. . .

I STAYED with her a long while, as the others filed in and back out again. When I returned to the waiting room, everyone was asleep except Dad, who sat in a stiff chair with Mums's head in his lap. He was stroking her hair. He turned his head as I entered and raised his finger to his lips, and I thought, that's odd, he looks ten years younger.

I knelt next to him and spoke in a whisper. "She's fine. Resting now. But I think she'll be all right."

Dads nodded. "Thank you." He mouthed the words.

I rose and kissed the top of his head and went to my own chair. I gathered up my coat and gloves, my hat and pocketbook. Dad cast me a curious look. I pointed to my watch and whispered, "Work."

I opened the door and bumped straight into Lily Greenwald. "Vivian! I just found the telephone message. How is she?"

"Awake now, thank God. Gave us a little scare. They're all sleeping now." I nodded to the room behind me.

She pressed her hand to her chest. Her cheeks were all flushy-peach, all luminous Lily. "Oh, thank goodness. The note said something about a coma. Scared me to death."

I laughed. "That's just Mums. She had a knock to the head, but she'll be just fine, if I know Aunt Julie. Go wake up Pepper. She'll clue you in."

"Where are you going?"

"I'm going to London, Lily."

Her head made a satisfying little jerk. "London!"

"Research, you know." Sophisticated working-girl wave of the fingers. "I've decided it's time to find out more about this Lionel Richardson."

"I see."

I laid my hand on her blue-woolen arm. "You'll take care of them while I'm gone, won't you?"

Lily took the hand and squeezed it. "Don't worry about a thing. I'll keep you posted. Just . . . well, enjoy yourself."

"Enjoy myself?"

"If that's the word. You're so young, Vivian. Just try to step back a bit and enjoy yourself."

A trolley clattered behind us, a murmur of voices. Rounds of some kind. I breathed quietly and allowed Lily's dark blue Schuyler eyes to draw me in, to connect with me. "I will, Cousin Lily."

"Good, then." She smiled and gave my hand a last squeeze.

"Oh. Wait. Lily. One thing."

"Yes, Vivian?"

"The Maxwell Institute. Paris. Ring a bell?"

The brow wrinkled. The eyes squinted. "Maxwell Institute? I don't think so. Why?"

I hoisted my pocketbook on my shoulder and smiled my Mona Lisa. "No reason."

I STEPPED outside and found that dawn was breaking all over Manhattan, the kind of fragile pearly pink sunrise that makes you want to climb on board a jet airplane and start a brilliant new life.

I looked down at my shoes, sensible old sneakers for once, the first ones that had come to hand when I left my apartment in a blurred rush seven hours ago.

Maybe I'll walk home, I thought. Five or six miles of therapeutic New York City sidewalks, as good as an afternoon with a shrink. I could buy my airplane ticket on the way.

A long walk. Just the thing.

Violet

Violet walks and walks. She reaches the outskirts of the city where the buildings begin to knit with one another and the patches of green to shrink and disappear. The sun burns the crown of her small hat, the perspiration wets her back and chest. She discovers she's hungry, and stops for a fat bratwurst from a vendor on Hohenstaufenstrasse. Perfectly cooked, the skin crisp beneath her teeth, insides rich and meaty. She washes it down with a bottle of cold lemonade and wipes her fingers on her handkerchief.

Her head remains clear. She is the old Violet, the scientific Violet, without emotions to cloud things over, to make her heart crash and her skin tingle. She searches for clues to Walter's behavior, for the little signposts that should have warned her. At this point she should have guessed *that*; with *that* sentence she might have guessed *this*; such-and-such action of Walter's should have instead provoked such-and-such reaction from her. All the myriad instances of her blindness and willful self-delusion: she catalogs them all in her orderly mind.

Her feet guide her to the Tiergarten. She sits on a bench near the Victory column, where the massive white columns of the Reichstag rise imperviously behind her. A restless crowd of Berliners mills about her; discarded newspapers litter the ground. The Balkans situation, she supposes. The little diary in her pocket is of no interest to these people. They are thinking about war, about treaties and mobilization orders, the course of history.

How long she sits there, she can't say. At one point she grows thirsty and buys another bottle of lemonade, which she drinks quickly and holds in her hand, rolling the smooth glass between her fingers. She is so young, and her fingers look so old. When did that happen?

The sun begins to darken and sink, flashing across the sharp points of Victory's wings. The crowd thickens, like a sauce does when it begins to bubble.

A shout: *Violet, my God, there you are!*

Four o'clock. Lionel was going to meet her at the institute at four o'clock. What time is it now?

Before she can pull her gold watch from her pocket, Lionel has reached her. She stands and takes his outstretched hands and looks into his familiar face, made unfamiliar by the hair in black disarray, by the heat in his cheeks and the almost maniacal wildness in his eyes. "I'm sorry," she says. "I lost track of time."

"What the devil, Violet! What happened?" His hands grip hers with extraordinary strength, as if he's holding himself back from some disastrous display of emotion. "They said you'd left hours ago, just walked out the door. I've been like a madman. I tried the flat, I tried the Adlon. I was on my way to the Reichstag to find—"

Violet wriggles her hands free. "I'm quite all right. I went for a walk, that's all."

"A *walk*! But why? What's the matter?" His empty hands rake his hair and land on his hips. His face is desperate. "Tell me. Second thoughts? You can't imagine what I've—"

She takes Walter's diary from her pocket and holds it out to him.

His gaze drops. "What's this?"

"A diary. My husband's."

"Hell."

She nudges it against his chest. "Go ahead. It's fascinating, really."

"Violet, I can't."

"I'm going to use it as evidence in the divorce petition, so you might as well know what's inside." She nudges him again, and this time he takes it, with an air of wary reluctance, and sits down on the bench.

He reads for a minute or two. She watches him closely for signs of surprise, of anger, but his face is already pink from heat and exertion. There is a dustbin not far away. She walks there and drops her lemonade bottle inside, and then she returns to sit on the bench next to Lionel.

He closes the notebook and hands it back to her. "Put it away. I can't look anymore."

She slides Walter's diary into her pocket.

"I'm going to kill him. I should have killed him already."

"Don't say that. It's done, it's finished. He's not yours to vanquish."

"Yes, he is. You're mine now, and he . . . he . . ."

"It's just Walter. It's who he is. I should have known, I shouldn't have been such a shorn little baa-lamb, bleating for more. It won't happen again."

"By God, it won't."

She rises from the bench and turns to him. "Really, Lionel? Are you really any different? Listen to you: *You're mine now.* Aren't you all the same, wanting to own a woman, to pretend to love her, while you wander off and . . . and *fuck* whomever you fancy?"

He leaps to his feet. "No, as a matter of fact. I *do* love you."

"Really?" She held up the diary. "Tell me, does any of this surprise you? Shock you at all? Can you honestly say you haven't done the same?"

"Have I been with other women? Yes, I have. I've been with many. Have I visited such houses from time to time, in the bleakness of life? Yes, I have. I admit it. I've done it all, God forgive me. But have I done any of these things since I first sat down with you in that laboratory, Violet?

Have I?" He snatches the diary and tosses it on the gravel. "Not once, Violet. Not once. Not even once, though I knew you were in Grant's bed, his wife, taking whatever he gave you. Not *once*. Do you know why?"

She makes a movement of her head, neither a shake nor a nod.

"Because I'm in love with you. Because you fill my head, my chest, until I can't even breathe without you. Because I thought, in my madness, that if I was true to you, if I kept myself whole for you, I might have a chance to deserve you. I hoped to God I would have that chance before the summer was over."

His eyes blaze; his hands fist. She feels the scintillation of his nerves beneath his layers of clothing. She can't disbelieve him, and yet she can't shake this stiffness in her muscles, this dullness in her bones. She cannot take a single step in his direction.

"And God gave me that chance, Violet, and I took it, and now I have you. Or it's the other way around, really. You have *me*. You *have* me, Violet, you have my life in your hands, my beating heart, and you've got to decide, you've got to tell me, I've got to know what you're going to do with me."

Violet blinks. Lionel swims before her, his pained face sharp and then blurry, and then sharp again. She brushes the tears with both hands. She takes a single step forward and presses her fingers against his dry cheeks. Her thumbs frame his mouth, his beautiful mouth.

"For now? I'm going to take everything you have to give me."

THE LIGHT from the window grows blue with age. Lionel stirs at Violet's shoulder and kisses her neck and ear and hair.

"Hungry yet?"

"Mmm."

"Is that a yes or a no?"

"Mmm."

He laughs and rises from the bed. "Let's go out. Our last night in

Berlin. We can pack when we get back. With luck, we'll be in London by midnight tomorrow, tucked into a suite at the Ritz."

"*Mmm.*"

He takes her hand and pulls her upright into his arms. "Are you always this sleepy after making love?"

THE CAFÉS ARE FULL, the streets humming with war talk. Serbia's reply to Austria was satisfactory, Serbia's reply was abject and humiliating, Serbia's reply was unacceptable. The Serbian representative in Vienna had been expelled from the country. No, he had been shot in the streets. A Serbian general had been arrested. No, he was released. No, he was shot in the streets. War was coming. War was impossible. War was already here.

Lionel drinks his wine and lights cigarette after cigarette. "I've got to get you out of here. Austria's going to declare any day. The borders will close."

Violet looks around her, at the golden room bathed in modern electric light, the animated faces, the excitement like a visible frisson in the smoke-laden air of the café. "How do you know?"

"I just know." He stubs out his cigarette and drops a few coins on the table. "Come along. Let's get a newspaper."

Potsdamer Platz is running over with war-fevered Berliners, with shouts and whoops and scattered singing. *Deutschland Über Alles.* Lionel keeps Violet's hand securely in his. He elbows his way through the jammed-up clusters of factory workers and brown-suited students and buys a newspaper from a high-voiced boy in a checked cap. He tucks it under his arm and takes up Violet's hand again.

"Aren't you going to read it?"

"I already know what it says."

"Then why buy it?"

"To give to our grandchildren one day, I expect."

. . .

"YOU DON'T look English." She strokes his lazy face. "Your skin, and your hair. You look wildly exotic for an English gentleman."

"I beg your pardon. Did I ever claim to be a gentleman?"

"Only your eyes are English, and even there you have these *eyelashes*." She touches them. "No proper Englishman would be caught dead with eyelashes like these. They're just excessive. You're nothing but a beast, Lionel."

"As it happens, my mother was quite notoriously Sicilian. Satisfied?"

She rolls him over and puts her arms around his neck. "No, Lionel. I'm not satisfied at all."

SOMETIME in the darkness, she reaches for Lionel and finds nothing at all, a cool sheet, slightly damp. She hears a noise through the plaster, though, and thinks he must be awake and packing, unable to sleep. Her brain is thick and love-blurred. She takes his pillow instead and folds it into her arms. London by tomorrow, the two of them, Violet and Lionel, a bright new life. She has no trouble sleeping, velvet and dreamless.

HIS HAND on her bare shoulder. "Violet. Violet, wake up."

"Lionel?"

"I'm sorry, darling. You've got to wake up, you've got to get dressed." His hands on her arms, her waist, lifting her gently.

"What time is it?"

"Half past three. We've got to leave now, Violet. I've got your things."

Violet is too sleepy to do anything except obey. He helps her with her petticoat, her stays, her blouse and skirt. Her vague fingers can't seem to manage the buttons; he does them for her. She needs to use the lavatory. Through the door, she hears him moving about impatiently, checking the drawers and wardrobes. She washes her hands, gives her teeth a quick brush, pins her hair, gathers her few toiletries into the case.

When she emerges a moment later, her head is clear. "What's going on?"

The lights are off. Lionel stands in shadow by the window, looking down at the street through the crack in the massive curtains.

"I'll explain later." He turns to her. It's too dark to see his face.

"Is something the matter?"

He hesitates. "Yes. Come along. I have your valise. Is there anything else you need?"

"Just you."

Through the window, a siren shrills faintly.

"Violet," he whispers. Somehow, he finds her mouth in the darkness, and then he leads her through the bedroom, the sitting room, the hall, where he closes the silent door behind them.

PART THREE

When my love swears that she is made of truth
I do believe her, though I know she lies,
That she might think me some untutor'd youth,
Unlearned in the world's false subtleties.
Thus vainly thinking that she thinks me young,
Although she knows my days are past the best,
Simply I credit her false speaking tongue:
On both sides thus is simple truth suppress'd.
But wherefore says she not she is unjust?
And wherefore say not I that I am old?
O, love's best habit is in seeming trust,
And age in love loves not to have years told:
Therefore I lie with her and she with me,
And in our faults by lies we flatter'd be.

—Sonnet 138, William Shakespeare

Vivian

y the time my BOAC 707 touched down at London Airport at
eight o'clock the next morning, rattling my sleepless teeth, I had
it all planned out. I'd go to the British National Archives and
track down Captain Lionel Richardson's war record, if he had one. I'd
locate his family—again, if he had one—and see if they'd be willing to
share any information. I'd scour every dispatch, read every antique newspaper if I had to. I'd stay at the Ritz. Because one should always stay at
the Ritz.

Oh, the wet-nosed innocence of me.

Everything was hunky-dory, right up until I prepared to waltz my
way through customs with a flirtatious wink and a salacious smile. You
see, I'd had this idea, this crazy sickness, this rare outbreak of sentimen-
tality, to bring Violet's suitcase with me. It seemed airworthy enough,
after all. It had a certain vintage charm amid the standard-issue Sam-
sonite. I liked the way the handle felt in my palm, solid and classy. We
were making a pilgrimage, that suitcase and I, filled with the relics of
Violet's old life.

But the customs official cast one beady eye on the beaded leather and
pounced with all fours.

"Is this your suitcase?" he demanded, and I was so surprised and flustered—I know, *me, flustered,* but you know how it is with customs officials—I said the most irredeemably stupid thing I've ever said in my life, before or since. The one thing you should never, ever say to a customs official.

I told him the truth.

I said: "No, not mine, it belongs to a friend."

Like red meat to a bull.

"If you'll step aside with me, miss," he said, in a way that brooked no sass, and you know those scary little rooms like in the movies, with metal chairs and a metal table and probably one-way glass on one side, though of course you don't know for certain unless you're on the right side of it?

I was on the wrong side of it.

The customs official stood on one side of the table, on which my aunt Violet's belongings were arranged in careful piles. He was a slight fellow, with pale orange hair and a nose bent creatively to one side. He held Dr. Walter Grant's 1912 diary open in his hands. I sat and stared at Violet's gold watch. *Why, then the world's mine oyster, which I with sword will open.*

"This is pornographic material," said the official; we'll call him Little Roger. I looked up. His face was flushed at the corners.

"I know. Good stuff, huh? Try August thirteenth, it's a doozy. Would you believe he was in his late forties?" Low whistle.

"According to United Kingdom law—"

"This is a private journal. Written fifty years ago for personal use. By a countryman of yours, I might add. Honestly, I'd heard British men were filthy perverts beneath all that cheerio and tally-ho, but I never quite believed it until . . . Now, hold on. That's fragile."

Little Roger was picking up Lionel's note, scattering rose petals to the wind, had there been any wind in that airless compartment of suffocation.

"You are responsible for every damned one of those petals," I said. "They're antiques."

He stared down his crooked nose. "Who's Lionel?"

"My aunt's lover."

"Is he the author of this diary?"

"No. That was her husband. It's very complicated." I was trying not to look at his nose. "You know, I know an excellent plastic surgeon in New York, does all my mother's work. Much better than these National Health quacks you've got here, by the looks of it." I tapped my own nose. "I'll bet you'd have much better luck with the ladies."

Without another word, Little Roger set Lionel's note on the metal table and walked out of the room.

And that, my friends, was the last I saw of Little Roger.

NEXT UP. The beanpole. He must have been seven feet tall, at least from my vantage point in the low-slung chair, and the sleeve of his poor uniform only reached the furry middle of his forearm. He had a head of sparse blond hair that spread in a wispy bowl from a point at the crown of his head, and he had even less sense of humor than that poor Little Roger.

"I hear you fancy yourself a bit of a comedian, young lady." He had one of those whiny provincial accents, which he wielded like an instrument of medieval torture. "We're not fond of comedians here in Her Majesty's Customs and Excise."

"Coming from a representative of the land that gave us *The Goon Show*," I said, "I find that impossible to believe."

He ran his gaze over the table between us. I pointed to Dr. Grant's journal. "That's the pornographic one. I'm sure you'll want to take a nice long look. Do you mind if I smoke?"

The official, we'll call him Long Peter, pulled a pair of glasses out of his uniform pocket and settled them on his nose. I took that as a yes. He picked up the journal; I picked up my pocketbook and lit a cigarette.

A companionable silence ensued. There was no ashtray. I flicked over the linoleum floor instead. Long Peter read slowly and avidly. I watched the back-and-forth progress of his eyes behind the glasses.

"August thirteenth. That's the real paydirt," I said. "But there's a three-night bender in October worth a look, if only for the description of the ladies involved. Go on. I won't tell."

He snapped the book shut and gave me the old official glare. "You do realize, miss, we're not impressed with you vulgar American girls who run around in tight skirts and make smart remarks and think they're so bloody clever."

I stubbed out my cigarette against the metal table and leaned cheerfully forward. "It's Miss Schuyler to you, bub, and you do realize that my father took a bullet in the oysters in defense of this great country of yours, so you could stand there and harass his innocent daughter on her perfectly legitimate overseas holiday, *hmm*?"

At this point, you might be wondering why I was being so difficult. Well. For one thing, I never could resist a deserving target. For another, I knew like I knew my own dress size that in matters like this, you went straight to the top. Never, ever mess around with your front-line civil servant, all juiced up on petty power and regular coffee breaks. You asked to see the manager, and make it snappy.

This was just my little old way of asking to see the manager.

He arrived shortly after Long Peter departed. I knew at once this was a man I could deal with. Eyes sharp and steely, middle-aged hair sleeked back over a bald spot the size and color of a ripe peach. His jaw looked as if it were missing an important section on the right side. An ex-soldier, without a doubt. He would dismiss all this nonsense in a second.

"Miss Schuyler." He nodded and addressed himself to the table.

"You know, I don't mean to tell you how to do your job, but I must say that Her Majesty isn't exactly putting her best face to the world with those two sad sacks you sent me earlier."

"You say this isn't your suitcase?" He fingered the handle.

"It belonged to my great-aunt. The contents, too. I'm planning to return them to her. The Maxwell Institute? In Paris?"

"I've never heard of it." He was rooting around inside the suitcase, making me feel rather uncomfortable, if you must know. As if he were violating my person somehow.

"It's a very small institute."

But he wasn't listening. He slipped a hand into the interior of his jacket and produced a penknife, and before I could leap to my feet and utter an outraged howl, he had sliced open the lining of Aunt Violet's suitcase and reached inside to the elbow with all the squalid enthusiasm of a veterinary midwife.

"Hello." He withdrew his hand and produced a leather envelope. "What have we here, my beauty?"

Violet

Lionel and Violet leave the eighth floor of the Hotel Adlon just before four o'clock in the morning, not by the lifts and across the elegant marble lobby, but down the back stairs and through the service door at the rear. A motorcar sits in the blackened alley. Lionel opens the passenger door and urges her inside.

"Lionel, what . . . ?"

"*Shh*. Later." He tosses Violet's valise into the boot and swings around front.

The car springs from the clutch. Violet grips the door frame. The air is cooler than she expects, rushing against the side of her face from around the windscreen. She leans forward. "Is it war? Are the borders closed already?"

Lionel glances in the mirror. "Just let me get us out of the city."

The car whips about a corner, and a shout echoes from the pavement. Lionel accelerates. The wind roars against Violet's eardrums. She puts up her hand to secure her hat.

"Is there anyone behind us?" asks Lionel quietly.

Violet cranes her head. A pair of headlamps. "Yes."

The engine growls ravenously. The door frame vibrates under Violet's hand. She focuses her eyes on the small winged figure perched at the edge of the bonnet, whose mercury body stretches forward in a perpetual leap of faith.

Another turn, and another, small narrow streets without lamps. Lionel drives at a ruinous speed, without speaking, without blinking, his eyes fixed and determined on the pavement ahead. Violet's feet are numb from pressing into the floorboards. Berlin passes by in a charcoal blur, the last she will see of it for many years.

The streets lengthen, the buildings thin. Violet catches a glimpse of the horizon, purple-gray in the moment before sunrise. As suddenly as they've begun, they're in the suburbs, and then a field opens up to the right, swallowed shortly by a forest. Lionel slows the car and pulls to the side of the road, beneath the black branches. For a minute, he sits still, breathing deeply, and then he asks Violet if she will find his cigarette case from his jacket pocket.

The jacket lies on the floorboard, inside out. Violet picks it up and finds the case. She runs her fingers over the engraved Roman monogram: LRP. The *P* must be his middle name. What does it stand for? She has no idea. Silently she hands it to him, and he selects a cigarette and lights it in methodical movements. The sky is beginning to lighten, illuminating the clean white of the cigarette paper, the slender stream of smoke.

"Grant's dead," Lionel says abruptly. "Your husband's dead."

The air stops in Violet's lungs. Perhaps her heart stops, too: she's not sure.

"Good," she says, but her voice quivers.

"The police have found out, obviously. We're heading south, to Switzerland."

"Why south?"

"We can't go north. It's flat and populated and obvious. And if Germany mobilizes, it will shortly be swarming with soldiers, and all the ports will close, and every train and road and bloody loaf of bread will be requisitioned." He sucks hard on his cigarette, staring ahead.

Violet gathers herself. Begins to breathe again. "How did it happen?"

"That's the question, isn't it?" He puts his two hands on the steering wheel and drums it with his thumbs. "Does it matter?"

She thinks for a moment. "No."

"Then don't ask any more questions, *hmm*?" He stubs out the smoke and turns the ignition.

Grant's dead. Lionel's flat voice. *Your husband's dead.* Her mind hovers numbly around the words, poking at them, trying to determine if they're real. Walter. Dr. Walter Grant, her husband, eminent physical chemist. His brilliant eyes shut, his famous and flexible brain locked in rigor mortis. This sick feeling in the pit of her belly: grief, or relief, or disbelief?

It could not be. Walter could not be dead. Surely she had misheard him.

The car bumps back onto the road and gathers speed. The sky is lightening more. Lionel switches off the headlamps. In the glow of sunrise, the dashboard gleams like warm honey.

Violet asks: "Where did you get the automobile?"

"I borrowed it," says Lionel.

THEY DRIVE for two hours before Lionel stops at a village for petrol. While he fills up the hungry Daimler, Violet finds a bakery and buys a dozen sweet rolls. There are apples in a basket on the counter, four pfennigs each. She buys six.

Lionel keeps to local roads, narrow and unpaved, consulting a map every so often. Violet eats two apples and a roll, but already it's too hot for food. She asks if they have any water.

"In the back," says Lionel. "I filled two jugs back in Seehausen."

Violet finds the jugs and opens one, and they pass it back and forth between them. "You can sleep if you like," says Lionel.

"You're the one who should be sleeping. I don't think you've slept more than four hours in the past three days."

"I'll sleep tonight."

Violet doesn't mean to sleep, she's never been a tremendous sleeper, naps are almost unknown to her. But somewhere in the low rumble of the automobile engine and the thick heat of the air and the nearby comfort of Lionel's body, her thoughts drift and settle. She wakes with a start when the car slows to a stop.

Words echo in her head, impossible words: *Grant's dead. Your husband is dead.*

They are surrounded by green shade, a small halfhearted orchard of some kind. Ahead, an old barn sheds paint into the grass. Lionel is already jumping out of the car.

"Where are we?"

"A kilometer or two from Hildesheim. We're going to leave the car here and walk into town for the train."

"The train!"

"It's the Frankfurt line, headed into Zurich." Lionel yanks at the doors of the barn. The old wood gives way in a rush of thick air. "They won't be looking there."

They. Who are *they*? The police, probably. She and Lionel are running from the German police. That is real, that is reality.

Violet opens the door and forces her stiffened muscles onto the carpet of sparse grass and rotting leaves. A few cracks of sunlight mottle the air before her. She watches Lionel as he forces the barn doors into submission and pauses, catching his breath a little, blinking.

"You're shattered," she says. "You should sleep a few hours."

"Not yet."

"When does the train leave?"

He takes out his watch. "Two hours."

"The walk into town will take a quarter hour. Lie down, Lionel."

He rubs his forehead. "If I sleep now, I might not stop."

"I'll wake you. I'll keep watch."

Lionel watches her doubtfully, exhaustion warring with his unstoppable momentum. His face is so drawn and quartered, his strong shoulders so gaunt. Violet straightens and fills herself with compassion. "Come." She puts her arms around him. "Come and rest. Let me do this for you."

"I'll just put the motor away first."

He drives the car into the barn. He's too long for the rear seat; Violet finds a pile of old straw and spreads the blanket on top. The air is warm and musty, smelling of ancient summer sunshine, trapped and released. Lionel arranges himself on the blanket, arms crossed on his massive chest, eyes closed to the rafters above. Asleep in an instant.

Violet settles her gold watch on his chest, against his knitted hands, so she can keep an eye on the time and on Lionel. He sleeps at a profound depth. His limbs are absolutely limp, his breathing so slow she keeps checking his pulse, as if he were a patient in a hospital, or a newborn baby. She watches the dust drift around his face, counts the motes as they strike his skin. She wonders, if she touches his forehead with her fingers, whether she can find his thoughts. Can make some sense of it all: his actions, her illogical faith in him.

Lionel's eyes blink open exactly two minutes before Violet intends to wake him. He lifts his head suddenly, as if he's shocked by her; the watch rolls off his chest and into the blanket. "What time is it?"

"Three-thirty."

His head falls back. "Damn."

"We can stay here. We can catch the train tomorrow."

"No. It's got to be this one." He heaves himself upward, stretches, and turns to fold the blanket.

On the road to Hildesheim, Violet's sensible black shoes turn white with dust. She holds her pocketbook and the small bag with the rolls and apples inside; Lionel carries her valise in one hand and his jacket in the other. The brim of his hat rides low on his brow, and he stares long down the road, as if trying to pick out some detail in the distance.

Grant's dead. The truth. *Your husband's dead.*

"I've changed my mind," Violet says. "It does matter. I need to know."

Lionel sighs. "Yes, I expect so."

"How did he die? Was it when you hit him in Wittenberg?"

"No." Lionel switches the valise to his other hand and flings the jacket to his shoulder. "He followed us to Berlin. Went to your flat."

"And he was killed there?"

"Yes. A gunshot to the chest."

"I see." But Violet doesn't see. Walter's chest torn open, his heart bleeding out into the calm parquet of their apartment in Kronenstrasse. She should feel something; she shouldn't be this clear. Numb and clear, both at once. "Did he suffer?"

"I imagine he died very quickly. There was a great deal of blood."

"You were there."

He stops and sets the valise in the dust. "Just ask me, Violet. For God's sake. Ask me if I did it."

Violet opens her mouth, and she only realizes she's crying when the tears run past her lips and onto her tongue. She tries to speak, but instead a shuddering sob of a gasp wracks her chest, and she puts out her hands to stop Lionel from reaching for her. "I can't. I can't ask you."

"Violet . . ."

"Don't tell me. Don't tell me any more."

He takes her in his arms anyway and holds her, there by the side of the dusty road, while she weeps for the husband she detested, for the lover she hardly knows.

"Just say," she says, hiccupping and sobbing, "just say you had no choice. He left you no choice. Just say you did it for me."

Lionel strokes her hair. "Violet, I did it all for you."

. . .

IN HILDESHEIM, they stand upon the empty platform. Lionel reaches inside his pocket as if to check his watch, but he pulls out a small gold ring instead.

"What's this?"

"Our name is Brown. Edward and Sylvia Brown. We're American, from New York." He takes her left hand and slides the ring on her fourth finger.

"Are you mad?"

"New papers. I had them made up just in case there was trouble leaving the country." He holds her hand for a moment, examining the ring as if to inspect its credibility.

"Because of Serbia?"

He meets her eyes. "Because of Serbia, and everything else. For one thing, if there's a war, I don't want to spend it in some damned German internment camp. Now, if they ask any questions, let me do the answering, all right? Swallow your marvelous pride and self-sufficiency this once."

"But you're not American."

"Honey, I can be as American as apple pie, if I have to." His accent is flawless. He reaches back into his waistcoat pocket, and this time he holds his watch. He flicks open the case and frowns. "German trains are never late."

"It's only four minutes."

A steam whistle pipes from the distant northeast. Lionel replaces his watch in his pocket, picks up Violet's valise, and turns expectantly up the platform. The rails shriek softly. The gold band weighs down Violet's hand with an unnatural mass; the thunderous approaching train makes the metal sing in sympathy.

Lionel draws her arm into his elbow. "Come along, Mrs. Brown."

The train shudders to a stop and releases an exhausted sigh of steam. Lionel leads Violet up the platform to a first class wagon-lit and hands her aboard. A steward greets them, clad in white. "Mr. and Mrs. Brown?"

"Yes." Lionel hands him Violet's valise. "I'm afraid our luggage was stolen. My wife and I will require two sets of pajamas."

"Of course, sir. Right away. I'm very sorry." The steward leads them to their compartment and tells them about the facilities and the dining car and the expectation for arrival in Zurich. Violet stares dully out the window. The train lurches forward, the steward leaves.

"You'll want to clean up before dinner, of course," Lionel says gently.

"Yes, of course." Violet opens her valise and finds a new dress and linens. Lionel helps her wordlessly with the fastenings. She opens the door to the washstand and cleans her teeth, takes the pins from her hair, brushes and repins. She turns to find Lionel, stripped to the waist, lifting his shaving kit from her valise.

"All finished?"

"Yes, go ahead."

He shaves as if there's nothing at all wrong, nothing at all unusual, only a married couple, Mr. and Mrs. Edward Brown of New York, preparing for dinner on the Hamburg to Zurich express. "By God," Lionel says, blotting his cheeks with a white Turkish towel, "there's nothing like a hot shave to make a man feel himself again."

"Yes."

Evidently Violet doesn't sound quite so sanguine. Lionel drops beside her on the seat. "I'm sorry about all this," he says quietly. "I know it's a shock. I'm reeling myself."

"You seem to be coping well."

He curls his hands around the edge of the seat and stares with her at the plush blue carpet. How she loves the smell of his newly shaved skin; she is like one of Pavlov's dogs, wanting to throw herself into his neck at the barest whiff of him, even now, even with her brain and her heart like double anchors weighing her to earth. His bare shoulder touches her dress; his trousers stretch under the pressure of his muscular legs. He asks, "Are you all right? Can you manage dinner?"

She nods.

"It will be all right, Violet. I promise, I swear it."

"I know. I know it will."

Lionel moves his hand to cover hers. "Though I'm afraid there *is* one more thing."

THE WHITE-CLOTHED TABLE in the dining car is not empty.

"Well, hello," says the Comtesse de Saint-Honoré, lifting her beautiful head from an earnest inspection of the menu. "If it isn't Ed and Sylvie. Fancy seeing the two of you here."

VIOLET MAINTAINS her composure throughout the soup and fish, the meat and dessert and cheese, throughout the trivial table conversation, throughout Jane's powder-scented kiss good night and Henry's firm handshake. Once the compartment door closes behind them, she flings her gloves against the window and turns to face her companion.

"What is going on, Lionel? What the hell is going on?"

He stands motionless, his back covering the small window in the compartment door. "You should call me Edward, for now."

"How dare you be calm. How dare you tell me to call you Edward."

He hesitates.

"And don't call me Sylvia!"

Lionel draws down the blind on the window and locks the compartment door. He takes her hand. She tries to pull it away, but he holds firm. "What do you want to know?"

"I don't know where to begin. Jane. Why is Jane on this train? Is she your lover, too?"

"Don't be ridiculous. Of course not. She asked me to help her secure a seat out of Berlin. That's what I was doing yesterday, while you were at the institute. Arranging everything for us."

"Oh, yes? And what made *her* decide to leave?"

"There's a war about to begin, if you hadn't noticed."

Violet pulls her hand away and drops into the seat, which has already been made up for the night by the steward. The sheets and blanket are pulled so snugly, she makes hardly a wrinkle. A suit of crisp blue pajamas lies folded next to her legs. "I don't know what to think. I don't know what to believe."

"Believe *me*."

"I am not stupid, Lionel. I know there's more. You and Jane."

"We are not lovers, Violet. There's only you."

"So you say."

He crosses to the washstand. "I thought we'd resolved all this last night. My God. How could you possibly think I'm holding a single piece of myself back, after last night? I gave you all I had."

She says nothing. The water runs softly at the washstand: Lionel brushing his teeth, splashing his face. While she sits on the bed, he moves about her, changing into the pajamas, slipping a matching blue dressing gown over his shoulders and belting it at the waist. "I'm going to visit the lavatory," he says. "You'll be all right?"

"Yes, of course."

He leaves, and Violet changes into her pajamas, brushes her teeth, lets out her hair. By the time he returns, she's turned off the light and settled into the top bunk, with the blanket up to her nose.

"Christ. Violet, don't do this."

She knows she should answer, she's being childish and stupid, but she can't think of a word to say. She feels as if she's lived a lifetime in this single day. She can't bear another moment. She needs to think; she needs not to think at all.

"Violet, I'm sorry. I realize I'm making a hash of this. I never meant . . . I can't explain it all, there's too much. You've had too much laid on you already. Can I ask you to trust me?" He brushes the hair at her temples. "Poor Violet. You've been through hell, haven't you? I'm sorry. I know I've no right to your trust, but I'm asking anyway. I'll tell you everything, I swear it. I'll make you understand. I'll show you, I'll lay myself bare. Once we're safe, once we're clear. Just let me get you safe, Violet. Can you give that to me?"

She listens quietly, while his fingers stroke her hair, his voice works in her ears. A tear escapes from one closed eyelid, and she knows that he sees it, because he catches it with his thumb.

"All right, then. Good night, darling." His voice is softer than she expects. He kisses her forehead twice, once on each side, and ducks into the bunk below.

Behind the curtains, the indigo fields rocket by. Violet's bed sways in time with the syncopated beat of the metal wheels, the endless modern *clackety-clack clackety-clack clickety-clackety-clack* that hurtles them through the German night and into a Swiss morning.

VIOLET IS NOT quite asleep when the knock rattles the compartment door.

"Papers!"

Lionel leaps out of bed. "Let me handle this, Violet. Don't say a word."

His voice is strict and sure. Violet sinks back into her pillow.

The train still careers down the tracks. They're not at the border, then: just stamping papers in advance to avoid waking passengers at three in the morning. Unless it's something else, unless it's the police.

"Here we are," says Lionel in his American accent.

"Hmm." The sounds of paper shuffling, grunts of official skepticism. "You are Edward Brown?"

"Yes, sir. I sure am."

"Your wife?"

"Sleeping right here, sir. She was taken a little poorly, if you know what I mean."

Violet imagines a wink of shared masculine understanding.

"Hmm," says the official.

Footsteps. Violet closes her eyes and arranges her face into peaceful misery.

Lionel chuckles apologetically and speaks in his American voice, Lionel and yet not-Lionel. "You know how it is with these female complaints, sir."

Violet makes a faint groan, investing it with as much misery as she can. She feels the bright beam of a flashlight on her face.

"Now, now," says Lionel. "We don't need to wake her up, do we?"

"Sylvia Brown?"

Violet groans a pitiful *yes.*

"From New York?"

Nod.

"Hmm." The flashlight moves away. "Very well, then. Your papers are in order. We cross into Switzerland at four o'clock. There exists a state of preparation for war—"

"Yes, sir. That's why we're leaving. Sounds like a real humdinger. I was just telling Sylvie over dinner, I said to her, Syvlie, honey, it's a good thing we—"

"—and there may be an additional stop at the border. I apologize in anticipation for any inconvenience."

"Yes, yes. Thank you."

The papers shuffle; the footsteps scrape into the corridor; the door snaps shut.

Violet opens her eyes and lifts her head. Lionel stands breathing in the center of the compartment, a few feet away. A crack of moonlight escapes the curtains and touches the outline of his still body with silver-blue.

"Everything all right?" he asks.

"Yes."

"Go back to sleep, Violet." He ducks into his bunk.

There's no question of sleep. Violet stares at the low ceiling above and listens to the jump of her heart, the *clackety-clack clickety-clackety-clack* of the carriage wheels.

"Lionel, what does the *P* stand for?"

"The *P*?"

"Your initials. Your middle name."

A sigh. "It stands for Philip, Violet. Lionel Philip Richardson."

Violet lifts the blankets from her legs and climbs down the ladder to the carpet below. The pile is plush beneath her bare feet. She kneels next to Lionel. In the thick warmth of the compartment, he rests on top of the covers, his long blue legs bent slightly because the bed is too short.

"What is it, Violet?"

She reaches for his left ankle and draws the loose blue-striped pajamas up above his knee. She traces the smooth skin, the wiry hair. "There's no scar," she says softly.

"No."

"You weren't in Berlin for surgery, were you? There was no doctor, no operation. You didn't need a cane."

"No."

"Our new papers. Edward and Sylvia Brown. Your American accent, your perfect German. The way you handled that official just now."

"Just ask me, Violet. Ask me."

"Who are you, Lionel? Or *are* you really Lionel?"

He laughs drily. "Oh, I'm Lionel, right enough. The Honorable Lionel Richardson, Captain in the Life Guards. I *did* murder my stepfather; you can look that up. I did study with Grant, back at Oxford. That's why I was in Berlin, because I knew him before, because my German was excellent."

"What do you mean?"

Lionel reaches for the cigarettes on the little fold-out table beneath the window. "Violet, Grant's a traitor. He was supposed to be gathering information on German war preparedness for us, except that he wasn't." He lights a cigarette and settles back against the wall. "He was playing us false, telling us what his generals and his officials told him to tell us. A double agent, to use the familiar term."

"Are you certain?"

"Yes."

"He was doing it on purpose? He wasn't . . . They weren't simply using him?"

Lionel reaches for the ashtray. "That was the question I was supposed to answer this summer."

"And you did. You found out."

"I did."

"That was why you killed him."

"Does that make it easier for you?"

Violet jumps to her feet and turns to the window. "And me. You seduced me in order to learn about Walter. Another reason to send you, of all men: you're irresistible to neglected wives."

He's behind her, covering her back, his hands braced on either side of the window. The smoke trails away from the cigarette between his fingers. "That's where you're wrong, Violet. Perhaps that was the plan, at the beginning, the *very* beginning, but then I met you—"

"Oh, yes. How could I forget? You fell headlong into love with me. Imagine the coincidence. You simply *had* to have me in your bed, to seduce me, to gain my trust."

"Violet . . ."

"Yes, the sacrifices one makes for one's country." She ducks under his arm. He grabs her elbow.

"Wait, Violet. Just listen to me."

"The way that official just listened to you and believed it all? Your perfect American act?"

"I've told you the truth. I've answered your every question, haven't I?"

"As you answered his."

"You can't leave. You'll be arrested without me, without our papers."

"I don't care."

"*I* care, by God! I risked my life to bring you out with me. To make you safe."

Violet stands with her back to the door, her eyes closed against him, sobbing quietly. "Stop. Just stop talking. I am so very *sick* of words."

"Oh, Violet. Violet." His hands on her face, her arms. "I'm sorry. I'm sorry."

"Just stop *talking*, Lionel."

THE BED is impossibly narrow. Violet sprawls almost entirely on top of Lionel, and still her foot bounces slightly over the edge, her back touches the wall with every jerk of the moving train. How she loves his strength, his bulldog chest and shoulders, the carnal muscles of his legs, holding her steady in her precarious perch. What heedless risk, to lie here naked with Lionel in the airless compartment, utterly vulnerable, when a single official boot could snap the latch on the door and expose them together. Why doesn't she care?

"I suppose Jane is part of it?" she says softly.

"Can we *not* talk about Jane?"

"Just answer me."

"Yes, she is."

"But why? She's American."

"She's also highly skilled, and paid handsomely for her services. Is that enough for you?"

Violet's ear lies exactly over Lionel's heart, which beats in the slow and measured thuds of recent climax. She counts them, one by one, waiting expectantly for each blow to strike her eardrum.

Lionel maneuvers his body around hers, until they face each other, breath on breath. "Is it, Violet? Is it enough? Do I have your faith yet?"

She wants to say *no*. She wants to place a square of gold foil between her heart and his, so she can't hear it anymore, can't feel it in her ears and bones, can't let it beat against her logic. But her body is too subdued by him, her needful flesh too triumphant over his. She is too soldered to Lionel. The line has been crossed; it was crossed days ago, at the precise moment when she leaned into Lionel and accepted his kiss amid the roses. She knows that. It's already too late. It no longer matters whether he's true or false. He's *here*, that's all.

"Violet, I need you. I need your faith in me. I can't live without it."

"You want me to trust you blindly."

"That's what faith is, Violet. Knowing what you can't prove."

She laughs sadly. "Lionel, I'm a scientist."

"I know you are. I'm asking you anyway."

Violet stares at Lionel's lips, still warm from her kisses. In the cramped space, she stretches around their damp bodies to pry the gold ring from her left hand. She perches it atop the crooked last finger of his right hand, just above the topmost joint.

VIOLET WAKES sometime later in the same reassuring nook of Lionel's body, while his heart strikes the same assured cadence against her ear. But his body is tense, his breath watchful in her hair. "What is it?" she whispers.

"The train," he whispers back. "It's stopped."

Vivian

One minute I'm cracking wise in an airless interrogation room at London Airport, the next I'm speeding down the A4 in a police car, lights flashing panic, siren practicing scales. What delight, *hmm*? This was London, it should have been raining, but it wasn't: the sky was picnic-perfect, blue space and puffballs. The traffic parted obediently before us.

"Far more convenient than a taxi," I said to Mr. Peach, who sat next to me in the backseat, looking as if he wanted to spring a set of handcuffs on me. Not in a good way. "I hope you're not going to bill me for the fare."

He went on tapping the leather envelope against his knee.

"Not a talkative chappie. I get it. We're not all at our best in the morning. Fag?" I held out a cigarette. He shook his head. "At least you can hear me. I so dislike it when people ignore me, don't you?"

No answer from Mr. Peach on that one.

I lit a cigarette and cracked the window without asking. Outside, the dreary suburbs passed by, wretched terraces and unhappy semis, backed by gardens in the last gasp of November dilapidation. I hadn't been to London in years, not since my parents took me to Europe the last time, the summer before I started Bryn Mawr. It had been late June, and I wore my one woolen sweater all week, before we departed in relief for Calais and tossed our umbrellas overboard into the channel. Besides the rain, I remembered the long rows of identical white pillar–fronted houses, the merry chaos of streets, the fragrant ceremony of tea in the afternoon. One morning we took the train out to Blenheim. The clouds parted magically, and when we walked through the gardens, we found the exact spot where Winston Churchill had proposed to his wife. My father had got down on one knee and took Mums's hand, and she, all blushy, had put her hand to her bosom and said *Oh, Charles.* Tiny wanted to take a picture, but by the time she got her Brownie all ready to go, the moment had passed. The clouds were gathering back together in a dull ceiling, and the first drops were smacking against our hats.

No sign of rain today. I finished my cigarette and smashed it into the tiny ashtray in the door, and when I looked up again we were speeding into central London. "Not to put my vulgar American curiosity on full display, but where are you taking me? Please say it's Scotland Yard. Such an honor."

"No." *Tap tap tap* went the envelope against Mr. Peach's knee. "It's not Scotland Yard."

Another flash of buildings, a sudden cataclysmic stop, and hustle bustle went Vivian out of the car and up some stairs and through a door and more stairs, all of it surrounded by strapping lads who looked as if postwar rationing hadn't blighted their growing years a bit. "Just inside here, if you will, Miss Schuyler," said Mr. Peach, and I went into another picturesque interrogation room.

"What about my suitcase," I began, but as I turned to address Mr. Peach directly, the door closed in front of me with one of those awful metallic clangs that tells you you're going nowhere in a hurry, Miss Schuyler, and you might as well sit down and have a cigarette and hope that someone in this joint knows how to make a decent cup of coffee.

WELL. Jet lag, excitement, et cetera. I fell asleep, head on arms, arms on picturesque metal table. I dreamed that my doctor and I were climbing to the dome of Saint Paul's Cathedral, hand in hand, and every time we turned the corner, an endless new set of stairs appeared before us, and I knew we were never going to make it, stone stairs ad infinitum unto rigor mortis, but for some reason we kept trudging on. Hoping the sublime would open out before us.

When I awoke, a man stood before me in his shirtsleeves, large hands on narrow hips, shoulders like battleships on either side of his navy-blue tie. His cropped dark hair absorbed the overhead light. His brow cast his eyes in actual shadow, or maybe it was a trick of the light.

"I think this is the part where I ask to see a lawyer," I said.

His left eyebrow scoffed at the very idea. The rest of his face remained serious as a heart attack. "Miss . . . Schuyler, I believe."

"Ah. Mr. . . . Bond, I believe. *James* Bond." I held out my hand. "A pleasure. I'm Vivian Schuyler, and I'm not going to sleep with you, no matter how bad a boy you are."

He gave my hand the briefest of shakes, and his eyebrow lost its scofflaw kink. "So. They weren't joking," he said.

"Who?"

"My colleagues. Please sit. You must be exhausted."

I sank gracefully into my seat and crossed the old legs. One of my stockings had developed a conspicuous ladder. I recrossed. "I was about to ask for coffee."

He nodded and walked to the door. Pressed a button. Asked for coffee for Miss Schuyler, on the pip-pip. I liked the man already.

"Now, Miss Schuyler."

"It's Vivian."

"Miss Schuyler. The documents hidden in the lining of your suitcase. Where and when did they come into your possession?"

"The irony here is that I don't even know what these documents are."

"Answer the question, please."

"Ooh." I shivered. "That was thrilling."

"Thank you. I practice."

"If you must know, they came into my possession at twelve sharp on October the fourteenth of this year, at the United States post office on West Fourth Street in Greenwich Village, New York City. Only I didn't know about them until a few hours ago, when your charming friend Mr. Peach—"

"Mr. Peach?"

"The fellow at the airport. With, you know, the . . ." I made a circular motion in the rear center quadrant of my scalp. "The peach."

A tiny flush marred the pallor of James's cheekbones. He raised his left fist and coughed, ever so posh. "Go on."

"Well, that's all, really."

"You must have received the suitcase from somewhere."

"Oh, that. Yes, my mother forwarded it to me. It had been sent to her apartment on Fifth Avenue by mistake." *By mistake.* Even as I said the words, their meaning struck me from a wholly new direction. Did anything ever really happen by mistake?

Particularly when secret compartments and leather envelopes were involved.

I was falling into a rabbit hole, had been falling since that first customs official pulled me aside, and another false bottom had just disintegrated below me.

James's right hand fell to the edge of the table and began to *tap tap tap* against the metal surface. His navy eyes took on a reptilian flatness, which might unnerve the sort of girl whose nerves detached easily.

James pulled out the other chair in a prolonged scrape. He sat down. The coffee arrived in a utilitarian white cup and pot, with cream and sugar. I ignored the fixings and lifted the cup to my mouth, black and hot and unalloyed. I had the feeling my counterparty took note of every detail.

"Miss Schuyler," he said, when the coffee lady departed for interrogation rooms unknown, "you strike me as a clever sort of girl. Why don't you do the clever thing and start from the very beginning?"

I bounced my foot. "I might, if I were to receive something from you in return."

"You're really not in a position to bargain, Miss Schuyler."

Bounce, bounce. Coffee. Smile.

Because I had nothing left in my bag but chutzpah.

"Oh, James. I think I really am."

JAMES—I still didn't know his name—drove me to the Ritz himself, three hours later. Not in an Aston Martin, alas: he drove a smallish boxy thing, a Rover, I think, which fit around him like a birdcage over a bulldog. "Now, James, I'm trusting you'll fulfill your end of the bargain," I said, as we pulled up before the entrance and half a dozen doormen dashed to our assistance. "Don't you dare disappoint me. The honor of the British intelligence community is at stake."

"Do you know the hotel bar?"

"I'm planning to make its acquaintance as soon as possible."

"I'll meet you there at eight o'clock this evening."

A man in a splendid red uniform opened my door. I levered myself out of James's car, crooked my finger good-bye, and struck out for the hotel reception.

"Schuyler. Vivian Schuyler," I told the dainty red-suited woman at the desk.

"Ah. Yes. Miss Schuyler. Your luggage has already been delivered. The Imperial suite, I believe."

"I beg your pardon?"

"The Imperial suite. Is something wrong, Miss Schuyler?"

"I'm afraid there's some mistake. I reserved a single bedroom, no view."

She looked down at the papers on her desk. "It seems your reservation was changed two hours ago. Will this be a problem?"

"Not at present, but it will be a significant problem in a few days, when I come downstairs to settle the bill."

"Oh, the room's been paid for already, Miss Schuyler, as well as any additional charges." She smiled her apple-cheeked English smile at me as if I were the first and honored concubine of the King of Morocco.

I removed my red leather gloves and tucked them into my palm. "In that case, there's no problem at all."

Now. It was almost worth the trouble of being kidnapped by the various loving arms of Her Majesty's snoopy government to walk through the double doors of the Imperial suite and see, foremost, a foil-topped champagne neck poking through a bucket of ice in the center of a mahogany table, and, hindmost, Buckingham Palace flirting wickedly through the bare gray trees. My luggage had been unpacked and put away in the closet. A room-service menu lay open next to the champagne. In the bedroom, a vase of pink-and-white stargazer lilies perfumed the air, newly spread, about as subtle as a banana dipped in honey. A note lay inside: *With gratitude. James.* How I loved a man of three words.

I opened the champagne with an expert whisper of a pop and ordered myself a breakfast of imperial proportions, even though it was one o'clock in the afternoon. It arrived a quarter hour later in silver domes. I tossed the waiter a few bob. Hoped I wouldn't need them later.

I ate every crumb of my imperial breakfast, including the parsley, and drank half the champagne, and then I fell face first on the imperial bed and didn't wake up until the sky was black.

TRUE TO HIS BOND, James was waiting for me in the hotel bar. Two drinks sat in front of him: not martinis, either shaken or stirred, but good old-fashioned whiskey. He pushed one glass in my direction. "I thought about ordering you a champagne cocktail, but reconsidered at the last minute."

"Good man." I sipped. "You have the suitcase?"

He patted the lump next to him. "Right here. Everything's inside, exactly as it was. Except the papers in the lining, of course. I hope you don't mind if we keep those."

"All right. Now suppose you start from the beginning, like a clever boy."

He smiled, all thin-lipped and masculine. "Has anyone ever told you you're the most extraordinary woman to cross an interrogation room since the Mata Hari? I don't suppose you're in need of employment."

"Now, James. Don't try to change the subject."

He gave my glass a little clink and drank his whiskey. "All right. I'll jump right in. The document you were carrying in your aunt Violet's suitcase, this document which has apparently been sitting in a godforsaken Zurich government warehouse for the past half century, is one of the most significant finds in the history of military intelligence. That document, if delivered to the British consulate in Switzerland as intended, might conceivably have prevented the outbreak of the First World War."

I might conceivably have coughed up a drop or two of whiskey. James might have been forced to pat my back.

"That's not possible," I said. "One piece of paper? There was no way to prevent the war. The . . . the dominoes . . ."

"There's no way to know for certain, of course. But that was the idea. That was why Lionel Richardson fled Berlin at the end of July 1914. He was trying to reach Switzerland before war was irrevocably declared."

"Lionel Richardson was a spy." I said it flatly, as a fact. Because I'd had several hours now to accustom myself to that conclusion, the only possible conclusion from the moment that envelope had been extracted from Violet's suitcase.

Unless Violet herself was the spy.

James nodded. "One of our best operatives in those years. He'd gone to Germany that summer to investigate Dr. Grant, who was supposed to be gathering information for us, but who we believed—correctly, as it turned out—was actually working for the Germans."

"Oh, stop. Walter was a *double agent?*"

"Yes."

I lifted my glass, but it was empty. James signaled the bartender.

When I didn't speak, he went on himself. "We'd heard that the marriage was an unhappy one, that Dr. Grant was . . . well . . ."

"A philandering pig."

"As you say. So Lionel was sent to . . . well, to work his way into the confidence of Dr. Grant's wife, to engage her trust."

"That's not true. He was in love with her."

James gave me an exquisite look. "Miss Schuyler, I'm sure your aunt was a lovely woman, but Richardson was a professional. He was extremely good at this sort of activity; he'd pulled it off countless times before. Naturally, he would have made quite certain she *felt* he was in love with her, that was part of engaging her trust . . ."

I shook my head. "No. He loved her. They were in love."

The bartender returned with fresh drinks. I snatched mine and downed it deep. James pulled a cigarette case out of his jacket pocket and offered the contents silently.

"The note," I said, after he had lit me up. "The note he wrote her. With the rose petals."

"As I said, he was very good at what he did. They say he was better than Olivier, he could make you believe anything. And of course he was the right sort, bad and dangerous, the sort the ladies love to ruin themselves over, God knows why." James lit his own cigarette and gazed across the room. "I'd give anything to have seen him in action."

"You're sick. All of you. I know he loved her."

"You have proof of this, Miss Schuyler?"

I touched my chest with my palm. "I know. Don't give me that smug smile, young man."

"I'm not smiling. In any case, the two of them had an affair, Richardson and Mrs. Grant, I think we can agree on that, and Richardson was able to get the information we needed to neutralize the husband. We planted some false information with him, which did a little good. But this was the real coup: there was a guest in Wittenberg, at the Grants' country house, a German government official who was ambivalent about the prospect of war. Thought Germany would ultimately suffer, that it would bring down Europe, that sort of thing. A real Cassandra. So Richardson made contact with him, and together they worked out an alternative scenario, by which Richardson proposed a British-led guarantee of autonomy for Alsace—"

"Alsace?"

"A French province, lost to Germany a generation earlier in the Prussian War. The prospect of wresting it away from German control would coax France to remain neutral, at least for the critical period. Meanwhile the German chap, Richardson's contact, constructed an alternative deployment for his country's troops that would send all resources east instead. The idea being, you see, that Russia would refrain from mobilizing because it could not count on French support, and then Germany would have no imminent threat to mobilize against. The chain of dominoes would be stopped in its tracks."

"Peter, Paul, and Mary," I whispered. "Are you kidding me?"

"No. Audacious, wasn't it? Richardson went to Berlin—"

"With Violet."

"With Mrs. Grant. She was apparently leaving her husband. He went to the British ambassador with the document, but there was nothing Goschen could do, he couldn't vouch for the integrity of the cables or the diplomatic pouches at that point, so Richardson decided to get it out of the country himself. That was his last communication from Germany, a coded cable he sent on the evening of July twenty-sixth, that he was on his way to the consulate in Zurich."

"That was the night Dr. Grant was murdered."

"Yes. So he fled with Mrs. Grant—"

"You see? He loved her. He would have left her behind at that point, if he didn't love her."

"He was using her, Miss Schuyler. He was using her as a courier, in case he was stopped, in case he was found out as a British national. That's what we discovered today. These documents, which had gone missing from history, he had sewn them into the lining of Mrs. Grant's suitcase."

"But why? If she didn't know they were there, if he was using her as you say, how would she know what to do with them?"

"I expect he gave her some sort of instruction. And he had another plan, a backup, as I believe you Americans call it, if he were in fact separated from Mrs. Grant."

"And what was that?" I stubbed out my exhausted cigarette.

James jiggled his ice and noticed my predicament. He took out another smoke from his case, lit it against the glowing end of his own, and handed it to me. A long scar ran across the back of his right hand, which I hadn't noticed before, thin and vicious. His fingers lingered against mine. Another hand appeared in my head, smooth and unscarred, with a surgeon's adept fingers and close-clipped nails. It lay atop my naked breast to count the strikes of my heart, *gathump gathump. A bit elevated, I think, Miss Schuyler. A bit overstimulated. Whatever shall we do to relax you.*

"Are you quite certain you want to hear all this, Miss Schuyler? All this ancient history. Because, to be perfectly honest, I'm finding the present moment decidedly more interesting."

I drew my hand away from his to lift the cigarette to my lips. "How interesting that you find it interesting, James. Still, I'd like to finish what we started, before we plot ourselves any brand-new shenanigans. I'm just orderly that way."

Our knees touched, stool to stool. James leaned his elbow intimately on the bar. His eyes were no longer flat and reptilian, but full of whiskey warmth.

"Orderly, are you?"

"Like a nurse with her favorite patient."

James plucked a chip of ice from his drink and drew it along the back of my hand. "All right, then. Richardson was working with another pair of agents that summer. An American woman and her son. A woman called the Comtesse de Saint-Honoré, except that the young fellow with her wasn't really her son. He was another agent of ours, an extraordinarily precocious young American chap, who was pretending to be a student of Grant's for the summer."

Violet

The carriage is as still as moonlight. Violet rises and sinks on Lionel's chest, listening to the motionless air.

A distant shout. A faint bang, like a carriage door.

Lionel slides out of the bed and pulls Violet with him. "Get dressed. No, not the pajamas. Your clothes. That's it."

She struggles to cover her guilt: her damp belly, her flushed chest. Lionel fastens her stays with calm fingers and hands her her stockings. He tugs on his drawers, his shirt, his trousers. He fastens his braces and slings them over his enormous shoulders. From the valise he takes a dark object and slides it into his waistband. Violet's breath sticks in her lungs.

Lionel slides on his jacket and snaps the valise shut. "Ready?"

"For what?"

He cracks open the compartment door and glances down the corridor. Violet hears another bang, louder this time, and voices hurrying in urgent German. "Christ," mutters Lionel. He draws her into the corridor and taps on the compartment next door.

It opens to reveal Henry's dark head. "Sir?"

"We're leaving."

"Leaving?"

Jane's voice. "The third rendezvous?"

"Yes."

The door closes. Lionel tugs Violet to the rear end of the wagon-lit just as the steward appears at the opposite end. "Sir? Herr Brown?" he calls.

"Just taking Mrs. Brown for a bit of air!" Lionel calls gaily.

"Sir! You can't! There is a police matter . . ."

Lionel forces open the door, tosses down the valise, and leaps to the ground. He turns and holds out his arms. "Now, Violet!"

She jumps into his chest, into the warm and shadowed night. Without a pause, he takes her hand and picks up the valise and runs to the edge of a dark-rimmed wood.

VIOLET STUMBLES between the trees, clutching Lionel's steady hand. "But the steward!" she pants. "Won't he raise the alarm?"

"Jane will take care of him."

Ahead, the trees open up into a clearing. The moon has vanished, but the faint light of the rising dawn illuminates the shapes around them. Lionel stops at the edge, takes out his watch, and makes a slow rotation, taking in every shadowy detail of the landscape around them.

Violet sinks atop a fallen log and draws in as much air as she can. They must have run a mile, at least. "Where are we?" she asks.

"Judging by the time and the mountains off to the south, I'd say we're about fifty miles from the border."

"Fifty miles!"

He turns and looks at her. "Are you all right?"

"It's nothing. Just . . . my stays, I suppose . . ."

"Oh, damn. Of course. I'm sorry." He unbuttons her blouse and pulls it apart, over her shoulders. His fingers find the tapes at the sides of her stays and loosens them. "Better?"

"I won't ask where you acquired your familiarity with ladies' underthings."

"And I won't ask why the devil you persist in wearing such wretchedly uncomfortable garments."

"Walter . . ." She stops. *Walter likes my waist small and my breasts high.* Or rather, Walter *liked.* What had begun as an effort to please her lover's exacting taste had become a habit, a vanity she could not quite shake, like the gradual lengthening of her hair. Her small waist and her high breasts had become as essential to her sense of herself, of Violet Schuyler, as her intellect.

Lionel buttons her blouse again. "When we're in Paris, Violet, replacing your lost wardrobe, you'll start fresh, won't you?"

"Yes."

"You'll buy whatever suits *you.* Because I don't happen to give a damn what you wear during the day." He winks a hungry eye and leaves the night unaccounted for.

"Yes." She smiles. They stand in the middle of an unknown woods, having leapt off a train in the night, pursued by German police, and Lionel is discussing her wardrobe. Making saucy remarks, as if nothing's the matter, as if everything is well in hand. As if the shops of Paris are only a mile or two away.

He does it on purpose, of course. To keep her calm, to keep her from panicking. We can't have the lady panicking now, can we?

Lionel picks up the valise. "Off we go, then. Thank God you've got sensible shoes, at least."

"One never knows when one's going to be tramping through the countryside at sunrise, after all." Violet takes his hand.

"One never knows."

AN HOUR LATER, they're riding bicycles, which Lionel has found in a shed. The shed was in the village of Gomaringen, which they reached just as the sun crowned the rooftops and turned the distant glaciers a delicate shade of pink.

Lionel whistles as he pedals. The valise is strapped to the back of his bicycle with a length of weathered rope, also from the shed. Violet insisted on leaving a few deutschemarks behind. "You're not cut out for this work, are you?" he said, shaking his head.

"No, thank God. I prefer my laboratory."

"And you shall have it, my love. By God, you shall have the finest laboratory in Europe, if I have to lay each brick with my own hands."

Violet flattens her eyebrows at his radiant mood, his happy whistling. Both bicycles are made for men, and she has gathered her skirts like harem trousers about her legs. She keeps her gaze pinned to Lionel's gray wool back as they pedal through the hot valley. She doesn't want to see the spectacular scenery, the triumphant surrounding mountains. After all, the landscape will exist forever.

She only wants to see Lionel.

IN THE AFTERNOON, as the sun burns through Violet's blouse and the perspiration rolls down her skin, Lionel stops by a river. "It's damned hot," he says, dismounting the bicycle. "Let's cool off."

Violet balances her feet on the pedals and glances about. There's nobody near, only the grass and trees, the broad cool river flashing white in the sun. Lionel is already pulling down his braces, unbuttoning his shirt. He looks at her and grins. "Come on, then."

"What, without any clothes?"

"Of course, without any clothes." He toes off his shoes and shucks his trousers from his thick legs.

"Here, in the open?"

"There's nobody here but us." The afternoon light covers his burly body in gold. Without waiting, he jumps into the water. A splash explodes in the quiet air. "Ah, marvelous. Come in, Violet. Swim with me."

Swim with me. Violet shakes her head and glances at the horizon. Her muscles ache, her skin throbs with heat, while yards away, the cool river beckons. Lionel beckons, with his long brown fingers and his cheerfully wicked smile.

Violet swings her leg over the bicycle, props it against a tree, and finds the fastening of her skirt.

When she looks over the bank of the river, Lionel is paddling on his back, gazing up at the pale sky as if he's not running for his life, hurrying to the border as fast as he can. "I thought we were in a rush," she says, covering her naked parts awkwardly with her hands.

Lionel's gaze finds her. He scrambles upright. "God, look at you."

"Aren't we in a rush?"

He holds out his arms. "You were about to topple off your bicycle. You need a rest. An hour won't make any difference."

Gingerly, Violet steps down the bank and into the water. "Oh, it's freezing."

"Come on, then. You do know how to swim, don't you?"

"Yes." Violet draws in her breath and pushes herself forward through the mountain-fed current, toward the radiant Lionel, whose arms are still stretched toward her.

Later, as they scramble dripping on the riverbank, Lionel drags her face against his. "You do believe me, Violet? You trust me, don't you?"

She can't answer. How can she answer, when his body is against hers, when they are soldered together like this?

He holds himself still and hot against her skin. "Violet, tell me you trust me."

She takes his face between her palms and kisses him.

"Violet cannot let a lie," he says, in his softest voice.

Violet's eyes are closed. Lionel's skin is warm beneath her cheek, smelling of grass and clean water. A drowsy bee lingers near her hair; she is too spent to brush it away. "It doesn't matter. We're together, here, right now. Does it matter if we can't read each other's minds?"

"I can read yours."

"And what do you read there?"

"Doubt."

"Yes. Can you say to me honestly, can you *promise* you've told me everything? There's nothing else?"

He lifts himself away and reaches for his jacket pocket. "To answer your earlier question," he says, lighting a cigarette, "it *does* matter, practically speaking. This isn't a holiday. We're on the run, Violet. If we get in another tight spot, like we did on the train, you'll have to do exactly as I say. Obey me without question."

She wraps her arms around her bare skin and watches him, the way the sun touches the tip of his nose, the sprinkles of hair on his unshaven cheek. "I obeyed you on the train, didn't I?"

"Why?"

"Because I know you wouldn't hurt me. You must have some sort of use for me, some feeling for me, or you'd have left me in Berlin."

"Christ, Violet. Some sort of *feeling* for you. Is that what this is, the two of us? Just some sort of *feeling* for each other?"

"Because God knows you're competent at what you do. You take care of those who depend on you."

"I'm flattered."

"And because, in the end, I don't care. Whether you really love me or not, whether you're telling me the truth about everything, or anything, or nothing. Whether or not you plan to go on your way once we're safe in Switzerland—"

"To *abandon* you."

"—once you've accomplished your mission, and begin another one. I've thrown my lot in, haven't I? I sink or swim with you. If I've only got a day of you left, I'll take it."

"What does that mean?"

"What do you think it means?"

Lionel stands with his hands linked behind his head, watching the sky. The cigarette dangles from his full lips. "Ah. Do you love me, then, Violet? Do I have that, at least?"

"I love you, Lionel."

He grinds out the cigarette against a tree and turns to kiss her. "There, now. That wasn't so hard, was it?"

VIOLET AND LIONEL cycle on, toward the mountains. The grassy hills pass by, the sweet-laden orchards, the abundant fertility of July. Every three or four kilometers, a village rises up along the road, gray-roofed and somnolent under the summer sun. They pass a few farmers, who wave and call greetings as if all Europe is not on the brink of war.

Violet doesn't want the day to end. She wants to cycle forever, exhausted and happy, watching Lionel's broad gray back shift with the effort of pedaling. They must stop for the night at some point, and he will make love to her again, as sure as the coming darkness, and perhaps even again before dawn. How many more times will Violet lie with Lionel? Twice? A dozen? A thousand? If she keeps pedaling, if they never stop, can they hold back the inevitable?

Evening falls softly. They find a barn and share a picnic dinner, nestled in straw. Violet aches in every bone. She has bicycled thirty miles at least today, most of it upward, winding around the Alpine foothills. Her blouse is unbuttoned, her dusty shoes and stockings laid out nearby. She watches in bewilderment as Lionel moves about the hayloft, checking the doors and windows, whistling softly as he examines his revolver. He's in his element, doing what he was born to do: the way Violet feels solving a page of equations, or calibrating a perfectly designed experiment.

He glances at her. "What's the matter?"

"Nothing. You. You can't really intend to give all this up and settle down with a dull woman scientist."

Lionel sets the revolver down on the wooden floor beside the straw and prowls toward her on his hands and knees, his teeth gleaming in the moonlight, like the panther she imagined him all those weeks ago in Berlin. "I can't think of anything more exciting," he says.

. . .

LIONEL COULD have broken her hold like a spiderweb, but he doesn't. He falls against her, shuddering like a dying man. "So you'll take *that* risk," he says, when he can speak again. "But you won't trust *me*. You want me to father a child on you one moment and betray you the next."

"I don't *want* you to betray me."

"But you think I might."

"All the more reason to want this now. To be selfish. To keep as much of you as I can."

Lionel's head sinks into the straw next to hers. His breath is still hard and rapid, his heartbeat like a bass drum. "You'll kill me, Violet."

He is so heavy, so warm and excessive. How can she ever be empty of him, in want of Lionel? It defies imagination. The straw prickles her back. His thick elbows stab her shoulders; his hands cradle her hair as if she were made of rubies.

He says, "We'll be married in Zurich. At the British consulate."

Violet doesn't answer. She tightens her arms and legs and keeps him safe inside her, as long as she possibly can.

The light retreats through the windows. Not a sound reaches them, there in the hayloft, as if they're the only two people in the world: only his breathing and hers, the rustles of straw, the tiny movements of their bodies in the loneliness.

Lionel lifts himself away and draws on his trousers.

"Where are you going?" she asks, half asleep. The sudden exposure makes her shiver.

"Just to smoke." He lays his jacket over her chest and shoulders. Violet listens to the creak of wood as he climbs down the ladder from the hayloft and crosses the floor below. In his absence, the silence is primeval. She curls herself into a ball, so that she fits entirely inside the weight of his jacket, and closes her eyes. She sees Lionel standing next to the barn, perhaps leaning his bare shoulder against the wall, smoking quietly under the sliver moon. His gray eyes squint into the darkness, and his arms are crossed, and the pale smoke drifts thoughtfully along the side of his face.

When Lionel returns some untold time later to settle into the straw, her mind startles awake. He curves his body like a protective shell around her. He's still wearing his trousers, but his chest is bare.

"I can't blame you," he says.

"Blame me for what?"

"It's a dirty business, isn't it. What I do. I lie, I seduce, I break faith. I change masks without a blink. Sometimes I kill."

"Not wantonly, surely. Only when you need to."

"And then there's you, like the new-fallen snow."

She works herself deeper into the shelter of him. Her legs ache from pedaling, her back aches from bending over the handlebars. She has been caressed and pummeled and made gloriously alive. She thinks for an instant of Walter and his more exotic demands, of her faithful acquiescence and her pride—oh, God, her ridiculous pride—in her own large-mindedness. As if obedience to the unspeakable were proof of worth.

"That's not true. I was no innocent."

"In the essentials, you were. You *are*. There's no pretense in you. The way you're lying in my arms now, lying here willingly with your head between my jaws. You astound me."

Violet takes his hand and holds it against her belly. She loves the sound of his voice, the cigarette-scented breath of him. The words themselves no longer matter.

Lionel tucks her hair over her ear. "You are so beautiful. Your skin and hair, all sunburned and lovely. Your marvelous mind, your practical fingers. You make me believe in things again. You make me think it's possible."

"What's possible?"

"Everything." He kisses her hair. "Anything."

. . .

LIONEL WAKES HER at dawn, bristling with energy. "You're not human," Violet says, rolling her face into the straw.

"Come along." He gives her bottom an encouraging swat. "We've got to cross the border today. I'd give anything for a newspaper this morning."

"I'd give anything for a bath."

"You can bathe in our hotel in Zurich tonight. I'll wash you myself. Up you get, or I'll be forced to take extreme measures."

Violet yanks him into the straw. He yanks her up again, and in a few minutes they're on their way, while the breeze pulls the stalks from her hair.

AT LUNCHTIME they arrive in the outskirts of the town of Blumberg. Lionel stops to consult a map, the bicycle balanced between his long flannel legs.

Violet brushes back her damp hair. She left her hat behind in the train compartment, and the sun is hot against her unguarded skin. "Where are we?" she asks, for perhaps the dozenth time that morning, though this time she knows the answer. Here, the streets are alive with the hum of commerce, the rattle of urgent travel. The gathering momentum of a steam engine chuffs over the rooftops. Violet cannot breathe.

"It's the main border crossing." Lionel looks up. "This way."

Violet seizes her handlebars and follows him about the streets, between carts and chattering pedestrians and the odd automobile, too exhausted to think. He pulls up before a small hotel and dismounts the bicycle. "Here we are."

"Here?" She looks up doubtfully at the ancient building, which looks as if it's been welcoming weary travelers since the days of the Grand Tour. A columned portico sags to leftward, dreaming of more elegant days, above a double entrance shut tight to the hot afternoon air. A cluster of agitated tourists huddles in the slanted shade.

"My dear Mrs. Brown." He helps her from her bicycle and kisses her hand, right atop the ring. "Do remember we're on our honeymoon."

In the absence of a doorman, Lionel ushers her through the entrance with her valise in his hand. The lobby is cramped and dark and blissfully cool. Two figures rise from the worn red velvet settee in the corner, flanked by a pair of valises.

"I might have known," Violet says with a sigh.

"I SUPPOSE you know more than I do about all this," Violet says to Henry. They are sitting at a small table in the dining room, sipping weak lemonade, while Jane and Lionel confer quietly next to them. Lionel's shoulder brushes her with reassuring nearness, and yet she feels quite apart from the two of them, a different world entirely.

Henry stares at the stained and pitted wood before him. "Not much."

"Does she usually drag you about on her . . ." Violet squints for a word. "Her missions?"

His dark head lifts, and his eyes examine her with an expression that seems far wiser than his years. All of him seems older and wiser than he did just months ago, in May. His shoulders seem wider, his jaw sturdier. As if his flesh is finally filling out the gaps in his long skeleton. "She's a force of nature, you know," he says. "She lands on her feet, every time. You can trust her."

Violet glances at Jane's animated face and back again. She smiles. "We're a great deal alike, aren't we, Henry?"

He manages a smile of his own and reaches out boldly to squeeze her hand. "I'd like to think so."

Lionel turns to her and speaks in a low voice. "Does that make sense, Violet?"

"Does *what* make sense? I'm sorry."

"Crossing here, instead of the smaller station near Stülingen. We'd stand out more among the locals."

Jane speaks up. "Henry and I went for a walk earlier. There's a terrible amount of foreigners crowding up here at the moment. Because of the emergency, I guess."

"The emergency?"

"Austria's declared war, Violet," says Lionel. His fingers drum against the wooden tabletop. "I expect Russia's mobilizing already."

"Good God. What does that mean?"

"It means we've got to move like lightning. We've already wasted enough time." Lionel rises from the table, without waiting for Violet's agreement. Not that it matters to her where they cross the border; not that she can possibly have an opinion on that point.

Outside, the bright clear air makes Violet blink. The streets are busy, full of hurry and a simmering sense of panic, quite out of place in the idyllic Alpine setting. A train whistle sounds shrilly, making her jump.

Lionel's hand touches hers. "Nothing to worry about."

Jane's arm loops through her other elbow. "What a grand coincidence, isn't it, Sylvie? Our meeting up here in Germany like this. What a story we'll have for them, back home."

"Yes, of course."

Jane keeps up her chatter all the way through the thickening crowds. They reach the border queue on the outskirts of town. It snakes down the road and around the corner of a squat red-tiled guardhouse. Henry sets down his two valises and dashes out to buy a newspaper from a busy vendor.

"They're disembarking everyone from the train and sending them through the crossing," he says, when he returns. "That's why the queue is so long."

"I see," says Lionel.

"What a nuisance to have our holiday spoiled," says Jane. "And these

Europeans claim to be so civilized. Is Italy going to be a part of all this? Maybe we can run down to Monte and stay there."

"Monte Carlo is in Monaco, not Italy," says Violet.

"Oh, that's right. But don't they speak Italian?"

"French."

Jane tosses her white chiffon scarf over her shoulder. "Well, well! Imagine that. I always thought it was Italian. I never can keep these lingos straight. I wonder if anyone knows anything." She taps the shoulder of the man before her. He turns, starts at the sight of her, and whips off his hat. She smiles with understanding. "Excuse me, do you speak English?"

To his obvious regret, he does not.

The queue edges forward. Henry finishes the newspaper and hands it to Lionel. "Not much new, sir," he says.

Violet peers between the restless bodies around her and spies the border guards. Nothing seems out of the ordinary. They're strapping fellows, of course; she would expect nothing less. They wear uniforms of dull field gray, stern and official as they examine papers in the dusty road. The one nearest has a pink and bulbous nose. His jowls dangle doubtfully over the papers in his large paw.

"Nothing to worry about," says Lionel in her ear, and she swallows her anxiety into her belly.

"The heat is terrible, isn't it?" Jane fans herself. "I do wish they would hurry along."

Lionel's hand finds the small of Violet's back. "How do you feel, darling? Are you all right in this heat?"

"Yes." She wants to turn into him, to cling to him and hold him here, to take him away from this ominous long queue and the guard with the bulbous nose. She wants to find their bicycles and pedal backward, back to the barn of last night, the riverbed of yesterday, the Hotel Adlon of two days ago with its indigo twilight and crisp linen sheets. *If I've only got one day of you left, I'll take it,* she said yesterday, but yesterday she didn't know what that meant. She didn't know that tomorrow would actually arrive. She had thought, somehow, that the clock would stop for her, and she would not actually be standing here before the border to Switzerland listening to the final minutes rattle past.

An automobile rushes by, raising clouds of bitter dust. A pair of uniformed men leap out and approach the guard with the bulbous nose. He looks up and scans the crowd before him. His mouth is working. What are they saying to each other? Violet gathers the alert tension in Lionel's hand at her back, in his body inches away, watching the exchange as intently as she does.

The guard bursts into unexpected laughter. The other men laugh, too, and head into the guardhouse.

"Well! I thought there was a war on," says Jane.

"Not yet." Lionel picks up the valise and moves forward in the queue. "Nothing's written in stone, is it?"

Another hour. The guards are working with remarkable efficiency; only one party stands ahead of them in the queue now. They are now being split between the two guards. Violet looks back and forth between them, trying to judge which will finish first. She doesn't want to go to the man with the bulbous nose; she doesn't like the keen squint of his eye, the bloodhound hang of his jowls above his stiff gray collar.

The other guard waves his party through the gate and calls over the next in the queue. Lionel's hand closes about Violet's, in a solicitous husbandly way. "Tired, my dear?"

"It's dreadfully hot."

"We'll be through soon, I promise."

Violet watches the guard. He looks up and jerks his head at the man who stands nervously before him, and the man picks up his valise and hurries with relief through the barrier. The guard turns his gaze to Violet, and then, more thoroughly, to Jane. He lifts his hand and motions them forward.

Jane thrusts her papers forward. "Jane Mortimer, of New York City," she says. "And my son, Henry."

The guard takes the papers and looks them over.

"What an adorable country you have," says Jane. "I admire your efficiency tremendously. Such a strong and muscular race."

He looks up. She smiles winningly.

His eyes shift to Lionel and Violet. "You travel together?"

Lionel offers the papers. "Yes. Edward and Sylvia Brown, New York City. Some crowd you've got here, eh? You'd think there was a war on, ha, ha."

The guard runs his thumb along the side of Lionel's false passport. He opens the leather cover and flips over the pages. "Edward Brown?" he says.

"Yes, siree. My wife, Sylvia."

The guard spares a glance at Violet and returns to his study. For some reason, the word *wife* comforts Violet, even though it's false, even though Lionel is telling a patent lie. She likes the way it sounds in his confident American voice. As if, in that instant, she really is his wife, and he really is her husband.

"I hope everything's in order," says Jane. "I can never keep all these official stamps straight."

The guard's gaze falls for an instant on her bosom, on the smooth skin of her neck. He turns to Lionel and Violet and jerks his head. "You, go ahead."

"But we can't—" says Violet.

"Let's go, Sylvie," says Lionel. "They'll catch up."

Jane says, "Oh, go on ahead, you two. I suppose I've left something out again."

Violet looks frantically at Henry. "But—"

"Let's *go*." Lionel's unshakeable hand surrounds her arm.

Violet gives way. Lionel urges her forward with swift American-like strides, toward the barrier, which lifts obligingly at their approach. Switzerland, safety, the end of the journey a few steps away. Violet's blood skids giddily in her veins.

A shout from behind. Violet turns.

Lionel tugs her forward. "Come along, Sylvie! Now!"

"Schliessen Sie! Schliessen Sie das Tor!"

The guard at the barrier brings down the bar with a thud. He looks toward the guardhouse. A swirl of dust lifts past.

Lionel's hand clenches like a vise on Violet's arm. "Look here, we've already been cleared."

The pair of guards—the ones from the automobile—stride toward the barrier, waving their arms. They shout to the crowd, in English. "No more! No more today!"

An outraged murmur passes among the hot and dusty crowd. Someone shouts out in furious Italian.

"No more today!" the taller one repeats.

"But we've already been cleared," says Lionel.

The guard shrugs. "By order of the state."

THEY SIT around a table in a bare room in the guardhouse, the four of them, Lionel and Violet and Jane and Henry. The guard with the bulbous nose overwhelms a chair in the corner. His eyes fix on Jane's swelling bosom with expressionless intent.

They have been picked out of the crowd, along with a few other parties, and brought here, while all the other travelers drifted off to the hotels and restaurants to nurse their official outrage. "This is ridiculous," says Jane. "We're American citizens. I demand to see the fellow in charge."

The guard doesn't answer. A clock ticks on the wall behind Violet, unnaturally loud in the overheated stillness of the room. She imagines a glass of water, tall and cool, on the table before them. She can almost picture herself lifting it up and drinking deep. Next to her, Lionel sits back in his chair, his jacket slung behind him, his muscular body at perfect rest.

Lionel will handle this. Lionel knows what to do. Invincible Lionel.

Violet crosses her hands in her lap and allows a long breath. The gold ring squats on her finger, fat and reassuring. Faith: whatever that is. Faith in this, at least: that Lionel will find some way to release them from this guardhouse. That this room and this moment are not the ones she has to fear.

The door creaks open. The guard scrambles to his feet.

A slim blond man enters, dressed in a dark suit, flanked by a man in a police uniform with a thick band strangling his arm. He bites out a command to the guard, who falls back into his chair with a bang.

"Now then." The blond man turns to the table and smiles. "Edward and Sylvia Brown, is it?" He speaks in perfect King's English.

"Yes, and I demand to know why my wife and I have been detained in this manner." Lionel sets his fist on the table.

"Tush, tush. You Americans." The blond man smiles. "The thing is, though, you remind me very much of a young man I knew at Oxford, when I studied there. A man named Richardson. Merton College."

"Richardson?" Lionel screws up his face. "I knew a fellow named Richardson at school. Two of them. Common name, Richardson."

"You come from Berlin, Mr. Brown?"

"We come from New York City."

A patient smile. "I mean most recently. You were in Berlin? So states your passport."

"Yes, yes. Seeing the sights. My wife and I are on our honeymoon." Lionel reaches over to pat Violet's hand. "Tour of Europe, except it seems you've got plans of your own this summer. I was just about to take Sylvie to see the—"

"Now, see here," says Jane, "if you're here to question Mr. Brown, why have I been stopped here with my son?"

"I beg your pardon, Mrs. . . . ." The blond man's gaze drops to the papers before him. "Oh, I do beg your pardon. Madame de Saint-Honoré, isn't it?"

"Yes, it is. And I'll have you know—"

"Do you not think, madame, it's a precarious time for a French citizen to be touring about Germany?"

"I was in Berlin for the summer. My son was studying there. Anyway, one little French husband doesn't make you a citizen forever, does it? So what's this about?"

"Yes," says Lionel, "either state your business or let us go, or I'll have the American consulate . . ."

The blond man waves his hand. "I shall be brief, then. My dear Madame de Saint-Honoré, I ask your pardon for the frank nature of this question, but I am afraid I must make the inquiry, for form's sake: When you murdered one Walter Grant, a British subject residing in Berlin, did you commit the act on your own initiative, or did you obtain the assistance of an accomplice?"

Vivian

I let James walk me to the door of the Imperial suite after a late dinner. "I don't even know your real name," I said, with my hand on the very knob, my voice merry with wine.

"Nor will you."

"You can't give me a hint?"

He angles his head thoughtfully. "My mother's mother was a Merriwether."

"Merriwether." I put on my deep voice. "*James* Merriwether."

He laughed, nice and throaty. I watched his Adam's apple bob pleasantly up and down. A lovely rugged neck, a little ruddy in the golden-dim hallway lights. I could see it dodging assassins' knives and producing all the necessary lies.

"So that's it," I said. "The trail ran cold somewhere around the Swiss border, and you never heard from Lionel Richardson or the others again."

"Not a word. But at least we now know someone made it to Switzerland."

"Do you think they survived?"

"I think Richardson was likely found out and killed, or he would have popped up again. As for the others, I can't say. There are ways to disappear, especially when Armageddon is breaking out. To be honest,

I don't particularly care at the moment." James laid his scarred hand atop mine, on the knob.

I studied his warm fingers with my wine-blurred eyes.

Friday night. Friday afternoon in New York. What was Doctor Paul doing right now? Were he and Gogo going out tonight? Had they gone out last night, had they gone to his apartment? They were engaged now, and everyone knew what engaged meant these days. It gave you sanctity. It meant even virtuous Gogo was free to slink after dark into Doctor Paul's apartment as I had, to lie on the floor with him and stare at the bumpy ceiling. And Paul? Well, he'd been paid handsomely, hadn't he? No backing out now. Been paid a down payment of half a million dollars to take care of Gogo, to make her happy, to buy her a big oak-flanked colonial in the suburbs and fill her womb with the babies she craved. Maybe he'd already made dutiful love to her on that white bed of his. Taken her virginity carefully—*It's all right, sweetheart, I'm a doctor, you won't feel a thing*—and held her afterward while she wept with joy.

Well. Maybe not. But he would. Eventually. Lightfoot would hold him to it.

And it was fine, fine. Gogo gets her man, her man gets his money, Vivian keeps her job. A nice square deal for all concerned. Everyone goes home with a prize.

I said, "Don't get your hopes up, Mr. Merriwether, *James* Merriwether. I already told you I wasn't going to sleep with you."

"I was hoping I'd contrived to impress you otherwise."

I turned to face him. My back rested against the door; his hand still lay atop mine on the knob. "I'm afraid we American girls are a little harder to impress than that."

James dropped Aunt Violet's suitcase from his opposite hand and laid his forearm against the door, next to my head. He kissed my neck, my mouth, forceful, confident, well versed, tasting like wine and *poires au Grand Marnier*. His torso was large, blocking out the hallway light as I lay back against the silky paint of the door, going through the motions of kissing and arching my back and enjoying myself thoroughly, until James stopped in his tracks and lifted his lips away.

"Open your eyes, Vivian."

Opened. Reluctantly. James's eyes were black and far too close.

"You don't really want this, do you?"

Some damned thing leaked out of the far corner of my right eye.

James swore softly and stepped away. I folded my arms and stared at the red carpet, slightly worn. The ribbon of light from under the door. I heard him rummaging around his clothes and expected him to say *Well, I'm off, then, pleasant evening, jolly pip,* but instead his body slumped next to mine against the wall and the orange newly lit smell of his cigarette filled the silence.

"What's the poor bloke's name?"

I snared the cigarette for myself. "Paul. He's a doctor. He took a million dollars to marry my boss's daughter, because his dad got in deep with the Vegas racket and he needed the money."

James snorted. "That's what he told you?"

"That's what he told me."

"Let me guess. Dad's severed finger arrives in the post one day, shock and horror, strike me down, he has nowhere else to turn . . ."

"It was the ear, actually."

"Oh, nicely done. Marvelous touch. Engages the sympathy, a detail like that. A real professional." He took the cigarette back. "So it seems he wants to have his million dollars and eat himself a little scrumptious cake on the side."

"The cake is not on the menu."

"Good. He's not worth it, Vivian."

"Are you worth it, James?"

"I expect not." He rolled to his side and laid his hand atop my left breast, as if to count the strikes of my heart through my dress. "God, you're astonishing. Look at you. Say the word, Vivian. Say the bloody word, please. We will be so *good* together in there."

"Damn it." I squeezed my eyes shut.

The hand fell away. "He's an idiot."

"Well, I love that idiot. That stinking idiot. I love him to death." I slid down the door and landed ungracefully on my bottom, legs splayed, as if that act of abasement would stop the tears, which ran right through the cracks in my eyelids, no matter how hard I squinted them, and down my cheeks and into my collar. "Why, James? Can't a girl catch a break once in a while? Does everything have to be so damned difficult?"

He slid down next to me, shoulder to shoulder. Violet's suitcase sat at our feet. "Because it's life, Vivian. It's just life, we're all out for ourselves. It's the only way you make it through to the end. You get lucky sometimes, that's all, and you enjoy it while it lasts."

"Poor Violet," I said.

A reassuring glassy patter filled in the silence. Rain, gentle and English, on the window at the end of the hall, the slate roof above us. We lay there listening to it, until James finished his cigarette and kissed my shoulder and rose to his feet. I didn't move.

"You'll be all right?"

"I'm always all right, James." Right as rain.

He was taking out a card from his inside jacket pocket, a ballpoint pen. "When you're all better, Vivian, ring me up. Sooner, if you need anything. If I can help you with something."

Tell me another one.

"Thanks." I lifted my hand and he slipped the card between my fingers.

"Stay here as long as you want. It's taken care of."

"So I hear." I looked up and found his face, which was all wrinkly with handsome worry. Another fine physical specimen, James Merriwether. Really, the world was full of them. Chockablock, dime a doozy. An endless supply. No need to worry. No need to pine for the one that got away.

His lips found my forehead. "Mind yourself, Vivian."

. . .

IN THE MORNING, I found a slip of paper under the door from the hotel reception. A Margaux Lightfoot had telephoned long distance yesterday evening at nine-thirty-eight. She would try again at noon today.

I crumpled the note in a ball and tossed it into the wastebin. A knock sounded on the door. *Bell service!* I opened with a shiny morning-glory smile.

"Take it all downstairs, please. And could you be a dear and have the doorman call me a taxi for London Airport?"

"Of course, Miss Schuyler. Where are you headed today?"

I slung my overcoat over my elbow and picked up my pocketbook.

"Paris," I said. "Where else?"

Violet

Violet leaps to her feet in the hot and airless room and turns to Jane. "*You?* You killed him?"

"Ah." The blond man squares his papers. "You are perhaps acquainted with the unfortunate Dr. Grant, Mrs. Brown?"

Violet opens her mouth. Every eye is fixed upon her. Jane is impassive; Henry, leaning forward in the chair next to his mother, looks flushed. She can only imagine the expression on Lionel's face. *This,* after all he's done, after all his careful preparations. Naive Violet tumbles without a bump into the most elementary of traps, clumsily set.

A chair leg scrapes briefly against the wooden floor.

"Yes." Violet hides her shameful damp palms in her skirt. "We know Dr. Grant. What shocking news. I believe we met the man at some party or another. At Jane's apartment, isn't that right, darling?"

"Why, I guess you're right," says Lionel. "Or maybe it was that evening with the baroness. Poor old fellow. You say he was murdered?" Lionel makes a *tsk*ing sound.

"Yes, he was. A most bloody crime, wasn't it, Madame de Saint-Honoré?" says the blond man.

"This is nonsense," says Lionel. "Jane wouldn't hurt a fly."

The blond man smiles at Violet. "And of course you must have met

Dr. Grant's lovely wife, Mrs. Brown. American, too, by a happy coincidence."

Violet resumes her seat. "I think so. I don't remember exactly."

His head dips once more to the papers before him. He sifts through them, one by one. "Perhaps this will help your memory. She is of above average height, with reddish hair and blue eyes. A pretty young woman, about twenty-two years of age." He looks up. "Rather like yourself, in fact."

"This is nonsense," Lionel says again. "What exactly are you trying to imply? That my wife is also married to this Dr. Grant? That she's somehow involved in his murder?"

The blond man smiles at him. "Your words, sir. Not mine."

Lionel's voice gains urgency. "Now look. You've detained a group of tourists on suspicion of capital murder—capital murder!—without a single shred of proof, let alone evidence. In America we have a little saying, sir. Innocent until proven guilty."

"Naturally, the system of American justice is the wonder of the world." The blond man's lip makes a little curl. "But, alas. I'm afraid we in Germany are in a declared state of preparedness for war, which allows the police a little more freedom to perform our duties. And I do"—here he patted the papers before him—"have a number of eyewitness accounts, of a man and a woman matching your descriptions, both entering and leaving the apartment of Dr. Grant around the day of the murder. Leaving the city hastily together that night, I regret to add. And there is the question of Mrs. Grant." He turns to Violet, and the curl in his lip becomes a full-fledged smile, the cat who happened upon the unguarded canary.

"What question is that, sir? What are you implying?" says Lionel.

"I am implying, my good fellow, that you are not Edward and Sylvia Brown of New York City. I am implying that you are the Englishman Lionel Richardson and his lover, Mrs. Violet Grant. That you are fleeing Berlin with Madame de Saint-Honoré, Dr. Grant's known mistress, having murdered him in cold blood in his own library." The blond man speaks passionately now, building to his thrilling climax. He rises to his feet. "And that you are now trying to escape German justice by entering Switzerland. And I promise you, Mr. Richardson, *that will not happen!*" His fist rams his point home on the table.

Violet cannot speak. This is out of her universe, beyond her experience. What did you say, in the face of accusation? What did you say, when caught in a trap, staring up at the poacher who planned to make a meal of you?

And they had been inches away. A few steps only, before the gate thudded down.

Lionel sits exquisitely still, watching the blond man without blinking. His quietude contrasts with the blistering passion that continues to echo in Violet's ears: *fleeing Berlin, known lover, murdered him in cold blood.* And the clock, ticking softly, somewhere.

Henry clears his throat. Lionel holds up his hand.

"Very well, Herr—"

"Von Engel." A look, meaning *as you know very well.*

"Herr von Engel. I am prepared to make a full confession, to cooperate fully with the police in this unfortunate affair."

"You admit you murdered Dr. Grant?"

"I am prepared to confess that I acted, and acted alone. I put myself in your custody. I do so, however, under a single condition."

Herr von Engel lowers himself in his chair with a flourish of immense satisfaction. "A condition, you say? What right have you to demand conditions?"

Lionel does not flicker. "I have every right. I can contest this matter fiercely. I can call in the American consulate. The British consulate. I can make any number of protests to any number of influential people. Or I can go willingly, cooperate without hesitation in your investigation, and praise your efficiency and professionalism at every level. But the decision, of course, is entirely yours."

Violet marvels at him: his calmness, the precision of his words, his air of disdainful superiority in the face of von Engel's blond doggedness. *Go willingly.* He will not go willingly, of course. There is a plan here, she's sure of it. Brilliant Lionel.

Von Engel picks up his pen and fiddles with it. A tic beats mercilessly at his temple. Those luscious words, *praise your efficiency and professionalism at every level*: he's slavering at them. Lionel knows his man.

"What is your condition, Mr. Richardson?"

"My friends go free. They are escorted by your guards to the front of the border queue, and allowed without further delay into Switzerland. I do nothing, say nothing, until I have watched them board the train for Zurich, in Swiss hands, in perfect safety and without harassment."

Violet's mouth freezes open. Jane starts to say something, but Lionel aims her a look of immediate and total command.

"This is impossible, and you know it," says von Engel. "They are suspects, witnesses in a case of capital murder."

Lionel shrugs. "Then I'm afraid your career will pay the price. Thank goodness there's a war about to start. You could join the Army. Pick up your rifle, dig a few trenches. Face down a machine gun or two."

The tic throbs away. Von Engel's forehead has taken on a delicate sheen.

Lionel continues: "It's a simple request, really. You have your suspect. You'll have a confession. You won't even need to go to trial. The hero of the hour, the intrepid detective."

Von Engel stands. "Very well. I meet your condition, Mr. Richardson." He turns to the guard and barks in German: "Take these three to the border and escort them through."

The guard's eyes widen. "Sir?"

"Immediately."

Violet has time to look wildly at Lionel, to plead with her eyes. He shakes his head. "Don't forget your valise, darling," he says, and he picks it up from the floor and hands it to her. The leather handle is warm in her hand. Their fingers touch. He leans to her ear and whispers, *"Wait for me in Zurich."*

Five words.

She repeats them on the way out the door, the confused bustle of guards and suitcases, the reassuring hand of Henry Mortimer at the small of her back.

She repeats them as they board the train, and she looks frantically for the low building near the border gate, where Lionel is surely watching from the window.

She repeats them all the way down the twenty miles of rattling track to Zurich, where they find a hotel and order dinner, and the setting sun turns orange in the peaceful west.

Wait for me in Zurich.

Vivian

Paris! City of love! Or was it lights? City of lights. Anyway. The lady looked splendid from the window of the airplane, even clothed in November gray, with that shining serpent Seine clutched to her breast and the grand boulevards crisscrossing her skin. You could not witness Paris from the air without a white ball of excitement going ping-pong in your chest. You could not help the *tap tap tap* of your pointy-toed shoe, eager to make tracks around the doo-doo to the nearest café and arrange itself for display with a miniature coffee and a long crisp cigarette.

But. First. Duty called, or rather I called Duty, waking it up at seven a.m. for an update on Aunt Julie's condition and a confession of my own whereabouts.

"For God's sake, Vivian. Paris?" scratched Mums down the line and across the Atlantic Ocean.

"Yes!" I shouted. "The Georges Cinq! You don't mind wiring a girl a franc or two, do you?"

"You are impossible, Vivian. I should have refused the call. I suppose you're continuing with that story of yours."

"The one you've forbidden me to write? Yes, indeed."

"You are impossible, Vivian," she said again.

"What, you're not giving me permission, are you?"

"Obviously it's not going to stop you if I don't."

In other words, *fine then, Vivian, go ahead with the damned story, ruin us all, see if I care.* I smiled into the receiver.

"Obviously not," I said. "How's Aunt Julie?"

"Much better. She's coming home tomorrow. Do finish up, Vivian. This is costing me a fortune. When will you be home?"

"That depends. I may stay forever."

"I beg your pardon?"

"Forever!"

Her sigh roiled the oceans. "I'll wire the money to the American Express on the Avenue de l'Opera. And for God's sake, don't sleep with any Frenchmen. You'll catch something hideous."

"So full of maternal advice. Good-bye, Mums. Give my love to Aunt Julie."

I lay on the bed for a moment with the telephone at my side. I loved high-ceilinged Paris hotel rooms, the feeling that you were sleeping in the middle of someone else's history. My cubbyhole here wasn't the Imperial suite, not by a grand *étoile*, but I subscribed to the general theory that the worst room in the best hotel was better than the best room in a second-rate hotel. For one thing, you had Pierre-Auguste, the Georges Cinq concierge. I picked up the receiver and dialed him up.

"Mademoiselle Schuyler! What may I do for you this afternoon?"

"My favorite words. Could you find me the address of the Maxwell Institute, please?"

"The Maxwell Institute. Do you perhaps know the quarter in which it is found, this institute?"

"I haven't the least idea, Pierre-Auguste, but I have every confidence you'll be able to find it for me."

"Right away, Mademoiselle Schuyler."

My second-favorite words. I thanked him, hung up the receiver, and swung my legs over the side of the bed. I was wearing my best Chanel suit—quality over quantity, Mums always said—and *naturellement* it suited me perfectly, down to the bracelet sleeves and matching pillbox hat. Look the part, that's what you did in Paris, or anywhere for that matter. But. Especially Paris. I lifted myself across the room to the mirror, where I reapplied my hat and reapplied my velvet pink lipstick. The phone rang.

"Pierre-Auguste?" I said.

"*Non*, mademoiselle. This is the hotel switchboard. You have a call from New York."

I sank into the chair and propped my feet on the bed. "Put her on."

But it wasn't Mums. It was . . .

"Hello, Vivs."

I didn't recognize the voice, all distorted from the overseas connection, all subdued and borne down by conviction. But no one else called me *Vivs* quite like that.

"Gogo! Dear. How are you?" I wrapped my hand around the arm of the chair to steady myself.

"Vivs. Honey. How are *you*?"

"Fine, fine. Having a marvelous time in Paris. Research for my story."

"Your mother told me where to find you."

A tremor of a pause. I imagined her winding the telephone cord around her finger, unwinding it again. The image was so vivid, I began to fiddle with my own cord, loop it round and round. Strangling myself.

"Good old Mums," I said.

"Why didn't you tell me, Vivs? Why didn't you? I thought we were friends."

"We were friends. We are friends. What's happened, Gogo?"

"David told me everything. Yesterday morning, lunchtime actually, he came by the office and we had coffee and he told me everything. Why didn't you tell me?"

"How could I tell you? You had your heart set on him. You were perfect for each other." I tightened the cord another notch. "You *are* perfect for each other. I'm just . . . I'm wild oats, Gogo. I'm nobody's true love. I'm a selfish old broad and always will be."

"Vivs, you're an idiot. You're beautiful and brave and magnificent and he loves you."

"Sweetie pie, there's love and there's love. If he's confusing the two, he's the idiot."

"Anyway, I gave him back the ring."

"You did what?"

"Gave him back the ring." A laugh came down through the snap crackle pop. She was strengthening now, strengthening and lightening all at once. "And then I marched down to Daddy's office and told him he could take his money and stuff it . . . stuff it in his mattress. And then I went out and got drunk, Vivs, drunk! With Agatha!" Another laugh. "And it felt good, and I called you in London to tell you, but you didn't answer."

"Jesus, Gogo. Are you all right?"

"I am a-okay, Vivs. Hunky dory. I really am. I am looking down at my finger, and I'm so glad, Vivs, so damned *glad* there's nothing on it."

"Gogo, listen to me. You need to sit down. You need to . . . to think this through . . . You're not yourself. I'm flying back to New York right now. Don't . . . Jesus, Gogo, don't even leave the apartment." I stood up, with the receiver caught on my shoulder, and reached for my suitcase against the wall. My hands were all a-flutter.

"No! God, Vivian. You think I'm a child, don't you? A helpless child. That's what all of you think. But I'm not, I'm really not. I'm a grown-up, and I'm not"—laughter again—"*not* going to marry a man my father bribed with a million dollars, a man who's in love with my best friend . . ."

My best friend. I put my hand on my eyes. "He does care for you, Gogo. It's not just the money."

"He doesn't care for me like he cares for you. You should have seen his eyes, Vivs." The last part was buried under a flurry of copper-wired inter-ference. "He was a wreck."

"A what?"

"A wreck! Anyway, I gave him back the ring. I made him take it. He told me he'd go through with it if I wanted, but I set him straight. I set him straight as a metal ruler." The transatlantic static was no match for Gogo's determination, not even close.

I caught a glimpse of myself in the mirror, my ashen face under my golden-yellow pillbox hat. "What did your father say?"

"What's that, Vivs? Speak up!"

"Your father! What did he say?"

"Oh, Daddy? He swore at me, of course." Laugh laugh. "And he said he damned well better get his money back from David. But David will give it back, obviously, and then . . . well."

"Well what?"

"Well. I just want you to know, Vivs, it's the reason I called, really, that the two of you . . . Well. You're free. Don't worry about little old me. I'm a big girl now."

"Yes, you are. You are the biggest girl I know." I pressed my fingertip into the mirror until it shone white and free of blood, and a ring of fog circled it on the glass.

Gogo, the only one of us who comes out of this smelling good.

"Well, good-bye, Vivs. Have a lovely time in Paris. I want postcards."

"You've got them."

The line clicked. I replaced the receiver and gazed at my pale mug in the mirror, my cat eyes reduced to roundness. My pink lipstick, gar-ish now.

He was a wreck. Well. Good. He deserved to be. We both deserved it. Wrecks, the two of us. Wreckers. We had our just deserts, our *poires au Grand Marnier* stuck with bitter cloves. I only hoped Paul really had been lying about the Vegas racket. I wouldn't want to be on the wrong side of Lightfoot's ledger. Not for a million dollars.

The telephone, still in my hands, startled me with a harum-scarum *ringringring*. I let it go until my heart steadied.

"Vivian Schuyler."

"Mademoiselle Schuyler! This is Pierre-Auguste speaking. I regret I cannot find any record of an institute Maxwell in Paris, or the suburbs. I have tried the telephone directory, the maps. I have asked the manager."

"Are you quite sure?"

"I can keep looking, mademoiselle, but . . ." He hung his silence expressively.

"No, that's all right. Thank you anyway."

"I am always happy to be of service, mademoiselle."

I turned away from the mirror. "Thank you, Pierre-Auguste. Oh! Wait a moment. Perhaps you could send a cable for me."

"But of course."

"It's for a Mrs. Julie . . . Oh, damn . . . Hadley, that's it. Mrs. Julie Hadley, the Lenox Hill Hospital in New York City."

HER REPLY arrived two hours later, at four in the afternoon:
NOT MAXWELL INSTITUTE STOP MORTIMER STOP GOD DAMN MORPHINE STOP LOVE JULIE

Violet

The telephone rings at four-forty-five in the afternoon, just as Violet is about to rise from her desk to retire for the day. She doesn't last as long as she used to, but she can forgive herself for that. One does not reach an age when one's joints rattle in their sockets without having earned the privilege of coming and going at will.

She picks up the receiver. *"Oui, j'écoute."*

"Madame, there is a young lady to see you. A Mademoiselle Vivian Schuyler."

Violet's body stills at the news. She hasn't heard that name in many years, and yet, like a scent from childhood, it awakens an instant chemical reaction inside her. The blood quickens, the ears sharpen. Her eyes fall upon the photograph on her desk, in its molten silver frame, and she studies it for a moment, counting the strikes of her heart, while Mademoiselle Bernard waits knowingly on the other end. Seventy-two beats per minute. "Vivian Schuyler, did you say?"

"Oui, madame."

Vivian Schuyler. That would be Charles's daughter, the one who went to Bryn Mawr and now works for some sort of fashionable New York magazine. Violet saw her photograph in the paper a few years ago, when she and her parents had been traveling through Europe. An exclusive party of some kind. She was quite lovely, Vivian. In the photograph, she was smiling, smiling with her black-and-white mouth just parted, as if she were about to say something unfathomably daring.

Violet rises from her chair with the telephone receiver still at her ear. "Make her comfortable, Mademoiselle Bernard, and tell her I shall be downstairs instantly. And could you discover my husband's whereabouts and tell him to join us?"

Well, not instantly. But Violet can still move about with briskness. She credits her active life for that, her years spent on her feet inside the laboratory and chasing her children around outside it. Her husband, who keeps her brain busy, who makes her laugh, who still, when the wind is north by northwest, makes eager love to her in their high four-posted bed on the second floor of what had once, in another age, been the Hôtel de Saint-Honoré, the Paris residence of the aristocratic family of that name.

She smoothes down her dress and looks in the tiny mirror on the wall, next to the door. Her heart beats in great smacks against the wall of her chest. She pinches her cheeks and adds a little lipstick from her pocketbook. This is a grand occasion, after all. She's been expecting it for years, decades, and now that it's here . . . well, she can't quite comprehend why the air still hangs about the furniture in the ordinary way.

Violet opens the door and makes her way down the expansive staircase to the salon on the ground floor.

A young woman in a fashionable golden-yellow tweed suit stands staring at the portrait above the mantel. She turns, and Violet catches her breath in recognition at her eyes, large and Schuyler blue, tilting upward at the corners in a catlike way that she's enhanced with artful black kohl and a thick lashing of mascara. Her wide mouth, slicked with velvet pink. Her brave cheekbones holding it all up. Her chestnut hair beneath her pillbox hat, flipping playfully at the ends to expose her dainty ears. Vivian is iridescent.

"Violet?" Her voice is rich and comes from her chest. Her eyes are shining, brimming over. "Aunt Violet?"

Violet whispers: "Yes. Yes, dear. It's me."

Vivian makes a movement with her torso, as if she wants to step forward but can't. She gestures to her feet, and for the first time Violet sees the leather valise on the floor next to her. "I've brought your suitcase."

"My suitcase."

"The one you left behind . . ." Vivian's voice falters at last. "Left behind in Zurich."

Violet wavers. "Oh. Oh, my dear girl."

And then Vivian is holding her up, crying and laughing, and Violet's nose is full of the cosmetic patchouli scent of her, the whiff of cigarettes and life, the soft scratchiness of her golden-yellow tweed shoulder.

"You're taller than I thought," says Vivian. "You're almost as tall as I am."

The door creaks, and Violet turns with pride to the salt-and-pepper man who stands with his hand upon the knob, watching the two of them with an expression of well-deserved bemusement.

"Darling," she says, "this is my great-niece, Vivian Schuyler. Vivian, my dear, I want you to meet my beloved husband. Henry Mortimer."

Vivian

The first thing I noticed about Henry Mortimer. He had no right arm.

Naturally, I kept my gaze on his face, which had filled out considerably since the sepia days of 1914 and had become that of a square-jowled and sturdy man, not unhandsome even in his dotage. But the empty sleeve. That. It lured my attention. When had he lost it? The war, obviously. How? A shell? Infection?

He took my hand with his left and kissed it. He exclaimed his delight, his enchantment at meeting one of Violet's nieces at last. He insisted I stay for dinner—oh, for God's sake, nobody gave a damn if I was properly dressed—and for that matter I shouldn't be staying at a hotel, even the Georges Cinq, when I had family right here in Paris. I agreed to dinner but refused to inconvenience them so far as to invade their privacy overnight. The arm, I now perceived, had been lost just above the elbow.

"We were married at the end of the war," said Violet, accepting a glass of Madeira and a slight caress from her husband. "Henry was wounded in the Meuse-Argonne, as you see, and when he came back to the Hôtel de Saint-Honoré to convalesce—Jane and I had turned the house into a private hospital, you know, when we first arrived in Paris in 1914—well, he wore down all my objections."

"For a scientist, she's terribly superstitious." Henry beamed at her. "But I pointed out all the logic of it. In the first place, we both wanted to turn the hospital into our own scientific institute when the war was over, and since we would be living under the same roof for the indeterminate future . . ." He shrugged.

"And in the second place, we were expecting another baby," Violet said calmly, sipping her Madeira.

I was just lifting my own glass and nearly choked. "Another? Baby?"

"Yes, the first was born in the spring of 1915. The end of April. A little girl. I believe Henry was Papa to her right from the beginning, weren't you, darling?"

"I was smitten, I admit."

"Charlotte was such a charming baby. And then she grew up!" Violet laughed, and Henry laughed with her. He was sitting next to her, on the arm of the decidedly English wing chair in which his wife was arranged, all alert poise and tip-turned Schuyler eyes. Her hair had turned white, like spun snow, but her skin was singularly smooth, radiant as a girl's. I hoped this was down to Schuyler genes, and that I was next in line to inherit, but I had a notion that the glow within her bones had something more to do with the feeling that existed between her and the man who sat protectively beside her, with the ions that frizzed happily in the atmosphere of the armchair. Violet went on, oblivious to her own good fortune: "Do you remember when she ran off with that package from Rutherford? The radium he gave us? A hundred thousand francs worth, and she takes it to play post office with her baby brother."

"We had the police here, crawling about everywhere." Henry shook his head. His hair was shot through with long bullet-trails of gray, but I recognized its darkness from the photograph. "Jane found it eventually, thank God, when she visited the nursery for tea. Luckily Rutherford's boys had lined the package properly."

"Jane?"

Violet's eyes turned quiet, and she nodded to the portrait above the mantel, a somewhat abstract interwar rendering with an enormous red-tinted left eye and a Dalí-eqsue alarm clock running around madly in the background. "She died five years ago. She deeded us the house as a wedding present."

"You must have all been very happy here."

"We were a family." Violet's eyes climbed to mine, Schuyler to Schuyler, communicating a fact that could not possibly be articulated, but instead lay along some section of a shared chromosome, some ancestral memory, and the recognition of it shocked me. "After Berlin, after everything that happened. You do know what happened, don't you?"

"In broad brushstrokes. That you left Berlin together, you and Jane and Henry . . . and Lionel." Well. I stopped there, because I couldn't exactly pose vulgar questions to my own great-aunt Violet, could I? Not even I, Vivian Schuyler, could do that. Especially not while Henry Mortimer's left hand curled and uncurled quietly on his quadriceps like that. I had to content myself with a questioning eyebrow, an air of longing curiosity.

"Henry, my dear," said Violet, "would you mind telling Madame Marone we will be adding another for dinner?"

Ah, the knowing chuckle between the fond spouses. Henry rose and made a little bow. "With pleasure, my dear."

"Now," said Violet, when his footsteps had faded down the hall, "let us sit together on the sofa. So much nicer for intimate chats, don't you agree?"

I agreed. I nestled next to her on the broad damask cushion, and she took my hand between hers, which were quite elderly. A life of useful work, had my aunt Violet. She began: "Now tell me, Vivian. Is this a story for your magazine?"

Mouth open. Closed. "Yes."

"I thought so." She tapped her forehead. "Deductive skills, you see. Honed over the years. Well, I suppose it does no harm, after all these years. What do you need to know?"

My stunned throat made some noise or another. Then: "Details, I suppose. I have a draft already, if you don't mind looking that over and filling in the gaps. Up to the point you left Berlin, of course. I don't really know what happened after that. You sent a postcard to Aunt Christina from a border town."

"I did. We reached the border, the four of us, and we were about to go through when the police found us. About the murder, you see. That was when . . . when Lionel confessed that he was the one who killed my husband—"

"Lionel killed him!"

"No." She smiled. "Lionel didn't kill him. But he wanted to throw suspicion on himself, so the guards would let the rest of us go."

"So you and the Mortimers would deliver the suitcase to Zurich—"

"Yes. So we would make it through the border. That was the deal, Lionel told them. He would make a detailed confession, cooperate fully, if they would let the three of us go through without any further delay."

"So what happened?"

"What happened? We went through the border and made it to Zurich, but it was all for nothing because the valise was lost." She looked in the corner, where it sat unopened. Neither she nor Henry had suggested I open it. "I can't believe it's there, after all these years. A miracle."

"Would you like to see it?"

She looked down at our hands, linked together in my lap, gnarled old and ink-stained young.

I squeezed. "You don't have to, if you'd rather not."

"No. No, let's look inside. I can hardly remember what's there."

I rose and fetched the valise and rested it on the cushion between us. "Shall I?"

"Yes, you do it."

I flipped the metal clasp and opened the sides, and one by one I laid the contents on her lap: clothes, notebooks, papers, jewels. I took out the gold watch and placed it into her hands, and she made a little breathless

Oh! and her hands shook, so violently that I thought she might drop it, but she held on gamely, staring, rubbing the glass case as I had done so often. Seven-oh-three unto eternity. She turned it over and read the inscription, and that was when the tears broke under her eyelids. I took a handkerchief from my pocketbook and handed it to her.

"I know it's silly," she said. "It's just a watch."

"But it's *your* watch."

"Yes, it is." She looked down at her lap, at the artifacts piled around her. She touched the blue gossamer dress with her finger. "I was wearing this the night we left Wittenberg, the night I left Walter. Lionel drove us. God, that drive. I remember every moment. We stopped to rest—he'd been up all night, the day before—and he slept in my lap like a baby. I would have died for him, right there. I was so grateful. He saved me."

I'll be damned if I didn't break out in goose bumps. As if Lionel's ghost were standing right there on the parquet floor, over my shoulder, smiling down on my pert bosom as I knelt next to his Violet in her chair.

"Is that why you brought along Walter's diary? To remind you why you left?"

She started, and then her body went quite still. "Walter's diary."

"Don't you remember?"

"Of course. But I . . . my God." She sorted through the notebooks until she found it, Dr. Walter Grant's filthy journal, his matrimonial testimony. She held it up before her as she might hold an infant's soiled napkin. "I suppose you've read it."

"I've read enough. Too wholesome for me, really."

She laughed. Really. "Do you know, I haven't even thought about him in years. Isn't that funny? And we shared a bed, we shared a life once."

I tapped a worn corner. "Don't tell me you took it for sentimental reasons."

"Oh, God, no. I only wanted evidence. For the divorce."

THE SECRET LIFE OF VIOLET GRANT

"So you didn't mean to kill him?"

Oh, the slightest pause, the telltale pause. The rotten fact. "No, we didn't. There was no point." She went on staring at the book, at the gold-stamped number 1912 in the corner. Her worn thumbnails dug into the leather.

"We?" I said.

She handed me the journal, and by *handed* I mean slapped me in the chest with it, case closed, keep your truffle-pig nose to yourself, Miss *Metropolitan*. "You can take this back with you. I don't need it any more, obviously." She picked up the watch again and wrapped it up in the tear-stained handkerchief.

I said: "There's one more thing inside. A small thing. I don't know if you still want it."

I took out Lionel's note, very carefully, so I wouldn't spill a single one of the fourteen faded scarlet rose petals.

For a second or two, she said nothing. I thought, maybe she doesn't remember.

"Oh, my God," she said, "oh, God, Lionel."

Her body shook with sobs, spasmed with them. Her throat was choked with shock, or grief, or whatever it was she was feeling. I was afraid Henry might hear her and return. I folded the petals back into the paper, but just as I opened the valise to tuck them inside, she took my wrist.

"Wait. I'm all right. Let me see."

So I opened the paper back up, and she touched each petal.

"Do you remember what the note said?" I asked.

She said, "What note?"

I showed her.

Ah! So Violet is a romantic after all
I have kissed each one to last you until I return

Lionel

409

This time, she didn't cry. As if her store of tears were exhausted, exhumed in their entirety, and she was scientific Violet again, examining a natural curiosity. She only touched the ink with her fingers, and then she said, dry-voiced, "The petals, they were in my hair, that night in Wittenberg. The night he kissed me. I folded them away in a leaf of notepaper. He must have found it, when he put the papers in my valise."

"You never saw him again, after the border?"

She held up a petal to the lamplight. "I never saw Lionel again. No. I think . . . I *know* he died that day. He would have tried to escape, of course. No, Lionel Richardson did not survive the night."

"Did you love him?"

"Love him. Yes. Oh, yes, I loved him with all my heart." She looked down again at the words before her. "But I will say this. The love I have for Henry, the love we share, it's so much deeper and dearer and finer. Wrought by a thousand fires. The flight to Paris, on foot for the most part, since all the trains were taken up for mobilization. All that awful uncertainty, knowing we'd failed with the valise, realizing I was pregnant with Lionel's child. And it was a difficult birth, hair-raising really, and he was so good, so loving to us both. He just worshipped Charlotte, right from the start. Then the war, my God, the war. We worked together in the hospital, side by side, until America declared, that was 1917, and his commission came through that very afternoon. The children—we had four, in the end. And then our work, of course. As Violet Mortimer I was able to continue on after the war, to publish our work under Henry's name with the help of the others."

"The others?"

"Lise and Otto. Max and Albert always encouraged us. They never breathed a word of what happened, though of course . . . well, they were all there in Wittenberg, except Max."

Her voice fell away, and I had the feeling she was seeing it all again, that summer. Across the room, an ormolu clock ticked softly beneath the piecemeal portrait of the Comtesse de Saint-Honoré. Dusk was dropping bleakly behind the tall windows, and I watched the glow of someone's headlamps grow and grow on the street outside, until the car itself flashed by, a taxi.

"Do you think . . ." I read the lines again, and again I wondered how a man could write such words and not mean them. *He could make you believe anything*, James Merriwether had said in awe. "Do you think he loved you? Lionel?"

She placed the petals on the paper and folded it up again. She took her time. When she spoke, it was as if she had hand-selected each word from a dictionary of mercy.

"I think he loved me as much as it was possible for him to love another person."

IT WAS nearly eleven o'clock by the time I stepped through the revolving doors and into the golden-lit lobby of the Georges Cinq. I was almost too exhausted to breathe. I stumbled for the elevators, and I hardly noticed the tall figure who rose from the red velvet bench near the bell station.

"Vivian," he called softly. If the lobby weren't empty, I might not have heard him.

I stopped. Turned. "You again."

Doctor Paul took off his hat, and the damned light gleamed on his too-long sunshine hair, making my ribs ache. He kept a respectful distance. As well he might. "I called your mother. She told me where to find you."

"And you just jumped on an airplane?"

"Found a taxi, straight to Idlewild." He shrugged.

"What about your job? Children are dying back home, Doctor Paul."

"I'm not the only surgeon in the world."

"No, you're not. Not by a long shot over the bow."

He rotated his hat in his hands. "Can we talk, Vivian?"

"You don't think we went over things pretty thoroughly already?"

"I spoke to Margaux the very next day. Thursday, whatever it was. I told her everything, and she said—"

"I know. She told me."

A startling of the old Doctor Paul shoulders. Oh, God! Those sturdy shoulders, holding up my parcel, holding up the world. "How is she?"

"Quite impressively well, I think. So you don't have that on your conscience, at least. Your ego, now, that's another story." I turned and pressed the call button. Remarkably, my finger did not betray a single tremor.

"Wait, Vivian." He stepped forward.

"Wait for what?"

"I just . . . I came all this way. Just to talk to you. Apologize, throw myself at your feet. Look at you, you look beautiful. I . . ."

"I look tired, Paul. Let's be frank. Very, very tired, and I'd like to go up to my room right now and fix that very problem. Alone."

The doors opened.

"Wait, Vivian!" Doctor Paul stuck his desperate gloved hand against the door.

"Mademoiselle! Mademoiselle Schuyler!"

I turned, because one doesn't ignore a frantic French voice sounding one's name in the plush money-scented lobby of the Georges Cinq in Paris, and well, well! Who had we here but Pierre-Auguste, I wouldn't say *running* toward me, no, but *striding aggressively*, that was the term, in his navy-blue concierge suit and neat red Hermès tie.

"Pierre-Auguste! What are you doing here, at this hour? You should be home in bed with your wife," I said. Instead of meddling in *affaires de coucher* that don't *voulez-vous*.

Gallic shrug. "My hours, they are over at midnight. May I have the honor of a private word with you, Mademoiselle Schuyler?"

I glanced at Doctor Paul's innocent expression, as he guarded the elevator doors. I turned back to Pierre-Auguste and his scheming French eyebrows. I threw up my hands. "If I wanted the Spanish damned Inquisition tracking me down at eleven o'clock at night, I'd have flown to Madrid instead."

Pierre-Auguste grasped my hand and tugged me gently, as one might lead a recalcitrant child to his *devoirs*.

"Mademoiselle, I do not mean to interfere—"

"And yet. You are."

"—but when Monsieur arrived an hour ago, in such a state, so, so desperate with love, I confess"—that damned shrug again, it should be outlawed, and now the hand on the throbbing chest, by God!—"my heart, he cooked."

"Melted."

"Melted, *oui*. Like the cheese in the fire." He took a key from his pocket and pressed it into my palm. "I have moved your items to the Imperial suite, mademoiselle, which by the good grace of God and the hotel management is not occupied at present—"

"You've got a nerve."

"—and taken the liberty of furnishing her with a few comforts. Please do not make the poor monsieur miserable, Mademoiselle Schuyler. He has traveled so far this day, on the jet airplane. He loves you so. Only look at him, mademoiselle."

I looked.

Doctor Paul stood in place by the elevators, leaning against the wall now, hands shoved in pockets, oh, the picturesque despair of him. He gazed back at me from under his downtrodden brow.

Well. I wasn't taking that lying down, so to speak. On the other hand, neither was I turning down the Imperial suite. I marched over and pointed my finger between the third and fourth buttons on Doctor Paul's thick wool overcoat. "You have ten minutes, Doctor. Ten minutes to make your case. So hop, skip."

He smiled a slow smile and stepped away from the wall, where he had been skillfully concealing the call buttons. With his thumb, he pressed the one on top. "I'm not here to make my case, Vivian. I'm just here to bask in your presence."

We basked in silence all the way up to the fourteenth floor (really the thirteenth, that should have made me suspicious) and into the Imperial suite. The sight of the champagne in its bucket didn't faze me, didn't faze me at all. I tossed my gloves and pocketbook on the entry table. Before I could reach for my lapels, Doctor Paul was helping me out of my coat and hanging it in the closet, next to his own.

"Thank you," I said.

He lit me a cigarette, then himself. He went to the liquor tray, the champagne bucket. "Drink?"

"Water."

If that surprised him, he didn't say. He added water and ice and handed it to me in silence, and then he made one for himself and leaned back against the wall and watched me drink, the old expression, a doctor observing his patient. "You *are* tired," he said.

"Concur."

"Are you all right?"

I jiggled my ice. Because yes, I did want to tell him. I wanted to kick off my pointy heels and tell him all about my evening, all about Violet and Henry and Lionel, how happy I was for her and yet how crushed with an odd and dislocating grief. I wanted to talk it out with him on the sofa, all curled up in our familiar Gordian knot, and hear what he had to say. And then make love and go to sleep, and wake up and make love again. Breakfast and lunch and dinner and breakfast once more. Bacon and coffee and a close-packed shower.

But.

Gogo. Lightfoot. The Vegas racket, such as it was. My sins, his sins. And everything else, the tug of guilt, the dread of further slings and arrows, the uncertain capacity of forgiveness. The quality of mercy. The strain of it all.

"I'm all right," I said.

He turned on his side, holding up the gold-flecked wallpaper with his shoulder. "No. You're not. You have that shocked look in your eyes. Your smile, it's all stiff."

"That's what happens when your ex-lover turns up somewhere he's not supposed to be."

"Vivian."

I looked into my glass. "I found Violet."

"You what?" He started away from the wall.

"Found Violet. She's been living in Paris all along, at the Hôtel de Saint-Honoré, Jane's divorce present, except they've renamed it the Mortimer Institute for Physical Chemistry. She's there with Henry Mortimer. They married in 1918. They have four children. Well, three. The first one was Lionel's, but he raised her as his own."

"Good Lord."

"Hiding in plain sight, you might say." I finished my water and crossed the room to set it on the drinks tray with a clinky old crash of ice. I stubbed out my cigarette and stared at the champagne bottle. Bollinger.

"What about Lionel?"

"He gave himself up at the Swiss border, so the others could cross. Never saw him again. Violet thinks he tried to escape and was killed." I dropped a bit of zing on the word *thinks*.

"What do you think?"

"I don't know, Doctor. I'd like to think he sacrificed himself. More likely he went back to work, doing what he did best." I opened my mouth to tell him about James Merriwether, and stopped the words at the back of my throat. "So. Did Lightfoot demand his money back?"

"Actually. Astonishingly. He didn't. The strangest thing. I gave him back the two hundred, told him I'd pay the rest when I could, and he said not to worry about it. A blank slate. I guess Gogo got to him, or else he just wanted to wash his hands of the whole thing. Anyway, I *will* pay him back. Set aside something every month, like a mortgage on my own soul."

Flippantly: "Or your dad could pay him back. It's his debt, remember."

He made some movement behind me. "Pops? No. Pops is dead."

"What?" I turned.

Paul was staring at me. His eyes were old and blue and something else. Glassy, if I had to put a name to it. His cigarette was almost out, burning right up to his fingers. "They think it was a heart attack. He didn't even know I'd settled the money for him, you know? So it was all for nothing, I guess."

My first bitter thought was *How convenient*. I know. I know. What a darling I was.

He tossed his cigarette in the ashtray just in time and dropped his gaze to his water glass. His beautiful finger circled the rim. I loved him, I loved him. Why was this so difficult?

He said, "I'm leaving first thing tomorrow to settle his affairs, arrange the funeral, all that. So you really don't need to worry, Vivian. I wasn't going to make a pest of myself. I just wanted to see you again, before I said good-bye to Pops. That's all. That's the honest truth. Tell you eye-to-eye, look, I did my best to make things right."

You know something? The oddest picture came into my mind just then. I saw Dadums in the chair in the hospital waiting room, cradling my mother's sleeping head on his lap, raising his finger to his lips so no one would disturb her. And. I heard Violet's voice in my ears, as kind and clean as water: *He loved me as much as it was possible for him to love another person.*

I thought, out of the blue, maybe this isn't so hard after all.

Maybe it droppeth as the gentle rain from heaven.

I removed my golden-yellow pillbox hat and shook out my hair until it released the smell of the cold Paris night. I braced my hands on the narrow table behind me, and I said, in the husky voice of compassion: "Would you like me to come with you? To pay my respects?"

Doctor Paul lifted his face to mine. The expression of wonder there made my heart fall and fall, still beating, *gathump gathump*.

"Vivian. More than anything."

AT TWO O'CLOCK in the morning, I startled awake in the grip of a sudden conjecture. I slipped out of bed, threw on a dressing gown, and went into the sitting room, where I picked up the telephone and asked the hotel to send a cable for me, to Mrs. Vivian Schuyler, Fifth Avenue, New York City.

The reply came in with the breakfast tray.

YES STOP SOLD A FEW OLD JEWELS STOP COMING OUT OF YOUR INHERITANCE STOP LOVE MUMS

"Something wrong?" Paul looked up from his coffee.

I slid the telegram under my plate and took the coffee cup from his hand.

"Look here!" But he was smiling. (Oh, how he smiled.)

I straddled his lap with my long bare legs, cupped his face in my hands, and kissed him. (Oh, how I kissed him.) "Nothing's wrong. Nothing at all."

AFTERMATH

O, never say that I was false of heart,
Though absence seem'd my flame to qualify.
As easy might I from myself depart
As from my soul, which in thy breast doth lie:
That is my home of love: if I have ranged,
Like him that travels I return again,
Just to the time, not with the time exchanged,
So that myself bring water for my stain.
Never believe, though in my nature reign'd
All frailties that besiege all kinds of blood,
That it could so preposterously be stain'd,
To leave for nothing all thy sum of good;
For nothing this wide universe I call,
Save thou, my rose; in it thou art my all.

—Sonnet 109, William Shakespeare

Lionel, 1914

The thin edge of a fingernail moon lingers above the roofline of the Hotel Baur au Lac. For an instant, Lionel recalls the last time he saw Zurich, my God, was it only the year before? It seems like another life, another Europe, another Lionel. He was just passing through. A few posh nights at the Baur, a few lavish dinners. There was a woman. She had dark hair and small, graceful breasts. A diplomat's wife, a Russian, enthusiastic and not very useful.

But the golden windows now before him eclipse the recollection of that distant Zurich. That other epoch. For one thing, he has a job to do, a last and vital task. (He repeats that to himself: *last*. For such a small word, it has a heart-stopping sound, glittering, final, the word of the future.) For another thing, behind one of those golden windows breathes Violet.

He cannot think about Violet. Not yet.

The water slaps quietly against the canal walls. Lionel concentrates on the classical white facade before him, blue-luminous in the electrified Zurich night, and the exquisite creatures who stream in and out of its doors. Everyone is having a smashing time. Everyone is wearing black tailcoats or jewel-colored dresses. You would never guess that armies throughout Europe were mobilizing for war. A few bars of Strauss dance through an open doorway, and then the door closes again.

Lionel leans his shoulder against the tree, smoking, waiting. His muscles ache from the abuse of the day, overcoming guards and leaping aboard moving trains, and he knows there is more to come. He holds himself still, hoarding every packet of energy, every kilojoule remaining to him. There is no human test quite akin to the certain expectation of pain.

The last of the moon slips behind the rooftop. A dark figure crosses the porte cochère and enters the garden where Lionel waits.

Lionel doesn't move. The profile, the gait, the carriage: it's Henry, all right, carrying Violet's valise in his left hand, down the gravel path to the Schanzengraben canal. His right hand is shoved in his jacket pocket, either casually or warily. The young fellow is still an enigma. Was all that awkwardness part of his cover, or not? When Henry has nearly reached him, when the crunch of his leather soles on the gravel is close enough to touch, Lionel steps from under the shadow of the tree.

"Good evening, young Mortimer," he says.

Surprise, surprise. The satisfaction of a good ambush never dims, does it?

But Henry composes himself quickly. "Richardson! Thank God! You've made it!"

"Miracle of miracles. I suppose you'd given up hope."

"On the contrary. I had every faith in you." Henry's hand moves in his jacket pocket.

Lionel nods at the valise. "I presume you're on your way to the consulate right now?"

"Yes. Of course. I took it upon myself in your absence. Jane agreed I should be the one to do it."

"You're going by boat, I take it?"

"What's that?"

"You're headed for the Schanzengraben. I presume you have a boat waiting for you?"

"Oh, yes. Of course." Henry's weight shifts to the balls of his feet.

"Well, then." Lionel tosses his cigarette on the gravel. "I'll come with you."

"There's no need. You must be shattered. Go in and join the ladies. Let me handle this one."

"What? Let you take all the credit, after all my hard work?" Lionel shakes his head slowly. *Tsk tsk.* He reaches for the valise. "I'll just take it from here, if you don't mind."

Henry bolts with astonishing quickness, such quickness that Lionel, even prepared, loses a few precious instants as he turns and forces his twisted right ankle into pursuit. In the darkness, he can't see Henry's long black back ahead of him. He runs by instinct, by the shift in the shadows, by the certain direction of the Schanzengraben ahead of them, and the imperative that Henry must not be allowed to reach it.

Henry runs fast and unhindered by the battering Lionel has taken that day. But Henry is burdened in turn by the valise in his two arms, and Lionel, catching a glimpse of the younger man's white collar, closer, closer, shoves his limbs past all limit of endurance and launches himself into the air.

He catches Henry by the waist and drags him into the ground with a marrow-loosening *thud.*

For a second or two, both men lie stunned, and then Henry rolls over and kicks himself free. Lionel lunges and catches him, and together they roll in the gravel, shoving and elbowing like schoolboys, flailing for a clear strike with a fist, a knockout punch. But while Henry is agile, Lionel is thicker and stronger, massive as a young ox, experienced in the brutality of hand-to-hand combat. On the third attempt, he catches the young man's shoulders in an oak-armed lock and places his knee against Henry's kidneys.

Dust fills his mouth. He spits it out and leans into Henry's ear. "Now. I must beg you to satisfy my curiosity before we proceed."

"What the . . . *bastard* . . ." Henry gasps. He strains against Lionel's arms.

"Did you alert the police in Blumberg for the sole purpose of having me killed, or was it the papers you were after?"

"I don't know what you mean."

Lionel jerks back Henry's head. He saws for air.

"I think you owe me an explanation, don't you? I was put to considerable hardship today. Had to kill poor von Engel, and I do dislike killing a Merton man. My temper is not at its best. So tell me. Who are you really working for? The Germans? The British? Yourself?"

"Fuck yourself."

"I would have suggested the Americans, but then we recruited *you*, didn't we? According to my information, you agreed because you wanted to help Britain, because your own country was enslaved to German interests. So you said."

"You don't know what you're talking about."

"Now, there *is* another possible motive. Violet. I've seen the way you look at her. Not that I blame you." He says, in a silky voice, provocative: "Trust me, lad, she's even better than you've dreamed."

A violent spasm of arms and legs. "Leave her out of this!"

"Ah! So we have a confession of *something*, in any case." Lionel digs a little deeper into the small of Henry's back, wanting to punish him for his thoughts, for the images of Violet that must lie in his male imagination. The anguish of Henry's cry soothes his rage. Just. "So. Now that we have your hopeless yearning for Violet sorted out, let's discuss your plans for her suitcase. You were intending to deliver it to the consulate as planned, were you not?"

"Of course!"

"Because we are all on the same side, here. Americans and British. We both want to prevent a war, don't we?"

Henry mutters something into the dirt.

"What's that, Mortimer? I can't quite hear you."

"I said, *fucking pacifist*."

"Ah! That's better. What I thought you said." Lionel's mouth tastes of copper. He must have bitten his tongue at some point, or else Henry's elbow has knocked him about more firmly than he thought. His face is such a mass of bruises already, he can't tell. "Let me guess. You're among those civilians who have never worn a uniform, never seen a man tattooed by a Vickers machine gun, who believe war is inevitable, even desirable. That a—what shall we call it?—an Anglo-American showdown with Germany should be encouraged sooner rather than later, before she gets too strong. Isn't that right, in a nutshell? Or were you playing a deeper game? Is it your preference that Britain and Germany and France and Russia all destroy each another, and leave the United States to pick up the pieces for herself?"

"You're a dirty bastard, Richardson. A fucking traitor. Going off on your own like this, contrary to orders. We were supposed to stop Grant, that was all, not . . . damn it all . . . go off and interfere in matters of state!"

"We *did* stop Grant. Or *you* did, with that premature shot to the chest. Nerves, was it? Or had you meant to kill him all along? Violet's husband?"

Henry bucks wildly, but Lionel holds firm.

"Not that it matters, really. I'm not a man who gives a damn about motives. What I care about is this: we recruited you for a single mission, because you were clever and American and could talk atoms and molecules, and you might simply have finished the mission and slunk back to your laboratory in peace, and have never heard from us again. And you had to meddle, Henry. Meddle in things that didn't concern you."

"Someone had to stop you, and Jane wasn't going to do it—"

"Because Jane is on my side, Henry."

"—and then you had the nerve, the fucking perversion, to use Violet to do it. Seduce her and use her, you loathsome dog, and then—"

Lionel places his lips next to Henry's ear and growls: "Do not ever speak her name again. Do you understand me?"

Henry wriggles furiously in his grasp. A voice calls out in German.

Lionel swivels toward the canal, and a white flash explodes behind his eyes. Henry breaks free.

Knifed. The devil. He bursts forward after Henry while his flesh burns, while the blood runs down his ribs. His own fault. Henry's hand moving in his jacket, Lionel's distraction over Violet. Own fault. Damndamndamn. Get the suitcase. Get the fucking suitcase before . . .

Splash.

Lionel reaches the railing an instant later, in time to see Henry flailing in the black water of the Schanzengraben canal, ten feet below.

Help! he calls.

Suitcase! Where's the fucking suitcase?

Lionel kicks off his shoes, tears off his jacket, and vaults over the railing in the wide gap between two moored boats.

The water is colder than he expects. He comes up gasping and dives back down in frantic strokes. Nothing. Black water. Nothing. An object strikes his cheek, a blinding second of hope, he grasps and tugs but it's only a foot, Henry Mortimer's shoe. He gives it a vicious jerk and shoots to the surface.

"Where is it?" He takes Henry by the shoulders and shakes him. "Where's the suitcase?"

"Fuck you!" A weak gasp.

Lionel shoves his head in the water and holds it down—one second, two, three, four. "Where's the suitcase?" he yells again, but Henry is coughing and choking, it's hopeless. Something dark runs down the younger man's forehead, not water.

Lionel lets him go and dives down again.

And again.

And again.

And

nothingnothingnothing

empty black water

it's gone

Lionel puts his head back and howls to the Zurich night sky.

Someone shouts out: *"Wer is da?"*

An unbearable pressure settles about Lionel's ears. Can't be true. All that effort, all that strain, all that pain. Not possible. All lost. A slim hope, a last slim hope, but then the world was built of slim hopes, and this might have been one of them.

Lost.

This unforgiving pressure about his ears, it's the weight of history. Of a million men in arms, ten million. More, if God, from His sacred distance, proved vengeful rather than merciful.

He strokes slowly back toward the canal wall, and something brushes against his arm.

Henry.

The faint light flashes against the back of his head. Lionel blinks, not quite comprehending, and then he wraps his arm around the young man's chest and continues, a little faster, until the rough stones of the wall collide with his outstretched hand. There are stairs here somewhere. Lionel drags Henry's inert body downstream, until the wall cuts away and his fingers find the first step.

He hauls Henry up the steps on his shoulder and pounds his back. No reaction, no vomiting of water, not even a spasm. Nothing more than a wet sack of flour, Henry Mortimer. He lays the young man out on the grass and checks his breathing, his pulse. Nothing. There is a deep cut on his forehead. How had the fellow managed to land himself in the canal? Swung the suitcase too hard, perhaps, and toppled over the railing?

Lionel stares for long moments at the shadow of Henry's body, and a little pinprick of an idea flares in his mind, like the lighting of a cigarette on a cold night.

No. Surely not.

But the idea persists, winding together with that seductive word *last,* that dazzling possibility of a future outside the scope of his present life, that determination to build a Lionel outside the scope of his present self. The knowledge of Violet, waiting for him in her unswerving innocence, behind one of those golden windows set inside the pale and perfect facade of the Hotel Baur au Lac.

The two of them, primary suspects in the murder of Dr. Walter Grant.

The opportunity is too perfect, as if dropped by heaven, by a God turned merciful after all. As a consolation for his failure. An act of compassion he can never deserve.

Lionel lifts Henry's jacket and finds the inner pocket, telling himself he must not hope, must not expect. His fingers encounter a packet of sodden papers, covered in leather. He pulls them out.

His heart bounds and rebounds against the wall of his chest. He feels its pulse in his ears.

He opens the packet, and inside, still damp but legible, protected by the leather binding of the notebook, is a United States passport for one Henry John Mortimer, birthplace Boston, Massachusetts, height six feet, weight a hundred and sixty pounds, hair dark brown, eyes gray.

Lionel tucks the papers in his inside jacket pocket. He removes the gold college ring from Henry's left pinkie finger and smashes it down the length of his own. He empties all the remaining pockets and fills the trousers with gravel. He peels away the jacket and shoes, the shirt with its embroidered monogram, anything at all that might identify the body. He drags him as far as he can to the end of the park, where the Schanzengraben canal empties out into the spreading Zurichsee, and with a whispered prayer he releases Henry Mortimer over the side.

He stares for a moment or two at the shifting water, the flashing glimpse of skin and hair bobbing away in some unknown current.

VIOLET ANSWERS his soft knock at once. He looks at her astonished blue eyes, her round red *O* of a mouth, her pale and guiltless skin, and he cannot speak.

"Lionel."

He steps inside, shuts the door, and takes her deep. As if he can somehow draw her into his chest and replace his soul with hers.

"Lionel, what's happened? You're all wet! My God! Your face!"

"Violet. There's been an accident. We've been betrayed."

A gasp from the other side of the room. Jane.

"Is it Henry?" she whispers.

Lionel lifts his heavy arms from Violet.

"Oh, God! You're bleeding! Lionel!"

He reaches inside his jacket pocket and withdraws Henry's passport. He fans out the pages, one by one, and lays it on the desk to dry.

"You're mistaken," he says. "I'm not Lionel. Lionel Richardson is dead."

THE NEXT DAY, in the afternoon, the captain of a small tourist boat in the middle of the Zurichsee notices a small brown valise half hidden in a coil of rope in the stern. He holds it aloft. "Has anyone lost a piece of baggage?"

The passengers look at one another and shake their heads.

The captain shrugs. He will bring it to the town hall at the end of the day. They have a special department there for lost items.

Violet, 1964

Violet watches her husband in the mirror as she brushes her hair. He's checking the windows before bedtime, as he always does: the force of habit and suspicion. It reminds her of the long-ago night in the long-ago German barn, the night they made Charlotte. (Well, she can't be quite sure, but the memory of that night is so particularly poignant, that connection so especially passionate, and this is what she likes to think.) She smiles at the reflection.

"I think she's beautiful. And not just beautiful; she's got such a spirit about her. I'll bet you were enthralled."

He abandons his windows and joins her before the mirror. With his good left hand, he lifts her hair and kisses her shoulder and replies as every wise husband should. "I am enthralled by you."

She taps him with her hairbrush. "You can admit it. I'm not offended. She's my great-niece, after all. And you'd have to be made of stone not to notice her, which you're most certainly not."

"Only because she reminds me of you."

"Oh, she's much braver than I was."

He takes the hairbrush from her hand and tugs her to bed. "Brasher, maybe, but not braver. You are, and have always been, the bravest person I've ever known, Violet Mortimer."

Violet follows him in and tucks herself into the familiar overhang of her husband's body. She clasps her fingers along the abrupt end of his right arm, the rounded stump. "Richardson," she whispers. How can she call him anything but Lionel when they're lying together in their bed? In all these years, she never could.

"Mortimer." He kisses her hair. "Why didn't you tell her the truth?"

"Because she's writing for her magazine. I didn't want to ask her to hide anything. Anyway, I wasn't ready." She doesn't need to say more; he knows what she means. This close and fragile secret between them, this intricate deception of which they, Lionel and Violet, form the living heart. Not even the children know the truth. This vivacious Vivian, this clever and radiant niece: Violet can't quite bring herself to share the terror of that night in Zurich with her. Stitching Lionel's skin together with her own shaking hands. Expecting the knock at the door, the shouts of police. Leaving the next morning, as if everything were quite normal, fearful of every glance at Lionel and his stiff gait, his glassy eyes. The fever that started the next day and lasted for a horrifying week, weakening him to a husk, not far from the hundred and sixty pounds his passport claimed. Jane's untiring support, her massive strength holding them together. And everything, everything else. Everything, my God. A dozen lifetimes' worth of everything.

How could she describe all this to Vivian?

Violet turns in her husband's arms. She wants to see him with her own eyes.

"But you must tell her one day," says Lionel.

"One day, I will."

AND THE FOLLOWING APRIL, when Vivian and Paul return to Paris, this time to marry in a small ceremony in the front salon of the Mortimer Institute, where a dozen or so Mortimer grandchildren dash about unchecked and nobody except the bride's mother minds that the bride's belly appears a little rounder than is seemly beneath the empire waist of her knee-length ivory satin dress, Violet pulls her great-niece aside and tells her the truth in hushed and reverent tones.

Vivian. Sweeping of eyelash, velvet-pink of lip, birdcage of veil. She rolls her joyous eyes beneath the netting. "For God's sake, Aunt Violet. As if we hadn't figured that out by Christmas."

A gentle trumpet sounds from downstairs. Vivian Senior calls out from the doorway, "Time to go, darling, before that impatient groom of yours gets a better offer."

Vivian notices Violet's astonished expression and laughs. She leans close and encloses Violet's shoulders with her ivory-gloved hands and whispers, "Darling Violet. Lovely, lucky Violet. I am so very glad you told me today."

HISTORICAL NOTE

Readers and interviewers often ask me where I get the ideas for my books, and the answer is simple: everywhere! I'm a literary magpie, grabbing historical nuggets here and characters there. *The Secret Life of Violet Grant* began with a family story, to which I added various bits and pieces: from a minor link in the chain of events leading up to the First World War, from the spectacular story of the men and women who explored the frontier of atomic physics a hundred years ago, and from a little-known Victorian sex memoir.

The family story described on the opening page of this book belongs to my husband's grandfather, the Mr. Henry Elliott caught in Europe with his extraordinary mother when the First World War broke out. The German government really did send him an unsolicited check for their lost luggage forty years later, though naturally my sense of drama required the actual suitcase to be delivered to Manhattan for the purposes of this narrative. Needless to say, neither Henry nor his mother were spies—at least as far as we know—and had nothing whatever to do with either murder or atomic physics.

I took even further liberties with the historical record in my description of the coterie of individuals who forged our understanding of the interior of the atom, and let me hurry to assure you that Dr. Walter Grant never existed, nor did any such scandal ever touch the legendary Cavendish Institute at Cambridge University, on which I based my fictional Devonshire Institute at Oxford. Credit for Dr. Grant's breakthrough in determining the existence of a solid atomic nucleus properly belongs to the great Dr. Ernest Rutherford and his team at the Cavendish. Since my own years of studying physics are far behind me, I relied on Brian Cathcart's *The Fly in the Cathedral*, a gripping (yes, gripping!) layman's account of the race to split the atom, both for its insight into the scientific process and for its memorable opening scene in the darkness of the experimental laboratory. As for the unprecedented gathering of scientific genius at the Kaiser Wilhelm Institut in the years before the war, I can only say that I wish I might have been a fly on the wall of Max Planck's drawing room during those musical evenings.

While Lionel Richardson and his race to Zurich are figments of my own imagination, that last-minute Alsatian solution to the July Crisis was, in fact, reported to have been proposed by an unnamed colleague of German Chancellor Bethmann-Hollweg, as Barbara Tuchman discusses in her monumental account of the war's outbreak, *The Guns of August*. "But," as she explains, "to seize it required boldness, and Bethmann . . . was a man, as Theodore Roosevelt said of Taft, 'who means well feebly.'" Nothing ever came of it, and war was declared on August 1.

I'm sorry to say that Dr. Walter Grant and his appalling journal were likewise inspired by a real-life counterpart. While researching Victorian bedroom habits, I came across the most staggering of sex memoirs: *My Secret Life*, by the pseudonymous "Walter," which spans over forty years of explicit antics by a garrulous and remorseless nineteenth-century sex addict. The read is not for the faint of heart, but as a window into the mind and methods of the compulsive seducer, into the fatal tendency of even the most intelligent and independent women to fall under the spell of his psychological control, and into the everyday details of life in Victorian London, it has few equals.

ACKNOWLEDGMENTS

With every book, my appreciation deepens for the extraordinary group of people who take my raw manuscripts and land them on readers' shelves, both actual and virtual. My heartfelt thanks are always and forever due to my matchless literary agent, Alexandra Machinist, and her crack team of professionals at Janklow & Nesbit, who open doors and smooth paths and allow me to concentrate on what I do best. I'm also deeply grateful for the support and talent of my editor, Chris Pepe, and all the marvelous people at Putnam Books: Ivan Held, Meaghan Wagner, Katie McKee, Mary Stone, Lydia Hirt, and Kate Stark, to name a few, and to say nothing of the copyeditors, proofreaders, and others who work all the magic behind the scenes. I owe special thanks to the Putnam art department, who gave me such a blindingly gorgeous cover for *A Hundred Summers*, and who possess an uncanny skill for capturing the heart of a story in a single image.

I'm fortunate to have the support of so many wonderful people in my writing career. Sydney and Caroline Williams, Christopher Chantrill, Vonnie Chantrill, Renée Chantrill Reffreger, Bill and Caroline Featherston, Edward and Melissa Williams, Chris and Elizabeth Fuller, Deborah Royce, David and Anne Juge, and the entire mom team at Julian Curtiss School: you're the best. Karen White, Lauren Willig, Mary Bly, Sarah

MacLean, Linda Francis Lee, Bee Ridgway, Susanna Kearsley, and my other dear friends from the writing world (you know who you are!): there are no words to describe how much you've enriched my life.

Finally, and most importantly, I thank my husband, Sydney, and our four precious children, for the love and commitment that make everything possible.